RICH BOY

RICH BOY

SHARON POMERANTZ

TWELVE

NEW YORK BOSTON

Twelve
Hachette Book Group
237 Park Avenue
New York, NY 10017

www.HachetteBookGroup.com

Twelve is an imprint of Grand Central Publishing.
The Twelve name and logo are trademarks of Hachette Book Group, Inc.

Printed in the United States of America

First Edition: August 2010
10 9 8 7 6 5 4 3 2 1

Library of Congress Cataloging-in-Publication Data
Pomerantz, Sharon.
    Rich boy / Sharon Pomerantz. — 1st ed.
        p. cm.
    ISBN 978-0-446-56318-5
    1. Rich people — Fiction.   2. Self-realization — Fiction.   3. Psychological fiction.
I. Title.
    PS3616.O577R53 2010
    813'.6 — dc22

2009032386

In memory of my beloved father, Julius Pomerantz (1926–2006), who believed that I could do anything.

"We'll be poor, won't we? Like people in books. And I'll be an orphan and utterly free. Free and poor! What fun!" She stopped and raised her lips to him in a delighted kiss.

"It's impossible to be both together," said John grimly. "People have found that out. And I should choose to be free as preferable of the two."

—F. Scott Fitzgerald,
The Diamond as Big as the Ritz

PART I

CHAPTER ONE

Oxford Circle

For as far as the eye could see were miles and miles of Jews, families of four, five, and more packed into long, solid-brick rows—so many 'Steins and 'Vitzes, Silvers and Golds—each house with its own narrow scroll of front lawn and a cement patio big enough for exactly two folding chairs. On Robert Vishniak's block, the 2100 block of Disston Street in Northeast Philadelphia, an Italian family lived three houses down from him. "Italian from Italy," his mother liked to say, born over there, unfamiliar with the lay of the land, and so no one told them until it was too late that they were buying on the wrong side of the Roosevelt Boulevard, a highway that might as well have been a river; Jews stayed west of it and Catholics east.

The area was known by residents as simply "the Northeast," and Robert's neighborhood was called Oxford Circle, named after a traffic circle that drivers had trouble navigating their way out of. Most of the fathers in Oxford Circle worked at government jobs or in factories, did physical labor, or owned small shops. The mothers stayed home with the children and were house proud. They hung their wet clothes on miles of line that stretched from house to house in the endless shared back driveway—the heavy canvas work shirts were spotless and the white bedsheets gleamed, as did the kitchen and bathroom floors that the women scrubbed, on their hands and knees, as if in worship.

The Vishniak family moved here in 1953. Before that, they'd lived with Robert's grandparents, Cece and Saul Kupferberg, in a three-story row house in Southwest Philadelphia. Robert made the fourth generation to reside in that overcrowded house, yet the adults greeted the arrival of the first grandchild as if he warranted his own national holiday. Saul—who worked long hours at the tannery and came home so tired that his dinner was often served to him in bed—asked that the baby be brought to him after his last glass of tea so that he might hold him for a few minutes before bed. More than once he was found with his arms locked around the infant, both of them fast asleep. When Robert's young uncle Frank, just a year out of high school, returned each day from his job at the supermarket, he lifted the boy into the air, parading him around the living room high above them all, where they believed he belonged. As Robert grew, his grandmother indulged him with endless home-made desserts, and his aunt Lolly, who lived just down the block and did not yet have children of her own, came over every afternoon to hold him on her lap and smother him with kisses while declaring Robert the most beautiful child she'd ever seen.

She was not completely biased in her assessment. He had a full face, with olive skin like his mother's and straight black bangs that skimmed large brown-black eyes. On his chin and on the right but not the left cheek was a dimple that, when it chose to appear, seemed to be awarding a prize. Mostly, the boy smirked rather than smiled, as if possessing a secret that might at any moment corrupt him. Women particularly responded to his charms. When walking the child in the stroller, Stacia and Cece were often stopped by strangers who wanted to smile at him and, in Stacia's words, "make fools of themselves." A neighbor once took a picture, hoping to enter him in a local contest for adorable toddlers, but his mother would not hear of it—there was no cash involved, so what, Stacia asked, was the point? She was the only one who didn't slobber over her son; for that matter, she didn't hug or kiss most people, be they child or adult. But affection is affection, no matter where it comes from, and in Cece and Saul's house Robert grew drunk on it.

Though Stacia worried that Robert would be spoiled, she could not deny that so many babysitters, cooks, and assistants made her life much easier. She would have been happy to live in her parents' house forever, paying no rent and letting others fuss over her firstborn, but then, when Robert was five, Stacia had another child, Barry. The second son brought none of the novelty of a first grandchild and was a loud, colicky baby who kept the house up all night. The adults were five years older, five years more crowded and tired. Cece's father, now age ninety-five and referred to by all as "the old man," was still occupying the attic and showed no sign of going anywhere. Frank was as yet unmarried and remained at home. Instead of happily making room for the new baby, the family wondered where on earth they'd put him. It was not that they were unloving, or neglectful, but they went about their duties this time with significantly less enthusiasm. Then Saul got sick, and it dawned on his wife that Stacia, her husband, and their growing family might stay forever, and Saul would never be able to retire. So she kicked them out.

Stacia argued with her mother and then, for the first and only time in her life, she begged—"We haven't saved enough for our own place; we'll pay more into the household expenses; I'll keep the baby quiet, I promise"—but Cece's mind was made up. She folded her arms over her significant chest, told Stacia to get a mortgage like everyone else, and declared the decision final.

They bought the house in Oxford Circle for $6,300 with 30 percent down. Even at six years old, Robert knew those figures because Stacia Vishniak believed that hearing what things cost was good for children, like castor oil. There was a mortgage to pay now, and Vishniak, who worked at the post office during the day, began moonlighting nights and weekends as a security guard. After Barry went off to first grade, Stacia took the school crossing guard job so that she could still keep an eye on her sons after school. Mornings and afternoons she ferried the children from Solis-Cohen Elementary School safely across Bustleton Avenue. It was a strange vocation for a woman who hated automobiles, considering them wasteful and dirty. But no crossing guard was more diligent, keeping her charges in line with only a look, and holding drivers to the school-crossing speed limit, memorizing quickly the license number of anyone who infringed. Robert's mother not only shopped for and prepared their meals and did the cleaning, washing, and general housework, but she also did all her own home repairs, fixing plumbing and unclogging drains, plastering and painting hallways and replacing light fixtures. Every other Sunday morning Stacia mowed the small front lawn with a rusty hand mower. She paid all the bills, too, squeezing twenty dollars out of each nickel. If the neighbors sometimes gossiped about her standoffishness, her plain appearance, she ignored them. No one's opinion mattered to her but her own.

Eventually Saul died, followed by the old man. Cece sold her house and moved to an apartment near Stacia. Then the rest of the family trailed after her to Oxford Circle, so by 1960 the Vishniaks and Kupferbergs—cousins and grandparents, great-aunts and great-uncles—were once again within blocks of each other. And for a long time that was all Robert knew—the embrace of family, blocks and blocks of people who if they were not related to him, might as well have been. But he was older now, did not need them as he had in childhood. No matter, they still crowded around, wanting to be close. On the streets, he heard his name called out too many times, noticed too many familiar, familial, faces always watching him. As he grew to adolescence, preparing for the ceremony that would declare him a man, he could get away with exactly nothing and he began to yearn, more and more each year, to be a stranger.

*　　*　　*

WITH SO MANY COUSINS, Cousins Club was an event to be dreaded but not ignored. Every few months his mother and her two siblings and most of their many cousins, and sometimes all the elderly parents as well, got together at someone's house. The system that determined who hosted was part economics and part caprice — some had it twice within a short time; others were overlooked completely. Eventually, though, when Robert was thirteen and Barry eight, the wheel stopped on Stacia and Vishniak.

His mother made the announcement at the dinner table that February. "The Cousins Club is here next month," she said. "Even the rich cousins, back from their fancy winter vacations, are coming to look us over."

"When was the last time we had it?" Robert asked. He could only remember his parents leaving for other people's houses dressed in their best clothes. They returned late at night, often waking up Robert with their fights; the evenings were not without controversy.

"We've never had the club," Stacia said. "When we lived with Cece we didn't have to. Now we have our own place and we can't escape. It's a family obligation."

"Jesus!" Robert's father said, suddenly pounding his hand on the table. The boys and their mother started in their seats and then looked at him, waiting for some additional verbiage, but he went back to his mashed potatoes.

"What does the club do, Ma?" Barry asked, hoping for special passwords, or time spent in a tree house.

"They play cards for money," Stacia said. "Too much money."

"They eat like pigs," his father added. "Like termites." He paused. "They eat like the Russians are at Camden Bridge."

"Great!" Barry said.

"It's not great," Robert replied, five years older and more in touch with the general sentiment. But he was desperately curious to meet the mysterious rich cousins—two of his grandmother's nephews who'd been in the junk business, barely making ends meet, when the Second World War broke out, bringing with it the incessant demand for scrap metal. What would prosperity look like on the face of a Kupferberg? How, he wondered, were these cousins made?

By now Robert knew that the children of Cece and Saul Kupferberg, while intelligent, did not have heads for business. At one time or another, all had tried their hand at entrepreneurship and failed. The Vishniak side of his family was no better—his father's father had a brief period of entrepreneurial success as a bootlegger during Prohibition, but then his basement still caught fire, forcing the family to make a narrow escape as the house burned almost to the ground. Stacia and Vishniak's story, while less dangerous, was no more optimistic. Just after the war they owned a candy store in South Philadelphia. A lover of sweets, Vishniak ordered too much merchandise and gave away endless samples, carried away by his own enthusiasm, insisting that generosity brought in business. Stacia, who operated the cash register, mostly stood up front, arms folded, glowering at the freeloaders. Vishniak hired his brothers to work for him, and often one or the other sat in the back reading books for their night school classes. After three years the store went belly-up, and all Robert's father had to show for his efforts was a bad case of diabetes and a garage full of stale Goldenberg's Peanut Chews.

Were these rich cousins somehow constituted differently than the rest of the family? Or was it, as his mother claimed, merely luck? The rich cousins lived in the far Northeast, meaning farther north on the Roosevelt Boulevard. Even that was a mysterious place to Robert, a distant neighborhood where, he'd been told, brave settlers carved aluminum-sided single homes and a shopping mall out of a virtual wilderness.

During the month leading up to their hosting of the club, Stacia was in a terrible mood. Theirs was a loud house with two boys, but in the weeks before the cousins arrived, even Barry did not dare set anything on fire, pass wind at the dinner table, or slide down the carpeted steps on his stomach yelling, "When the hell are we finally going to buy a used car?"

Generally his mother could always be counted on to cheer up when his father returned from work with new treasure — a broken but serviceable umbrella, a man's watch with a cracked face that still ran, a pair of barely used pantyhose, or a lady's scarf, sometimes monogrammed, often still smelling of its owner's perfume — all left behind by passengers on the bus or elevated train. His parents kept these collectibles in the drawers of the china cabinet in the dining room, where most people would keep their good silverware and cloth napkins. In the week before Cousins Club, Robert noticed Vishniak making a particular effort, but even when one of that week's scarves turned out to be silk, Stacia said barely a word, her eyes scanning the living room in search of excess dust.

Stacia cleaned and vacuumed, not to please her sister or brother or mother, or even the various cousins who lived blocks away and were seen with regularity; her worry focused utterly and completely on the two rich cousins, their wives, and a third man, a brother-in-law, who was also a distant relation. In their family, out of either habit or tradition, cousins often married cousins.

The much-anticipated Saturday night arrived, and despite the constant shortage of parking on the block, the rich cousins somehow found spots in front of the house. Robert looked out the window and saw three Cadillacs in a row: pale blue, silver, and pink. His parents and aunts and uncles waited in the living room, assembled near the bay window, peering as if at a passing parade. He heard whispers of "those earrings" and "that coat" and "with all his money you'd think he could buy a better rug."

The rich cousins burst through the door, the men first, wearing leather jackets and jingling the change in their pockets. The wives had blond hair the color of yellow corn before boiling; all three wore long furs of varying colors and patterns. They shook hands and smiled and kissed the air like movie stars as the crowd gathered around them. Barry and Robert stood by to take their coats.

After exchanging fast greetings, the men went downstairs to play poker and the women remained in the living room, sitting around a spread of food on snack tables—chopped liver and herring, creamed cheese stuffed inside olives, knishes and kishke and pumpernickel and all kinds of fruit. This was only the hors d'oeuvres. The real food came out after the men finished their game and joined them. It was a basic rule of all family functions that no one skimped on food, his mother and grandmother least of all, even if for the next six months they all ate leftovers and bought dented cans from the discount bin.

All night, Barry and Robert made trips up and down the stairs with sweaters and overcoats, but the long furs and leather jackets of the rich cousins weighed as much as all the other coats combined and needed two trips. The silk linings of the three minks smelled of cigarettes and heavy perfume. Robert put them on top of the stuff on his parents' bed in a heap, a mountain of coats.

In the master bedroom, Barry tried to entertain Robert with his skill as a mimic. His newest impression was of an old man who lived down the block, an epileptic who a few months earlier had had a fit while walking his dog on Disston Street. The drama of the event—the barking, his wife rushing out of the house with a butter knife to put under his tongue—had been the talk of the neighborhood for weeks. At recess, Barry now fell to the ground regularly, wriggling, groaning, and foaming at the mouth to great applause from his peers; he repeated the performance for Robert that night, having achieved a kind of studied perfection through practice, but Robert was already bored with his brother's small repertoire.

"Try someone else already! What about your gym teacher, the one who's always got his hand down his pants? Or the cashier at Shop N' Bag, with the lisp, who hates when Ma comes with all her coupons?"

But Barry would please only himself and fell onto the coats, cookie spit erupting from his mouth as he kicked out one leg in a series of scissorlike motions and almost tumbled off the bed.

Robert left his brother and went out into the hall, sat on the landing where no one could see anything but his feet, and listened to the hum of female chatter down below and the high-pitched exclamations of delight. *Fake*, he thought, *all fake*. With the arrival of the rich cousins, the other women, when they bothered to say anything at all, spoke in high, strangled voices. His mother was talking about how well Robert did in school, that his teacher had suggested he apply to Central, the city's academic magnet high school. How strange to hear her talking of him this way—she never did, never called him smart or praised him in any way.

One of the rich cousins talked about a trip she'd taken to Florida and plans she and her husband had to visit South America, where gambling was legal. All the rich cousins were big gamblers, his father had told him. Was that not a lesson in itself?

Robert walked carefully down the steps to where the women sat. Aunt Lolly winked at him and spread her arms wide. When he got close to her, she smothered him against her enormous bosom. Cece took his face in her hands and kissed him wetly, and Uncle Frank's wife pecked his cheek. Then one of the rich cousins put her hand on his arm, a small hand with long fingers, nails painted red.

"So handsooome," she purred, clamping her fingers around his wrist, "he looks just like Monty Clift." Finally she released him and he walked into the dining room.

"What good will his looks do him?" Stacia asked. "They won't help him earn a living. As it is the girls run after him. Only thirteen years old and they call the house. Call the house!"

The other women laughed, though Stacia had not meant to be funny.

Robert mulled over their comments as he walked through the kitchen, stopping to pour himself a glass of orange juice. At school he'd heard his English teacher, Mrs. Markowitz, tell his history teacher, Miss Taft, that one day Robert Vishniak would be a lady-killer, a term that rang in his ears like a threat. When boys and girls had to pair up to learn square dancing in music class, four or five girls would rush to his side, so that he had to make none of the effort of the other sweating, red-faced males. Those same girls sometimes wanted him to walk them back from school, and twice he'd made out with Margie Cohen behind a tree in the school yard, and he'd liked kissing her but was uncertain what to do from there. Miss Taft, the youngest of all the teachers and the prettiest, would sometimes brush the bangs off his face and, smiling sweetly, tell him to get a haircut, even when he'd gotten one the week before. The sensation of her fingers on his forehead, and the light scratching of her fingernails, gave him a pleasurable chill. Other female teachers seemed to like to put their hands on his shoulders, giving them a momentary squeeze. Yes, women liked to touch him, but what his part was, how far he might go in response to their caresses, remained unclear.

While thinking of the mysteries of women, he descended slowly into the dark basement, the realm of men, and his feet made a hollow clomping sound on the stairs. The room was filled with cigar smoke and, as if inside a cloud, the men around the table hunched over their cards, shoulders stooped in concentration. In front of Robert's father were only four chips. Uncle Frank had a few more chips than Vishniak, and Uncle Fred was doing the best of the three, but nothing compared to the chips in front of the three guests on the other side of the table. Robert stood behind his father, looking over his shoulder at his hand: two of hearts, two of diamonds, four of clubs, eight of spades, and a king of spades. What could Vishniak do with such a hand? From the glass next to him, Vishniak took a few sips of cherry brandy, sweet as syrup, which Robert knew he was not supposed to do, on account of his sugar. His father's face was red, his forehead sweaty. Unlike the women, the men were mostly silent — a grunt here, a cough, a random obscenity mumbled.

Barry came down moments later eating a *mandelbrot* cookie, the crumbs clinging to his sweatshirt. They stood together and watched their father ask for three cards, which improved his hand only slightly, then silently throw a chip into the pot in the center of the card table. "Is he winning anything?" Barry whispered. "He's not winning anything, is he?"

"Shut up," Robert replied. For the first time in his life, he saw nobility in his father, who was mostly a shadow presence in his life, a sweaty mumbler of greetings who came in from work as his sons were leaving for school, was asleep by the time they did their home-work and ate dinner, and left for a second job as they were going to bed. But suddenly Robert saw how his father could be strong, losing money without speech or expression, swallowing his shame.

And he wanted to help him. He stared at the cousin who was win-ning, at his big, shiny face, his cigar, the calm of his expression, the confidence as he upped the ante, then stopped to mop his brow with a handkerchief. Because the basement was cold — only a curtain divided this room from the garage — Stacia had felt the need to spring for two space heaters, which were surprisingly effective, and the cousin who was winning took off his sport jacket and put it over the back of his chair. Robert stared at the jacket — navy blue with a pink-and-white-striped silk lining. He'd never seen anything quite like it before. One side sagged with weight, a lump created by something in the inside pocket. *A wallet,* Robert thought. *He keeps his wallet in his jacket, not in his pants. He can't sit on his money because there's too much of it.*

Barry, bored with it all, had wandered over to the other end of the room, to the table where unopened bottles of liquor, the accu-mulation of ten years of Christmas gifts from Vishniak's various supervisors at the U.S. Postal Service, sat on a table. Barry tried unsuccessfully to reach an open bottle but was too short. He sig-naled to Robert, but Robert, lost in his own thoughts, didn't see his brother, so Barry crossed the room.

"Throw a fit," Robert whispered.

"Now?"

"Yeah, a big one. Lots of spit. Throw your leg around like you did upstairs."

"Whadda I get?" Barry asked. "I'm not doing it for nothing."

"This is for Pop," Robert said, motioning toward the game. "Think about someone else for a change."

Vishniak had only two chips left now. He took another sip of his brandy, then pulled a handkerchief out of his pocket and mopped his brow.

"I want a drink first. The gold-colored stuff in the fancy bottle." He pointed at the makeshift bar.

Robert went to the bar — the men oblivious, grunting and scratching, a few moans as they lay down their hands — and filled about a third of the cup with black cherry soda, Barry's favorite. Then, as Uncle Frank dealt a new hand, Robert picked up the bottle of Crown Royal and quickly poured to the top of the cup, then replaced the cap and brought it back to Barry.

His brother tilted his head back, gulping down as much as he could, then gagged softly, and burped.

"All right, hurry up," Robert whispered, and pushed his brother closer to the men. Barry took a deep breath, as if plunging into water, and fell to the ground, groaning and convulsing, his foot catching on a metal folding chair that hit the floor with a loud clatter. There was some commotion, a few cousins got up, but Uncle Frank and Vishniak glanced at each other with a certain understanding, and Frank shook his head, smiling to himself. The rich cousins did not even leave the table, and Robert feared his plan would not work; how could he get at the jacket if everyone refused to be distracted?

Then Barry, taking his performance to a level beyond the Method, rolled over and groaned, crawling to the poker table on all fours. When he got close, he grasped at a chair and began to pull himself to his feet. He opened his mouth, about to say something, and cherry-red vomit spewed out in a great arc, some of it raining down on the table and its inhabitants, some of it traveling all the way to the distant curtain. As if under fire, the men ran for cover in the garage. Vishniak spotted the cup of mud-colored liquid by his son. As Frank ran upstairs to get towels, Vishniak went closer. Those in the garage, including the owner of the navy jacket, now searched for a sink rumored to be in the back, where Stacia still did her washing. When they found it, the pipes made a loud squeaking sound as the slightly rusty water emerged from the spigot.

Robert knew that it was only a matter of minutes before his father figured out what Barry had been drinking and who'd given it to him. Across the room, Barry sat on the ground, clutching his stomach, too stunned to comment on what he'd wrought. Vishniak picked Barry up by the arm and, as he hung in the air, struck him several times on the behind.

"Shitfuckhellpiss!!" Barry screamed, over and over, so that Vishniak had no choice but to hit him again, across the mouth.

His father and brother occupied, Robert slipped a hand into the jacket, too scared to look around him or even to breathe. He felt for the lump, felt the momentary relief as he pulled out the smooth leather of a packed wallet and took half the contents, dropping a bill on the ground, then put the rest back. Quickly he retrieved the five from the floor and shoved the money down the front of his pants just as the men began to file back in from the garage, their faces, hair, and clothing all soaked with water. None of them looked pleased.

The pale eyes of his victim seemed to watch Robert closely as he rushed up the basement stairs and through the kitchen, then walked as calmly as he could through the living room where the women still sat. Avoiding his mother's glance, he ran up the steps to the second floor. In his bedroom he fished the wilted bills out of his pants. They smelled of his skin, the newly pungent adolescent odor of damp yearning, of sweat socks and Ivory soap. He counted out three fives, a twenty, two tens, and four ones, and placed the bills on his desk to look at them. He was rich.

"You jerk!" Barry yelled, rushing up the steps. When Barry got to Robert's bedroom, he climbed up on a chair and pounced on his brother. He smelled of vomit, and of cherry soda and whiskey, and it was all Robert could do not to gag as the two rolled around on the floor. "You set me up!" Barry said, crying as he punched and kicked his brother.

It took Robert some time to pin his furious brother down, holding his arms over his head. "Listen to me. I got us money. Lots of it."

Barry struggled for a little longer, until he noticed the desk and the crumpled bills. "I want some," he said. Robert released him, and he got up to touch the cash. "Half of that's mine. I want what's coming to me."

"I have to think," Robert said. "We need to be careful."

In his short life, Barry had never been careful and did not intend to start now. He jumped onto the bed, yelping with delight. As miserable as he'd been a moment before was as triumphant as he was now. He used the mattress as a trampoline, falling to the floor with a loud thump and then jumping onto the bed again, then back to the floor. Suddenly they heard their mother's fast and frantic footsteps on the stairs. Robert and Barry grabbed the money and shoved it into a drawer, but Barry held one bill back, slipping it into his pants pocket.

"What's going on here?" Stacia asked, pulling at the door, which did not lock but rather stuck closed, the frame warped from dampness, so that it opened with a *thwack*.

The boys stood at attention next to the bed like soldiers during inspection. Vishniak's anger was tame — a few slaps that barely stung — but their mother used a belt with a big, aggressive metal buckle. Even worse was the sound of her shrill voice, and her disappointment.

"We could hear you jumping downstairs. People thought the ceiling was gonna come down," she said, moving toward the bed, her hands on her hips. "Barry, I told you to wash your face and change your shirt! Robert, comb your hair. You've been fighting, haven't you? I can't turn my back for five minutes—" She rushed at Robert but instead of hitting him, as he expected, she sat down abruptly on the bed and stared at the opposite wall. "Christ," she added, putting her head in her hands, "what a disaster, from start to finish!"

The room was so silent that Robert could hear the ticking of the plastic alarm clock on the desk and then the *click* as the minute hand struck half after nine. His mother pulled briefly at her short black hair, and then she was still. Perhaps she didn't want to go downstairs any more than they did. Robert walked over to the drawer, opened it, and took out two crumpled tens, then moved cautiously toward his mother. "Here," he said, and put the bills in her lap.

"I'm not giving my half!" Barry said, but then Robert walked back to the drawer and took out the rest, dropped it into Stacia's lap, and retreated to the opposite wall.

Stacia looked down at the money and began to straighten out the crumpled bills. "Where—?" she asked, but by then she must have thought of the commotion in the basement. There were few people in their family who carried so much money with them. Often these poker games ended in a flurry of IOUs that were paid, always, over time.

"Did you take everything?" she asked.

"I left half," Robert said. "To make up for Pop. So you won't be mad at him."

"I didn't bring you up to steal," she said, but then she looked at Robert and something strange happened, something he rarely saw—she smiled. A half smile, really, because his mother had, years before, suffered an attack of Bell's palsy, and her face never completely returned from the paralysis, so that her mouth sometimes went in two directions at once—just then, one side of her face was entertained, but the other turned downward, a mix of shame and mortification that would stay with her all night, so that from the time she served the food, to the moment the last guest took his coat and left, Stacia would not make eye contact with a single person.

But that was later. Right now, the boys stood by the bed, wondering what would happen to them. Robert elbowed his brother to tell him to give back that last bill, but Barry would have none of it. At age eight, Barry was already his own man, his behavior hard to predict. Like their mother, he always wanted what was coming to him — but then, like their father, he could turn around one day and hand you everything he had for no reason at all.

Stacia's hands shook slightly as she gathered the bills into a pile, then folded the pile in half and put it into an apron pocket.

"You gonna give the money back?" Barry asked.

"Don't see how I can," she said, "without having the two of you admit what you did. And you're not apologizing to the likes of them. A bunch of thieves with their government contracts."

"I don't wanna," said Barry. "Apologize."

"Well then," she said, "the men are coming upstairs to eat with us now, so go wash your hands. And don't forget to use soap."

CHAPTER TWO

Domestic duties

The girls continued to call Robert's house, asking him to walk them to school, and he even made out with a few more in the private corners of the school yard, but all that was interrupted when, encouraged by a guidance counselor, he applied and was accepted to Central High School. Central drew the brightest from all over the city, but it was also all male. Across the street was its counterpart, the Philadelphia High School for Girls, known as Girls' High, but the two schools had little daily contact, so that in ninth grade the only females Robert got close enough to touch were those he was sometimes pressed up against during the crowded morning rush hour on the bus that took him to school each day.

This should have been a proud and happy time for Stacia and Vishniak, but from the moment Robert got into Central, they became racked with anxiety. Central graduates often went on to college. And if Robert went to Central, Barry would want to go, too; his first statewide test scores were surprisingly high, and he got grades as good as his brother's with little effort. Two boys in college—how would they ever afford it? The assumption was that

Robert would go to Temple University, the cheapest local state school, and then there would not only be tuition, several hundred dollars a year at least, but he'd also have to get there, and would likely demand a used car to get back and forth.

The very thought of so many expenditures shook Stacia Vishniak to the core. Her husband took on as much overtime as possible, and Stacia clipped twice as many coupons. At night she turned the thermostat down so low that Robert and Barry swore, upon rising in the morning, that they could see their breath. She insisted that they reuse everything from tin foil to dental floss. For Robert's fourteenth birthday he got a birthday card, signed by his parents, along with several pairs of socks and some underwear. After he'd read the card, it went back in the drawer, only to be taken out again for the following year's birthday, and the one after that.

Happy to share the wealth of her endless anxiety, Stacia drove Robert, and later Barry, to make as much money as possible. The kinds of jobs Robert got in the neighborhood—delivering groceries, stacking books at the library, shoveling snow in winter and raking leaves in fall—never satisfied her. Each Saturday morning, she stood over his sleeping form, shaking him awake, incanting over and over: *You have to make money, you have to make money, I ain't running a welfare hotel here. You have to make money.*

Though she ran her house with the authority and efficiency of a general in wartime, Stacia Vishniak was not without her hobbies. Like most of the women in Oxford Circle, she collected green stamps. And being a saver of unusual energy, she not only saved her own, which she got mostly at the supermarket, but also those of anyone she knew who had a car, bought gasoline, and could be persuaded to hand the stamps over to her. Slowly, and then all at once, the books accumulated on top of the breakfront in the dining room. By the time Robert was in his first year at Central, the books of green stamps had gotten so high as to block out the light from the room's only windows. And then, just as they threatened to spill onto the floor, the stamps began to disappear, sent off through the mail with mysterious purpose.

The aim of her new project, she announced to her family one night at the dinner table, was to spruce up the house and give it a needed touch of class. Robert wondered if his mother's announcement had something to do with his getting into Central. He was now meeting kids from all over the city—had already received invitations to homes in Chestnut Hill, Germantown, and beyond. He'd even gone once to listen to records in the house of a boy named Andrew Malkin, who lived in a single house on the very edge of the city, a house so close to the Western suburbs that the front yard looked across City Line Avenue to the mansions of the Main Line. Though it was facing a highway, Andrew's house had a circular front driveway and enough lawn to accommodate a touch football game played on grass, as opposed to the cement or asphalt Robert was forced to play on at home. Inside the house, Robert was introduced to wood paneling and something called a family room. But after the first visit, he found a way to decline further offers. Without a car, getting home took forever, requiring three switches on public transportation; with homework and all the other things he had to do, he simply didn't have the time. He might have asked the boy's parents for a ride, but then he'd have to admit that his own family had no car, and as much as he wanted to branch out beyond Oxford Circle, he would not do it at the cost of his dignity.

Could his mother, for the first time ever, be giving some thought to other people's opinions? Was she worried that having experienced such heights, he'd find their house somehow lacking? Or, worse, that Robert would invite Andrew Malkin to Disston Street some afternoon? Mulling over this puzzle, he quickly decided that no, his mother would not give the likes of Andrew Malkin a second thought. This was simply an extension of her obsessive tidiness, her floor scrubbing and rug vacuuming at all hours of the day and night. Having finally purchased a house, his mother was as caught up with her investment as any other woman in the neighborhood. Here was her chance to beautify—for free—and any project that took her focus off finances could only be a good thing.

After much fanfare, the first painting arrived in the mail, covered in brown paper, then unveiled to great ceremony. Hanging in the bathroom was now a topless African woman painted on velvet, her hair bound up in a head scarf, her breasts round and high, with prominent dark purple nipples. The picture became the bane of Robert's existence. Given his choice, he'd have stayed in there forever, his mind caressing those breasts over and over again, but there was only one bathroom—three others had to use it, too—and he had an after-school job at the supermarket, and so much homework. Then there were meals that his mother insisted he attend, household chores, friends who sometimes knocked on his door and wanted his attention—in other words, a life that he now sandwiched in dreamily between his needs to visit the bathroom. And that was how things would have remained until, weeks later, another picture arrived in the mail. This one was large and rectangular in a thick gold frame, an acrylic painting done with heavy brushstrokes that reminded Robert of whipped egg whites. He and Barry stared, mesmerized by the woman and man, both on their knees in front of a palm tree, pressing their pelvises toward each other. Around them were strange swirling bits of color, which his mother informed them implied movement.

"Why are they moving?" Barry asked. And Stacia told him to shut up, commanding Vishniak to hang the picture in their room, over the bed. Relatives caught on quickly and began to give them gifts—particularly as that year marked their twentieth anniversary. Eventually, a series of topless native women in grass skirts lined the wall along the steps leading to the second floor, dancing what Vishniak joyfully referred to as the Hoochie Coochie. Then a large pink and red flower came to hang over the couch. It bore, in color and shape, a remarkable resemblance to female genitalia.

Robert began to wonder if, rather than beautify the house, his mother was trying to torture him; there was hardly a corner that did not now inspire in him a profound and urgent reaction. But she assured him that while nudity in Tahiti, Provence, or any other place she had no chance of visiting was art, nudity on Bustleton Avenue was filth. He found little comfort in her philosophy; Robert's life at home now became unbearable, a series of physical embarrassments, and life at school was not much better, as he was born with a fertile imagination. Very quickly he came to the conclusion that what he needed was a real live girl.

Pretty much any attractive live girl would do. They had wanted him before, back when the classroom had been coed, so surely he could land one now. He settled on Margie Cohen, the same girl he'd slobbered over during seventh-grade recess. He had a history with her and, best of all, she waited with him most mornings to get the bus. The Cohen girls were known in the neighborhood to be smart, like the Vishniak boys. Margie attended Girls' High, as her sister had several years before. She was a tall, talkative girl, with pale brown hair, wide-set brown eyes, and long legs. And she lived on Knorr Street, just a few blocks away, which made her a convenient choice.

Robert formulated a plan. After school three days a week he went to work at Shop N' Bag, where, as he often remarked to Barry, his job focused on the "bag" part of the equation. But on the other two days he generally got home at three fifteen, and Stacia did not return until around four. He would try to get Margie to his house on one of his free afternoons and see what could be done.

On the morning that he was to ask her, he stood in front of the only mirror in the house, which was on the medicine cabinet above the bathroom sink. Due to the close proximity of the topless woman, hung on the wall to the right of the toilet, he had barely bothered to look at anything else in that room, and even now it was difficult to look away from her. She stared at him, half smiling, as if she knew him well. But he managed, for a moment, to break away and look

23

at himself in the mirror. He brushed his hair with a wide wooden brush of hard bristles and noticed the dark hairs on his upper lip and around his jaw. He would be shaving soon, perhaps should be shaving already. His body had filled out, was less of an outline now, and his shoulders were getting broader; his mother had complained recently that he was growing out of his shirts too quickly. His nose was longish and leaned slightly to the left — it was as if one day he had a small, childish button nose and the next, this one, a man's nose (though actually it was remarkably similar to his mother's). He did not mind. On the contrary, the nose made him feel mature and worldly, like a prizefighter, and it kept his face from a certain kind of prettiness — the fullish lips did not help, nor the dimple on his chin and cheek — and prettiness would have been death in his neighborhood. He tilted his head and looked up into his nostrils, made sure both the airways were clean, nothing hanging out, and then he brushed his teeth and left for school.

It was Tuesday morning, and the bus arrived as always at seven fifteen. The aisles were already packed with men holding thermoses or paper bags with their lunches inside and women of all ages — cleaning women and clerks, salesgirls and the occasional teacher — nodding off every few minutes in their seats, or standing and clutching at the handles above them as if for life itself. With some clever maneuvering he found himself pressed closely against Margie, willing himself not to think of the painting in the bathroom, or any picture in his mother's house. He did not whisper compliments in her ear — Steve McQueen didn't utter compliments, yet he got women. Instead he told her, his voice forceful and dramatic, that he *needed* her to come over after school, it was just that simple, he could not live without seeing her.

Margie looked up carefully, as if examining his face and intentions under a microscope. His black-brown eyes, staring back at her, were so dark that iris and pupil were almost one, the expression intense and unreadable, almost angry, and then his eyes suddenly

24

softened and filled with longing. Variations of that look, and its pleading vulnerability — the vulnerability of a boy whose own mother had so often ignored him, leaving him to beg for love elsewhere — had drawn women to him, starting in Cece's house, where aunts and cousins first took him on their lap, kissing him and hugging him as he nestled into pillowy laps of generous thighs and large breasts. He could feel the echoes of those sensations now, albeit in a more dangerous form, could still be that boy without even trying. The paintings in his mother's house had only awakened him to what he always knew, even as a child, and knew now with the force of revelation: he loved women. Loved how they smelled, and the rhythm of their walk, and how their voices could go very high while laughing in surprise or making an emphatic point, and then transition effortlessly to a thrillingly low whisper. He loved all their mysterious secrets yet to be discovered, and having been introduced to those pictures on Stacia's walls, he loved the curves of their naked bodies, though he hadn't so much as touched one. And in return they would love him back, as they always had, because he needed them to so much.

Margie finally agreed, yes, she would come to his house after school, but then she turned away, either to look out a window or to contemplate other options, and when she turned back her expression was all business. She had questions: Could she use his phone? Would he help her with the paper she had to write on *Great Expectations*? Would there be cake?

There was hardly time on the ride to answer everything but he was persistent, talked fast, slipping his hand around her waist, lapping at her earlobe with his tongue. "Stop it," she said, giggling. "You're making me think of Ruff, our dog." She paused. "He died last year. I opened the door for Grammy and he ran into the street and got hit by a car. Isn't that sad?"

He nodded.

In homeroom at 8:00 a.m. he wondered how on earth he'd ever

make it through the next seven hours. All day — through his test in pre-Algebra, then a salami sandwich he had no hunger for at lunch, and a game of volleyball in gym where, distracted, he'd gotten hit on the head with an oncoming ball — he could think of nothing but the bell signaling last period was over. He had a secret and this, too, was an aphrodisiac — what wasn't?

On the way from the bus stop to his house, Margie raced to keep up with him. "Could you slow down just a little? You know my mother doesn't let me go to boys' houses when no one's home, but since I've known you all my life, I mean —" She paused to catch her breath. They were almost at the door. "Anyway, you're not like that, I mean, is there anything to eat?"

He took her into her mother's kitchen and brought out various ingredients for a sandwich. "Why don't you make us each one?" he asked her.

She obliged, finding it not in the least bit strange that she, a guest in his house, would be asked to make her own food. No one's father or brother in any house she knew of actually made his own sandwich, or even toasted his own bread. She stood at the counter, smearing mustard on the rye. He came up behind her, cautious at first, and then he moved aside her mane of thick brown hair and put his lips to her neck. She giggled, as if ticklish, and then he moved his hands slowly around her waist, holding her from behind. His hands moved under her shirt, touching her stomach, as his erection pressed against her low back. She turned around, confused, and he kissed her. It was an awkward kiss, slobbery, not much different from the one she might have received from Ruff before his untimely demise. Robert was not thinking of romance, or a long, languid buildup; he simply wanted to get her upstairs and undressed as quickly as possible. It was already three thirty. But as he tried to unhook her bra, she told him to stop.

"We can't do this unless you promise to be my boyfriend," she said. "And only look at me, and not at other girls. And not go all the way."

26

These promises he made, quickly, telling her to bring her sandwich with her — no, he replied, he wasn't hungry — as he pulled her toward the second floor. She was still chewing when he took the plate from her hand, put it on his desk, and shut the door. He shut it hard, as necessity dictated. If shut with enough force, the door would stick, supplying several necessary seconds of warning. He moved quickly toward her. Using both trembling hands to unbutton her blouse, he reached inside and touched the thick cotton of her training bra. He couldn't get the thing unhooked and had to ask her to take off her own underwear. It was a torturous conflict, his desire to stand back and look — to take in what was his first, full-fledged topless girl, the real thing, with a kidney-shaped birthmark by her collarbone and tiny breasts with pink, budlike nipples — and his need to move the process along. They had ten minutes left. She refused to take off her skirt, and when he tried, she shook her head.

"Come on," he said, his eyes on the clock, "just down to your panties," and without waiting for her to comply, he pulled up her skirt and began to tug at her stockings. He could not be doing anything so wrong, he told himself, because she kept interrupting him to demand kisses. But as he pulled down her underwear, she reminded him of his promise.

"Just for a minute," he breathed in her ear. "I'll be careful. I promise." But she was a woman of her word, and she pushed his hand away, then stood up and began to put her clothes on. "Remember your promise," she said, pulling up her pantyhose — which her mother, she informed him, had only recently allowed her to wear to school — and then quickly fastening her bra. "I have lots of friends I'm going to tell now."

"About what exactly?" he asked.

"That we're going out," she said, pulling a sweater over her head, her face emerging a moment later. "We're a couple now."

"We are?"

"We are," she said triumphantly, and pushed past him. She was

27

remarkably strong, able to pry the door away with both hands after only two tries, and then she was gone.

It took two more Tuesdays until he finally lost his virginity, at three forty-three. It was she, strangely enough, who after endless mornings of ignoring his begging and pleading at the bus stop, led him upstairs, took off her clothing, eyes downcast, and stood before him, naked, biting her lower lip.

"If I give you what you want," she said, "you have to promise that you love me."

What a strange manual she was working from. She assigned him oaths, and he mumbled them mechanically, hardly aware of words as more than sounds repeating. Where did this knowledge come from? Certainly not experience. She was remarkably practical about the whole thing, too, as when she requested a towel, informing him there'd be blood.

"Blood?"

"Mine," she said, fear creeping into her tone. He went to the linen closet to find a towel. Rushing back, he was out of his clothing in seconds. He kissed her, his hand traveling down her soft flesh, his fingers clumsily stroking her thighs until she laughed and told him she was ticklish. "Don't touch me there," she said. "Just do it now if you want to."

"Really?" he asked. He understood vaguely the concept of fore-play, though not, logically, how any man actually put it into practice, particularly a man whose mother was expected home in seventeen minutes. Not that he needed more than two. And then it was over. He unloaded the burden of his virginity all over her pale, white belly and lay next to her, breathless and exalted.

"Kiss me," she said, "on the lips." He did so gladly, for he was feeling a combination of gratitude and warmth toward her that surely could be called love. But love, as Margie had warned, was a wet and bloody mess. They snuck the towel out in her book bag and buried it in a neighbor's trash can, hoping that his mother would not come looking for it.

The next time they did it, she had somehow acquired a condom. "My sister mailed it to me," she informed him.

Robert heard her as if from very far away. He was racing to get his own clothes off as she got under the covers of his single bed. "Draw the shades. There's too much light," she said.

He did as she asked and got quickly into his childhood bed, drawing Margie's body close to his. But when he touched her small breasts, took her tiny nipple gently in his mouth, she began to ask questions about the poster of the Brooklyn Bridge that hung over the bed. He stroked her inner thighs with his fingertips, and she talked about a trip she'd taken with her mother to visit an aunt once, in New York. He placed a finger between her legs, exploring the area, as she talked about Barnard College, and a girl her sister knew who went there, whose parents let her live in an apartment. Nothing he did got her attention, until he had no choice but to do as she urged and oblige himself quickly. During the act itself, she was silent. All she asked of him was the kiss, afterward, on the lips, and that was the only part she approached with any relish. Then she got dressed.

The news that Robert and Margie were officially "going together" spread to every girl, boy, and adult in the neighborhood. Even girls he'd never seen before, Margie's friends from Girls' High or her ballet lessons, girls from as far away as Welsh Road, so many he couldn't even keep track, stopped to talk to him on the street, knowing his name. Had they all moved in while he sat in all-male classes, did his homework, and worked at the Shop N' Bag? Had he just not been watching carefully enough? When they spoke they ran their fingers through their hair, and touched their necks, pulling seductively at their clothing, until he could barely stand it. More than a few offered him their numbers, but now he was roped in, he belonged to someone, and he could only contemplate those other girls in his imagination. It was his own fault; he had made a promise.

On Saturday nights before it got too cold, he was required to pick Margie up, shake hands with her father, and take her on the bus to Adams Lanes for bowling and candy; she liked snowcaps. Or they'd go to Lenny's Hot Dogs for orangeade. Once winter came, they sometimes sat on the couch in her parents' house and watched *Perry Mason* or, more often, her father drove them to a diner on the Boulevard where they met a large group of her friends, and then some parent or another showed up to take them all home. He had not been aware, when he chose Margie, of how much she cared about her social standing. She and her girlfriends traveled in a pack. Even when doing their homework, they were on the phone with each other, and Margie once mentioned falling asleep with the receiver by her ear. How much, he wondered, could one girl possibly say?

She was the first of her group to have a steady, and this fact, when spoken aloud by Margie or, more particularly, by any of her girlfriends, made her eyes shine and her cheeks flush. He wondered if there was any way he could do that for her in private, but he was beginning to doubt it. Just as she met his demands in the bedroom, uncomplainingly but with little enthusiasm, he appeared with her on weekends wherever she asked, which was always in crowded places where Robert and Margie would spend half the night in groups of her friends, hardly speaking to each other. When, in their booth at the diner, one of her friends pressed closely against him, or put her hand on his arm when making a point, then and only then would Margie move in very close or, for a few teasing seconds, put her hand on his thigh under the table.

Her parents seemed pleased that Margie had a boyfriend, having no idea what was actually going on. They saw him as a steady boy, smart, college-bound, from a decent if slightly peculiar family. And they themselves had met in high school, as had many on that block. His own parents were less enthusiastic. Stacia swore she'd never give him a cent to take out a girl — was this how he was going to burn up his paychecks? He reminded her that most of his paychecks went to her, for the college fund, but this made no impression. A girl, she continued, would only disrupt his schoolwork. When he came home late on Saturday nights, she looked at him as if she could read his mind and see into his very soul, told him more than once that he was not to bring that girl, or any girl, above the first floor. But Vishniak, passing Robert in the living room one morning — the exhausted father on his way to sleep, the drowsy son on his way to school — put his hand on Robert's shoulder and handed him a few dollars, adding, with no explanation, that Robert should take it easy.

Sex with Margie did not take away Robert's desire for other girls, but it did calm him down, allowing him to function in his own home. Within a few months, he grew used to the activity on his mother's walls. Real flesh was what held him in thrall now. His first winter exams at Central came and went in several feverish weeks of studying. During that time, his family left him alone, and if he was studying he could make demands, even on his mother: to eat dinner upstairs by himself, to skip putting out the garbage, to get some quiet. He spent hours in his room reading British novels and thick history books, taking notes, doing algebra problems and, every few hours, jerking off to relieve the tension he felt at the thought of so many tests.

That winter the resulting good grades, and the twenty-cent hourly raise that he got from his boss at Shop N' Bag, brought him the first respect that he had ever earned from Stacia. He gleaned this mostly from overhearing her occasional telephone conversations with other members of the family. It was Cece who came over and kissed him and praised him and handed him a dollar.

One afternoon just before the Christmas holidays, Margie told him that her family would be spending the week at the Jersey shore, visiting her grandmother. She was dressing at the time, and he watched her pull the season's thicker winter tights slowly up her long, shapely legs.

"It's not fair," he said. "Almost a week. How can I survive without you?" He was aware now that when he talked to her, he said things he didn't quite mean. He felt guilty about this, for he'd come to like Margie and, in moments, to wonder if he loved her. He certainly respected her opinions on things; she believed that space travel was inevitable and that someday people would see Truman as a much better president than Eisenhower. She introduced him to her favorite books, J. D. Salinger's *Franny and Zooey*, and *On the Road* by Jack Kerouac. But despite her fascination with eccentricity in literature, she was not an adventurous girl — amazing that she'd given up her virginity before marriage — and she seemed to talk all the time, except when he wanted her to; in the act of making love, she was silent as a corpse.

That day would be their last for over a week, and as she pulled up her skirt, glancing over her shoulder at the clock, he put his hand on her back and asked: "Am I doing something wrong?" He still had no idea.

"Isn't it enough that I let you do it?!" she asked. "Do we have to talk about it, too?" She pulled on her sweater, adjusted her hair in the mirror, and walked toward the door.

"I'm sorry," he said, seeing that she was on the verge of tears. "We'd better get out of here. I'm just sad that we'll miss six days."

"Of what?" she asked. "Of me or of doing it? Is it me you'll miss?"

He said what she wanted to hear, aware that he had a schedule to keep, aware that the truth and the lie were now so intertwined in his mind that he could not separate them. Ushering her quickly down the steps, he grabbed his coat and shut the front door behind them, leaving the key, as always, under the mat. They walked the three blocks to her house in silence, and when they arrived at her doorstep, he kissed her good-bye. Only on his way home did it dawn on him that his mother, too, would be home over Christmas, as would his brother. How strange that this had never occurred to him. How thoroughly his desire now blotted out everything in its wake, even thought and reason. It was like a giant tank, unmanned and rolling relentlessly toward its destination. Would he ever, he wondered, be in control of himself again?

During Christmas vacation, he tried to block all thought of sex out of his mind. He got extra hours at the supermarket, spent his days helping old ladies load bags into their rolling carts and carrying boxes of soda to people's cars. The weather was freezing cold, and with the doors opening over and over again in the market, he had to wear his coat and gloves all day long. For his hard work, he was rewarded with Christmas tips and a busman's holiday: on his one day off, he and his brother went with Stacia back to the same market to help her carry the groceries home. At least it was a triple-coupon day, which guaranteed she'd be in a good mood.

Finally, there were only two days left until Margie returned. He had gotten one postcard with Mr. Peanut on the front — the giant plastic nut with legs and a top hat that stood out on the Boardwalk in rain or shine. She lamented that it was too cold to go to Steel Pier or the beach. She would bring home saltwater taffy, she said, and signed her card "with love."

New Year's Day, Robert's father was off and so was everyone else; the entire family was to come over to watch football and eat dinner. His mother needed more folding chairs, and she sent him two blocks away to pick up a few from a cousin.

He never got there.

He was walking down Bustleton Avenue when he spotted a familiar form across the street; it was Margie, wearing the pale blue coat and the white wool hat that she'd worn every winter day for the past two months. Worse, she was strolling along as if nothing were the matter.

"What the hell happened?" he yelled. "Did you get back early?

Why didn't you call me?!" Had she lied? Why had she said she'd be gone until after New Year's? Could the postcard have been sent by someone else? Scenarios of betrayal struck him again and again, like blows.

Margie, uncharacteristically, was silent, did not even run toward him with her arms dramatically outstretched, as she often did, imitating a perfume ad that she liked in a magazine. Instead, she continued walking slowly, in a rhythm he did not recognize. And then, as she got within twenty feet of him, he realized that something was very wrong. It was not Margie at all.

"Robert Vishniak, right?" the girl asked, removing her hat. She wore pale pink lipstick, and her hair was streaked blond in places and flipped upward. Margie, at five foot six, was one of the taller girls in her class, but this girl was over five ten, about Robert's height, so that the two of them stood eye to eye. Her face was broader and her entire form more filled out, as if Margie were only a pencil sketch of a person. "I'm Donna. Her sister. I've heard all about you." She took out a cigarette and lit it. "I guess it was the coat. She let me borrow it while I'm home."

He noticed how differently the coat fit her, straining the buttons across the front.

"You're fourteen, too?" she asked.

He nodded.

"You look older. You could pass for eighteen, easy."

"I guess because I'm tall," he said, pleased by the compliment. "Back from college?"

"Penn State. I just finished my first semester."

Robert had never met anyone before who'd left home to go to college. The few college students he knew in the neighborhood stayed local, going to Temple or Drexel, or in one rare case, the University of Pennsylvania, and commuting from home. Penn State had a nearby campus, but Donna had gone to the main campus, hours away. He had much to ask her, but before he could, she announced that she was walking to a place on the corner for a beer — did he want to come along?

"I'm underage."

"You'll pass," Donna replied, and put her arm through his. He was aware of the heavy smell of hair spray, the sound of snow crunching under their boots, and a lovely pressure creeping up his spine as she put her hand in his jacket pocket — she had not brought any gloves.

At the restaurant, he held the door for her and then followed behind to the small bar. They sat down and she signaled to the bartender. It was a Wednesday night, not very crowded. She ordered a beer for each of them and asked for some peanuts.

"He legal?" the guy asked. She handed him her ID. "I'll buy both," she added, and leaned over the counter, smiling, waving a bill. Two tepid beers and two glasses appeared in front of them. She poured half the bottle into the glass, tilting it expertly to cut back on foam. She had learned to drink at school, she said; in college people drank beer as if it were as necessary as the air they breathed. Before he took a sip, he asked her to tell him more about Penn State, peppering her with questions about the level of difficulty, and how she got her parents to let her go away.

"College," she said, and sighed, then spun him around on his seat to face her, their knees touching. She told him about football games and frat parties, which she called moronic, and people who thought they knew more than they actually did. Then she took out a cigarette, and the bartender came over and lit it for her, plunked down an ashtray. Robert made a note to himself — carry a lighter, light their cigarettes.

"You might be able to get money," she added, taking a drag, "if your grades and SATs are high enough. And then it's a lot of paperwork, tons of forms."

"I'd do anything to get out of the Northeast," he said.

"I can understand that." She leaned back in her seat, her face turned toward the ceiling, exposing her smooth throat as she blew a series of intricate smoke rings. Then the door opened suddenly, and the cold air erased her efforts.

"Why aren't you with the rest of your family?" he asked.

"Now that I'm in college, I do as I please. I'm like a god to them." She took another sip of her beer and added: "I don't think she likes it much."

"Who?"

"Margie," she said. "My sister. How many other girls are you doing it with?"

"Just her," he whispered, horrified. How much did Donna know of his failings?

"She'd never have agreed if it weren't for me."

He stared at her. "You told her what to do?"

"She wanted a boyfriend so badly — something to do with those twits she hangs out with. I said if she didn't do it with you, you'd dump her for sure."

He had never met a girl like this before. She told the truth, effortlessly, as if it were easy.

Donna was right; had Margie said no, he would have moved on. He was a terrible person. A terrible person who could not stop staring at his girlfriend's sister's breasts, which now strained against the buttons of her pink blouse. The buttons stood up, as if about to pop off at any moment, exposing what he could only imagine. He felt dizzy.

"But I couldn't exactly be there to instruct her," she said, putting out her cigarette in the glass ashtray. "To be honest, I can't stand her. She's always getting the parents in an uproar. So uptight about everything. Always competing." She leaned closer. "I thought it might help her loosen up, you know, to break the rules for once. And now I understand why she chose you; you have physical magnetism."

From the depths of a thick cloud of lusty thoughts, he heard her words, and his pride was injured. "I chose *her*," he said.

"You never choose us," she said. "We always choose you. Don't you know that by now?" She laughed, and her laugh was deep and a little dirty. "I'm home all alone. Nothing to do but smoke and watch TV," she said. "Why don't you come over? If you've got an hour?"

As he helped her on with her coat, his longing was excruciating, so much so that he could no longer speak. She threw a few more dollars on the bar and they left.

What a relief, he thought, walking with her to the Cohen house — Margie utterly vanquished from his mind. There might be more to the thing than met the eye. And someone was going to show him. He grabbed her hand and they ran toward her house.

Once inside the living room, she made no pretense of offering him a drink, or wanting to talk, only looked over her shoulder and walked up the steps to the second floor, expecting him to follow, which he did. Their house was the same model as his, and it was a strange feeling, both familiar and utterly new, walking up those same carpeted stairs to the bedroom that, in his house, belonged to his brother. "The first thing you need to learn," she said, standing in front of him in her bedroom, "is how to stop staring at my breasts. Women don't like that. They'll show them to you in a million ways, but you have to pretend not to look." Slowly she unbuttoned her blouse. Underneath was a tiny, lacy sort of undershirt the likes of which he'd never seen before, and under that was a black lace bra. He got up and stumbled toward her, but she held him back. "Come stand behind me, and unhook it."

"I can't," he said. "Just take it off."

"No." Her voice was firm. "You'll thank me for this some day."

He complied, though it took several tries.

"Slow down, it'll work better. Now try with one hand. When you've done that, we'll move on to the next lesson. Panties: how to remove them."

There was no thirty-minute limit, no fear of his mother running up the steps or his brother returning from school. The hours flew by like minutes. Her body was like the bodies that had first tempted him on his mother's walls; her breasts were round and heavy, her hips curved out from her waist, expanding to make way for the roundness of her behind. All of this held his attention as if she were the only naked woman he'd ever seen or would see again. She stood in front of him, aware of what she had, letting him look at her for a while, and then suddenly, with no warning, she licked two fingers and slipped them between her legs, closing her eyes and moving rhythmically, moaning in a way that he found both frightening and beautiful, until her voice got louder and then, with a long sigh, she was quiet.

"What was that?" he asked.

"That's the object. The object, and your job. And now, before you explode all over the rug, let's get on with it."

He began to wonder if what he'd had with Margie was even sex at all, so different was it from this other loud, wet, and powerful choreography. She taught him to list the U.S. presidents to keep himself from coming too quickly, and what it meant to go down on a woman—fellatio, she mentioned casually, was still illegal in many states, wasn't that thrilling? Then she gave him his first blow job.

She owed it all, she said, to a series of dirty books that her father kept hidden in the basement broom closet in a Korvette's bag. Practical experience had arrived in the form of her philosophy TA, visiting from Canada. Her mother demanded that she be a virgin, of course, but anything her mother demanded couldn't possibly be right. The only person more in need of straightening out than her mother, she insisted, was her sister.

The idea occurred to Robert—was this all a way to get at Margie? Was he part of some strange sisterly competition? He didn't know, and for much of the afternoon he didn't care. He might never meet another such girl again, and so it obliged him to seize the opportunity until, as the sun set beyond a distant window, he felt that he had somehow left his body, abandoned it on her bed, as if discarding a useless husk.

He walked back to his house just before dinner, missing the chairs he'd been sent for — Stacia's request felt like weeks ago — and he received a loud, public scolding from his mother as Cece tried to silence her, and Robert begged to be able to go upstairs and sleep. His brother sat in the corner, grinning at him sinisterly, as if he knew exactly what had distracted Robert for the last three hours. Why hadn't Barry gone for the chairs? Why was he expected to do everything? "You're not going to eat anything?" Cece asked.

"I'm not hungry," he mumbled. All around the room, his relatives stared at him, surprised, abashed. Why was he separating himself? He was already taller than most of the men in the family, and even standing on a lower step he seemed to look down upon them from a great height, and they wondered: Did he think himself too good for them?

He walked into the center, moving around the room as he bent down to kiss his aunts and uncles and placate various cousins. But they were right; he did feel separate from them and had for a long time. He did not belong here. Upstairs, he fell fully clothed into bed, rerunning the events of his day in his head, certain of one thing as he nodded off to sleep: no matter what it took, he was going away to college.

THE NEXT DAY DONNA WAS back upstate, and he was unenthusiastically reunited with Margie. A heavy snow fell, and they spent the last weekend of vacation at the movies. Once school started again, he did not press her to come to his bedroom, knew from her sister that she didn't much like it — not that this hadn't always been somewhat obvious; he just didn't want to see it. His eyes were open to women now, to how they worked, to their desirability over girls. But after two weeks back at school, thinking day and night of Donna, sitting in class day after day with a hard-on, he was ready for any pallid substitute. One afternoon, possessed as if by a demon, he rushed home and called Margie.

"Is there any chance you can come over now?" he asked.

"I figured," she said, her voice tense, "that maybe there's some-body else."

He used whatever flattery was at his disposal, telling her that he was holding back because he wanted to get to know her better, consider her, perhaps, for something more serious.

"More serious?" she asked. "You've hardly talked to me all week."

"That's not true and you know it."

"Anyway, it's quarter to four. By the time I get there —"

"Then run," he replied. In his mind's eye, he spoke to Donna, who was moving her tongue in slow circles up his thighs, kissing and teasing him, moving her finger up into his — "It's a matter of life and death!"

When she arrived, he rushed her up to his bedroom, knowing the house would not be empty long. He slammed the door but did not want to take the time to put anything in front of it. Quickly he removed her clothes; expertly he got her bra off with one hand, then kissed her as he removed her corduroy pants and pulled down her underwear. He began to try, in a manner rather rushed, some of the techniques Donna had taught him, but Margie only moved his hand aside and whispered that he should get on with it. They moved to the bed. He had learned something more of timing, of the ben-efits of not rushing, and yet every time he opened his eyes, the clock made a click for another minute passed. He was cutting things far too close, but he couldn't stop himself, and then he was calling out that name he'd been trained to call out, just weeks before, and had been thinking of nonstop for days now—Donna. His eyes closed, his body rigid with pleasure, he called to her over and over again until Margie, lying underneath him, began to cry.

As he rested on top of her, unsure for a moment what had happened, or even where he was, he heard his own name as if from a great distance. "Get the hell off me," Margie hissed, just before they heard the terrible squeaking, the door coming away on its warped hinges, then Margie screamed his name, his mother screamed his name, and his brother, peering underneath his mother's bent arm to get a better view, laughed their father's horrid, raucous Vishniak laugh.

"Get your clothes on, both of you! Margie, don't think your mother won't hear about this," Stacia said, her face twitching. Margie, eyes downcast, quickly pulled her pants up as Stacia grabbed Barry by the elbow and shoved him toward his room. "Not a word out of you!" she said, but that was futile. Barry was already moaning Donna's name over and over again, in case, as she rushed by, Margie had missed exactly what had happened the first time.

Robert stood in only his boxers when his mother came at him. She slapped him across the face, hard, and then again. His nose started to bleed, but he did not move a muscle.

"Too much time on your hands," she said, handing him a tissue. "I thought you said you were joining the debate team!"

"That's in tenth grade. Don't slap me again." He paused. "I'm sorry. I shouldn't have brought her here." He pressed the tissue up against his nose.

"You better not get her pregnant, mister. I'm not raising any more babies."

"You never raised any the first time."

She raised her hand and this time it was not a slap, but a full-fledged punch. He slumped against the wall, but would not let himself stay there. His jaw ached, but he got up and walked back to where she stood and faced her; he in his underwear and she still in her navy blue uniform with the badge over the pocket. The room shifted a little under his feet. He picked up his bloody tissue and waved it at her. "Hit me again," he gasped, "and all bets are off." He'd never have hit his mother, but she got the point, and the two sank onto the bed, exhausted. Robert heard a high-pitched sound and realized it was coming from him as he struggled to breathe. He felt as if his lungs were slowly closing, and he began to panic, coughing and coughing until he ran to the bathroom and threw up. When he came back, weak and tired but able to breathe again, his mother was still sitting on the bed. She handed him his pants.

"Your grandfather used to make a sound like that, with the hay fever."

Robert remembered the doctor coming, and Saul's helpless wheezing. But there was no talk of doctors now. Stacia did not believe in them — doctors had never done much for her father, and they were all just out to make a buck. He was hoping that the interruption had derailed her, but once he was breathing again, she picked up where she'd left off.

"All this funny business with girls will distract you from your schoolwork," she said. "I want you to make something of yourself. Look at your father, working two jobs and driving himself into the ground to save money for you and your brother. This is how you repay him?"

He wished she would go back to slapping him instead. It would have been easier. How had he ever imagined that she wouldn't get in the last word? She stood up, ran her fingers through her hair, and walked toward the door. Then, over her shoulder, she called, "Your nose is bleeding again. Sit with your head back and I'll get you some ice."

He closed the door after her, suddenly remembering Margie. He had hurt her, and apologizing would probably only make it worse, though he would have to try. That it was over between them he knew, but then he had another, more chilling thought: *She'll tell all her friends, and they'll set up a damned committee. I'll be ostracized and never get laid again.*

Robert spent the next few days at school trying to be as inconspicuous as possible. He called Margie's house a few times, but she wouldn't talk to him, even walked to a different stop, careful not to meet him on the corner. They avoided each other in the neighborhood, too. When he thought of her, he felt sick, achy all over, as if guilt were a virus. But his fear that the girls in the neighborhood would ostracize him could not have been more wrong. If anything, more girls approached him, and now he knew just what to do with them. By tenth grade, he had learned how to control his stare, the intensity of it, the softening of his eyes. He needed only to affect such an expression and, like magic, almost any girl would come toward him. All the physical pleasure he received seemed only to make him taller, more confident, and better-looking. Girls now invited him to *their* houses after school and on weekends, and most of them had no scripts and demanded no loyalty oaths.

By age sixteen, he'd made out with most of the girls over thirteen in Oxford Circle; a substantial number had given him hand jobs, and more than a few had sex with him. He had become what his English teacher predicted, a full-fledged lady-killer, confident in his abilities, understanding, finally, that while his looks were not something to be catered to or even acknowledged, they had their advantages and should be put to good use. He would never lie to a girl again — or so he told himself then — not when the truth would do so well most of the time.

Just before he was to take the SATs, he announced to his parents that he would apply to schools as far away as New England. To their credit they did not discourage him. His mother said simply that he would have to get the money in the form of financial aid, and the result was out of their hands, like a gamble. Maybe he would win, maybe he wouldn't. Perhaps they allowed him to try because they didn't really believe that any Kupferberg or Vishniak could have such a triumph. No believer in God, Robert found himself praying each night in the darkness: please, please, let me get the hell out of my parents' house.

His prayers were answered. He got into more than one college and was offered financial aid and a scholarship, and even some money from the Masons—the mysterious meetings his father went cheerfully off to every few weeks, insisting that he'd joined for the cheap rates on life insurance. Who were the Masons to help him? His gratitude knew no bounds. The news was equally remarkable for his family. How would they resolve the fact that one among them had been elevated? Or rationalize Uncle Frank's motto that nice guys finish last?

Robert went with the best financial-aid package offered, from Tufts University in Boston. A college had accepted him, and then he had accepted them. It was all such a satisfactory, reciprocal relationship that he could not help but be suspicious, though only for a moment, as he signed the papers. The next night, Stacia had the family over to celebrate. Good news! It put the color back in their cheeks, and the talk and laughter were so loud that the walls seemed to vibrate with joy. Everyone looked happy except for Barry, who sat on the couch silently nursing a black cherry soda. How could Robert abandon him? Here?

"Maybe you'll come visit me in Boston," Robert told him, knowing that it would never happen. Stacia would never pay the bus fare, or send a thirteen-year-old off on a Greyhound to wreak havoc, and they both knew it. "And in a few years it'll be your turn. You'll be lucky, too."

Barry seemed for a moment not to hear him. He was distracted, his dark eyes staring off past the stairs. Was Barry afraid that Robert had sucked up what little luck the family had, sucked it up all for himself, just like, as a child, he had sucked up all the affection and love from their extended family, before Barry even arrived?

Barry took a sip of his drink, and a red mustache of bubbles clung to the thickening fuzz on his upper lip. Then he belched, as if to clear his thoughts. "I don't believe in luck, brother," he said. "People make their own luck."

While Vishniak toasted his son, filling everyone's paper cups with cherry brandy, Cece, now close to deaf, came and sat next to him. "In the town where we lived when I was a girl," she shouted, resting her small brown hand on his knee, "everyone fought over who would shine the shoes of the town doctor. It was an honor!" Her dream was that Robert should become the one whose shoes got shined instead of the one doing the shining. Vishniak, having downed his brandy and poured another shot, said that a doctor took too much schooling, why not a lawyer?

"Lawyers are crooks," a cousin blurted out. "Have an accident at work and they come out of the woodwork."

"Stockbrokers," said Aunt Lolly. "A license to steal."

"Politicians!" Uncle Frank snorted.

"They're all shysters," Stacia yelled from the kitchen. Her feelings about doctors were known by all. Still, she told Robert to listen to Cece; medicine was a brilliant racket, one of the best, and why shouldn't he profit by it?

As for Robert, he gave little thought to the fact that the family had gathered to celebrate his launch into the world of the college-educated, a world they believed to be rife with corruption and dishonesty. Only the world of working people — the world of suckers, as Vishniak put it — was an honest one. But they wanted something easier for him.

"Better to be the Man than serve the Man," Vishniak said, and everyone raised their glasses in a toast. Robert drank, too, believing every word.

A few months later, Frank drove them to the bus station. Vishniak bought Robert's ticket, and then they all walked to the gate. The driver stowed his duffel bag while Stacia cautioned him to budget his money carefully and work hard. His father patted him on the back and nodded; Barry rubbed his face in the crook of his elbow, trying to camouflage his tears. As the bus pulled out of the Market Street station, and Robert's family stood waving at him from the pavement below, he knew that he'd never live in Oxford Circle again.

CHAPTER THREE

Roommates

Having taken the Greyhound bus and then the T to Davis Square, and then dragged his duffel down College Avenue and through the university gates, Robert Vishniak paused for a breath. He was just about six feet tall, and his slimness made him appear even taller, but his shoulders were broad, and his back muscular, from all those winters of shoveling snow and years of carrying heavy bags of groceries for the patrons of the Shop N' Bag. As a result of his mother's insistence that he and Barry take dancing lessons at the YMHA — a by-product of her cultural push that he had faced with particular dread — Robert's posture was excellent and he had a certain grace, if not on the dance floor, then in his general walk and deportment. He had shaved at six thirty that morning and it was now almost 4:00 p.m.; there was a vague shadow around his jaw. He wore his one pair of dress pants, which were dark gray and a little too short, with a white dress shirt. In the heat and crowding of the bus, he'd rolled up the sleeves.

Robert bent down and heaved the duffel onto his shoulders, then walked in the direction of the hill that he thought would take him to his dorm in West Hall — on the bus, having nothing but time, he had assiduously studied the campus map included in the package of papers he'd gotten with his acceptance. With that duffel on his shoulders, he might have made a good extra in *On the Waterfront* or, with his slimness, a dancer in the chorus of *West Side Story*, more Shark than Jet. The collective impression created by his size and the intensity around his eyes, the sensuality of his full lips contrasted with the longish, slightly crooked nose, and then the dimple on his chin, like the last perfect stroke of a sculptor's knife, all this meant that he could not walk through a crowd completely unnoticed. The occasional mother stopped to look, and so did the occasional daughter, but mostly people rushed by: freshmen preoccupied with their tasks, snapping at fathers and siblings, comforting emotional mothers, complaining to each other about the heat, and carrying stereo speakers, suitcases, typewriters, desk lamps, garment bags, skis, tennis racquets, golf clubs, and hockey sticks. He had never seen so much stuff. In addition to three pairs of slacks, counting the ones he now wore, he owned exactly four T-shirts, two dress shirts, a pair of shoes, underwear, some sneakers, and a sport jacket, already too short in the sleeves, left over from his high school graduation. His mother was predictably strict about purchases. Devotee that she was to the hand-me-down, she had never forgiven her sons for not being able to share clothes — Robert being tall and thin, and Barry short and round. She might as well have had a girl, she often said, for all the clothes those two demanded.

Despite the ninety-degree temperatures, the boys around him wore coats, ties, starched cotton shirts, trousers, and shiny loafers. His pants, at least, were not wrinkled, due to his mother's belief in the sanctity of permanent press, but he'd spilled a Coke on himself when the bus came to an abrupt stop, and his legs felt vaguely sticky. The duffel was getting heavy now and, crossing under a series of archways, he could see that the service elevator was mobbed; he would have to carry it up three flights. He found his key in a mailbox by the steps and made his way quickly, wanting to get the last leg of his journey over with as soon as possible.

He found his name written on the door along with that of his roommate, Sanford Trace, who had been a last-minute substitution. He'd heard about the change only a few days earlier, and so they'd exchanged no letters or further information. Up until then, he was to room with a David Hersh from Bayonne, New Jersey, but Hersh was no more and Sanford's name was now coupled with his own on the door, for better or for worse. His roommate had already taken the bed by the window, so Robert, feeling the end near and his strength waning — he had not slept a wink on the bus and hardly at all the night before — dropped the duffel and dragged it to the bed against the far wall, then hoisted it onto the naked mattress.

He walked over to his roommate's bed. Lined up next to it were five suitcases in descending size, all in pale, butter-colored calfskin with red stitching. Each piece was embossed in gold with the letters TSA and the Roman numeral III. He picked up one piece; it had already been emptied. There were several books on a small table next to the bed. One was *The Fountainhead* by Ayn Rand, another was a French dictionary, and the third was titled *Folie et déraison: Histoire de la folie a l'age classique* by Michel Foucault. He picked up the dictionary, looking for some of the French words — he had studied Spanish in school — figuring out enough to know that the book was a history of madness.

Well, he's a reader, Robert thought, *bilingual, and possibly insane.* He walked back to his bed and lay down, using the unpacked duffel as a headrest. His body ached. What he really needed was a shower. No, he needed to sleep. No, a shower. His mind went back and forth, unable to decide, until he had no choice and gave in to his exhaustion.

He was awakened by an explosion and sat up abruptly, wondering where he was. Someone yelled the word "score" and then "my shot!" A ball bounced hard against the other side of the thin party wall; Robert could feel the reverberation with each toss. Then the noise stopped, and he fell off to sleep again. Now someone was calling his name, shaking him to consciousness. A tall young man stood over him. He had a square jaw dotted here and there with acne. His features were small and compact, making his chin and forehead look much larger, and he wore his blond hair, so pale as to look almost white, slicked off his face. His clothes were pressed and new, but not *too* new — white shirt, crisp khakis, and a yellow, blue, and white tennis sweater tied over his shoulders. "Vishniak?" he asked, pointing to the word that had been written, in large block letters, across the top of Robert's duffel, next to where he now rested his head.

Robert wondered if he was really awake. "Who the hell are you?" he asked.

He heard loud chuckles and snorts; two more guys stood by the other bed. The boy standing over him smiled; his mouth was full of blindingly white teeth. "I'm your roommate, Sanford Trace. Tracey for short."

"Oh," Robert said, propping himself up on an elbow. "Guess I was asleep."

"You missed orientation."

"What was it like?"

"I have no idea," Tracey said. "I missed it, too. Something about blue and brown beanies, no members of the opposite sex past the lobby, the usual." He paused, furrowing his brow. "Do you mind if I ask where you slept last night?"

Robert stared at him, puzzled.

"Forgive me, Robert, but you stink."

Tracey's two friends laughed loudly.

"I suggest a shower," Tracey continued, as Robert finally stood up and stretched, moving away from Tracey, wondering if his comment was merely humiliating or a little bit funny. He wasn't sure, but decided not to be angry.

"Anyway, I stopped by to get the introductions over with before I go back with those two wastrels over there."

"Back to where?" Robert asked.

"Harvard," said the small guy who sat now on Tracey's bed, flipping through *The Fountainhead*. He was awash in color — madras pants, a striped shirt half tucked in, and canvas boat shoes. "I'm Mark, by the way. Mark Pascal," he continued. "This clown over here is Cates. First name is Benoit, but we only call him that when he's misbehaving, or his mother is visiting."

Cates, tall, thin, brown-haired, with a deep tan and copious freckles, was, like his companions, very bright in his red-and-white-striped polo shirt, white shorts, and tennis shoes that were scuffed just enough to prove that he, in fact, played tennis, but he was much less animated than either of his companions and less inclined to smile. Still leaning against the wall, Cates nodded almost imperceptibly in Robert's direction, and then added, "This is a damned small room for two people. We've got a freshman suite three times this size."

"If you're going to live with Tracey," Pascal said, sounding like an overzealous tour guide, "then you're going to be clean, whether you like it or not. Just ask Van Dorn. You had him taking how many showers a day?"

"Who's Van Dorn?" Robert asked.

"My roommate at school," Tracey replied, "and I never forced Van Dorn to take a single shower. He took it upon himself to, um, improve his hygiene."

Pascal continued flipping through *The Fountainhead*. "You read all these books, Tracey, and they still wouldn't let you in, huh?"

More laughter. Robert wondered what exactly they all had to be so cheerful about. "Let him in where?" Robert asked.

"Harvard again," said Pascal. "Sanford Trace is the only one in five generations to get the ding."

"I got lousy grades in high school," Tracey announced cheerfully.

"Who the hell cares? We're off to have a few beers. Why don't you get yourself cleaned up and come meet us?"

"I have to be somewhere at eight."

"Somewhere, eh?" Cates asked, standing up straight and glancing toward the door. "Very mysterious."

"So meet us after that," Tracey persisted. "You can bet we'll still be there. Come on. One drink? For roommate goodwill and all that."

Robert was certain his new roommate was only being polite, if you could call his manner polite, but he didn't want to get off on the wrong foot. He had noticed how Cates and Pascal had directed most of their comments back to Sanford Trace, as if for his approval. He could not help but feel a little fascinated by the kind of person who would inspire such behavior.

Tracey now stood at his desk, scribbling something on a piece of notebook paper. "I'm writing down the directions to the bar," he said, "so maybe we'll see you later."

"Maybe you will," Robert replied as the three boys left, first Tracey with his easy, confident gait, then Cates following quickly, hands in his pockets, his mouth set in what seemed to be its natural frown, and finally Pascal, still absorbed in *The Fountainhead*, which he now took with him as he slumped out of the room, shoulders hunched.

Quickly Robert unzipped the duffel. His clothes, which had been folded carefully by his mother, were now a wrinkled mess. In one corner she had shoved a series of bath towels and washcloths, thin and scratchy, some of them belonging to an elderly Kupferberg cousin who had recently died of a heart attack. When someone died in his family, everyone divvied up their towels and sheets, and no one was faster to the scene of tragedy, her arms laden with empty shopping bags, than Stacia. He took a towel, a fresh shirt, and some underwear with him, too, and a bar of soap and some shampoo that had come from a much larger bottle and been transferred into this smaller one, with a scraped-off label, doubtless as part of some new system of his mother's for shampoo economy. Then he walked out the door and down the hall to the bathroom.

The place was a dazzling white, the tiles sparkling under the glare of artificial light. The urinals were empty, and so were the stalls and showers. Everyone must have been at dinner or out with their families. The floor's occupants had hung their towels on rows and rows of hooks. A long shelf above the towels held their shaving cream and razors, hair cream and toothpaste. A trusting bunch, Robert thought, already they were treating the place like home.

There was one hook left if Robert cleared the way by moving aside the slack of so many big, thick aggressive bath towels. And there would be his, probably once brown but now barely beige, the edges unraveling, fringe hanging from the bottom. He snatched up the towel and pulled; it gave way almost immediately, and he threw the pieces into the trash. He would buy a new one, first chance he got; even if it came from Woolworth's, at least the thing would be new. He looked only momentarily over his shoulder before grabbing the bath towel of one of his neighbors and heading for the shower.

HIS MEETING WAS FOR students who would work in one of two campus cafeterias. He arrived a few minutes late. A large crowd of boys stood in the entrance to the kitchen. Robert placed himself with a group of stragglers in the corner. They introduced themselves. Zinnelli was from outside Providence, Rhode Island, a place called Warwick. Goldfarb was from Brooklyn. "Flatbush Avenue," he said, with a New Yorker's confidence that Robert would know what that meant. The boy next to Goldfarb was Cyril Dawkins. He was the only black student Robert had seen all day. Dawkins stood with his shoulders squared as he shook Robert's hand; his father, he told them, was a Marine. He folded his hands in front of him and spoke not another word.

To their right was a huge metal box. "Demonstration on that thing," Goldfarb said. "That's the rumor, at least."

"I've used one of these before," Zinnelli said. "My pop's bar, we have this kind. It's old. They must have the bigger, modern ones back there."

"So why don't they train us on one of those?" Goldfarb asked.

"Because they don't want us to break anything important on our first day, you dingleberry," Zinnelli replied.

"I have no idea what a dingleberry is," Goldfarb said, and Zinnelli told him to look it up.

Like Robert, the boys' shirts were part polyester to make washing and ironing easier. They wore lace-up oxfords because loafers were impractical and provided less support. They slouched against cupboards and walls and tried to look casual, though all were in various states of nerves. Nobody wanted to do anything wrong on the first day. Nobody wanted to do anything wrong, period; they had gotten this far by never being wrong.

The kitchen supervisor finally arrived. She was a small, compact older woman in a gray cotton dress and a hairnet. Her name was Agnes; she had an accent that reminded him of Cece, and the accent made him think she would be a kind boss. Agnes told them that the dishes had to be rinsed first, and then she pulled a hose down from over her head. The box opened and closed by a lever, allowing the boy who was washing to stack the bottom with plates and silverware. When she'd closed the giant box again, she pressed a button underneath the sink. The box traveled on a metal track down the length of a long sink, oozing steam. She warned them not to stand too close when they pulled the handle, and not to grab the clean plates right away or they'd burn their fingers. She insisted on the use of rubber gloves for anyone on scraping or loading, and most particularly on pots, where you had to hand-wash the huge cookie sheets and industrial-size pans that were too large and encrusted with food to trust to mechanization. There was a sink for this in the back with boxes of steel wool. Gloves would be provided.

Agnes left to get a sign-up sheet. While they waited for her, a few of the others attempted to do the elephant walk, taught to them at the orientation Robert had missed, and Zinnelli asked no one in particular if they minded if he smoked, even though there was a sign directly over his head announcing that he couldn't, and he never actually lit the cigarette. Goldfarb looked at Robert and asked if he, too, was planning to go premed. Cyril Dawkins remained silent.

He already felt that he knew these people. Goldfarb had the same glasses as his uncle Fred and cousin Harry, the only style offered on the Utility Workers' vision plan. And Zinnelli, pretending he was about to break the rules, though of course he never would. These boys were the strivers at the public magnet high school, bused out of their communities because they were smart, arriving home each night, trying to blend in with their neighbors and families whom they secretly wanted only to abandon. He knew them because he was one of them. It was painful to see these things and realize how other people would see him. At home none of this would have been painful — none of it would have occurred to him. Now he wanted to hide from them, but he could not.

Quickly he signed up for three shifts in the coming week, knowing that Goldfarb would partner with him — there was no need to even ask. He walked out of the building with Goldfarb, Zinnelli, and some others. They paused on the steps.

"Any takers for a pizza in Porter Square?" Zinnelli asked. "I know a place where you can get an extra large for two bucks." Word spread fast and about half of the original trainees walked together toward the college gates. Robert told Zinnelli that he'd like to go with them, but he had other plans. Goldfarb looked dejected. Zinnelli finally lit the cigarette he'd been holding for so long and said, "Suit yourself." Robert walked with them toward the Red Line, but when they'd gotten about a half block from the school he let the others get ahead, watching their swagger as they moved up College Avenue. Stopping at the traffic light, he heard a noise and glanced back over his shoulder, watching Cyril Dawkins soundlessly rush away in the opposite direction.

It was barely light as he came up from the T stop. Harvard Square was teeming with noise and activity. A guitarist on the corner played a bad rendition of "I Wanna Hold Your Hand," his guitar case out for change. Students lined sidewalk cafés, walked arm in arm, or simply plopped themselves on the curb. A skinny guy sat Indian style on a blanket, quietly hawking issues of *Life* and *Look*. He was the first man Robert had ever seen with long hair. By his junior year, almost every guy on that square would have followed suit.

No one he knew had ever traveled beyond Atlantic City, New Jersey. Why bother, his parents had always said, when all that the world had to offer was right on Bustleton Avenue. Here was immediate proof of what he'd always suspected but never known for sure: where he came from was unvarying and gray, polluted by the smell of the nearby refineries, circumscribed by the disappointment of too many people living too close to each other. Where he was going now, he told himself, was fresh and open, filled with music, color, and endless possibility; the air smelled fresh and everyone was young and beautiful.

In reality, where he was going was down an alley that smelled of urine, past a coffee bar and a Dumpster, to a storefront with an illuminated beer mug. Inside, he heard the din of loud voices and smelled generations of fry grease mixed with cigarette smoke. He began to cough. Three girls sat at the bar drinking shots, but most of the patrons were young men.

He found his party, relieved when Tracey waved him over. On the table were several pitchers of beer and a few extra empty glasses. In front of Tracey, Cates, Pascal, and a fourth boy whom Robert didn't know, were plates littered with the shiny remains of hamburger buns, stray bites of uneaten beef, and the occasional lonely French fry. Robert took the empty seat between Tracey and Mark Pascal, then poured himself a glass of beer, hoping a drink would stop the coughing.

"You all right?" Tracey asked, patting him on the back.

"It's the smoke," Robert said. "Happens sometimes."

Tracey had been smoking a large cigar, and he looked at the lit end as if contemplating life without a dear friend, then ground it out on the table. He introduced the guy sitting next to him: this was the formerly dirty but now scrupulously clean Van Dorn, Tracey's high school roommate. He had a broad, strikingly homely face, with thin lips and narrow gray eyes that tilted downward on either side of a flat nose. He was enormous, and he shook Robert's hand, enveloping it, his fingers thick as sausages. Cates mentioned someone named Harkness who hadn't shown for orientation, and then there was the matter of four others who were expected the following week. As they spoke, Van Dorn refilled Tracey's water glass and mopped up some spilled beer by his place. Was this something Tracey demanded in a roommate? Robert sure wasn't cleaning up anyone's stains; he didn't care how nice his clothes were.

All talk was of Harvard. The Harvard dorms were a joke, but for sophomore year they'd apply to houses. Eliot was deemed the best, along with Lowell, but Dunster was to be avoided—full of theater people. They discussed the Harvard/Yale game—no discussion of the Harvard/Tufts game—and the various fraternities. All the while, the group ordered rounds of whiskey shots to chase down the beer. Robert thought politics might bring him into the conversation, and asked what they thought of Westmoreland requesting more troops to send to Southeast Asia. No one offered any opinions.

"Don't mind these illiterates," Mark Pascal said, shouting to be heard over the noise. "They don't read newspapers."

"Johnson promised to end the war," Robert said. "He doesn't seem to be ending anything."

"I don't really want anyone to end the war," Pascal said.

"Why not? You want to go to Vietnam?"

"Not as a soldier," Pascal replied. "A war correspondent, writing from the thick of it." Though small, Pascal seemed older than the others. He was losing his hair and had the pallor of someone who didn't get outside much.

"You a journalist?" Robert asked.

"I'll be starting on the *Crimson*. And I'm applying for a summer job at the *Globe*, too, just in the mailroom," he said, then added, "My father's apoplectic."

"Why?"

"He wants me to go into his business, real estate," Pascal said. "It's all a trap, ask Tracey. Our fathers hate their work and want us to be just like them, as if we haven't been watching."

"What's Tracey's family do?" Robert asked, lowering his voice; Tracey was absorbed in his shot glass, playing a game with Cates and Van Dorn, but Robert felt strange asking someone else when the man himself was sitting just on his other side.

"Ships. Commercial, military," Pascal said. "At least that's where they started, but now they're diversified." Robert nodded, pretending to know what that meant. Pascal leaned closer and whispered in Robert's ear. "Tracey's family *is* the military-industrial complex."

Robert wanted to ask Pascal more, but a ruckus had started on the other side of the table. Cates was trying to get the phone number of a waitress, but she rolled her eyes and rushed away.

"Cates is a philistine," Pascal said quietly, "but he does have one advantage."

"What's that?" Robert asked, sneaking a glance at their already inebriated subject.

"His sister. A real stunner. Women! They're a beautiful mystery, aren't they?"

With an attitude like that you'll never get laid, Robert thought, though he was grateful for Pascal's attention. The others made no effort whatsoever. Why had Tracey even invited him?

"Your parents have something in mind for you?" Pascal asked.

"No expectations, really," Robert said. "Except that I graduate. And don't go to war."

Tracey turned abruptly and faced him. "A bunch of pacifists in your family, Vishniak?"

"No," Robert said, "cowards."

Everyone laughed. He had made them laugh by selling his family down the river. There was something satisfying in their approval that also made him feel a little sick. He took a fortifying swallow of beer. They began to talk about girls. Cates stubbed out his cigarette and lit another. Van Dorn lit one, too, then offered the pack to Robert, who declined, but Tracey accepted.

"Notice how they all start sucking down nicotine at the mention of a female," Pascal said. "Oral fixation."

"Thank you, Freud-by-numbers," Tracey snapped. This was the most spirited comment he'd made all night. He looked at Robert. "Anyway, Vishniak can't take the smoke. So don't aim it in his direction. Van Dorn, why don't you open the front door? It's hot as hell in here."

Cates took a second cigarette from Van Dorn's pack on the table. Now he had one in each hand. "Yes, sir!" Cates said, saluting Robert. "I'll blow it up your ass instead, sir!"

Robert pointed his middle finger at Cates, then saluted him with it. There was more laughter, and he felt that he'd passed another test.

Cates stood up slowly, pushing back his chair, and glared at Robert. His eyes bore into him and his posture signified a dare. Robert stood up, too, just as he would have at home. He leaned on the table, trying to look menacing, and waited for something to happen.

"Hey, moron," Cates said. "It's not *High Noon*. I'm just going to the john."

And now all of them were laughing at him. He had misread something. Or perhaps not. For whatever reason, Cates already did not like him. Robert sat down sheepishly.

Van Dorn returned, limping because he'd used his shoe as a doorstop. "Whatever you say about frats," he announced, unaware that the topic had changed, "they get girls to their parties."

Robert wondered if Van Dorn had even so much as talked to a girl. Pascal repeated that Cates was lucky; his sister was at Smith and could invite him to weekends and introduce him to women. Then he went into further raptures about Cates's sister, something he probably wouldn't have done if Cates were not in the john. Tracey had just broken off an engagement with a girl named Annabeth. Engaged at eighteen? Tracey? The idea seemed ludicrous. Had the girl been knocked up? Robert asked. Tracey smiled. "No, it was just, we knew each other since we were five and we were either going to get married or, well——" His voice trailed off.

"I think you made a mistake breaking with her," Pascal said. Van Dorn mumbled something about a bird in the hand, and Tracey told them to shut up. The table went immediately silent. The waitress brought over the check and Tracey picked it up, then took out his wallet and threw a handful of bills on the table. Robert did a quick calculation——at least fifty dollars, maybe more. How could four boys eat and drink that much in an evening?

"You sure I can't give you a few dollars for my share?" Robert asked.

"We take turns," Tracey said, as Cates returned from the john and he and Van Dorn walked toward the door. "It's a tradition. So we don't bicker over a dollar here or a dollar there, like a bunch of schoolteachers."

Robert thanked him and they walked out into the hot, muggy

August night. He would make about seventy dollars a month working in the kitchen. He wasn't sure he'd had a good time with them, but he hated to think that he didn't have the option to figure it out. Well, in this and all things at college, he'd reserve judgment and decide, along the way, what was worth paying a price for.

CHAPTER FOUR

Robert learns a few things

Fall came early that year, New England fall with its pallet of red and salmon, pale yellow, and burnt orange. Robert walked the footpaths, feeling the brisk autumn air on his face, staring up at the enormous trees, first so lush and then, suddenly, so bare. He loved the morning frost on the windows and the distant smells of burning leaves, loved the fact that it was his option not to go to class, and so he never missed a lecture, for having been raised under his mother's strictures, he had a habit of trying to do the opposite of what was enforced. He liked Introduction to Psychology and Biology respectively, ran hot and cold with Economics, but his favorite was European History. He read about nihilism, and felt that as a way of looking at the world it was somehow familiar, originating in Russia, his family seat of origin, but no, he'd been raised by believers — his grandfather had trained as a very young man to be a rabbi — whose belief in God had been inverted in America by capitalism and the demands of making a living, but no, he was being solipsistic. Or was this about inbreeding? Had the marriages of so many cousins weakened the gene pool? On and on it went, new words, new viewpoints and philosophies ricocheting around his head until he felt like his brain might explode.

Meanwhile, his family sent only scant letters—his mother preferred penny postcards on which she wrote him instructions about laundry or saving money. She used envelopes only when enclosing coupons, which she did about twice a month. Barry did not have the patience to write. Only his father surprised him with words, letters about the politics at the PO, details about Robert's many Vishniak uncles. He asked Robert endless questions about what the place looked like, and how a college classroom functioned, questions that Robert did not answer, hardly writing home at all. For the first time ever, Vishniak told Robert that he loved him, words he could only write on paper but never say, words that brought Robert to tears, yet he replied only a few lines. Something held him back. He was having enough trouble adjusting to this completely new life—bringing his father along, even in letters, felt too exhausting to even attempt, like trying to haul a very heavy sack up a steep hill.

The challenge of that year was, among other things, learning to live in a small space with a boy who took three showers a day and had a habit of scrutinizing Robert when he least expected it. The first time this happened was just after the first week of classes. Robert had been sitting at his desk reading a course syllabus; pausing for a minute, he felt Tracey's eyes on him. "Something wrong?" Robert asked. "Why are you looking at me like that?" He had not forgotten their first meeting, when Tracey announced that Robert stank. Tracey was right—Robert had stunk that day—but Robert did not want such moments repeated.

"Actually, I was looking past you, out the window," he said, "or trying to. You think they'll ever wash it?"

But it happened a few more times. He'd be searching in his drawer for a pair of matching socks, or just sitting and reading a book, and there would be Tracey, looking him over. Robert would immediately check his shirt for stains. Or was he humming and didn't realize it? The two of them occasionally ate a meal together — always, they either went out or ate in the student center, because Tracey didn't like the cafeteria. During these times, Tracey would raise his eyes from his plate and look at Robert's face, and then at his own plate, and then back to Robert's face. This time, Robert knew exactly what Tracey was staring at; he had grown up eating like a pig.

It wasn't their fault. The men came home hungry after working long shifts; the women were good cooks. And the object, at the family table, became shoving as much food into your mouth with as little effort as possible. The fork was not so much an instrument for spearing food as it was a shovel, or a forklift. But now, he saw how his roommate cut his meat with a remarkable delicacy. Tracey kept his elbows close to his body and pointed his fork tongs down, always gathering the vegetables close, using the knife to organize the food and cut it, but no more — no licking the knife or scraping it against the plate. And then there was how Tracey coordinated eating and talking — remarkable! Nothing spewed from his mouth or rolled around on his tongue. He seemed hardly to be eating at all, as if it were all a sleight of hand.

Realizing all this, Robert felt as if someone had raised a window shade in a dark room. This was something he could correct about himself, but his fingers rebelled against the new way of moving and gripping. He wanted always to put the knife into a different hand, to move the fork in another direction, so for a while his habits were a hodgepodge and he felt muddled even in the simple act of eating.

Often when Robert came back to the dorm he found Tracey lying on his bed still in his pajamas, his cheeks pink from a slow, pleasant inebriation. Had he even gone to class? Under his bed he kept several different kinds of liquor and a large bottle of Wild Turkey, which he poured into a shot glass that he washed each night before bed, no matter what state he was in. In the beginning he always offered Robert a shot but soon gave up. More than the drinks themselves, Robert liked the accoutrements of alcohol, liked the martini shaker and triangular glasses that Tracey kept on his bookshelf. Or the silver flask he sometimes carried, given to him by his grandfather.

Tracey spent much of his time reading, but not for classes. Robert found Tracey's tastes both varied and puzzling — what exactly united them? The first half of the first semester, Tracey was slowly making his way through Proust's *A la Recherche du Temps Perdu*, which he translated for Robert as *In Search of Lost Time*. Robert was interested in any book with a section called "Sodom and Gomorrah," but when Robert asked Tracey to tell him what the book was about, he replied that Robert would have to read it for himself.

"I'll never get through a book that thick in a language I don't understand," he said. "Is it at least dirty?"

"The part I'm on now," Tracey said, "there's some stuff about your man Dreyfus."

"He's not my man," Robert snapped, surprised Tracey knew who Alfred Dreyfus was — surprised, too, that Tracey knew Robert was Jewish. Though of course he would, from Robert's last name, and his face. All his life, variations of that face had stared back at him from Cece's photo albums, the pictures sent decades ago from faraway relatives — boys playing violins, frowning women wearing kerchiefs — people frozen in time. He'd been taught to expect that any comment from an outsider would be hostile, but there was nothing unkind in Tracey's remark; only a statement of fact. "Sorry," Robert said. "I just mean that he died before I was born."

"I'm merely listing what's in the book," Tracey said, "no need to get your feathers in an uproar. The narrator is a clever little man who hides behind pillars and listens through walls, spying on people."

"Doesn't sound like my kind of thing," Robert said. "What happened to Ayn Rand and how man struggles alone — what happened to Howard Roark?"

"I gave the book to Pascal—I think I've already outgrown Rand. She was timelier in the nineteen forties. I have an agile mind, Vishniak. That's why I shouldn't be in college at all. College is the death of an agile mind."

"Why are you here?" Robert asked. "If you feel that way?"

"Because being here keeps my parents at bay," he said. "Anyway, I can think of worse places than here—there's a good library, and I can do as I please."

Robert admired Tracey's sophistication, his fluency in French, the outward sheen on even his smallest actions, but when Tracey talked about the world Robert sometimes felt as if his roommate were trying to spoil the ending on a story that Robert still wanted to read for himself.

"Sure wish I could write like this," Tracey said, having put down Proust and taken up Zola's *Germinal*. "Amazing how real he makes these people's suffering, the coal miners, I mean."

Robert looked up from his note taking—he had a paper due on the French and Indian War. "You sure read a lot," Robert said, though he wondered if it counted that Tracey never quite finished the books. "Maybe you'll be a novelist."

"Never happen," Tracey replied.

"Why on earth not?"

"I've never been very good at wanting things for more than a day or two. I can conjure up the desire, say, for a sailboat, or an ice cream. But then I get it and move on."

Oh, that's one I could teach you, Robert thought, *how to want.*

"I think I'm scared of being a certain kind of person," Tracey said.

"What kind?"

"The kind who spends his whole life trying to do something very *meaningful* and *important*, but never quite does, and becomes miserable, always reaching for what he can't grasp. Or he strives for years and years, and finally achieves that wonderful thing, cures that disease, writes that symphony, then looks around and says — 'Is this all there is?' "

"There has to be a third option, right?" Robert asked. "I mean, come on. What about doing something just because you love it?"

"Like what, exactly?" Tracey asked.

"I don't know, I haven't found it yet," Robert said. "We're only in the first semester." There was sex, of course, but he couldn't exactly do that for a living.

"Think about it," Tracey said, picking up his book again. "Someday you'll see I'm right."

The only class Tracey went to consistently was French Literature; the only paper Robert saw him writing during that first semester was on Sartre's *Nausea*. The whole time he typed, with two fingers on a brand-new electric typewriter, he complained to Robert that the problem with writing papers was that they sucked all the life out of books and ruined the whole experience. "A waste of my time," Tracey said after he'd handed in the paper and received a B+. Robert wondered exactly what Tracey would be doing with his time, in lieu of writing papers.

After that, Tracey found a guy willing to type his essays for seventy-five cents a page and write the whole thing for twenty dollars. That guy, Robert found out later, was Goldfarb, who occasionally farmed his business out to his compatriots in the kitchen. Robert could have used the money, but he always declined, not out of a sense of honesty but more because the chain of command made him uncomfortable. When Goldfarb delivered one such paper to their room, he nodded at Robert, looking as ashamed to be seen as Robert was to see him. Only Tracey was genial and welcoming, unruffled as he reached for his wallet.

As the weather grew cold, Tracey announced that no matter what his parents said about it, he had no intention of washing his own laundry. Robert offered to show him how to use the machines in the basement, where you could do a load for a quarter but had to keep your coat on, as the heat never seemed to work.

"It's a waste of my time, washing shirts like a charwoman," Tracey said, and Robert wondered, yet again, exactly what Tracey did with his time. Several nights a week he went out with his friends, but mostly he was in the room. He made no reply to Tracey's laundry declaration, fearing that Tracey would then offer to employ him and he would have a dilemma; again, he could use the money, but his pride would not allow it.

Tracey's solution was to wear a shirt a few times, until it was no longer clean enough for him, and then throw it down the garbage chute and buy a new one. Robert paid attention to these intervals and was sure to go to the chute himself, late at night when the hall was empty, or early in the morning before Tracey got up. Garbage often stuck there for days, and he could reach down and retrieve the shirt, wash it, and wear it as his own. At first he was secretive about this, and he hid the shirts in a box under the bed, wearing them only when he knew Tracey would be gone. As the collection grew larger, Robert noticed that when he wore Tracey's shirts he felt different, more confident. Then he wanted to wear them all the time. It was inevitable that he'd get caught, but when Tracey finally saw him in one of his own discarded shirts, his face registered no recognition. "New shirt?" he asked, and Robert mumbled a faint yes. How had Tracey, normally so observant, not noticed? Some of the shirts even had Tracey's initials on them, but they were so soft and so beautifully cut that Robert could not let them go to waste.

CHAPTER FIVE

Robert takes a road trip

In 1965 Tufts was considered coed, with the Jackson College girls living on campus but in dorms guarded by housemothers who took their job seriously. Boys visited officially on Sunday afternoons; they sat in the living room and talked to their dates, drinking nonalcoholic punch and eating cookies while a chaperone looked on. The girls had to sign in and out at night—at the end of a Saturday night date, boys were permitted only up to the dorm entrance, known as the fishbowl, where they said good-bye amid a flurry of public scrutiny.

The first year of college provided even less privacy and freedom than his parents' house, at least in terms of girls. The only sex he was having that first semester was with himself. And he was not alone. The halls of his dorm were filled with the sexually frustrated; in the morning they rushed to the toilets and showers, barely meeting each other's glances. Grade stress did not make things any easier, nor did having a roommate. Robert could not fall asleep anymore without jerking off, but he had to wait until he heard the low snoring on the other side of the room. Sometimes he was certain Tracey was sleeping, and suddenly the snoring would stop. Had Tracey woken up? He was a restless sleeper. Once he thought he heard Tracey whisper his name. Was it in his sleep? Or was he annoyed with the rustling of sheets? The slight squeaking of the bed?

He had only begun to ponder the implications of this problem when the opportunity came for him to visit a campus filled with nothing but girls. Just after Thanksgiving, Tracey invited Robert to go to Smith College for winter fling. They drove in two cars: Robert and Tracey went in Tracey's MG, and Van Dorn and Cates followed in Cates's Citroën, with Pascal sandwiched in the back. Tracey's crowd liked small, fast, and somewhat uncomfortable sports cars. The MG was dark green and the Citroën pale yellow with a black-and-white racing stripe down the middle. Both boys had gotten the cars as hand-me-downs from their fathers, so Tracey's MG had a small dent on the door and Cates's car had several long scratches across the hood. Because they saw their cars as castoffs, the owners were careless. Robert had seen Tracey double-park and run into shops, leaving the key in the ignition, or he would drive up on the campus lawn and coat the tires with mud, or miss the ashtray with his cigarette, leaving it to burn a hole in the carpet. That night Tracey sped through rain and salt and stop signs, his foot heavy on the gas, uncaring about the notorious speed traps on I-91, until just outside Springfield, when the rain turned to snow and the cars around them slowed to a crawl.

Over two hours after leaving Boston, they drove into the town of Northampton, down Main Street with its narrow storefront shops aglow in Christmas lights, then up a hill and through the tall iron gates to the campus. Robert looked out the window at the odd mix of architectural styles: the slope-roofed wooden and brick houses with big front porches; then the library with its dignified sandstone pillars; and then a group of modern, boxy buildings. Ancient oaks lined the streets, their bare branches frosted with a thin layer of white. The car rounded a curving road beside a frozen pond slick as a layer of glass; two skaters, arms clasped, spun round and round as if in a snow globe.

Tracey parked in a large lot—the others were already there, waiting—and they all got out of their cars, their breath clouding in front of them as they walked into a vast quadrangle, the kind of square Robert imagined in cities in Europe, and then they trudged up the high stairway toward the neo-Grecian entrance to Gardner House. Inside an elderly housemother checked their names off a list and told them to remove their wet shoes. She pointed to a fire going in the sitting room where, she said, they could warm their feet. Beyond the French doors, a group gathered around the grand piano singing "White Christmas," though the holiday was three weeks away. In front of an enormous Christmas tree two couples posed for photos.

They all removed their shoes and the others quickly dispersed to look for their girls. Robert took the housemother's advice and went to stand in front of the fireplace. The flames threw blue sparks, and the heat slowly licked at the edges of his icy toes. He'd always been fascinated by fire—as boys he and Barry had sometimes set pieces of paper alight, dropping them into an old ashtray in the basement. Why shouldn't he have a fireplace someday? If he really wanted it? He noticed a hole in his sock, the sole clue that gave him away—Tracey had lent him a navy blazer to go with the shirts he now regularly purloined. His pants were serviceable but not conspicuous. He reached down and pulled the material around his naked toe.

"Say cheeseburger!" someone called, and a flash went off.

No one at home would have believed that such a world existed, except in the movies. They'd have argued with him if he tried to tell them about the polished floors and Persian carpets, the low whisperings and polite laughter. On top of the tree a gold angel tilted precariously. In the corner a middle-aged woman in a dark uniform, her face etched with heavy frown lines, ladled eggnog and handed it to thirsty guests.

That night he met the mysterious Annabeth, her blond hair twisted on top of her head like an enormous pastry, and Claudia Cates, whose large hazel eyes looked out serenely from beneath a fringe of dark bangs, her legs long and shapely in lace tights worn with a short pink dress. There were a few other girls with them as well, but Robert wasn't introduced; Tracey spent his evening with Annabeth while Cates, Van Dorn, and Pascal kept the others in a tight circle.

Still, there were plenty of pretty girls to go around, creamy-skinned girls in lush fabrics like cashmere and velvet that hinted at the rewards of further softness underneath. Would he have the nerve to kiss one? He would have to try. They were girls, after all, and he knew all about girls. But the place made him antsy. Tracey and Annabeth walked arm in arm around the ground floor, whispering to each other. They seemed awfully friendly for a couple who'd just broken an engagement; he wondered if he'd ever find out what had really happened there.

He wasn't the only one who was curious. The dining room doubled as the dance floor, and a boy stood in the corner spinning records. The music was wonderful that year — the Beatles, the Rolling Stones, and Roy Orbison — music that college students would dance to for generations. Robert asked girl after girl to dance and was surprised to find that they all said yes and they all knew he was Tracey's roommate.

"We saw you come in," said a girl named Audra, who danced with him to "Look of Love" by Lesley Gore. "What's it like living with Sanford Trace?"

"He's nice enough," Robert mumbled.

"Is it over with him and Annabeth? She came to school with a ring and then a few days later it was gone."

"I don't know anything about it."

"I'm no gossip, but she's so closemouthed that she invites it. And he's, I mean . . ."

"What?" Robert asked.

"Tell me, do you know what kind of cookies he likes?"

"Cookies?!" Robert asked, unable to keep from laughing. "I suppose you can never lose with chocolate chip. But why don't you ask him yourself?"

Every girl he danced with that night—even those who danced very close; even a girl who'd gone to the balcony with him to kiss—still managed to ask about Tracey and Annabeth, or just Tracey. Until finally he could conclude only that either the girls at Smith College did nothing all day but talk about each other, or Tracey was a more important person than he'd realized. Certain girls talked about Robert's roommate the way they'd discuss the son of a film star or a rock musician. They told him of Tracey's attendance as Annabeth's escort when she came out at something called the Autumn Ball, and of his mother's appearance in the society papers, but mostly, there were questions—what kind of girl, exactly, was Sanford Trace looking for? Blond or brunette? Northern or Southern? Sporty? Bookish?

Did Tracey know that girls talked about him this way? Was that why he let so few people into his circle? Had Robert been in his position, he'd have used his popularity very differently indeed.

Robert spent much of the night silently casing Claudia Cates. Her brother dogged her every step, dragging her off every time Robert approached, or pushing her to dance with Pascal or Van Dorn. Robert finally got his chance when the Amherst Glee Club arrived to sing in the living room with the Smith singing groups and the dance floor began to empty. Cates left to get a good seat and Robert approached Claudia as she lingered near the door. "I'm the one your brother hates," he said. "So how bad could I be?"

To his relief, she laughed. "You look just fine to me. More than fine, actually."

"Dance?" he asked. "Before they close up for the night?"

She nodded and followed him onto the floor. They heard the opening beats of "The Shoop Shoop Song," by Betty Everett, garbled at first, then loud and clear. He took her hand, silently thanking Stacia for making him and Barry take those dreaded dance lessons. Dancing, he'd known even then, was just a way of touching a certain kind of girl — the kind you might not get near otherwise. Robert spun Claudia round and round, and she laughed and threw her head back in a pretty way.

"Full disclosure, Robert," she said breathlessly. "I'm engaged to a boy at West Point."

"Congratulations," Robert said. "There goes my plan to propose when the song's over."

"Was that wrong to say it so quickly?"

"You must love him; you want to do the right thing," Robert said. "When's the big day?"

"April."

"So soon?"

"Charlie leaves for Vietnam just after graduation."

"Are you worried?"

"Not at all," she said. "He's sure it'll all be sewn up in a few months."

Robert dipped her half-comically and then pulled her up. She was very close to him now, and then she moved gracefully away. He watched her slim hips moving to the music, her head bobbing up and down. Fiancé or no fiancé, he wondered if he could get her alone.

"I bet women really go for you," she said.

"Yeah, I'm smooth, all right," Robert said, moving closer to her. "Maybe that's why every girl I've danced with only wanted to talk about Tracey."

"They're all trying to get their hooks into him. No one thinks of poor Annabeth. Engaged one minute, disengaged the next."

"She doesn't appear to be suffering," Robert said. Just then, Tracey and Annabeth were in conference on the edge of the floor. As if hearing his name, Tracey looked up and waved at them in a mocking way, then the two left the room. "I suppose they're all going to hear the castrati from Amherst."

"Everyone loves the singing groups," she said. "It's a tradition."

"But you're in here getting dizzy with me," he said, spinning her around again.

"You clearly have charms far beyond those of mortal men," she replied, stumbling and then grabbing his arm for support. "Tracey hasn't made a friend since the eighth grade."

"I'm not sure Tracey considers me a friend, more of an appendage."

"He wouldn't have invited you," she said, letting go of his hand, "if he didn't like you."

"Can I ask you something? Why do those guys, your brother, Van Dorn, Tracey, why do they do *everything* together?"

"I suppose you didn't go away to school," she said. "Crazy loyalties, like a family in a way. I think it's worse with boys than girls, and those boys particularly. Van Dorn got picked on as a kid because he's funny-looking, and Tracey took him up and protected him. My brother thinks Tracey's the be-all and end-all. They were all supposed to room together at Harvard."

"And I ruined everything, as your brother so often reminds me."

"It's not your fault Tracey flunked out of school," she said. "When we all know how smart he is, all those deep books of his. It's like he wanted to fail."

"Maybe he didn't want to leave high school," Robert said. "If he was that popular."

The song was coming to an end. He held out his hand and finally she let him hold her fully in his arms. He slowly moved his fingers up her back, felt the muscles tense. She pulled away and shook her head at him, half mocking as she chastised.

"Any chance we can go somewhere to sit down? Not the living room. I'm not much for the harmonizing Rice Krispies."

"You're awfully cynical for someone so young," she said, as they walked to the edge of the floor.

"This is about musical taste," he said, slipping his arm around her waist. "I'm no more cynical than you are."

"Probably true," she said, removing his hand from her hip. "But I believe in true love."

"So no regrets about marrying what's-his-name?"

"Charlie? Not a one," she said. "Lots of girls get engaged just so they don't have to be the last ones left single senior year. You can see it in their eyes, you know?"

"But not you."

"I'd have said yes to him three years ago," she said, "when we first met."

"Lucky Charlie," he said, and bent down, kissing her very lightly on the lips. She let him, but only for a few seconds, then the lights came on and the guy began packing up his records. She looked quickly over her shoulder and, to his amazement, led him down a back corridor and up a staircase off the kitchen, to a landing where it was quiet and they could listen to the singing.

"You can't go above that step," she said, pointing to the second from the top. Then she sat on the top step herself. "I'll stay up here. It goes without saying that you'll be honorable."

"Scout's honor," he said.

"I doubt you were ever a Boy Scout," she replied. He knew when he was being flirted with, knew he'd been flirted with for some time now. He did what he would have done at home, got up and placed himself next to her, wedged himself in on the same step. She did not tell him to move, and so he kissed her again on the lips, very softly, the way he'd found worked best with girls when you were first kissing them. Just when you wanted the most to rush things along, experience had told him, was exactly when you needed to hold back. And you needed to listen to them, even when you least wanted to. If you listened, it was like magic — they would do anything you asked. Would she be the same as all the others? She kissed him back, and he took her lower lip gently between his before she pulled away, talking quickly, nervously about Elizabeth Taylor and Richard Burton. The two had stayed on campus the summer before, making a film just outside a house on Green Street.

"What's the movie about?" Robert asked. Distracted by his desire and her proximity, he told himself to slow down, his arm now around her waist.

"Something about Virginia Woolf," Claudia said, leaning away from him.

"Sounds kind of slow to me." He put his nose to her neck, inhaling her perfume.

"A girl I know came back to school early and she saw Elizabeth, I mean Miss Taylor, I mean, Mrs. Burton——" She sighed. "Stop that, you're distracting me. Anyway, she saw her coming out of her trailer in a bathrobe and slippers."

"How'd she look?"

"Frowsy. My friend said she looked a little bit fat and very frowsy." The idea pleased her. She smiled at him, finally looked into his face, and told him he needed a haircut. Then she reached up and, with two fingers, brushed the hair that had been hanging, arched ever so slightly over one eyebrow, back into place. He kissed her once more, touching his tongue to her own. Just below them, deep male voices crooned "I'll Be Home for Christmas."

"Oh, I love this part," she said, breaking away again and leaning forward, putting her elbows on her knees. "They pick a girl in the audience and sing to her."

"It's usually you, I bet."

"This year it'll be Annabeth," she said. "She's a freshman. New face."

She sat back and they began to make out in earnest, lips and tongues touching then darting away. He stroked the back of her knee, and then his fingers made their way slowly up her thigh. She whispered that he should probably stop but he continued to kiss her. He could barely stand it, and so he was hurrying things along much faster than he would have even a few months earlier, when girls were more plentiful and she would not have felt like the last beautiful girl on earth. He had his arms securely around her now, his hand underneath her sweater. His erection grazed her thigh.

"Stop it," she said, and then louder, "Don't be disgusting!" She shoved him away with force, and they both stood up awkwardly.

"Claudia," he stuttered. "That was, I was—"

She didn't say anything, only moved up almost to the landing on the floor above. He moved to a step below, leaned himself against the banister as if he'd been injured. "I think I misread things," he mumbled. "I mean—" He could see it all in her expression: moments before he'd been fascinating to her, like no one she'd ever met, and now he was a stranger.

"Please don't tell Charlie," she said. "Don't tell anyone."

"Of course not."

"You can love someone and want to marry them and still be curious, I mean—" Her words broke off and she began to cry. "Girls who do more than kiss are not marriage material. That's what Tracey told Annabeth!" And then she turned and rushed up the stairs.

Only later would Robert wonder why on earth Tracey would tell a girl something so ridiculous, so counterproductive. Perhaps Annabeth had misunderstood. Either that, or Tracey had a different girl stashed somewhere and was looking for a fast getaway.

DOWNSTAIRS IN THE LIVING ROOM, the singing had ended, the groups had left, and couples were saying their last passionate good-byes in the hallways and out on the balcony, as the housemother prowled the downstairs. Cates, it turned out, was too drunk to care about his sister, or anyone else, for that matter; Van Dorn and Tracey lay passed out on either end of the chintz couch. They'd all signed out for the night and were supposed to stay over; Annabeth had gotten rooms for them, but she was nowhere to be found, and Mark Pascal, now at Robert's side, wanted to go back to Boston. They'd be past curfew, and there'd be no sneaking Tracey and the others into the dorms in their condition, but they could stop at an all-night diner, he insisted, ply them with coffee and food, and get back before dawn, then sleep all day.

Robert was relieved not to have to face Claudia again, but they had to get the others to the cars. He and Pascal half-carried first Cates, then Tracey, and finally the enormous Van Dorn down the slippery steps and across the parking lot.

"I hope you can drive," Pascal said, holding out Tracey's keys. "I've had a hell of a lousy night. What a bunch of awful girls." He paused. "I saw you go off with Claudia."

Robert snatched the keys from Pascal's hand. "All she talked about was Charlie."

Pascal laughed, cheered that Robert also had a bad time. Robert was exhausted—he'd done the bulk of the heavy lifting, and getting Van Dorn down the steps just about killed him. But he now held Tracey's car keys, and the thought of driving the MG did much to erase all that had come before it. He had driven only three times in his life, counting when he took the test, and that was in his uncle's old Oldsmobile that bucked and stalled every few blocks.

If only Barry could see him now. How easy it was to adjust to a fine automobile, to be the one in control. The snow had stopped long ago, and at 1:00 a.m. there was little traffic. He sped east on I-91 with the radio blasting, ignoring Pascal's warnings about traffic cops posted along the roads, ignoring the signs to proceed with caution, ignoring Tracey snoring in the front seat. Why *had* Tracey chosen him to be his friend? It was a mystery. They were all a mystery, the men and the women, so cryptic and yet so certain of how things should be. Who, exactly, had written their rules, and why didn't he know them? He was enjoying himself too much to give the question much thought, only floored the gas, racing as fast as he could into the darkness.

CHAPTER SIX

Home away from home

That first year, the kitchen behind the dining hall became exactly what kitchens had been to him his whole life — a respite, a place controlled by older women who spoiled him. Three or four nights a week he ate an early dinner in the back, and then set up for dishes. By October the work was so predictable that Robert found it comforting, for what else at college had a beginning, middle, and end? Often he worked side by side with Zinnelli, who tended, as Robert did, to pick up as many shifts as he could get. Since coming up with his paper-writing business, Goldfarb had all but disappeared from the kitchen, preferring the cleaner work of the ghostwriter.

The students who handed him plates across the pass-through could see parts of him — his eyes and hair and hands, for instance — but he rarely looked up. People moved past him quickly, and he told himself that even those he knew probably didn't recognize him, seeing only parts of his face and generally rushing by on their way to somewhere else. Tracey had never seen him in the kitchen; he rarely ate there. This suited Robert just fine.

Zinnelli liked to dress up for holidays. Before Thanksgiving, he'd worn a plastic cockscomb fitted like a hat over his ears and now, the week before Christmas break, he wore a Santa hat that hung limply over one eye. As Robert loaded the dishwasher, Zinnelli picked up his towel, leaping across the kitchen on one foot, losing the hat and then bending over and putting it back.

"I don't see what's so thrilling about the Beatles," Zinnelli said. "If money can't buy you love, then what about prostitutes, huh?"

Robert treated such comments as rhetorical. Zinnelli was a natural-born arguer and he liked to shock. His father had dreams of law school for his son, but Zinnelli had recently confided in Robert that what he really wanted to be was a cop, an unpopular choice for the time. He mentioned it in a whisper, and then asked Robert for strict secrecy. Mostly, though, Zinnelli talked about girls. That was the one thing all the guys he knew had in common — they talked about girls. Confounded by the dorm rules, Zinnelli was thinking of high school girls. "Easier access," he said, picking up a dish towel. "Boston Latin? Cute seniors."

These days Robert concentrated his efforts on the library, the last place anyone seemed to be looking for women; every guy he knew spent weekends rushing to frat and sorority parties, or driving to neighboring colleges. But in the university library, Robert could drop his pencil, pick it up, and ask a pretty girl if it belonged to her. Or sit across from her at a study table and place his hand by hers, hoping she wouldn't pull away. Perhaps it was the romantic lighting that gave him courage, but his risks were often rewarded. He'd made out behind the stacks with several girls. One had asked him to take a walk with her and they'd gotten carried away behind a tree and, had it not been for the cold, he might have had quite an evening. But Robert did not discuss these encounters with Zinnelli or anyone else.

"A car would be a big advantage," Zinnelli continued, placing a stack of dry dishes on the shelf. "Speaking of which, I saw you the other day, driving down College Avenue. It had to be his car, right? The green MG?"

"He lets me borrow it sometimes," Robert said. Though Robert rarely spent time outside the room with Tracey, his roommate was generous with his things.

"My roommate won't lend me so much as a goddamned T token," Zinnelli spat. "Tell me, how does the military-industrial complex manage to have a car on campus freshman year?"

"Parks it in a garage in Davis Square."

"Must be nice," Zinnelli said. "Anyway, you looked good in that car."

"That's a laugh," Robert said, though he knew it was true. In Tracey's car, like in Tracey's shirts, he felt like a better version of himself. Once he'd heard Tracey on the hall phone with Mark Pascal: "You never met anyone who loves to run errands as much as my roommate. The guy comes back from buying typing paper, or mittens, and he's whistling."

Still, being Tracey's roommate cost money. He refilled the gas tank if he drove the car for too long, and with wearing Tracey's fancy shirts, he'd found it necessary to buy a few pairs of pants. Then sometimes he'd eat out with his roommate, insisting that they split it because Robert did not feel right letting Tracey always pick up the tab. Books were more expensive than he'd expected, too, and on and on it went.

"Almost four weeks off," Zinnelli said, whistling, as they walked outside into the cold.

"Not at my house," Robert replied, watching his breath freeze and then disappear.

"Mine neither," Zinnelli said. "No such thing as a holiday if you own a bar. My old man works me like a slave."

Robert nodded. Zinnelli took off his mitten and shook Robert's hand formally. "Let's hope for a good 1966," he said. "Let's hope the war ends."

*　　*　　*

HOME WAS SOMETHING VERY different to him now, even as everything and everyone seemed exactly the same. The smells were the same, the family party to celebrate his arrival, the food, cooked for days in the narrow house, his grandmother coming toward him, her hands outstretched. For the first day all was joy and congratulations, but he'd hardly unpacked his fancy shirts when his mother was back to her usual song.

He'd stayed at school until as late as possible, making good money shoveling snow and working for the maintenance staff. "They paid you so well," Stacia said, "you couldn't stay longer?"

"The buildings close," he said. "Even janitors get to take a fucking Christmas holiday."

"Is that how they teach you to talk at college?"

For the next three weeks, every time he made the smallest mistake she would go back to the same refrain: "For a boy who's in college, you act like an idiot." Or "Smart college brain, do it again!" He felt as if she was somehow proud of him for forgetting where she kept things, or how she liked him to do certain chores, as if his confusion was a sign of his superiority, his education — and at the same time she was punishing him for leaving. On New Year's Day, before the family dinner, she gave him a list of things to do. He complained that he deserved a few days to sleep in, that Barry hardly did anything around the house and, anyway, she had no idea how hard college was. In response, she simply pointed to the living room recliner where Vishniak had passed out snoring because he was so done in that anywhere he parked himself, for even a minute, resulted in his nodding off.

Evenings Robert worked bagging groceries, but during the day he worked at his uncle Frank's appliance repair shop, clearly doomed as all his family's endeavors seemed to be. There were few customers, and Frank made him do so little that Robert felt guilty taking the money. He tried to clean and organize the dusty back room, coughing and suffering with his breathing, convinced he was at least helping his uncle, but he soon saw that he had made things worse — for weeks afterward Frank couldn't find half his supplies, and he even lost customers, thinking he had finished and returned a toaster or a Mixmaster that had been there all along.

But life was most uncomfortable with his brother, who had leapt into puberty with nary a clue. One afternoon, with an hour off between jobs, Robert came home to find Barry sitting in the kitchen with a girl named Mary Ryan, the two of them eating cookies and drinking milk. Barry was trying to take advantage of the forty-five-minute gap before their mother came home, but he was not doing it as successfully as Robert had, and Mary Ryan was a tough case. Robert had gone to Central with her brother, Owen, who was now at Villanova; Mary was at Girls' High. The Ryans, who came from the other side of the Boulevard, were smart and sarcastic, and if Mary was anything like her brother, Barry would never get her to bend to his will. Robert sat down with them for a minute, surprised to see that Barry could barely make eye contact or conversation with the girl. He talked his brother up, trying to make Barry's job easier. Mary turned her chair toward him and listened, hardly saying a word. When he asked about her brother, she said that Robert should come over and visit while he and Owen were both at home. Robert said he would, knowing he wouldn't, and got up to leave, thinking nothing of it. But according to Barry, from then on Mary went home each day after school, hoping upon hope that Robert would stop by. She blamed Barry because Robert never showed, and Barry blamed Robert when Mary said she only wanted to be friends.

"What would I want with some pimply-faced fourteen-year-old?" Robert asked, annoyed that his good deed went unnoticed. In response, Barry gave him the finger and ran up the steps, humiliated. When had his brother ever acted humiliated? Where was his spirit? Knocking on Barry's door, Robert was told to go fuck himself.

"I'm sorry," he said to the door. "She's a very attractive girl."

Had he returned home solely to be the family scapegoat?

Even his old bed felt too small for him. His feet hung out, and there was no way that his mother would ever buy a larger one — he did not even ask. Each morning of his vacation he woke up with a stiff neck, and when the day came for him to go back to Boston he felt as if he'd been rescued all over again.

CHAPTER SEVEN

Mrs. Trace

Toward the end of freshman year, Tracey announced that his mother was coming to Boston. "My father's sent her," he said, "probably to get me to study harder. Her errand is futile, Vishniak." But futile or not, she wanted to take Tracey and his roommate to lunch.

Tufts and Harvard had their official visitation weekends back in October, but plenty of parents came on other weekends as well. Just after Christmas break, Robert had met Mark Pascal's father, and Van Dorn's mother arrived in March. Both had taken out large parties of their sons' friends, including Robert and Tracey and five or six others. The group was big enough that Robert could blend in, required to say no more than "Pleased to meet you" and "Thank you for inviting me" to the adults at the table. Both times they went to a popular steak restaurant in Cambridge that required he wear a jacket and tie, and both times, to Robert's astonishment, the parent involved picked up the check for eight or ten hungry boys as if it were nothing at all.

They were to meet Mrs. Trace at a Chinese restaurant about halfway between Chinatown and the red-light district. Robert was surprised but also intrigued—it was not exactly an upscale part of town. He had never been to a Chinese restaurant before, did not know what to expect; it was hard enough eating American food in front of Tracey, and the best he could hope for was to get through the afternoon without making a fool of himself.

"Mother's on an Oriental kick," Tracey explained, as he parked the MG off a fishy-smelling alley. "When I was six, it was astronomy; she had to have a telescope. Two years later, she enrolled in cooking school. I could go on and on. She has a lot of energy."

Robert didn't know how to reply, but then they were at their destination, a nondescript red door. Inside, the tables were set with white tablecloths, their plates and delicate teacups decorated with intricate patterns. At each setting was a pair of red ceramic chopsticks. On the walls hung framed pieces of parchment, each with one Chinese character drawn in the center. Waiters in red jackets glided along polished dark wood. When she spotted the two boys, Mrs. Trace stood up to greet them. She was tall and thin, with a strong jaw and long neck accentuated by straight, pure-white hair that came just to her chin. She took Robert's hand in both of hers, and her palms were warm. The waiter arrived, and she ordered food for the table in halting Chinese—she had a tutor for the language, she told Robert, was leaving for Hong Kong in just a few weeks. There wasn't much authentic Chinese food here in the States, she complained, and this place, recommended by a Chinese friend, was the closest she could come in Boston.

Robert liked the freckles across her narrow nose, and how she bounced up and down in her seat when she said something emphatic, which was often. She made "You must try the duck feet!" sound as if world peace depended on it. Tracey was silent, which gave Robert permission to do the same, and they became her attentive audience.

The waiters filled their glasses with white wine—had there even been wine on the menu? Then they brought bowls of clear soup with vegetables and chunks of fish. Tracey took up his chopsticks and Robert did the same, struggling the first few times, dropping a stick in his lap, and finally managing to imitate how Tracey picked out pieces of food from the broth. After a few minutes Mrs. Trace picked up her bowl, blew on the contents, and drank from the rim. Robert looked to Tracey for direction as Cates came through the entrance. As he got closer, Mrs. Trace patted the empty chair on her left. Tracey had not mentioned that Cates was invited.

Cates settled himself, declining soup as two waiters arrived now with an endless stream of dishes covered with domed lids that were pulled back one by one to reveal: a whole fish; thick violet slices of eggplant dotted with scallions; piles of curling squid sautéed in spicy brown sauce; a bowl of vegetables that looked like tossed blades of grass, and pieces of chicken on a nest of transparent noodles that were thin as human hair. Robert watched Mrs. Trace fill a small bowl by her plate with rice and spoon delicate portions of food into the bowl. As she ate, she talked about Claudia Cates's wedding, which had taken place the week before at a country club in Baltimore. She was enraptured, motioning her chopstick in the air like a conductor. The bride looked gorgeous! The groom grinned endlessly! Young love, so refreshing! In between such exclamations, Robert also learned that Cates's parents were divorced and didn't even sit at the same table at the reception. "You'd think, for Claudia's sake," she said, as Cates stared into his plate, and Tracey told her to change the subject.

"You're right, dear," Mrs. Trace said, then went on as before. "Claudia and Charlie! So happy! So chic! None of the usual 'going to the gallows' expressions on either of them. Tracey, you should have seen your father at our wedding. Sweating, checking the fire exits like he was about to run for it." She looked at Robert. "I converted for him, you know. I was raised in the Russian Orthodox Church, but that wouldn't do. Too much smoke and mirrors! Too much Byzantium! Plus it was his second marriage, and my church didn't approve of divorce —"

"Mother," Tracey interrupted, finishing off his wine and refilling his glass.

"So Mr. Trace had plenty of reason to fear it wouldn't work. And I had reason to fear eternal purgatory." She laughed loudly. Was she drunk? Or was this her natural state? "And then men so hate to fail and, well, here we are, twenty years later." She paused for a moment. "So Robert, let's hear about you." Then, not allowing him time to reply, she added, "Where are you from? What's your major? I bet you have a girlfriend, more than one perhaps?" She scooped up some rice and a piece of eggplant from the small round bowl by her plate, and Robert thought he'd been forgotten, but then she added, "And your family? What does your father do?"

Robert looked at the fish in the center of the table, the body stripped of its meat so that nothing but a long spine of bone and a few strips of shiny gold skin were left to connect the head, with its watery black eye, to the tail. A waiter refilled their tea and brought more wine. Cates and Tracey looked at him intently. Mrs. Trace waited, for once, silent. No one changed the subject.

"My parents work for the government," Robert finally replied.

"Oh?! We have a history of public service on my side of the family, too," Mrs. Trace said. "I tell Tracey all the time — a diplomatic career is a wonderful way to see the world."

"I've already seen the world," Tracey mumbled.

Was she just being polite? She seemed to genuinely believe he could be the child of diplomats. He looked across to a mirrored wall and, seeing his face, had an urge, almost, to wink at his own reflection.

"You boys have to get back to your studies," she said, ceasing, all at once, to be interested in them. Robert had no idea why. Cates excused himself to use the men's room. Mrs. Trace got up, smoothed out her clothes and walked toward the door. Robert grabbed Tracey's arm. "Don't we have to pay?"

"She arranges it beforehand," he whispered. "Hates seeing bills. You worry too much."

Cates joined them out on the sidewalk. It was a cloudless early-spring day, and Mrs. Trace was now emphatic about going to the Commons to see the swan boats. She apologized that there wasn't more room in Tracey's car to give them both a ride, but Cates reminded her that he had a car. She kissed each boy on the cheek as they thanked her for lunch. Robert watched the pair drive away, wondering what it was like having such a sophisticated, attractive mother, even if she did seem easily distracted.

He and Cates walked in silence. They passed a strip club. The neon signs promising Sexy Girls and Live Nude had been turned off so that the words appeared as nothing but empty glass tubing. "You must be hungry, Vishniak," Cates said. "You dropped half your lunch on the floor."

Robert, still feeling relieved and elated after his performance at lunch, laughed. "I *am* hungry, come to think of it."

Cates, getting so little reaction, did not give up. "Nice how you get these free meals."

"I notice how you're always in the john when the check comes," Robert replied.

They had arrived at Cates's car, and he took out his keys. Robert offered him his hand to shake — he was in too good a mood to let Cates ruin his day — but Cates stared off toward the distant skyline, not seeming to notice Robert's offering, or purposefully ignoring it.

"Hey, Vishniak," Cates said a moment later, as if suddenly remembering Robert was standing there. "Don't spread it around. You know, about my parents?"

Before Robert could answer, Cates got in his car, slammed the door, and started the motor, about to drive off. Robert walked quickly to the driver's side and knocked hard and repeatedly on the window until Cates rolled it down.

"What now?"

"You want a favor? How about waiting for my answer?" Robert asked. "Or offering me a ride?"

"I'm not going your direction," Cates replied with a slight smile. "Now get the hell out of my way before I run you over." Then he sped off, leaving Robert on the sidewalk, puzzled and annoyed. Cates and his sister were some pair — they wanted him to keep their secrets yet offered him nothing but contempt in return.

HOURS LATER, ROBERT CAME back from the library to find Tracey lying on his bed, the reading lamp on, though he did not appear to be reading. On his chest he balanced a shot glass with a thin line of gold-colored liquid. "What time do you get up in the morning these days, Vishniak? Seven?"

Robert nodded, and to his surprise Tracey told him to wake him at the same time. He was going to the library. "Don't let me wave you away," he added, "no matter what I say."

Tracey didn't look so well. His expression was uncharacteristically serious, as if he'd been chastened by his mother's visit, which clearly wasn't so futile after all. Robert flopped down on his bed and the springs made an awful sound under his weight. "How long you been here by yourself?"

"Hours."

"Doing what?"

"Thinking"

"What about?"

Tracey sat up and finished off his drink. "That story Mother told at lunch? About her converting? It's true, you know. She was a believer but she gave it up for Father. And she's been grabbing at distractions ever since, so as not to notice how miserable she is." He stood up and poured Robert a drink, though Robert had not asked. Then he walked over to Robert's bed and held out the glass, which Robert was forced to take though he did not want it. Tracey pulled up a chair and sat down. He put his feet up on the edge of Robert's bed and then leaned forward, assessing him. Had Tracey noticed all the food he'd left on the floor at the restaurant? Should he not have asked about the check? Maybe Cates had said something to him. Robert's behavior might have passed muster with the mother, but clearly not with the son. So why tell him all this?

"Actually, Father never asked her to convert," Tracey continued. "Never said a word."

"Then why'd she do it?" Robert asked, closing his eyes, hoping for relief from Tracey's unrelenting focus. No wonder Van Dorn had taken three showers a day.

"My father can look at you in this very particular way he has," Tracey said softly, "so that pretty soon you're sure he knows everything that's wrong with you, or ever will be wrong with you, in your whole damned life. And you want to do whatever you can to make that look go away. It could drive a person crazy, Vishniak. Take it from me."

"I think I understand," Robert said, opening his eyes.

"You do?" Tracey asked, his question balanced there, gratefully, in the air between them.

"Yeah," Robert replied. He had lived with that look for months now, hoping that by self-correction he could make it go away.

Tracey stood, picked up the blanket at the end of Robert's bed and, to Robert's surprise, covered him with it, thanking him for he knew not what.

CHAPTER EIGHT

Summer of '66

By the time he got home, his mother already had a plan for how he could make more money over the summer. Within a day of his arrival, she reminded him that he would have to make as much as possible, as much as all the other years combined, because of how much he'd overspent. If only she'd known all the parties, movies, all the drinking he'd passed up—but she could only see the bank balance, and the four hundred dollars asked of them for next year, plus the books he'd have to buy if he were to go premed. He'd promised his uncle Frank he'd work for him again, but Stacia had talked Frank into taking Barry instead.

She had contacted Vishniak's baby sister, whom everyone called Henry, and her husband, Danny, a musician who drove a cab in New York and always knew about underground work. The couple lived in the West Village because it was cheap then, and Danny said he could help Robert get a hack license. Vishniak's siblings were all for repaying their debts to him and his family—Vishniak had supported and counseled all of them for years, even after his marriage, giving advice and, at times, small handouts. Even Stacia had never objected to this — blood was blood. But now it was time to cash in on those favors.

Robert could sleep on the couch of their place, Henry said, on West Fourth between Sixth Avenue and Washington Square Park. Frank tried to persuade them it was too dangerous, a young man that age driving by himself around a city like Manhattan at night. Stacia ignored him. She was certainly nothing like the other women in her family, who held on to their children for as long as possible.

Robert was happy to have an excuse to leave — would have jumped out of airplanes that summer, or swallowed fire, not to have to hear her with those words, the imploring angry chant *make money, make money, make money,* and the lectures that went with them. Barry got around Stacia by staying out of her way, hiding mostly in the basement. Barry had discovered drugs early, and that summer he showed his older brother how to roll a joint.

The fourth-floor walk-up was a sweatbox; even Henry and her husband called it that, affectionately. They were so in love that nothing seemed to bother them. He'd known before he even arrived that he'd be in good hands. The youngest of seven and the only girl, Henrietta had been so named because after six boys, her parents were not optimistic and wanted a name that was flexible. The family always called her Henry, part nickname and part ironic joke. As a child she'd been doted on by her older brothers, and as an adult she was easygoing and optimistic, incapable of criticizing others or herself. The house was a mess and neither Henry nor her husband seemed to care — roaches crawled on the baseboards, dirty dishes sat in the sink, and mold covered the shower curtain. Every chair was piled with newspapers. "Do anything you like here," she'd said a few minutes after he arrived, "so long as you don't get arrested."

"He won't have time to get arrested," Danny had said, taking his duffel. "He'll be too busy."

They'd been married for only two years, were not much older than Robert, and right from the start he envied them. So this was love. Their eyes followed each other hungrily, covetously, even around the apartment. They sat close at the dinner table, even though during his first dinner with them, he had to stop eating to mop the perspiration from his face with a napkin, or else it would mix with the food. On their days off, Henry informed him, they went across the street to the movies. "Air-Conditioning," she whispered, as if incanting the name of God. *Duel at Diablo* with James Garner and Sidney Poitier was playing at the Waverly, and that summer Robert would see it at least twenty times; some nights, after work, even the loud, bloody battle scenes could not keep him from falling asleep in the back row.

That first night, he slept on the pullout couch, inhaling the smell of reefer from the park mixed with industrial soap and steam from the Laundromat below. It was too hot to sleep more than a few hours anyway, and he wanted to be the first in the shower, while the couple still slept, so as to be out of their way and ready for work.

By 6:00 a.m., Robert was already shaved and dressed, and he sat in the dark apartment with his young uncle drinking instant coffee. Danny slid something to him across the breakfast table. "Take it," Danny said. "It's loaded, and small, but there's a clip on it. Keep it strapped to your leg, you see the holster? And if anybody scares you, just bend down real casual-like and wave it around. That scares them and they stop."

"You think I'll get held up?" Robert asked.

"Happens to most people at least once," Dan said. "It's like popping your cherry or something. You know, breaks you in." He smiled. "Don't be scared, kid. You'll make fifty dollars a day minimum. Get that hag off your back."

For his first month, just finding his way around, avoiding traffic, picking out customers who looked like tippers, staying awake at odd hours—all of it kept him so absorbed, his body rigid with adrenaline and fear, that he lost track of time, was done before he realized he'd been in the cab for twelve straight hours. By early July, still no holdups, no flat tires, nothing bad beyond being stiffed occasionally for a tip. He rarely worried about who he picked up anymore, knew instinctively which customers were desirable, when to stick with the avenues, and when to get on the highways. He got casual, and that was his mistake.

There were three of them that night: two young ones, with dirty blond hair, tall and skinny — their clothes hung on them — the third man, black-haired, solidly built. The two young ones got in the back. They wanted Ninety-sixth near Broadway, a tough neighborhood back then, not the famed Upper West Side that it would later become. The bigger man started to get in up front.

"I'd rather you get in back," Robert said.

"Oh, yeah. Well, they bug me, and I'm here, so drive." He shut the door.

They were in Midtown traffic on a Saturday night, cars honking. He had the right to ask the man to leave his cab, but it seemed ridiculous to lose a fare over a feeling. He reminded himself not to get paranoid, like the guys who'd been doing this for years. Paranoia, they claimed, saved you: if you had a funny feeling, don't accept the fare. But he kept driving.

When they got to Ninety-sixth, a brownstone, the two young ones gave him their money. They tipped Robert well, handed him a twenty, and told him to keep it. He accepted the bill, thinking that he'd been right not to make a fuss. There was nothing to be afraid of; they were his age, young guys, going, they informed him, to a high-class whorehouse.

The man in the front seat wanted to go thirty more blocks. Robert had relaxed by then; the big tip from the other two helped. The man was fat, well fed, a white man in a black suit going to Harlem late at night — likely he was a cop, or at worst a bookie — nothing to worry about, Robert thought. At a red light, he noticed that the man was missing the lower half of his ear.

They sat in silence all the way up Broadway. At 122nd Street the subway emerged from underground and showed itself, then crawled toward the Bronx. Underneath those aboveground tracks men were gathered in twos and threes, passing a bottle around. He turned right on 126th Street. At the other end was an abandoned lot and then some crumbling apartments near Amsterdam, the man's destination. The customer pointed to the doorway, and Robert pulled up in front, announcing the fare. When the man went to pull his wallet out of his pocket, he moved forward in an abrupt way as if reaching for something near his feet. Robert, misinterpreting the gesture, panicked and drew his gun.

The minute he did it, he knew he'd made a terrible mistake. The passenger looked at him and grinned. "If I was going to hurt you, I'd have done it blocks ago," he said. Robert was about to apologize when the man wrenched the gun from his hand, bending Robert's fingers until he screamed. He held the cold muzzle under Robert's chin. Robert apologized and begged—he'd been driving for fourteen hours straight. The man jerked the gun slightly and Robert heard a click and the bullet falling into place. "You in the mood, kid, for a wager?" Seconds later, he fired, the bullet piercing the left corner of the cab's windshield, sending spidery cracks in every direction; Robert was sure he felt it whiz by him, missing his face by inches. The man threw the gun on the dashboard and left without paying. When he was gone, Robert locked the door, made a U-turn, and broke the speed limit all the way down Broadway and then over to Eighth Avenue. In Midtown, he pulled into an alley behind a diner frequented by drivers, rested his arms on the steering wheel, and wept. His knees were shaking so badly that it was hard to operate the pedals. As he drove back to the southern tip of the city, he wondered if he would have to pay for the cracked windshield. How much would it cost? He was too tired just then to worry about it.

He got back to the Village around 3:00 a.m., his legs shaky as he came up from the subway. All he wanted was a shower and that damned uncomfortable couch. His clothes and hair were soaked with sweat, and he stank. Crossing the street, he heard a familiar voice calling his name. Looking over his shoulder, he saw Tracey crossing Sixth Avenue, waving vigorously, pulling a girl behind him, a girl in a short green cocktail dress.

"We went to the Vanguard. Some singer. Can't remember her name. God, Vishniak," Tracey said, weaving suddenly, grasping at the girl's waist for support and then righting himself, "didn't know you were in the city. Why didn't you call? This is Crea, by the way. Crea's still in high school, you know, so watch your language—"

Under the soft glare of a streetlight, Robert and the girl nodded at each other. She had pale skin and long, reddish blond hair.

"We were taking in the local color, right, honey? She called it . . . what was it?"

"A freak show," Crea said, laughing.

"We're gonna get one more drink at a place she likes," Tracey said. "Come on, Vishniak, one drink? You look like you could use it. I speak the truth—you look like hell."

"Three's a crowd. Gotta go," Robert mumbled, walking quickly down West Fourth. Then, aware of his rudeness, he paused, yelling over his shoulder: "I'll call you tomorrow!"

Tracey was too drunk to realize that Robert had no phone number for him; the Traces were not listed, and Tracey, more inebriated than usual, would retain no memory of the evening. Only Robert and the girl with the strange name would remember the encounter.

WHEN HE CAME HOME before Labor Day for a visit, he found himself even more distant from his parents than he'd been in the winter. He did not kiss either of them when he arrived, though even Stacia expected such formalities after months of separation. Over the next few days, he uttered only criticisms. "How much money can you save from those ridiculous coupons?" he asked his mother that Sunday, as she sat in the dining room with her scissors and newspaper, increasing her files. "If you add it up by the hour, you're wasting your goddamned time."

When she told him, as she had before, to watch his language, he replied that he was a real wage earner now, could talk however he pleased. His father had always been colorful with his language. Barry had cursed like a longshoreman since kindergarten. Why was Robert so special? All week, he and Barry went to the basement to get high. Where had his brother gotten all this grass? Barry would not tell him. Marijuana made Barry funnier, more relaxed, but Robert became even more sullen. The walls in the house were thin, and one night, lying awake in his room, he heard his parents talking.

"It's what we wanted, right?" Vishniak asked. "That he'd be too educated to speak to us."

"I didn't raise him to be stuck up," Stacia replied. "He's always been difficult. They're both spoiled."

"Jesus, Stacia, let me get some sleep!" Robert yelled. "Your insights are riveting, really, but these walls are for shit!"

Where did the rage come from? That summer, when he should have been growing into a man, Robert felt an adolescent level of anger that he couldn't shake. When he saw his father coming in late from the night shift, exhausted, he couldn't ignore Vishniak as he did as a kid, couldn't put his head in his breakfast and read the paper. He knew something of what happened to his father now, understood some of the brutality of work, and what men had to endure. How could his father make such sacrifices, years of them, for his family?

He left after Labor Day with only a backpack. He would hitch to New York, meeting up with a guy in his dorm who was driving up to school. His parents were now the ones who looked relieved to see him go. His father shoved a ten into his hand and told him to keep his grades up, but his mother folded her arms over her chest. In a sudden moment of regret, he put his arms out, about to hug her, but she placed her hand on his chest and held him at arm's length. "Get some manners next time," she whispered, "or don't come home at all." Then she smiled, a hard, distant smile, letting him know that she had won again—he had not shaken her one bit.

CHAPTER NINE

The world comes crashing in

In the fall of 1966, sophomore year, Robert came to understand dread. He had started Organic Chemistry. He spent his hours trying to redo ruined recrystallizations and puzzle through nonsensical NMRs. He was taking Calculus as well, walking with his head down, rehearsing formulas in his head. He wrote home that perhaps Vishniak was right; it was too much work to become a doctor.

In the second semester, he took an elective — Life Drawing, a popular course that had been excoriated in the local paper because it used live models. His teacher said he had some talent, but as Barry put it to Robert in a letter: "You're not exactly the starving-artist type." Robert knew he was right — memories of his summer still lingered, even as he knew that this coming summer would be no different. But a life of such summers? Just so he could have the freedom to draw and paint in his off hours? Not for him. By the end of the semester he began to doubt that he'd have enjoyed the drawing studio half so much if he hadn't had the miseries of the lab to compare it to. How on earth was he supposed to choose, at nineteen, what he wanted to do for the next forty years? How was it even possible?

If he couldn't choose, if he didn't have a career lined up requiring a graduate degree, then what would happen to him? In his first two years, he tried not to think too much about the war, told himself that maybe it would be over before he graduated. Tufts, tucked away on a bosky suburban campus, was known more for its premeds and Hawaiian-luau-themed fraternity parties than for its radicals. As a freshman, he had noted only the occasional, predictable outburst—a small group of students picketing over a popular philosophy professor not getting tenure; an editorial in the paper about dorm food—but by 1967, the end of his sophomore year, the atmosphere on campus was starting to change, if only in small ways. Students for a Democratic Society increased its membership; more school events featured antiwar speakers. In the fall of his junior year, on his way to class, Robert passed ten or so black students and a few whites outside Ballou Hall. A guy in a leather jacket and a wool cap was up on a chair yelling into a megaphone. "We have lived in Uncle Tom's Cabin for too long!" the deep voice intoned; the small audience applauded and cheered. Robert went closer, and the man took down the megaphone, moved back his cap, and nodded at him. It was Cyril Dawkins.

Tracey, too, was going through a transformation, though it was more aesthetic than political. He had shown up for their junior year with his hair longer, wearing the kind of flannel work shirt that Vishniak used under his uniform on cold days. This was the new style among those who kept up with style, and Tracey would not be left behind. He still drove his coveted green MG around campus, but as if to make up for it, he added a series of antiwar bumper stickers. Robert found this strange, considering what Pascal had told him about the military-industrial complex. But Tracey confided in Robert that he found his family history embarrassing now, and could Robert not mention to anyone that a company with his family name on it made warships?

Just after Thanksgiving break, Robert came home from the

library and found Tracey stretched out on the bed in his usual position, smoking pot. This was not surprising; grass was everywhere these days, and harder stuff not so difficult to locate, and so slowly Tracey had begun to intersperse booze with drugs or occasionally mix the two. But there was a young man lying on the floor next to him, someone Robert had never seen before. He was blond and thin with narrow blue eyes. He wore a pair of beat-up blue jeans and a striped T-shirt, and he lay on the rug caressing a guitar but not playing it. They were listening to an album and Tracey told Robert to come in and shut the door. He didn't introduce the boy — who was certainly more a boy than a man, didn't look to Robert to be more than sixteen — and when Robert started to say something, Tracey placed a finger over his lips and pointed to a chair. Robert went instead to lie down on his own bed. The music was strange and wonderful — a strong electric guitar behind a woman's voice that was sad and pleading, needy and angry all at once. He asked who the singer was.

"It's Janis," the kid said, putting the guitar down on the floor. "Janis Joplin. Big Brother and the Holding Company. Outta San Fran. Something else, ain't they?" The boy had a high-pitched, scratchy voice, like a scary elf in a children's story.

Tracey held the album up to him. "She's white. You ever heard anything sound less white in your life?"

Robert wondered what Tracey knew about any of it. He'd come to college loaded down with the Dave Clark Five. The song was ending. Was she singing "don't own me" or "down on me"? It didn't much matter. Her voice was like nothing he'd ever heard. Pleading and angry and victorious all at the same time. "Can you play that song again?" Robert asked.

Tracey reached over and put the needle at the start of the album. Then he ruffled the boy's hair, looking over at Robert and smiling. Having finished the first joint, the kid took another out of his pocket and lit it. He and Tracey passed it back and forth, then the kid came over and handed the roach to Robert. He sat on Robert's bed while

Robert finished it off, then the boy stretched out, getting comfortable. His sharp knee momentarily grazed Robert's thigh.

"Go over there," Robert said. The boy gave him the creeps. His fingernails were dirty and his eyes wild, but it was his voice that Robert couldn't stomach, as if his words were poised in the air, always trying to decide whether or not to break.

"He's not much fun," the boy said, standing up.

"Don't you have parents to go home to?" Robert asked. "It's almost one in the morning and I have an economics exam tomorrow."

"Vishniak, some manners," Tracey said, but he complied, getting up to walk his guest out. Robert walked behind them, continuing on to the bathroom. When he came back a few minutes later, ready for bed, Tracey was still gone.

Two more weeks went by and Robert did not see Tracey. He assumed he was spending time with his friends — certainly he came in very late and left early, or perhaps he didn't come in at all. Robert now freely borrowed Tracey's typewriter and played his records. Tracey was not there to give him permission but had always been so generous. Robert felt self-conscious each time he used what was not his, even as he could not resist.

This was the year that the students began to protest parietals. Robert went to meetings to talk about how to end the separation of the sexes, and found that the mood made everyone amorous. He picked up girls as easily as he had in Oxford Circle; they were willing to sneak into his room, coming up the fire escape or crawling in a lower window. People cooperated; there was a spirit of civil disobedience in the air, and he was suddenly grateful that he had no roommate to speak of. On one such afternoon, he'd snuck a redheaded, voluptuous girl named Jill Jamison into his room. The two of them were making out on his bed. She'd already told him she was on the pill, God's newest gift to mankind, and he'd just gotten her bra off when they heard a loud knock at the door. He told her to ignore it, his hands on her breasts, but then the knocking got louder, more aggressive.

"Vishniak!! Open this damn door!!" There were several voices. Then more pounding.

"Don't move!" he commanded the half-naked girl, who lay on top of him, her hips pressing so deliciously into his. But then the pounding started up again and would not stop. "Go answer it," she said, rolling off him. Robert obeyed, mumbling that it had better be important.

"Doesn't anyone on your floor answer the phone?" Cates asked. Van Dorn stood behind him. "We've been calling for days. We're looking for Tracey."

"He's not here," Robert said as Jill, now dressed, gathered her coat around her.

"You can stay," he said again, but she was already at the door, shaking her head. The two boys stood aside to let her go, Cates looking satisfied and Van Dorn watching her hungrily as she disappeared down the steps.

"I see how you've been using the damn room," Cates said, as Van Dorn pushed his way through, mumbling that it was hot as hell in here.

"Our heat is either blasting or nonexistent," Robert mumbled, trying not to think of his lost opportunity. "I told you, he's not here."

Van Dorn sat down at Tracey's desk and put his face in his hands. No one knew where Tracey was. The dean wanted to see him. He was on the verge of flunking out and his parents were calling Van Dorn and Cates and Pascal.

"If Tracey wants to disappear, you can't do anything to stop him," Robert said. He was sure Tracey had been back a few times. "I haven't been here when he came in," he said, "but it was clear that he took clothes and his mail."

"Then why wouldn't he contact us?" Cates asked.

"I don't know," Robert said. "Maybe he's off with a girl, maybe he's getting high in a hotel room, maybe he's found some new friends he likes better."

"Fuck you," Cates said, but he sounded half afraid that Robert was right.

"Where's Mark Pascal, the voice of reason?" Robert asked.

"Off writing about panty raids for the *Crimson*," Cates said, kicking at a warped floorboard with his foot. Van Dorn cursed Pascal as no help at all. "Call if he comes back," Cates added, and wrote down his number. He had once wasted energy disliking Cates, hating him even, but as he watched Cates and Van Dorn leave, they seemed to Robert stuck in time, lost without their leader, and suddenly very young.

Tracey did finally turn up a few days later. Robert had handed in a series of physics problems that all but killed him. He'd felt the relief of, at least, finishing the test, no matter what the result. To celebrate, he and Zinnelli went out after work. They had a few drinks in a local bar, then came back to Robert's room and smoked a joint that Zinnelli had bought off one of the full-time kitchen staff. The heat went out again, and they sat with their coats on. By the time Zinnelli left, and despite the bracing temperature, Robert's body was heavy with exhaustion.

After a quick trip down the hall to brush his teeth, he piled Tracey's quilt on top of his own and got in bed. His eyes were heavy and he huddled under the warmth. Suddenly he was with Margie Cohen. She had her clothes on but was lying on top of him, kissing him, unbuttoning his pants. He was aroused but also frustrated because she wouldn't let him touch her. "You've betrayed me," she whispered in his ear. "And I'm calling the draft board."

A loud whistle pierced his consciousness. He awoke into blackness, his heart pounding. A shadow danced on a distant wall, cast by the light below their window, lit to bring last-minute stragglers safely back to their rooms. Then the radiator sounded again, and the pipes shrieked and knocked. He was awake in his dorm room. The heating had come on. Warm now, he pulled off the top blanket and rolled over onto his side.

"Leave the covers on," a familiar voice said softly.

An arm was around him in the darkness, a body pressed against his. "Don't move, Vishniak," the voice pleaded. It was Tracey. He reached down and began to stroke Robert's thigh. "I'll give you anything," he said. "Anything I own. But don't pull away."

Could he be dreaming? *I'm awake for Christ's sake and Tracey's hand is on my thigh.*

Tracey's touch was light, tentative. He smelled of alcohol. "Just pretend, Robert, pretend I'm a girl." Tracey moved against him, moaning softly, his erection pressing against Robert's lower back. His hand moved along the waistband of Robert's boxers. "Anything you want," he repeated, and Robert wondered, *What would I be willing to do for that MG?*

"I'm sorry," Robert said, finally grasping Tracey's wrist. "I don't think much would happen, even if I could bring myself—" He sat up, pushed the covers back.

Tracey turned to the wall.

"I'm sorry," Robert repeated, getting out of bed and turning on the desk lamp.

"Turn it off," Tracey snapped. He had grasped his knees up to his chest like a child. "Turn it off! I don't want to look at you right now. I've had to look at you for two and a half years. Two and a half goddamned years!"

Robert turned off the light and walked to the other side of the room, got the bottle from Tracey's desk, and came back with it. Unfortunately there wasn't much left. Why had the idea never occurred to him? He had been so sure that Tracey was scrutinizing him, correcting him, pitying him even. He approached the bed where Tracey, still curled up and facing the wall, had begun to cry softly.

"There's bourbon for you on the desk," Robert said. "Maybe it'll help."

"I don't want it."

The room was now very warm, the air rank with the remnants of pot smoke, alcohol, dirty laundry. Robert went over to the windows and began to yank each one open in turn. What was he to say? He hadn't known what was in front of him all along—and yet, how could he have seen it? He hadn't known to look.

Tracey finally rolled over and reached for the bottle. "Promise you won't tell anyone," he whispered.

"I promise," Robert said, turning around as a thought occurred to him. "The others, do they know?" Of course, they must have known.

"Pascal has no idea. The other two, they're not like me," Tracey said. "It was different for them."

Robert didn't say anything, waited for Tracey to continue.

"Cates would have to be very drunk; Van Dorn just wanted someone to like him. They outgrew it long ago. It *is* possible to outgrow it? Right?"

"I don't know," Robert said. "Where were you all these weeks?"

"Hotel. That dirty little boy took fifty dollars out of my wallet. Threatened to tell my father. Like my father would take a call from him. Like he hasn't known longer than I have—"

Robert walked over to his desk, took a swig of bourbon from the bottle, and turned on the desk lamp. Tracey was now sitting in his bed with the covers pulled up to his neck, despite the heat, as if he were trying to cocoon himself. His hair was disheveled and his face looked ghoulishly pale under the harsh light. Robert tilted his head back and let the last of the liquid burn his throat. Then he put the empty bottle down, turned out the light, and went over to Tracey's bed to lie down.

"You won't tell anyone about this—about any of it?" Tracey asked again.

"No," Robert repeated. "I promise."

"All right then," Tracey mumbled, "I believe you." Within a few minutes, he was snoring, but it took Robert some time to fall asleep. He lay on Tracey's mattress, staring into the darkness. For the last two and a half years, Robert had been convinced that something was wrong with his behavior, his speech, his eating, and his manners. What he'd seen as Tracey's scrutiny and hesitation was really a kind of love in disguise. And now, finally, he could be himself. Only he'd changed into that other person so thoroughly — gotten rid of the long Philadelphia vowels, held his fork and knife differently, dressed differently, walked differently — that he couldn't have summoned up his old self, the boy he'd been when he arrived with the duffel, even if he tried.

The next day they acted as if nothing had happened. Tracey did as he always did at the end of term — raced to make up for all that he had neglected, exhausted himself with cramming. There was no talk of whether they'd live together the coming year. No talk really, of anything much after that. Tracey made a show of giving up drinking entirely, though he seemed always to be leaning out the window, blowing pot smoke into the courtyard. And when Tracey was in the room, Robert no longer wandered down the hall from the shower in only his towel. Instead, he bought himself a bathrobe, like a man from an earlier era.

CHAPTER TEN

The natives are restless

Few that day had actually shown up for the cause. They were for the cause, of course — few their age wanted the war — but most were not organizers or screamers, were not angry enough, or idealistic enough, or maybe just didn't like public speaking. Robert, for instance, was sleeping with one of the organizers, and she'd begged him to come and bring friends. He was planning to dump her and he figured he could, at least, do her this one last favor. And Tracey came because Robert invited him, and because it was an exceptionally warm day for early April; he liked the idea of sitting outside on the banks of the Charles, listening to music — plus his sailing plans had fallen through. And if Tracey went, then Cates and Pascal and Van Dorn were not far behind, not just because they followed him everywhere, but because these days Tracey always had a stash on him. Goldfarb knew a guy in one of the bands that was playing, and Zinnelli agreed to make his appearance because Robert was always making it with some gorgeous girl, and gorgeous girls tended to have gorgeous friends; these events, everyone so high-strung and emotional, were a great place to pick up chicks.

They all stood together—Robert, Zinnelli, Goldfarb, Tracey, Cates, Van Dorn, Pascal. They looked more alike now than different with their long hair, torn jeans, and sloganeering T-shirts—the slogans mostly proclaiming, in endless variation, the importance of individuality. Flyers for the event promised an appearance by someone famous—Peter, Paul and Mary were rumored to be making a surprise visit. Someone else swore they'd heard it was Country Joe and the Fish. But the only musicians who played that afternoon were student musicians, and not very good ones. The sound system malfunctioned, and most of the student speakers, those who could be heard at all, lost their voices from screaming. Meanwhile, the Harvard rowing team glided along the Charles, impervious to the small crowd on the opposite bank. Shoulders squared, oars hitting the water in a tight synchronicity that obliterated individual need, they looked to Robert as if nothing could touch them.

By midafternoon the protest resembled nothing so much as a group of picnickers sitting on blankets or cardboard signs, eating sandwiches and rolling joints. Robert had fallen, that semester, under the spell of speed. Marijuana had begun to irritate his breathing, and quaaludes made him sleepy at a time when he was far too sleepy already. He felt that he had to be on his toes in class, could not afford to be hypnotized by the blowing of a curtain, or the lines etched in a desk. He liked the energy of speed, and found that he could go for a day without eating if he needed, could write papers with remarkable clarity, had an ascetic's lack of desire for anything but movement; his thoughts raced, all self-consciousness gone.

But that afternoon, his heart pounded and his hands shook. "Got anything to calm me down?" he asked Tracey, who was now as generous with his drugs as he'd been with his other possessions.

"Here," he said, handing Robert a 'lude. Then Tracey stood up and looked into the crowd. "Hello, Boston!" he shouted. "Here's my contribution to social equality!!" He reached into his backpack and threw handfuls of pills into the bored, stoned crowd. A sea of hands rose everywhere, people scrambled over each other, pushing and shoving. Tracey, having caused the chaos, sat down and watched. "Look at that, man, like mice with the cheese," he said. "Well, at least they're moving around."

A girl two rows in front of them, searching for the source of the beneficence, turned to smile at them, popping several pills in her mouth at once, washing them down with a green liquid in a bottle next to her. Then she stood up, squinting into the sun.

"Look at that," Cates said.

"She's an angel," added Pascal.

"Fuck me," mumbled Zinnelli.

She was, Robert would think then and for the rest of his life, the most beautiful girl he'd ever seen. For a moment, he wondered if he could be hallucinating. *Come this way,* he thought. *Look at me.* He made a wish and reached out his hand, wishing that if his looks had ever worked for him before, *dear God*, let them work now. She saw the yearning in his expression, the furrowing of his brow, as if by force of will he could move her toward him, and then she noticed his lips moving, as if in prayer. She stumbled over legs and heads and butts, then half-sat, half-fell, right in his lap.

"Sorry about that," she said, and scooted over to a space between Robert and Tracey. Robert was unable to speak, still feeling the moment when she'd fallen on him, the softness of her hair as it skimmed his face, the smell of her lavender shampoo. Tracey mumbled something under his breath. The girl turned to him. "Thanks ever so much," she said. "So generous of you."

She had a British accent, and her skin was creamy smooth, her cheeks flushed. She took a half-eaten bag of potato chips out of her backpack and offered him one. He stared into her honey-colored eyes, still unable to say a word. When he didn't respond, she took out a chip and ate it, licking the grease from her fingers. Finally, he leaned over and took one himself, glancing down her peasant blouse at the hollow of her cleavage. No bra. What felt like hours went by, and still he just looked at her.

"This is just awful," she said.

"What is?" he asked, hands in his lap, afraid to touch her because he wanted to so badly.

"All of this. The terrible music, a gathering with no real purpose. Hardly any mention of the war. Just an excuse to get high and make new friends. People are dying in Vietnam, but in Boston, it's all a big party."

"There are worse things," Robert said. She was not looking into his face the way women usually did, but seemed to be staring over his shoulder, at the rowers.

"Yes, what do you care that they're sending so many black boys off to die? You've all got your student deferments, and when that's finished you'll find something else. It's worse because you all *think* you're so noble."

"I don't think I'm in the least bit noble," Robert replied. He had spent the last three years studying people for clues to their origins. Despite the changing times, he had never given up the habit—even high, filled with lust—it was like swallowing. He knew, from her accent, from the casual way she wore her shabbiness, from the light, clean smell that clung to the edges of her, that she was one of them. A wealthy girl masquerading. But there was also something fragile about her. Her wrists were so narrow, he could have snapped them like twigs. He took her hand, turned it over in his lap and looked at the blue-green veins running under her pale skin. He wanted to protect her, though from what he had no idea. "What is your father, a duke or something?" he whispered, and his words came out sarcastic, annoyed, though that wasn't his intention.

"No, he's in department stores," she said. "Mother's beginnings are a bit more posh, I suppose. You haven't told me your name."

"Robert Vishniak."

"I'm Gwendolyn Smythe."

"Well, Gwendolyn Smythe," he said, summoning his courage now, taking a deep breath. "Wanna get out of here?"

In front of all of them, he helped Gwendolyn to her feet. She was the one who was shaky now, but he felt suddenly alert. A boy lying in front of them grasped her ankle, not letting go. Robert stepped hard on the boy's wrist, ignoring his groan of pain as he moved Gwendolyn out of the way. Then he put his hand around her waist and felt the eyes of all he knew watching.

Cates moved over next to Tracey, occupying the space Robert and Gwendolyn had left. Robert could hear his voice floating up through the crowd. "They were your 'ludes, Tracey," Cates said. "Fucking Vishniak. After all you've done for that phony."

CHAPTER ELEVEN

Gwendolyn

Gwendolyn told Robert that she was studying at Boston University and she took him, that first night, to a roomy two-bedroom, two-bath apartment in a doorman building on the fancy end of Commonwealth Avenue, away from the noisy fraternities and crowded dormitories of the university. To Robert the apartment was very adult: the living room had a nonworking fireplace and was furnished with a flowered couch, a coffee table, a wing chair, and an apricot-colored area rug. The pale wood of the floorboards seemed to gleam even in the late-afternoon light.

"All this is yours?" Robert asked.

"I rent it." She took his hand and led him down a long hallway and into an enormous white bedroom, big and high with a canopy bed, like something out of a children's story. Certainly she could have been a princess to him, as much a mirage as the ones in stories, with her accent and how she'd fallen on him seemingly out of nowhere. He stepped close to her, wondering why the stench of the afternoon had not clung to her. He could smell his own sweat, and the smoke that had been all around them, felt embarrassed by it, but Gwendolyn made everyone she came near smell a little of her perfume, a mixture of her lavender shampoo, a certain mysterious foreign soap she used in the bath, followed by a lavender talcum powder, and then her body itself—her very own particular smell, as individual as a fingerprint.

"Why were your lips moving?" she asked him, as if out of nowhere.

"What?"

"Your lips. Out there at the concert, when you put your hand out to me, your lips were moving. Are you religious?"

He laughed. "No, but I think I was praying."

"For world peace?" she asked seriously. She stood closer, her hips almost but not quite squared against his thighs, her fingers now at the back of his neck, touching him lightly with her fingertips.

"For you to notice me, and walk over," he breathed.

"That's sweet," she said. "What I noticed were your lips, you know? Such full lips, as if you've just eaten something very juicy. I wondered what it would be like to feel those lips all over my —"

He kissed her, ran his fingers through her hair, then pulled at the arms of her loose blouse to reveal the whiteness of her shoulders, and her collarbones and neck.

"You're awfully slow about all this," she said, and reached over her head, removing her shirt altogether.

They spent most of those first few weeks making love; he wanted her all the time, and she was obliging. No one interrupted. No one pounded on a door or barged in. There were hardly any phone calls, and when the phone rang they ignored it. He had chased women, and women had chased him, but often, when he got down to things, many of them seemed to be submitting. Even the girls who announced they were on the pill, who were reaching for something modern and new, still made him feel that they were giving in for him and not for themselves. This had not stopped him from enjoying himself, hardly, but afterward he felt the slight twinge, the ego, the man's peculiarly secret insecurity—had he done right by her? How to respond when a woman says yes as if for something larger than herself—a cause, a birth control pill, a domineering sister, or the urging of a man's insistent desire?

But Gwendolyn said yes because she wanted him; he felt that, felt the wonderful selfishness of her desire existing next to his. She was not aggressive, and rarely did she approach him first, but when they made love she moaned and whispered obscenities in his ear, and tore at his clothes and sometimes even sobbed, so taken over was she by her climax. After making love, he held Gwendolyn in his arms, startled by the emotion of the whole experience, and told her that he'd never leave her—which he'd whispered to more than a few women already—and how strange, all of a sudden, to mean it.

They did not say much about themselves in the beginning. Gwendolyn, like many of her peers, saw little distinction between the political and the personal, and so they listened to records, talked about articles in the paper, and she tried to explain her politics—a patchwork concoction that seemed half Socialist, half whimsy. She knew all about Vietnam, for instance, but had not heard of Laos; she was devastated by the recent death of Martin Luther King, believed that the Black Panthers were onto something important—the bookstore where she worked was the first in the city to have a section of writings by colored writers—but had no knowledge of Jim Crow. He chalked it up to her being a foreigner—she read newspapers, but for someone who'd spent her whole life in fancy schools, her education seemed scattered, slipshod. But mostly, in those early weeks, they made love, showered together, watched television, and said very little. It was a great thing to be able to be quiet with a woman. Girls had always tired him out with so much talking, but being with Gwendolyn was all patient calm and quiet. He could be himself.

They met in early April, and by the end of the month Robert had moved in; he had more or less been living there anyway, and she had plenty of room. Luckily, only three weeks remained in the semester and it was the girls, mostly, whom the school went after for cohabitation. He did not think of Tracey, whom he never seemed to run into when he returned to the room. He didn't think of Cates or Zinnelli or any of them. His mind was utterly singular — it was as if these others had never existed.

But once ensconced in the apartment, having moved all his things from the dorm, he did not see as much of Gwendolyn as he'd expected. She maintained a very busy routine, running from one activity to another. There was her job at the bookstore, and she went to various political meetings, including those held by that same group of draft resisters in Arlington who had come to Robert's dorm the year before. That she, as a foreigner and a woman, was a tourist in all this and would never be drafted did not seem to matter to her.

When four from her group were put on trial in Boston, including Dr. Benjamin Spock, the famous baby doctor, Gwendolyn's zeal knew no bounds. She spent hours making posters, circulating petitions and going to rallies outside the courthouse. Everyone around them seemed caught up — the fever for change had even spread to Europe. In France student riots broke out — on television they looked much like the riots and takeovers in Berkeley and Columbia and now Harvard, except in another language with subtitles and better-looking girls. President Johnson announced that he would not run for another term and promised that the bombing in North Vietnam would come to a halt — but a few weeks earlier Westmoreland had ordered another 200,000 troops.

Robert wanted to believe that his generation's actions might actually change something, but more than anything he found himself searching, not for a larger truth but for a loophole, an angle, a way out of his own dilemma. He reminded himself that he still had time, that he was resourceful and would figure a way out. Zinnelli told him that if he lost fifty pounds, got down to 120, he'd be turned down as useless. The campus rabbi suggested he get ordained. He was still a Vishniak, certain that if he let down his guard for just one moment, gave up self-interest for that of the collective, he'd be fucked.

Loving Gwendolyn was the closest thing he'd found to a cause. Let those who could afford it have their revolution. When Gwendolyn invited him to her meetings, he told her that going into churches made him uneasy, and he sensed he'd get little solace in a place where people advocated going to jail. If there was one place he knew he'd never survive, it was prison.

But Gwendolyn was energized, engaged utterly by the issues of the times. Robert had no real sense of what she was studying. When he asked her, she said that she was taking a variety of courses. But there were no books of hers around the house, only various periodicals. She had at least three newspaper subscriptions — to the *Globe*, *New York Times*, and *International Herald Tribune* — yet the place was rarely cluttered. Back issues disappeared as new ones arrived. He assumed that the maid took them away, but Gwendolyn didn't even bring books home from the bookstore where she worked, though she got them practically for free. Finally, trying to figure out where to put the cumbersome boxes of his own books that now lined the halls, he asked her at breakfast one morning, not sure when he'd see her again that day: When on earth did she study? Where were her books?

"I keep my books in my library carrel," she told him. "It's too quiet to study here."

Robert laughed. "Is there a party at the BU library that no one's told me about?"

"Don't tease me," she said. But she looked at him uneasily, biting on the skin of her thumb, which she did often, so that it was thick with callus; the only ugly part of Gwendolyn was her hands, fingers pink and calloused, cuticles ripped, as if repeatedly gnawed on by small animals.

"Put your books on the empty shelves in the living room. Then we'll have books around. Since you have these decorating prejudices."

He took a deep breath. He was not used to giving real information about his family or how he'd grown up, but Disston Street was always on his mind in one way or another — compare/contrast/ compare/contrast; then and now, then and now, like an endless freshman literature paper. "We never owned any books," he said quietly. "The shelves were for the television, or knickknacks. No one I knew growing up owned any books of their own."

"How'd you learn to read?"

"Library," he said. "Every week we took out books and returned them."

"Libraries are so much *fairer*, don't you think?" She got up and immediately began uncrating his boxes. "I can leave a little later today," she said. "I'll put them up there myself."

HE LIKED TO PRETEND that they were alone in the world, on an island with soft, flowered sheets, sweet-smelling soaps in the bathroom, and thick, oh, such thick bath towels. Even the air felt different at Gwendolyn's. He did not yet understand the severity of his childhood allergies, the sensitivities he had to dust mites and various cheap chemical cleaners. He did not think about the proximity of dorm rooms with teenage boys sandwiched in together, the air heavy, rank, and filled with cigarette smoke. Nor did he connect the weekly arrival at Gwendolyn's of the middle-aged Czech maid, Dana, who banished dust and scrubbed floors with rigor, using homemade concoctions and pine oil, with the fact that his nose and eyes hardly ran, and his chest felt lighter. He only understood the final effect — for the first time in his life, he could really breathe.

A doorman held the door for him when he came with groceries, and on days when he had no classes or kitchen work that doorman was the only person he saw other than Gwendolyn. Whatever friends he'd had at Tufts he met only in classes or for the occasional beer after work. Tracey extended a few invitations, which Robert declined because it was one of Gwendolyn's nights off or because Gwendolyn had asked something of him — and then Tracey stopped asking. Robert found himself relieved by this, happy to be away from them all. Had he just been pretending for the last three years? Was this love? Or a reaction to the times?

The only person Gwendolyn ever mentioned with any consistency was Bruno, the manager of the left-wing bookstore where she worked three nights a week. After Robert had lived with her for a few weeks, he asked to meet Bruno and see the place she talked about with such affection. She told him to come to the store that Thursday night; Bruno was there until closing.

The bookstore was just off Brattle Street. Posters of Chairman Mao, Che Guevara, and Malcolm X lined the front windows, their faces staring at him, backlit by a harsh neon bulb. A Closed sign had been hung on the front door; the lights were on but the shop seemingly empty. He found the front door unlocked — had it been left that way for him? — and turned the knob, entering to the sound of wind chimes. "Hello! Anybody here?"

Pope Paul VI looked down at Robert from the wall of the entrance, his hands outstretched above the caption "The Pill Is a No-No."

Bruno came out from behind a curtain in the back and walked toward him. He was big and beefy, with wild, curly hair and small, slightly crossed blue eyes. His belly hung over his jeans, seemingly pinned up by the enormous peace sign that was his belt buckle. He put out his hand and, instead of shaking, made a fist. Robert knew he was expected to do the same, but he simply took his hand away. He had no desire to play at being a Black Panther.

"Gwen, he's here! Your fucking Prince Charming!" Bruno yelled, and Gwendolyn rushed out from behind that same curtain.

Had they been back there together in the dark? Before she got across the room, Bruno took several steps forward, met her halfway, and touched her arm. "We got those bags to sort through tomorrow." He turned to Robert. "Prof at Harvard donates the stuff. Modern Soviet fiction mostly. We're low on that."

"The happy Soviet workers in the fields? Or reports from the Gulag?" Robert asked. "Isn't that where they put all their writers?"

"Our government feeds us lies about Russia," Bruno replied. "The whole Cold War is just lies piled on top of lies."

Robert stood near the door hoping that Gwendolyn, looking over the piles of new books, would hurry up and get her coat. The place smelled of old books, dust, and a clientele that didn't bathe. He bristled as Bruno ran his eyes up and down Gwendolyn's body.

"You got it all wrong," Bruno continued. "In Russia everyone has plenty of food, free medical care, nice apartments. They got the longest life expectancy on earth. Why do you think that is?"

"I don't know," Robert said, signaling to Gwendolyn to hurry along.

"I'll tell you why," he replied, banging his hand on a shelf so that the books shook. "They don't have to answer to the Man over there! He don't exist."

Robert had been hearing about the Man all his life. He felt certain he knew more about him than Bruno. More and more lately, Robert had been forced into conversations about the evils of capitalism and the glories of being poor. In Harvard Square, anyone with a leaflet about class oppression made a beeline for him, as if his face gave him away as an immigrant from the other side, a betrayer of something he didn't even understand. Or did he just look confused? "What do you call the secret police and the purges?" Robert asked. "A man can't listen to Miles Davis over there without getting arrested."

"There's no use talking to someone like you!" Bruno bellowed. "Go home, rich boy!"

"Happily," Robert said, aware that Bruno easily had eighty pounds on him and that his chest felt heavy. "What is your father anyway?" he asked. "A dentist? From the accent, I'd say Great Neck."

Bruno grabbed Robert by the collar and backed him up against a shelf of LPs. "You seem a little gray all of a sudden, man," he said, as Robert heard a rushing sound in his ears.

"Brun, we're leaving now," Gwendolyn said calmly. "Go in the back and smoke some dope. Relax." She put her hand on Bruno's arm. "And here I was hoping you two would get on."

Back out on the street, she scolded him for contradicting Bruno. "He's a smart man."

"No," Robert said. "He's a large man." Now Robert knew why Gwendolyn had such confused opinions. Clearly it was Bruno's fault. "And he's an idiot."

"You don't understand. He trained me for my job, and he looks after me."

"Yeah, I'll bet he does."

"He's my friend!" she said. "I didn't hear any complaints when he was giving us all that grass, and the hash, too."

"You paid for that stuff, if I remember."

"At a discount. He has to eat," Gwendolyn said, raising her voice. "You don't know what this job means to me. Robbie, what's wrong? All the color has left your face."

"Happens," he gasped, coughing. It had never been this bad before. Usually the heaviness went away after a few minutes, now he felt himself unable to take even small breaths, felt as if someone were holding his head underwater. He heard that sound, the awful, squeaking sound of his desperation to breathe.

"Try to relax," she said, taking him by the elbow and settling him on a bench nearby. Sinking. He was sinking deeper. The sidewalks and people weaved and dove.

She took his hand in hers and began to massage the palm,

pressing on the center, and then she went to each finger, massaging the knuckles and joints. "Breathe, Robbie. The air is so clear tonight. Slow down. Breathe." She had her fingers around his thumb, and as she squeezed it between her fingers, strong fingers that seemed to loosen something inside him, he felt himself calming, the rushing sound abating. Air. He felt it slowly at first, as if through the cracks of an old wall. Then his chest began to expand.

"A nurse taught that to me once. The hand has a lot of nerves."

He leaned over and kissed her as she continued to knead the base of his thumb and then the sockets of his fingers. Yes, the hand did have a lot of nerves and now he was horny as hell. "How about we go home?"

She agreed, and they walked off quickly toward the T.

PERHAPS SHE ENJOYED THE bookstore because of the company, even if that company included Bruno. She seemed so thoroughly on her own. No parents called—no letters, not even checks in the mail. He had no idea where her money came from, and after a month he began to worry about it. If his mother had known that he was not living in his room at Tufts—a room that was paid for at the beginning of each year—she'd have been very angry, but there was little chance of her finding out. She'd never call the dorm.

His board about to end, he needed to begin paying his way at Gwendolyn's place, yet he had no idea what that entailed—how much, how little, what he might already owe her. He had wanted to discuss money with her before he moved in, but there was that first rush of enthusiasm to be together, and the narcotic effect of sex. They had known without words that they could not be parted, and he hadn't wanted any impediments; everything was about speed and urgency. But how had *she* not brought it up? Perhaps she was waiting for him because he was the man. Could that be true? He had no idea. If there was one thing everyone talked about in his family, it was how much something cost and what was a person's share. Such conversations were never sentimental; no one hesitated or faltered. The shame was in *not* talking about it. Yet since leaving home most of the people around him talked of money in whispers, or not at all — and he had adopted this feeling, as he'd adopted so many others — so that he could not blurt anything out, kept the adding and subtracting of dollars and cents to himself, as if his head were a giant cash register camouflaged by a human face.

There were thirty dollars left in his bank account, until he was paid for his campus job, when the thirty dollars would likely be gone, and he'd get another seventy-five dollars. His mother wanted him to go to New York again to drive the cab. But how could he leave Gwendolyn? How could he stay? Insisting that it was for a friend, he had inquired about a newly empty one-bedroom apartment on a lower floor. The doorman had said it was already rented, for five hundred dollars a month. Their place was on a higher floor and was bigger, over 1,000 square feet. Surely it would be closer to six hundred? Even with a decent job, he'd come away with little if he had to pay that much for his half of the rent. How could he offer what he did not have? He would have to, somehow, to preserve his self-respect.

April came to an end, and the question of funds was on his mind every minute. Outside, it was raining for the fourth day in a row, and Gwendolyn had a cold. He got up early and made both of them strong tea with lemon; her mug rested on the bedside table, his on the windowsill. She'd come home from the bookstore the night before with a big bag of candy — a customer had given it to her — which now rested next to her on the bed. In between sips of tea, she fed him bits of a Mounds bar, her fingers slick with melting chocolate.

"Not our most nutritious breakfast," he said, as she put a piece in her own mouth.

"Didn't your mum ever tell you?" she replied. "Chocolate is excellent for a cold."

He took the candy bag and placed it on the floor. "We need to talk about something."

"Something that won't be improved with candy?! Robbie, give it back!"

"I'm serious. We need to talk about money."

"Oh, let's not."

There was the tone again. Tracey's tone when anyone argued over the check. "We never talked about it before I moved in, and now we're coming up on the first of another month and I feel weird," he replied. "I have to figure out what I'm doing for the summer. You see——"

"You're not sure you can stay here and pay," she said. "But why worry about it, when I have so much to spare? If it weren't for me, you wouldn't even be thinking of this, would you?"

"No, but that's not the point," he said, trying to follow her logic. "You exist, and so I do think about it. I don't want to freeload. And I don't want to leave you."

"It's not my money, anyway," she said. "To be honest, Robbie, I'm not even sure how it gets into my account. I wish I didn't have to take it from them——"

"You don't get along with your folks?" he asked. "You never mention them."

"They're all right," she said, taking another sip of tea. "But we're better off, the three of us, on different continents. Certainly they would say so. Oh, let's not spoil everything by talking this way. If my parents knew you were here, they'd probably pay you just to babysit me."

"Stop making jokes," he replied. "I need an answer."

"Enough!" she replied, raising her voice to him for the first time. She pushed some hair out of his eyes and kissed him on the forehead.

"Shall we go out for some breakfast? I'm getting my appetite back and I want masses of eggs and toast."

He read want ads and campus postings, asked everyone he knew about summer work. Returning to his old dorm room, hoping to find Tracey, he saw his old mattress now piled with Tracey's T-shirts, saw Tracey's books on his side of the room, as if he had never lived there. Certainly Tracey had to be happy to have the place to himself? He sat down and wrote his old roommate a note asking him if he knew of any work in Boston. "You've always been so generous to me, and I'd be grateful," Robert added, and signed his name. Then he wrote Gwendolyn's address. He knew that he was displaying bad manners; you didn't ask favors of someone you hadn't seen in weeks, and certainly not in a note. But all of that, the code he'd worked so hard to learn, was certainly over. The times were different now. He would try what he'd been taught at home — to ask and not care how people saw it, no, how Tracey saw it.

Three weeks later, a typed note arrived at Robert's new address. It said that Tracey would be moving to an apartment for senior year; he wished Robert luck and signed his name. No mention of Robert's request. All very polite and formal. Robert couldn't blame him, really, and he threw the note in the trash, wondering if he'd ever see Tracey again.

He already had his aid package for the following year, which included room and board. He wanted the option to continue working in the kitchen and have the free dinners available before work, or the occasional breakfast when in a hurry, which meant that it was easier for him to go on pretending to live in the dorms. He asked Zinnelli to be his roommate; Zinnelli was happy to cover for his absence and get a single for the price of a double.

In May he got himself a waiter job at a fancy seafood restaurant in Newton Center in which one of his professors was a silent partner. He and Gwendolyn did not talk again about the rent and when, on June 1, Robert put his half of the rent, a little over three hundred dollars, on a table in the living room, it sat there for so long that eventually he was forced to take it back and give up, living rent free in this paradise on Commonwealth Avenue. Even with the guilt he felt about the money, even with a fear of the draft hanging over him, he knew that he had finally grabbed hold of something—something as elusive as air itself—that he wouldn't let go of, not even for a summer. He told Stacia that he was house-sitting all summer in exchange for rent. He could do as he pleased, she wrote back, so long as he didn't ask her for money during his senior year. She could not complain about his grades, which had gotten very good that semester—he had given up, finally, on applying to medical school, and was taking courses almost exclusively in his decided-upon major, history. Other departments, in reaction to the times, were more modern in their approach, with rap sessions and professors called by their first names. But the history department still clung to some old fragments of order—and so did Robert. He was determined to end college with a decent GPA, even if the future was unclear.

And so, as summer began, he could think only of the misery of his past two summers, of his time in New York, in the heat and dirt, and before that of the tiny house on Disston Street. Even his room in the dorm now seemed ridiculously uncomfortable. How had this happened? Gwendolyn beside him each night in a queen-size bed, an apartment so well air-conditioned that they slept under a comforter in July, and a job that paid well and even fed him dinner. He knew that this was the happiest he had ever been. No, he understood that he was happy for the first time ever, and he went off to his job every afternoon waiting, like his mother's son, for the bad news to arrive.

CHAPTER TWELVE

Senior year

By the fall of 1968, Robert's senior year, half a million soldiers were in Vietnam, and injuries and deaths were reported in the thousands. His fall semester disappeared through his hands like so many grains of sand, and his head filled with plans for escape. Stacia's letters were full of news: a boy he went to Hebrew school with had chopped off his own thumb to get out; a distant Vishniak cousin faked insanity and, to everyone's surprise, was proclaimed of sound mind. Stacia had the whole family working on it; every Vishniak and Kupferberg was asking coworkers and neighbors, butchers and bookies, if they knew anyone who could help keep Robert out of the war.

He was so absorbed in the problem that at first he hardly noticed the changes in Gwendolyn. Her routine had, if possible, sped up — through the bookstore, she and Bruno organized various local protests against the draft, and a march to the statehouse. One day Robert came home to Gwendolyn shearing off Bruno's mop of hair in their living room, the thick black curls falling onto the wooden floor. The two would be campaigning door-to-door for Eugene

McCarthy, Gwendolyn explained. It bothered Robert that they were together more. And she couldn't seem to sleep without the help of pills—pills for sleeping, and for getting up, too. He worried that she wasn't eating. Their apartment was now filled with protest posters; mornings, Robert stumbled into a sunlight-filled living room that seemed to be shouting at him—Down with the Pigs! Stop American Imperialism! Remember Chicago!

Gwendolyn's morning reading took hours—when on earth did she go to class?—and she often cut out articles, underlining sections with a ballpoint pen. The periodicals no longer quietly disappeared—they were everywhere, accumulating so fast under tables, overflowing from bookcases, finding their way into the kitchen cabinets and, once, the freezer. The maid couldn't keep up. She was miserable, too. Students in Prague had occupied the university to protest the Soviet tanks rolling into the city; a nephew was missing. Then Nixon won the presidency, and at about three in the morning on November 9, Gwendolyn woke him up out of a sound sleep.

"Robbie, I have an idea."

"Can't it wait until morning?"

She turned on the light and he braced himself for news of yet another event or project. He had lost count and wondered when, if ever, he would have her full attention again.

"I want us to go to Philadelphia," she said. "For Thanksgiving."

"Oh, please," he groaned, putting the pillow over his head. Not that. "You're going to meet them anyway in six months. They'll be up for graduation." That would be hard enough, but at least fast; he'd intended to stay in Boston over Thanksgiving. "Can't I go back to sleep now?"

"I want to go now," she said. "I want to meet them at *home*."

"Well I don't want you to," Robert said. "I have enough on my mind now; don't ask that of me." He kissed her and begged her to come to bed, but she only went back to the living room.

Robert had come to hate Bruno now—yes, the emotion was

hate — for giving Gwendolyn all the pills, making her beholden to him and, most of all, giving her such crazy ideas. He felt sure that Bruno was the one who suggested she meet Robert's family. He knew this was irrational, but his jealousy knew no bounds. The next day, when he was sure Gwendolyn wasn't working, he went to the bookstore to tell Bruno to butt out of his life, but he found the place closed for the afternoon, the door locked. He went around to the side of the building — there was a window in the storeroom, and if he stood on tiptoe he could see inside.

There was Bruno, pacing the room and talking, only Robert couldn't see anyone else in there. Was he ranting to himself? Or were there others whom Robert couldn't see from his angle, with the boxes obscuring his view? He banged loudly on the frosty window, but Bruno seemed not to hear. He tried again and again with no result. He'd forgotten his gloves, and finally he put his hands in his pockets, went back around to the front, and knocked again on the door, staring into the display window. There were copies of a book lined up, framed by black velvet cloth. Gwendolyn did the windows, and they were always artistic. Too good for the shop, he thought. The book title was familiar: *Madness and Civilization*, by Michel Foucault. It was the English translation of one of the books Tracey had been reading, or trying to read, their freshman year. All around the display were questions, painted in orange on white cardboard: "Is it sane to be crazy in crazy times?" and "Who are the real crazy people? The suit on the subway? The boy with a machine gun and a weekend pass? Look around, brother — maybe it's you."

He walked quickly up the street, telling himself he'd go back, figure this all out. There was some puzzle here, with Gwendolyn and Bruno, with this place, just as there had been with Tracey. Again he couldn't understand the signs, didn't know the answer. His head hurt as he stumbled back to the T — he wanted some dinner, then off to the library; the apartment had become too crowded. Easiest to put one foot in front of the other, do what needed to be done.

Past midnight, he came home to find the apartment still empty. He ate a piece of cold pizza and crawled into bed. Gwendolyn had left the bedroom window open. A cold wind blew the lace curtains into the air like apparitions, but Robert liked a chilly room for sleeping. He got under the comforter, so light yet remarkably warm. He drifted easily off to sleep only to be awakened by a fire truck speeding down Commonwealth Avenue, sirens blaring. He sat up, looking around the dark room. Something was wrong. A lump on the floor caught his eye. For a moment he thought that an animal had gotten into the apartment, but when he got up and went closer he realized that it was Gwendolyn on the floor by the foot of the bed, no pillow or blanket, legs folded under her like a child.

"Baby, what are you doing down there?" he asked. He took the comforter off the bed and sat down next to her on the floor. She was shaking, and he put it around her, then curled himself up against her and held her, trying to keep her warm. "What's wrong?"

"I don't deserve to sleep in the bed, Robbie. I don't deserve it. Not any of it. I'm guilty, you see, I'm terribly guilty."

"Sweetheart, you've been watching too much news on television."

"All the children on fire, and the women screaming, and when they part, the machine guns are behind them. They weren't distributing flowers, they were working for the Vietcong."

"Who was?"

"I could have stopped them, you know, I might have."

"Stopped what?"

"All those souls. The souls are evaporating. Where do they go — ?"

She babbled on like that, and he couldn't comfort her. She seemed to think that she'd done something wrong, something more wrong than everyone else. "If there's anyone who deserves to live like this, Gwendolyn, it's you. You deserve everything lovely in the world," he insisted, but she would not come to bed. He couldn't leave her down there, so he slept beside her on the floor, his body wrapped around hers. In the morning, the only thing that calmed her, the only way he could get her to take any breakfast, was if he promised her, yes, he would ask if he could bring her home. He knew Stacia would say it was a waste of money; that he would see them at Christmas and she didn't like strangers sleeping in her house. He'd have the satisfaction of having asked, and the relief of not having to go.

But his mother was in a good mood when he called, and when he asked about coming home, she told him to do it. "We're having fifteen, at least." She paused. "How are you getting here?" Her voice was suspicious, as it got whenever she suspected she'd have to part with money. But he told her he was coming with a girl, and they'd rent a car.

"Expensive, ain't it?" she asked. "To rent?"

"It's her money." Robert said, "Tell my brother he better be on good behavior." How could he explain Gwendolyn and what she was used to? It was all cursed from the moment he began. The weekend would be a disaster.

"We know how to behave here, mister," Stacia said, and hung up the phone.

CHAPTER THIRTEEN

Holiday

They found a spot on the street, near the house, and Gwendo-lyn pronounced it a good sign. She kept asking him which house, exactly, was his.

"What difference does it make when they all look the same?" he snapped.

"Because it's yours, my love." She squeezed his hand. "You grew up there."

They arrived at night, just after eight. The tiny yellow patio lights were on, shedding their fuzzy glare up and down the block. They'd stopped on the road for dinner—Robert had insisted to his mother that this was the earliest they could get here when in truth he'd had no exams that day, classes were empty, but he didn't want to lengthen this ordeal any more than necessary.

Barry stood watch at the bay window. He wore a maroon sweatshirt and ate a kasha knish, and as Robert made his way up the walk holding Gwendolyn's hand, he could see that his brother's shirt was covered in stray pieces of grain. Then Vishniak joined Barry at the window and they waved—his father was wearing his undershirt and, Robert hoped upon hope, pants—and then the door opened and there was Stacia, her arms folded in front of her, face twitching.

"Oh, Christ," he whispered to Gwendolyn, who'd walked ahead of him and took the screen as it was held open to her. She walked inside and stood near the entrance, as Vishniak, wearing his slippers and pajama bottoms, ready for bed, fell on Robert and hugged and kissed him. Barry, usually the first to come forward, stood back, licking his fingers. Stacia assessed Robert, pronouncing him too thin, asking if he was hungry, and frowning at his answer.

"You'll have to take that car around and park in back," she said. "I don't know why you didn't do that to begin with."

Because he hadn't wanted to drop Gwendolyn off to face them alone; because they'd never owned a car and so he'd forgotten, in the moment, that they even had a garage—to him it was a basement—and because dread always drained him of reason. All these things he thought but did not say. Gwendolyn removed her ski jacket—it was white with fur around the hood and underneath it she wore a black turtleneck and dark jeans, boots, her face scrubbed clean, no makeup, and slightly pink from the cold. Her lips were shiny with gloss, something from a clear tube that she'd put on just before leaving the car. He saw them all looking at her and then at the ground, not sure what to do—was it her beauty, how natural she was? Or the fact that they'd had so few visitors who were not family? Something froze them in place.

Gwendolyn moved toward Vishniak and said hello, kissed him on his cheek—then she tendered her hand to Barry. He lifted his gaze slowly from the floor, his eyes wider and darker even than usual, and shook. Barry's eyes remained on Gwendolyn, so hungry, so lascivious, that Robert stepped in between them. "Keep your eyes in your own goddamned head," he whispered.

"Fuck you," Barry replied, and ran up the steps.

"I don't know what's gotten into that boy lately," Stacia said, shaking her head. "He's always running up the steps or down to the basement."

"Tits," Vishniak announced. "That boy is just helpless in the presence of tits. The nicer they are the more helpless he is." He paused meaningfully, as if for Gwendolyn to take in the compliment. "Did I tell you about the time that Jayne Mansfield walked into the PO? Looking to buy stamps, I think, but she made a beeline right for yours truly—"

Robert rubbed his eyes. He was getting a terrible headache.

"Thank you for having me," Gwendolyn said softly. "I hope I'm not putting you out."

Stacia did not know what to do with such a display of manners. Was she supposed to admit that having a guest sleep over in a house their size was some trouble? Or acknowledge that with so many coming for dinner, what was one more mouth to feed? She put her hands inside her apron and took them out again. "I wouldn't have told him to bring you if we couldn't handle it," she replied, and told Robert to take her bag to Barry's room.

"Let's get one thing straight," Robert said. "She's staying in my room."

"I'm happy to stay wherever you like," Gwendolyn said.

"Gwendolyn has her own place. You think we don't fuck whenever we like at home?" Robert asked. "Don't make me into a hypocrite."

"A hypocrite!" Vishniak said, laughing. "Is that what they call it these days?"

Gwendolyn shook her head at Robert and frowned, then took her bag out of his hand and walked toward the steps. It was Hermès, named for Princess Grace. He'd seen it in a shop, more expensive than a month's rent. He had brought a girl to this house who carried such a bag as casually as his mother carried out the trash. "I think I should stay wherever your mother says. It's her house." She walked up the steps, hand on the banister. He watched her until all he could see were the heels of her boots.

"Do whatever you like," his mother said, "you always do."

Had he actually won? Or might the issue not have been as important as he made it? He should have taken Stacia aside, just the two of them, and said something. He'd embarrassed Gwendolyn — she didn't know how they talked to each other, didn't understand that something came over him when he got into this house; he couldn't always control his language or himself. He'd been here for five minutes and already he was making a mess of things.

"Tell the girl I made pound cake. I'm just cutting it if she wants a piece with some milk."

"Her name's Gwendolyn," he said. "Not girl or girlie or hey you or you there. Proper names for purposes of identification! Give it a try. So civilized. So now."

Stacia turned and walked away. "Just tell her, and don't make a federal case."

He found Gwendolyn sitting in Barry's room on his bed, her bag at her feet. Barry sat next to her, clearly enthralled as they talked softly, though Robert could not hear about what.

Robert cleared his throat. "May I interrupt?" he asked. "Ma wanted me to tell you that there's pound cake and milk downstairs for you, if you're hungry."

"Brilliant," Gwendolyn said. Barry frowned as Gwendolyn got up to leave the room. He was staring at her ass. Robert felt furious, yet he remembered what it was like being sixteen. He wondered if Barry had been with a girl yet. He doubted it.

Gwendolyn stopped at the doorway and kissed his cheek, then walked gracefully down the steps.

"They wanted Gwendolyn to sleep in your room," Robert said, coming in and sitting in the chair in the corner, "but I talked them out of it."

"I don't think Stacia much cares," Barry said. "She hardly cleaned this room. Not like she scoured the rest of the house. I don't think she ever expected Gwendolyn to sleep in here. And now you're beholden to her, you know. You gotta do every damn thing she asks for the rest of your trip. On account of how grateful you are to be able to screw your girlfriend in your own house." Barry smiled. "If you ask me, you're the one who's screwed."

"You mad at me?" Robert asked, taking Gwendolyn's bag in his hand and standing up.

"Not mad," Barry said. "I just want to know how the hell you do it. You're not such a prize, you know."

"Do what?"

"Get a girl like that."

"A girl like what?" Robert asked, walking toward the door.

"Perfect," Barry said. "Fucking perfect! In every way."

A few hours later, Gwendolyn came back from the bathroom in cotton pajamas he'd never seen before, tops and bottoms. "Hands to yourself," she said, when they got into bed. "I just couldn't. Not with everyone so close."

"The walls are thick," he lied. "No one can hear."

"Good night, Barry!" Gwendolyn yelled cheerily toward the opposite wall.

"Good night, Gwenny!" Barry chimed back.

Gwenny? When had that happened? "Okay, okay," Robert said, "you made your point."

She allowed him exactly as much physical interaction as was necessary for two tall people to sandwich themselves like sardines into a single bed. Most of the night he stared at the ceiling, head pushed against the wall, feet hanging off the end, then got up and went to the bathroom, jerked off, came back to bed, and slept the rest of the night on the cold floor.

Robert couldn't ever remember Gwendolyn sleeping through the night. Always she got up, came back, tossed about, ground her teeth. But in his ancient child-size bed she slept like a corpse. She was up early, too, while he slept late, because he had taken until almost dawn to finally doze off, and now it was past ten. He dressed and washed quickly, knowing that she was alone with them, and dashed down the steps. He found Gwendolyn in the kitchen, at the sink, using tweezers to get at the last pinfeathers on a large duck.

In the last few weeks, Gwendolyn's hands had begun to shake, but now she was steady as a surgeon. She wore a pink gauzy blouse, very loose, a type that she owned in many different colors, with a pair of much-worn jeans, skin peeking through the knees, and a pair of flip-flops. She could dress modestly, and still the lines of her body were apparent to him, every curve of it, as if she were standing there naked in the kitchen. He told himself this was not a time to be turned on, not now, but he'd gone two days without touching her. She had rolled up her sleeves and tied her hair back with a rubber band from the newspaper his father now sat at the kitchen table reading.

His father was reading in the kitchen? Robert was shaken from his erotic reverie by the oddness of this detail. It was strange enough to see Vishniak home in the middle of the day—had he taken the day off? No, it was a holiday. Stranger still that he was not reading in his chair with the TV on. All this togetherness in such a tiny space, yet his mother was not yelling, or ordering anyone out. She stood at the opposite counter, cracking eggs into a bowl of warm noodles.

"Robbie!" Gwendolyn exclaimed. "Your mother's going to show me how to make all kinds of things today, all your favorite dishes."

His mother did not turn around, only continued her mixing.

"There's just about another cup left in the pot," Vishniak said, raising his face from the paper. He pointed to an empty coffee mug on the table. "I saved it for you."

Stacia turned around, stood behind Gwendolyn, and said calmly: "When you're done with that, you can start cutting up the carrots and onions."

Jesus, who were these people?

"Stop daydreaming!" Stacia said. "Since you got a car with you, Mr. Big Shot, go get extra chairs from Lolly, then pick up your grandmother and bring her here. She's helping me."

His grandmother loved this American holiday, even if she replaced turkey with duck, and runny cranberry sauce and tasteless mashed potatoes with kishke and kasha wrapped in pastry dough, recipes passed down through the generations, spoken only, never written down, the official Oral Torah of his family. The Oral Torah of food. Were they going to induct Gwendolyn? No, he feared, they would merely let her see the extent to which her membership was impossible.

"Fine, I'll get Cece," he said, pouring himself some coffee. It was cold.

"I'm not done yet," Stacia said. First he could get her best screwdriver and some WD-40 from a neighbor who'd borrowed them weeks ago. The front door had been squeaking, she told him, a sound imperceptible, Robert believed, to everyone but her and the German shepherd next door. But she had several other tasks for him as well.

"If I'm going to do all that, I should have gotten started yesterday," he said. His brother was right; he was now her slave. He lowered his voice. "I have that other thing, too, you know."

"What other thing?" Gwendolyn asked, looking up.

"Nothing," he said.

"You have plenty of time for everything," Stacia replied. "They won't be here until four."

"Barry?" Robert asked. "Where's he?"

"Over at Victor's," his mother said. Victor Lampshade was Barry's best friend, a boy almost seven feet tall at age sixteen, with an enormous head of bushy blond hair. Standing together, they reminded Robert of the number ten. While Robert ran around doing Stacia's bidding, his brother likely lay stoned on Victor Lampshade's basement floor, counting ceiling tiles and listening to Jimi Hendrix—how did Barry always get out of everything?

"Victor's coming for dinner," Stacia said. "His parents and Ocky are in Miami and he didn't want to go." She snorted, a noise reserved for those who flew to warm climates for no apparent reason other than enjoying themselves.

"Three main courses!" Gwendolyn chimed in. "Chicken, duck, and brisket. Twenty people! Have you ever heard of anything so wonderfully generous?"

Robert's parents looked at her as if she were speaking a foreign language, then they looked at each other. The idea had never occurred to them. The adjective and all its implications. *Generous.*

His appointment was with Dr. Oppenheim, his grandmother's physician, long ago retired. He had agreed to see Robert as a favor to Cece—just as he'd once filled out Robert's college medical forms, claiming to be the family doctor though he'd never seen Robert before as a patient, had only heard about him over the years.

Dr. Oppenheim's office was across the street from the seafood restaurant where Robert had gone with Donna Cohen. Today, the doctor was opening up the office just for him. Attached to the corner house, it was at the basement level: a dark pair of rooms, reception and examining. Once bustling with patients, the rooms now sat empty. According to Cece, Dr. Oppenheim's wife had died the year before, and he was about to put the house on the market and move to a retirement home.

The elderly doctor wore a coat and tie and stood very straight as he shook Robert's hand. He'd come from Germany in the early 1930s, settled in Southwest Philly, near Cece and Saul. A man with luck and a skill, Cece had said, but most of all, excellent historical timing. His wife was American born. They'd moved here when everyone else moved, and never had children of their own, but he was the practitioner of record in Oxford Circle. As a kid, Robert had heard that Oppenheim gave a peppermint sucker after an exam, and that he could be cruel. But what child doesn't think a doctor, by definition, is cruel?

"Ah, you got so tall. The grandmother is so short." The doctor chuckled, directing him into the examining room, telling him to strip to his underwear. Robert obeyed, standing in pale blue boxer shorts, his eyes watery from dust. This seemed an ideal environment for his task. Surely whatever was wrong with him would manifest here.

The doctor came back a few minutes later and asked Robert what was wrong exactly. Robert tried to describe the occasional, mysterious episodes, moments when he was sure that his lungs were closing. Often this feeling seemed to be aggravated by dust and cigarette smoke, sometimes cold weather.

The doctor shook his head. "Can't hear you! Hold on!" he called back. "Hate hearing aids! Hate the buzzing." He went to a drawer and took a long trumpet out of his desk, then held it to his ear.

Was he being examined by a Victorian doctor in a stage play? "You're the only doctor I have any record with!" he yelled. "They tell me I need documentation. Years of it."

"Documentation of what?" the doctor asked, his voice low. Only Robert had to scream.

"You tell me!" Robert replied. "Something's wrong with my lungs!"

The doctor thumped his chest, listening to it with a stethoscope. He looked in Robert's ears with a tiny flashlight, stuck a tongue depressor into his mouth and held down his tongue, then shined his light again. He made Robert cough. Then he asked him to step onto a scale, an ancient one, then run in place for five minutes and count backward from a hundred.

"Your grandfather suffered with hay fever," Oppenheim said when Robert was done. "Your family had the first air conditioner in Southwest Philly. We all went over to look at it. Enormous machine. Size of a refrigerator. People thought the Kupferbergs had come into money. But it was needed, after that time they brought him home in the ambulance. You were a very small boy."

He's old, Robert thought. *The past and the present are the same thing for him.* He wondered if he could use this to his advantage.

"Anyway," the doctor continued, "maybe hay fever, maybe dust." He paused. "Not bad enough to get you out of Vietnam."

"What about my lungs?!" Robert yelled louder.

"You ever had pneumonia?"

"Not that I know of."

"Childhood respiratory infections?" he asked.

"I don't know. I guess. Probably."

"I suppose I could X-ray, but I don't hear anything."

"What about a specialist?!" Robert shouted. Of course he didn't hear anything.

"Get dressed," the doctor said. "Meet me in the living room."

Robert was happy to get his bare feet off the freezing linoleum and did as he was told. Upstairs, the house looked almost exactly like the house he'd grown up in but with the steps on the other side. The furniture was ornate and dark; the room depressed him. The doctor sat in a wing chair. In front of him on a round table sat a blue china teapot, two cups.

"I don't have much time," he said, but noticed Oppenheim hadn't brought his trumpet.

"Good, I'll pour the tea. It'll warm you up. Sit down. Relax."

Robert did as he was told, his leg jiggling up and down impatiently.

"I know why you've come," the doctor said, placing the tea in front of Robert.

"I have no medical history!" Robert shouted. "It's a problem. But then, it could also be a solution—"

"You're not the first to ask," he said. "They're very suspicious now. A few months before the physical, you suddenly have a condition, they ask questions."

"But if I had a history?!" Robert shouted. "If it was a condition from years back—"

"But you don't," the man said. "You don't have a condition. As far as I can see."

"Then what have I been feeling all these years?"

"Allergies, to dust," he said. "I told you already."

"There was no dust in my house growing up," Robert said. "She cleaned night and day."

"Some say that can be the problem," he replied.

"So if I'd grown up in a dirtier house, I wouldn't be sick?"

The man smiled mysteriously. Had he even heard?

"You're retiring," Robert said, trying another tack. "Moving away."

"It took me years to get my medical license in America," he said. "I die without scandal." He paused. "I love this country."

Robert put his head in his hands.

"Maybe it won't be so bad."

"Easy for you to say, old man," Robert said, and stood up. The doctor got up, too, smiling politely as Robert turned and left.

CECE MET HIM AT the door in a hot pink dress, slippers, an apron. She lived in a small garden apartment. The salty sweetness of constant baking had become part of the walls, the carpet, the furniture, as if his grandmother lived inside a giant loaf of bread. He bent down and kissed her. "Come in the kitchen," she said. "I'll make you an omelet."

"We're eating dinner in less than two hours."

"You're hungry, I know you're hungry. I'm making you lunch."

He shrugged and gave in. He *was* hungry, actually. She brought out a bottle of milk. There was already a glass on the table. She scooped out a slice of homemade apple strudel that had been sitting on the stove, and brought over several slices of rye bread and a block of butter, as if he might expire from starvation while waiting. Then she got eggs and cheese out of the refrigerator and bent down to pull out a frying pan. Her kitchen was kosher, unlike his mother's. That was the one rebellion that he'd noticed in his parents' generation: they ignored the dietary laws. In old age, Cece could not be as scrupulous about her kitchen; she was losing her sight to cataracts and glaucoma. In her own place, she could manage by feel, though she admitted to sometimes confusing her pots. And she had to put her hand over the flame to tell how high it was, which made Robert nervous. She cradled the bowl in her arms and whipped the eggs with a fork.

"*Nu*, what did he say?" she asked. "Oppenheim?"

"No dice," he said, hearing the eggs sizzle as they hit the pan. "Said it's too late, a letter would look suspicious."

She shook her head. "Your mother said he wouldn't do it. She never liked him. Maybe we can find someone else." She bent close to the pan, then scooped up the omelet and flipped it over. Moments later she placed it in front of him, dripping with cheese, and then she sat very close, watching him eat. By the last few bites he felt sick, but still he kept going until the end. Afterward she stood, took the plate in her hand, and felt her way to the sink.

When she was done, Robert followed her into the large bedroom. Clothes were strewn on the bed. The dresser was covered in makeup brushes, powder, perfume, and a few scarves, everything scattered. In the center of the room lay a single shoe. He retrieved it quickly.

"Shoe, Cece," he said, holding it up in front of her. "Dark blue." He put it on the dresser. As a child, he'd thought her invincible, preparer of Sunday lunches for thirty, the only person who could order around his mother. Now a stray shoe imperiled her existence.

"Go in the closet. Find a silver shoe box," she said, sitting down on the bed. "It has English letters on it." His grandmother could not read or write English, had signed an X on his birthday cards his whole life. He pushed aside mountains of dresses, the dry-cleaning plastic sticking to his arms and face. A person could asphyxiate in such a closet. "Get Barry to help you clean this out!"

There was an overhead lightbulb. He turned it on. "How do you reach your shoes? You're not climbing on any ladders, are you?"

"The ones I wear are on the back of the door," she said. "Those are extras."

He found two silver boxes and brought them to the bed. The first one contained a pair of white sandals. She shook her head. The second he suspected was empty—it had felt that way when he took it down. She smiled and told him to open the lid.

A box full of money.

"You count," she said. "I've been saving since it began. The conscription."

All dollar bills. He did as she asked, laying the bills out on the bed.

"You take it, sweetheart," she said. "You find the man."

"What man?" he asked. "Another doctor?" It looked to be about a hundred dollars. How did you bribe a doctor for a hundred in ones? The doctors he'd heard about cost fifty times that.

She leaned closer, lowered her voice. "Don't tell nobody you're going."

"Going where?"

She paused. "Be very quiet. He'll put the blanket down so they won't see your footsteps. That's important. And make sure your little sister don't sneeze."

"Cece?" He put the box down. "Where are you?"

She took his hands and kissed them.

"It'll be all right," she said. "Only the old women got seasick."

CHAPTER FOURTEEN

Revelations

Cece leaned on his arm. He thought of weddings and funerals, the only time anymore that men led women in such a way. He had to walk slowly. His mother came to the front door for the handoff. "Park in the back and bring the chairs up through the basement," Stacia said.

"Where the hell is my wastrel brother?"

"Upstairs," his mother said, lifting Cece into the living room. "With her."

"I assume by 'her' you mean Gwendolyn and not, say, Lady Bird Johnson or Marianne Faithfull, or perhaps Mrs. Lepcheck my fourth-grade teacher?"

"Don't forget to bring in the chairs."

He parked the car in back then came in through the basement, walking up the steps, through the kitchen, and into the living room. His father was in his usual recliner—that was more like it—watching football, oblivious to his presence. Robert walked back up another set of steps to the second floor. His bedroom door was open, but Gwen wasn't in there. Then he heard voices coming from behind Barry's door. It was slightly ajar and he stood in the hall and watched.

His brother sat on the bed, opening a flat white box tied with a large red ribbon. Gwendolyn stood a few feet from the bed, smiling. Barry had never gotten a gift in a box like that, a box that actually fit the gift, not something patched together. He pulled away the paper, held a shirt out in front of him, a white linen shirt, collarless, a more masculine version of the type Gwendolyn favored herself. She shopped at department stores. Retail. There was a name on the box but he couldn't see it, knew Barry had never held a shirt like that in his hands — sewn with care, a shirt that hung on a person right and fit them. How had she known his size? From the picture he had of the two of them, taped to the mirror?

"Wow," Barry said. His eyes were wide, staring at the shirt, staring at Gwendolyn, then back to the shirt. But he could not keep his eyes off her long. Vishniak was right. The boy saw only one part of a woman, but did not seem to know a thing about actually talking to the opposite sex. Sure, he knew what sex was. Barry, too, had been schooled on Stacia's artwork, his father's basement *Playboy* collection. But when it came to talking to women, winning them, he was lost. Why hadn't he come to Robert? Why had they never talked about this?

"There's no secret, really," Gwendolyn said. "With girls, I mean. You just have to act like they don't matter to you and then they'll come running." She paused. "You might try taking an extra shower or two. A little of that lovely green soap they sell here. The manly stuff advertised on television. You know, the fellow chopping trees? Robert uses it. They make a deodorant, too."

She said these things so delicately, without judgment. Whereas another person, Robert or his parents for instance, might have said that Barry stank. Gwendolyn would never say that.

She put her hand on his shoulder. "You have your own qualities that Robert doesn't have. You have something, too, that's very attractive. That's just yours." She leaned over, kissed him on the forehead. "Soon you'll be going to university. The girls are better in university. Trust me."

"Okay," he breathed. In her hands, he was docile, pliable, drugged by lust. "I trust you, Gwendolyn."

"I'm going to take a shower now," Gwendolyn continued. "Your mother said to go while the hot water's not in use. Robert washes so much, he's practically antiseptic."

Barry laughed. Either she had won him over or else he was thinking of her in the shower, her white skin against the pale yellow tiles, and was too preoccupied to speak.

"I'll see you later." She got up to go.

Robert ducked into his room and waited for her. Inside his bedroom, the light seeped through the window blinds. It was the graying afternoon light of his childhood, a specific light that happened at around four o'clock in a neighborhood of row homes, the endless blocks where the sun never seemed to shine directly on furniture or floors, not like the glare in single homes or high-rise apartments. The light made him think of enforced naps, of homework and retreating to his room in the agonies of adolescence, made him think of his whole life in this house. When Gwendolyn entered in a sexless blue terry-cloth bathrobe that she'd bought for the trip, he put his arms around her, kissed her, and started to undo the belt at the middle, but she would have none of it. She had to talk to him about his family, she said, it was terribly important.

He braced himself.

"You have it all wrong, Robbie," she said. "About them. All wrong."

Then she told him how they really were. Stacia wasn't cheap; no, his mother was a brilliant home economist, able to make enormous meals on little money and stretch what needed to be stretched. She should run the government! And his father, reading for hours on his day off—in the kitchen, the living room, the bathroom. And so many interesting stories. Vishniak was so terribly imaginative, so literary. Sad that he never got a formal education, was always looking after his brothers. And Barry, such a sweet boy. Such big shoes for him to fill, being behind Robert, and Barry was competitive by nature, more than Robert realized, but he'd be fine, she said, the two brothers were more alike than different.

She remade them all, seeing only what was admirable, shining a light, retelling the story for him.

That night, they were all on best behavior, trying to fulfill her expectations. They knew somehow that she'd remade them, and they liked seeing themselves in her eyes. The extended family all kissed her and clawed at her and asked her about England, and the children made her say things over and over again, just to hear the accent. A Vishniak brother asked her to say, "The rain in Spain stays mainly in the plain." She did as he asked, smiling in her slim royal blue wool dress and pumps, pearl earrings; she had dressed for them, and they appreciated such niceties. They would talk for weeks about her perfume — what was it?

"Chanel Number Nine," she said.

They nodded solemnly, as if in prayer.

"Don't you think," he heard one female cousin say to another, "that she looks just a little bit like Jacqueline Kennedy?"

"Oh, what we once had in her!" proclaimed Aunt Lolly.

Every woman wanted to sit next to Gwendolyn, every child wanted to crawl onto her lap, every man congratulated Robert for having found such a girl. By the time the first course was served, they had decided unequivocally on the question that had puzzled them on the way over — of course Gwendolyn was Jewish. That much was obvious now. Stacia passed around gefilte fish, big heaping balls of carp covered in *drahlis*, the thick, runny fish jelly that Vishniak pronounced as looking "oh so much like dog shit," and Gwendolyn didn't even flinch. Not so much as a shiver as she picked up her fork. Oh, she was a Jew, all right.

They passed her the rest of the food: The soup with matzo balls because the Vishniaks never met a holiday, American or otherwise, that did not like a matzo ball, big as a baby's head, floating in a river of chicken soup; two kinds of kugel—sweet and vegetable; and kasha in pastry. Then green beans with almonds, carrots with pineapple—in their family, all vegetables had to be adorned—and the three main courses, including the duck in orange sauce, then the chicken for those who didn't like duck, and the brisket. The passing went on forever, and Gwendolyn laughed and laughed as uncles and cousins heaped more and more food on her plate.

"Robbie," she whispered, "I'll never eat all this."

"Just try," he said. "They only want to see you trying. And whatever you don't eat, pass over to him." He gestured to the enormous Victor Lampshade, whose plate was piled so high that someone had just given him a second dish to contain it all.

Where had that girl gone, the one curled up, crying, on the floor? Clearly, he had misjudged. She was not fragile. She was strong, stronger than he was, with a well of inner resources and a gift of seeing people as they wanted to be seen. She filled in the middle where others saw only outlines.

Gwendolyn ate delicately, as Tracey had, cutting the meat into small pieces, nodding at the others' conversation with her mouth closed. She ignored the food that shot across the table, or dropped from people's tongues, the food visible as it was chewed, his family digesting great hunks of meat then crunching on the bones, sucking out the marrow, devouring as if eating were work. Vishniak started to do the spoon trick, something he did every year involving an olive, a spoon, and a glass of seltzer, and, inevitably, dropping his pants. But he glanced at Gwendolyn and told the children to eat their vegetables. He would show it to them another time.

Instead of Pilgrims and Indians, John Smith and Pocahontas, they talked of Richard Nixon. Once they got started, they were on fire.

"A friend of Joseph McCarthy, that's what he is."

"A friend of Roy Cohn, that traitor, that *shandah fur die goyim*."

"Where were the young people? All their marching and yelling for the vote."

"Don't go blaming the young," said Aunt Lolly, as she leaned over and wiped a glob of potato from Uncle Fred's shirt. "They have enough to worry about."

"The war," whispered one of the children. She said it like a hiss. "The war."

"What will you do?" Uncle Frank asked Robert. "I read how more died there now than in Korea."

Robert nodded, unsure what to reply. But Gwendolyn put her hand on his leg, leaned across him and said, "Robert and I are going into the Peace Corps."

"We are?" he whispered.

"The Peace Corps?" Stacia asked. "What's he going to do there?"

"It's the perfect solution!" Gwendolyn yelled, for now she was raising her voice to compete. "He won't have to carry a gun, and we can help the poor."

"Robert help the poor?" Barry yelped. Vishniak, too, and several of his brothers joined in, laughing and snorting. "My brother?" Barry asked, chomping on a sour pickle, the juice running down his chin. "Don't you know, Gwendolyn? Robert is his own favorite charity."

Robert looked over at Gwendolyn. He expected her to fall apart, hearing them all laugh at her idea. But she was unchanged. Her eyes blazed with vision. They were going into the Peace Corps, she whispered to him again, and he'd finally be safe.

That night, after the others had gone, she lay next to him, so certain, so convinced. She could remake the war, the killing, now, as she'd remade his family. "If we went into the Peace Corps, we could make good out of bad, we could be together," she whispered, "and travel."

"You'd never get in," he said. "You're not an American citizen."

"I would be," she said, "if we got married." She began to kiss his cheek, and then moved down his neck. She held herself over him, arms taut, her tongue licking down his chest to his stomach, her long hair hanging over his body, softly stroking his skin. His thighs ached.

"Think about it, Robbie," she whispered. "Think about it."

CHAPTER FIFTEEN

Graduation

Even at 7:00 a.m., they could see the haze, the air thick with humidity. KYW News Radio predicted record-breaking temperatures, and Uncle Frank's car—the black Pontiac with the black bench seats—had no air-conditioning. Six of them had to squeeze into that car—Cece, Lolly, Stacia, and Vishniak, Frank at the wheel, and his wife, Lillian. Only Barry was absent, home studying for the SAT, and Uncle Fred had to work. The women wore stockings and hats and dresses with jackets; the men were in dark wool suits, the same ones used for funerals and weddings, not exactly appropriate to the season. Right from the start they all took their jackets off and laid them carefully in the trunk.

Cece, being the smallest, sandwiched herself in between the men in the front seat. In the back, Stacia and Lillian, both thin, were bookends to the heavier Aunt Lolly. They tried not to touch each other, their skin already sticky. Lolly made waves in the air with a stiff Chinese paper fan Fred had once brought her from a gas station. It was trimmed in red and featured a single, drooping branch covered in blossoms. At noon they pulled into a rest stop to eat the bagels spread with cream cheese and jelly that Stacia had prepared that morning, washing them down with iced tea from a large thermos.

Despite starting out at dawn, and giving themselves over an hour to spare, they got lost on the New York Thruway and went round and round for hours until they could get back on track. They arrived just as the ceremony was starting, slid into the back row, tired, sweating, the men thirsty and the women in need of the bathroom, but full of anticipation.

For years now, they'd been waiting for this, the first college graduation of their lives. A distant music started and the students walked in two at a time carrying flowers instead of programs. A few girls were barefoot, some were barefoot but wearing a cap and gown, and others appeared to be wrapped in bedsheets. A few of the boys wore T-shirts and torn jeans. "Where are the rest of the caps and gowns?" Lolly whispered to Stacia. "Did they run out?"

The students settled down in their seats and immediately began to boo various members of the administration, and then the guest speaker. The reason was never quite clear to the Vishniak party. The class valedictorian, a woman, spoke of how colleges kept students politically ignorant, and students needed to kick big business out of the academe. Stacia and Vishniak, like the other parents, stared down into their laps.

Afterward, overheated, disappointed, they found Robert and Gwendolyn and asked only for the use of the closest bathrooms and then a fast campus tour. Their favorite part was the library, with its rows and rows of thick books, the echoing halls, the ancient desks. And air-conditioning. They breathed in the quiet and the cold, cold air and were back to the parking lot within three hours of arrival. Cece dabbed at her eyes, saying that she was glad to live to see the first college graduate in the family. "You did graduate, right? That was it?"

"Yeah, Cece, it's over," Robert said and collected his five-dollar bills from each of them. His parents handed him a wrapped box. He unwrapped it and stuffed the paper in his pocket.

"It's waterproof," his father announced.

"It was on sale," his mother added.

His parents had bought him a Timex watch. He thanked them with as much enthusiasm as he could muster. By the time Gwendolyn hugged them good-bye, he couldn't wait for them to drive away.

GWENDOLYN DID NOT GIVE UP on her desire to enter the Peace Corps. A recent Peace Corps alumnus named Jerry Stiles showed up at the bookstore. He had just returned from the Peruvian Andes, and each time he came to browse, Bruno and Gwendolyn treated him like a celebrity. Gwendolyn set up a meeting so that she and Robert could ask Stiles questions about his experience. They were to meet in a café in Harvard Square, a place where Gwendolyn and Robert went when it was warm because they could sit outside together on the small patio and watch the parade of Cambridge humanity, most of it under age twenty-five.

The coffee was cheap and inky black, and Robert held a cup of it close to him as he made his way across the crowded patio, stepping one way to avoid a mutt tethered to his master's chair by a red rope, then ducked another way to avoid the heavy, nauseating scent of patchouli that hung, like a nuclear cloud, over a particular table. He spotted Gwendolyn in the corner and waved, but she did not see him. She was leaning in toward a tall, gaunt man with a heavy blond beard; the man looked at her intently, utterly absorbed. There was a third chair, and on the back of it rested Gwendolyn's old, weathered jean jacket. She had saved that chair for Robert, but what became clear to him, as he came closer and put out his hand and introduced himself, was that Jerry Stiles had thought he was meeting with Gwendolyn alone. Jerry shook Robert's hand — half-smiling, half-grimacing—and then he stared into his iced tea. He had been off in the wilderness for years, and his level of disappointment was serious indeed.

Gwendolyn got herself, and subsequently Robert, into these situations too often. She didn't understand how the average male heard the word *friend* when used by a woman who looked like she did. "Can I buy you something to eat?" Robert asked, hoping to show that he meant no harm. And the man needed a meal; Robert looked positively obese standing next to him. "Gwendolyn loves the pound cake," he added, "but I'm a doughnut man myself."

Jerry unfolded his endless legs from under the table, legs so long and thin that they made him look, as he stretched, like a being half man and half insect, and then informed them that upon his return from Peru, ten different worms had been found in his stools. Removing a small vial from his pocket, he lined up a series of tiny pills on the table and, adding that he still had to be careful what he ate, proceeded to swallow each one in turn.

Robert took a sip of his coffee, simultaneously reaching over to grab a hunk of pound cake off Gwendolyn's plate. She slapped his hand playfully. "Get your own," she said. Jerry hardly noticed Robert, or the implied intimacy of the gesture; his eyes were fully on Gwendolyn. She was so damned trusting. What would happen if he had to leave her for weeks or even months? Would she stay faithful? Whatever he did to escape the draft, he would have to bring her with him.

But no, Jerry insisted a few minutes later, they should not apply as a couple. It was harder that way. Even if they got married, he said, Gwendolyn's visa status would still be a problem. "Bureaucracies don't like complications," he mumbled.

Robert wondered whether or not to believe him. How did he know that Jerry didn't have plans for Gwendolyn when Robert was off in God knows where? When he imagined her with other men, he was so overwhelmed with jealousy that he could hardly think straight. It was in these moments that he became aware of just how covetous he really was, a bottomless pit of need, desire, greed. Why should the Peace Corps take him? What could he even give, when mostly what he wanted was to take?

Jerry had been a physics major at MIT before he joined the Peace Corps, and the lines on his face, the constant frown of his mouth, gave the impression of a man endlessly wrestling with a complicated mathematical problem. Had he been this serious before he left? Though the purpose of the meeting was for them to hear about his experiences, he was hesitant to talk much about the Andes until Gwendolyn encouraged and cajoled for a few minutes, patting his hand gently. He sat forward and spoke to her alone, the words hesitant at first, even slightly stuttering, but then his impressions suddenly came tumbling out in paragraphs, as if the information had been stored away in there for months and needed only the right person to coax it out.

He began by talking about the rigorous three-month training he had done with twenty-four other trainees in the jungles of Puerto Rico, a place picked to simulate the jungle climate they'd find in Peru, except that most of them wouldn't be assigned to the jungle because Peru had more climate variation than any other country on earth, from tropical jungles to frozen mountaintops. For those months, they spent six hours each day in organized physical exercise, including a ten-mile hike before dawn. When they weren't exercising, they were poked and prodded endlessly by psychiatrists, and every few weeks candidates were eliminated in a process with the Orwellian title of "deselection." They also had three hours of daily Spanish lessons, but when Jerry eventually arrived at the Andean village where he was to spend two years, he discovered that the Indians spoke their own language, called Quechua, and he had to start learning all over again, on the job.

He was to teach in the local school and do "whatever else was needed," and he decided that what this town needed was latrines — most residents used the nearby river for everything from sewage disposal to bathing. The rainy season lasted for months, and the children had to be kept from the puddles — if they played in them, they picked up parasites that blew up their legs and gave them disfiguring diseases. But that was assuming they lived past three, which more than half did not. The economy of this town worked on a feudal system; peasants worked for food and beer. All of the land in the region was owned by five families, banking oligarchs. When these families needed workers, they brought in more labor from the higher elevations. There was an inexhaustible supply of miserable, starving people who strapped pieces of rubber tire to their feet in lieu of shoes and chewed coca leaves in lieu of eating.

There had been victories, certainly, moments when he felt he was accomplishing something. "But by the time I left," Jerry said, shaking his head, "I knew I hadn't accomplished a damn thing. Not really. I taught five or six children to read, built some outhouses. So what? I was like a few drops of rain sent to quench an endless drought."

If this was what Robert had in store for him, though, he need not be too worried — his chances of getting accepted, according to Jerry Stiles, were not very good. Nixon had just appointed a new director, Joe Blatchford, and the rumors were already flying: The Peace Corps would have less money, accept more volunteers over age twenty-five, and reject more liberal-arts majors, or "BA generalists," as they were called. Only those with specific skills — agriculture majors, engineers, city planners — would be accepted. In other words, the Peace Corps would cease to be a shelter for draft dodgers.

By the time they left, Jerry was hoarse from talking, and Robert could not wait to get away. They thanked him and left the café, Gwendolyn drawing her jacket around her shoulders. Robert pulled her close. "I guess you're disappointed," he said, as they walked to the T stop.

She did not reply, did not even seem to hear him as she stared off in the other direction.

"And I suppose you shouldn't apply to go with me."

Finally she turned her head toward him. "Apply alone," she said casually. She would join him there after training; there was no law against traveling on your own.

Robert liked this idea even less.

She acted as if the evening had never taken place. Every week after that, she asked him if he had finally finished his application. He knew by now that when she decided something, she had a will of iron, could wear him down, all the time believing it was for his own good. And part of him wanted to be worn down. What was love, if not the desire to give the beloved what she wanted? He could not buy her gifts; could he not give her this? That she wanted so much?

She might have wanted it, but he feared that the Peace Corps would be their undoing. His mother lived in a place like the one Jerry Stiles had described, if only in her own mind. Why else would she collect the castoffs of the dead? And Cece had fled starvation and poverty, never speaking a word about where she had been. But Robert at least knew what he feared. Gwendolyn had no fear, and that couldn't be a good thing. Could she really survive in a lean-to in sub-Saharan Africa? Or deal with Brazil's street children, or India's untouchables? She was still a rich girl at base, never had to pay a bill or think about what anything cost; she even sent her laundry out to be washed and folded. The closest thing to hardship she'd experienced was sharing a single bed in Stacia Vishniak's house. Surely, there was another way out?

THERE WAS ONE PERSON he hadn't yet tried. The one person who surely had the power to help him—he would have asked months earlier, but for the awkwardness of the silence that he himself had created. He would go to Tracey. He would go humbly. If need be, he would beg.

Robert took barely a day to summon the courage to call the last number he had for Tracey; a girl answered and said that Tracey had moved out, was staying in a hotel in Cambridge. Robert called the desk and left a message. No response. He called again and again over the next three days and finally, on a Friday night, went himself, lingered in the formal lobby, finally approaching the desk to give his name. He was surprised when, after the clerk called up, he directed Robert to the elevators.

Tracey greeted him at the door wrapped in a white terry-cloth robe, his hair still wet from a shower. "You'll have to take me as I am," he said, ushering Robert inside. The room was a suite with a view of the Charles. In the corner were some overstuffed chairs, a beige couch. The door to the bedroom was ajar, and Robert could see an unmade bed, clothing and towels strewn around as if the suite were just another dorm room.

"You look well," Robert said.

Tracey did not reply to that remark but instead offered to make them martinis. If Tracey was mad at him, he wouldn't show it with rudeness. That was not his style. Robert's mouth was dry and his heart pounded in his chest.

Tracey was having trouble opening the bottle of olives. Robert came up behind him and took the bottle, cold and wet with condensation, out of Tracey's hands. He banged it on the top of the bar, heard the vacuum break—his mother's trick for recalcitrant lids—and handed it back.

Silently Tracey used toothpicks to spear the olives, putting two in each glass, then shaking up the mixture and apportioning it. They moved to the two chairs in the sitting area, sat facing each other. Tracey crossed his legs and sat back, but Robert perched nervously on the edge of his seat. "You know," Tracey said quietly, "there's nothing I can do for you."

"What do you mean?"

"You want me to help you get out of Vietnam, don't you?"

Robert stared into his drink.

"You think you're the only one to ask? My father's driver's kid — he got him into the Reserves. Took a lot of string pulling. Plus my uncle's barber and my parents' minister both have teenage grandsons. You're too late. My family has now officially gone out of the favor business. Everything's tighter since Nixon, since those fathers got arrested for bribery — a lot of resentment about people trying to get out of their duty."

"And you?" Robert asked. "What are your plans?"

Tracey ignored the question, running his fingers through his damp hair. It occurred to Robert that Tracey was nervous, too. "You look tired," Tracey said. "Careful or you'll lose your looks."

Robert, sallow and careworn, slumped in his chair, all his natural intensity turned in on itself. "Who gives a damn what I look like?" he mumbled.

"You've never cared, have you? I suppose it's half your charm."

"Thanks."

"Don't be too proud of yourself," Tracey snapped. "Anyway, if you can hold out for six months or so, Father says that Nixon's working on something. Wants to revise the 'sixty-seven draft act. Go to a lottery system. Everyone participates but some people won't ever have to go, if they get a lucky number. Much more fair that way."

"What am I supposed to do for six months? Go into hiding?" Robert asked. "Anyway, I'm not staking my future on a lucky number."

"Then you shouldn't have crawled inside that girl's cunt and disappeared," Tracey said flatly.

"Don't talk about her that way," Robert said. "We're engaged." If being married would not help them get into the Peace Corps, in the end, he had found that he liked the idea anyway. His love for her was the one solid thing in a future that felt murky and uncertain at best.

"Congratulations."

"You're very angry at me, aren't you?"

"Why?" Tracey asked. "Because I thought you were my friend?" Tracey didn't have to say what he was thinking; Robert knew. Tracey had told him the biggest secret of his life — had handed him, in effect, his soul — and Robert, having heard the information, promptly disappeared.

"I was your friend," Robert said. "I *am* your friend."

"The only times I've heard from you in the past year and a half were when you needed something. First a job and now a deferment."

"What about Cates and Pascal?" Robert asked, trying to steer the conversation back, trying to neutralize Tracey's tone. "What are they doing?"

"Cates, it turns out, is a diabetic. No wonder he was so moody. And as of last week, Pascal developed a sudden thyroid disorder. Van Dorn is going into the Guard." Tracey glanced behind him at the bar. "Can I freshen your drink? Now that you know your errand is futile."

"This isn't a game for me," Robert said. "It's not like in school, where you can pay someone to write the paper. I can't pay someone to die for me. This is my fucking life!"

"I'm afraid there's nothing I can do," Tracey said. "But I sense I'm not your last resort."

"You are."

"Please, Robert, spare me. You're a college graduate now. Like it or not, you've joined the club. No college graduate in this country goes to Vietnam if he can help it, not if he's even slightly cunning or the least bit resourceful. You don't even have to be very smart. Just drop a dictionary on your foot, preferably the *Oxford English* hardcover. That'll get you out of the physical and then you can enter the lottery, and if that doesn't work, well, you can break something else. Or steal a car, or claim you're queer. You may be a lot of things, but you're not out of options."

"I'm considering the Peace Corps," Robert said, standing up, knowing that if Tracey could not help him, he would have to try every other possible option, even those he didn't like.

"You see?" Tracey said. "I knew you had a trick or two up your sleeve. Not exactly what I pictured. But maybe the Peace Corps will improve your character."

"There's nothing wrong with my character."

"No," Tracey said softly, and got up, took their glasses back to the bar so that once again Robert was looking at his back. "There's nothing wrong with your character at all."

"I fell in love, that's all," Robert said. "I fell in love and I got selfish about my time with her. Maybe love makes you selfish."

"Maybe it does," Tracey said, his back still to Robert. "You can go now, if there's no other reason you came. Much as I've enjoyed this trip down memory lane, I have dinner plans."

Robert walked to the door and opened it. "I never told anyone, you know. I never told anyone and I never will."

As he left, Tracey was washing glasses in the sink. Robert assumed that he was doing it to keep busy — then again, Tracey had always been meticulous about glassware. Robert walked down the hall and pressed the button for the elevator. He wondered if he'd ever see his roommate again, and just as the question crossed his mind he heard a voice behind him:

"I hope I won't regret this someday."

Robert turned around. Tracey, still in his robe, leaned up against the wall, lighting a cigarette. "Won't regret what?" Robert asked.

"Leaving you to your destiny."

"If it's really my destiny," Robert replied, "then there's nothing to be done."

Tracey nodded, and Robert nodded back, as if they were two acquaintances who'd run into each other on a streetcar. The elevator opened; it was empty and Robert stepped in. As he turned around, the doors were already closing, and Tracey was gone.

PART II

CHAPTER SIXTEEN

The drawing

A gentle snow had just begun to fall, and already Robert could see a thin layer of white frosting the windowsill. It was the first night of the last month of 1969, a Monday, and they had the television on in the living room. Gwendolyn sat cross-legged on the couch with a bag of potato chips on her lap — she called potato chips "crisps" — and just then she shoved several into her mouth at once. She hadn't eaten much lunch or, from what he'd seen, much dinner; she was a lousy eater who found solace in junk food, and she often ate snacks in front of the TV on Monday nights, when they watched the eight o'clock movie together, Mondays being his only night off. But tonight was no movie.

This was the draft lottery and in every bar frequented by the young — and in every college dorm, fraternity house, and household with at least one adult male under twenty-six — the TV was tuned to it. Pacing in front of the screen, he thought of the Israelites in Egypt putting the lamb's blood on the doorposts of their houses so that the angel of death might pass over and spare their firstborn sons. If lamb's blood would have gotten him out of the draft, he'd

have happily drenched the place in it. He'd tried just about everything else.

"I don't see why you're so nervous," she said, licking the tips of
her fingers, as she'd done that first day he met her, a lifetime ago.
Even stuffing herself, she was somehow dainty. "Next year at this
time, we'll be on the other side of the world, and all this will be
behind us. Wouldn't it be wonderful if we wound up in Peru, like
Jerry?"

"The Peace Corps isn't a travel agency, Gwendolyn. Just because
you've decided you want South America doesn't mean that's where
they'll send us."

Gwendolyn slept through the night these days, though with the
aid of sleeping pills. The scraps of endless paper, newspaper and
magazine articles with paragraphs underlined, had slowly disappeared, much to the delight of Dana, the maid. She still went to
endless political meetings, still got high too much and took mysterious pills he didn't approve of, but while his life was teetering,
Gwendolyn went about her day cheerfully. She was full of energy
again, and all of it seemed channeled into her desire to leave the
country and follow him into the Peace Corps; her hopes fell on
South America, perhaps because Jerry Stiles was in the bookshop
at least once a week, embellishing his stories, feeding her ideas. He
pictured Jerry and Bruno always at her side, like mismatched bookends, as she went about her work.

"You know, in the Andes, they have shamans that cure illness
and exorcize demons? Sort of half priest, half doctor. A shaman
might be able to help your breathing problems."

"Oh, yes, a witch doctor, that'll do it," he said, taking a chip
from the bag in her lap. He had made yet another unsuccessful trip
to the doctor, a young internist recommended by a friend at the restaurant. He'd paid cash and again been told that nothing appeared
to be wrong with him. The man had suggested an allergist, but then

added that his allergies would have to be serious indeed to get him out of Vietnam. Doctors were suspicious these days of men his age. What Robert needed but did not have was a family physician, someone trusted, who cared about his future. But he didn't have that and couldn't pay to bribe the other kind.

Gwendolyn poured herself a shot of scotch from the bottle on the table. The phone rang but he didn't answer it. His parents. He let it ring and ring, while Gwendolyn stared at him helplessly, until the ringing finally stopped. He could not listen to the fear in their voices. Only Barry was calm and focused these days. The 1969 draft act had transformed him — specifically the announcement that by 1971 the draft would take only nineteen-year-olds. Barry would turn nineteen in 1971, and he was determined not to get stuck. Robert had never seen him so focused — sending away for applications, researching scholarships, writing essays; he was determined to have that educational deferment in hand by September. He had always wanted out of Oxford Circle, but now he had added incentive: he didn't want to die. Meanwhile Stacia and Vishniak drove Robert crazy with their endless suggestions — as if he and his draft counselor had not explored every possible avenue of escape, from starvation diets to felony convictions. The week before, his mother had called to tell him to come home; the Pennsylvania draft board was slower, she insisted, citing the example of a neighbor who'd been out of school for two years and still hadn't been called for his physical. Robert could transfer his residence. Then Vishniak got on the phone and told him to ignore everything his mother had just said. "What does she know? Boston's gotta be the most crowded, all those kids, and the most liberal, the most likely to cut you a break. Stay where you are." And then, as Robert heard Stacia yelling in the background, Vishniak hung up.

" — they have a potion, the shamans, sort of like LSD," Gwendolyn was saying. "You drink and vomit and supposedly you can see all the lives you've had, and all the lives you're going to have. Isn't that fascinating?"

"All you need is more drugs," he snapped. "And I'd never survive the air in the high altitudes!"

"Don't talk to me that way, please. None of this is my bloody fault."

"I know," he said. "I just wish you wouldn't get ahead of yourself. Right now, we're in Boston and my life is in the hands of a Republican congressman from New York. Can you stay down here with me in this life for now? Just for tonight?"

He was a coward; he still hadn't told her about the thin envelope that had come the week before, which he'd immediately shoved into his jacket pocket, disposing of it later in a public trash bin. The first rejection letter of his life. Perhaps the Peace Corps had sensed his ambivalence, though by the time the letter arrived he would have taken any offer that spared him from having to depend on the capriciousness of a drawing. The letter had suggested he apply again after acquiring additional skills, but he didn't need to get in later; he needed it now. Jerry had been right about one thing — the Peace Corps didn't want any more draft dodgers. How could he tell her, when she had made the last year of her life about this? How could he even begin?

"Darling, for the last time, would you please sit down?" she said. "You're blocking the screen. And here it is."

Alexander Pirnie's face had a hangdog quality, made worse by the presence of thick, black plastic glasses. His salt-and-pepper hair was arranged in a way that looked as if he'd been growing out a crew cut for the last twenty years, and he wore a black suit and frowned.

"At least he's properly solemn," Gwendolyn said.

But there was nothing solemn about this process. It played more like a dull game show where the winners got nothing less than their very futures and the losers were taken off in chains. The eligible birthdays, 366 of them, had been placed in individual blue plastic capsules. The congressman plunged his hand into a large cylindrical bowl and then called out the first birthday. An announcer then echoed the birthday for clarity's sake: September 14. The date was now posted on a large tote board next to the number one. Robert's birthday was May 9. He poured himself a shot of whiskey. Safe. He did the same for numbers 2 and 3. He was so tense that the alcohol seemed to have no effect at all. More numbers. They were up to 10, 11. Safe.

Gwendolyn took a joint out of her pocket and lit it. "Bruno gave it to me. For you. For tonight." She held it out to him.

"Bruno's not worried?" Robert said, taking the cigarette.

"Bruno?" she asked. "Whatever for?"

"He's young enough to go, isn't he?" Numbers 21, 22, 23. Still no May birthdays.

"I don't know how old he is, but he's a Communist." Numbers 26, 27. "The poor Commies," she added. "Nobody wants them. Except when everybody wants them."

He inhaled, shallowly, hardly able to get much into his lungs.

"Try it again," she said. "You know what happens when you get upset. You stop breathing. Breathe, Robbie."

He inhaled more slowly this time, holding the smoke in his lungs. What was in this stuff? Within minutes he felt calmer, could hear the numbers as if from far away. Numbers 39, 40, 41. She took his hand and massaged the joints of his fingers, like she'd done that time last winter after he'd gone with her to the bookstore.

"They seem to be taking a lot of fall and winter birthdays. Don't you think?"

"Don't say that," he replied. Old superstitions. He'd grown up with them. Don't ever think you're safe or lucky or privileged in any way; you invite the evil eye. Women would spit three times to keep it away. His heart was still pounding. She passed him back the joint.

By the time his birthday was called, he lay on the floor, so drunk and stoned that when he sat up the room tilted. "Was that me?"

"You're safe, Robbie. Number 197. It's 1 to 122 that has to worry."

"I'm safe?" He lifted his head cautiously.

"Yes," she said, and kneeled beside him, kissed his cheek. Then she helped him up and they walked to the window. The snow had dusted the lawns, houses, and railroad tracks in a comforting, uniform whiteness, illuminated by the streetlights. Across the street, a group of young men had formed a conga line and were dancing their way down the street — Robert and Gwendolyn had never seen them before. A few others wandered aimlessly, as if shell-shocked; one boy in a wool hat and scarf, jeans, a flannel shirt, and no coat got down on his knees in the middle of the busy avenue. At first the cars didn't see him, and whizzed by. "Is he — ?" Gwendolyn asked, as a car obliterated their view for a moment, and then his kneeling form was visible again. "Thank God," she whispered. The next car had spotted him and stopped. Others were honking, backed up, but the boys on the lawn still danced, hardly able to hear above their own screams of happiness. Suddenly, two men rushed out — one of them was Tommy, their doorman — and yanked the boy up, carrying him by his arms and legs. He'd gone limp, like the protesters carried away by the cops on the news.

"Poor sod," Gwendolyn mumbled. "It's so awful, isn't it? I sometimes feel like this war is all there is."

"I'm safe, Gwendolyn." He whispered the words into her hair and hugged her hard, feeling both guilt and relief, repeating again and again, "I'm safe, I'm safe."

BUT AS IT TURNED out, he wasn't so safe after all. Within twenty-four hours of the lottery, the papers began to report a different story. Those who drew between 1 and 100 were said to be making plans—escaping to Canada, or exploiting a medical condition. The Defense Department would likely need more inductees by summer, would call up those with numbers between 120 and 200. Men in that category, men like Robert, were deemed to be in something called "the sweat zone" because they would have to sweat it out for another year.

CHAPTER SEVENTEEN

The sweat zone

January arrived; it was now 1970, the start of a new decade, and Gwendolyn never stopped talking about the Peace Corps. Each morning she rushed to the mailbox, convinced that his acceptance had come. "Isn't January the month for acceptances?" she asked him. "No, that's April," he replied. "The month of college acceptances and income tax." Each day that the letter didn't arrive, she moped around the house for a bit, but by the time he got home at night, she'd talked herself back into optimism, chatting at him a mile a minute, as if driven by a motor. He tried to prepare her, asking what she would do if he got rejected. "You won't get rejected, Robbie," she said, looking up at him, her expression utterly trusting. "You never get rejected from anything."

Had anyone ever believed in him so much? And then she went on again, speaking about a travel book she'd read, and how guinea pig was a delicacy in Peru and Ecuador, but she didn't think she could eat guinea pig, but then, she supposed, if she were hungry enough she might. On and on she went, and he had not the heart to stop her.

By the first Saturday night in March, when he still hadn't told her, the gods took their revenge, or so it seemed to him. The head chef and one of the waitresses at the restaurant had broken off an affair, and the chef seemed determined to wreak havoc, resulting in an evening where orders were filled late, if at all, and tips were terrible. The manager screamed at him in front of a customer. The waitress who'd broken off the affair sat outside the kitchen sobbing. He got to the T stop past midnight, just missing his train, and had a long wait in the freezing cold.

When he arrived home, exhausted and wound up all at once, with a terrible headache, he found her in the kitchen, spooning yogurt into a dish. She began to say something and he stopped her. "Don't say another word to me about the Andes, please," he said. "There is no letter of acceptance. My rejection came months ago and I hid it from you. They rejected me."

She did not reply, only stared at him, still holding the spoon.

"Don't look at me like that. I know you heard me." He went to the refrigerator and poured himself some orange juice, then added a shot of vodka from the freezer. "Didn't it strike you as strange that I'd applied almost a year ago and still hadn't heard?"

"You didn't apply in March of last year or in April, either. You applied in July. I found the application in your jacket," she said casually. "Anyway, we don't need the Peace Corps. We can go off ourselves. I have money and we can live on so little in Peru. I've been reading all about it." She put the lid on the yogurt, returned it to the refrigerator. Then she went to the sink and began to wash dishes.

"We're not going anyplace," he said, coming up close to her. "Except maybe Canada, where I speak the language and can get a job. And that's only as a last resort. I don't want to be a fugitive and neither do you. And I won't live off of you, not anywhere."

"The world is falling apart. There has to be some way. If I don't find someone to help . . ." Her words trailed off.

"Then what?" he asked. "Can't we just take care of each other? Isn't that enough?"

"No," she said quietly. "It's not enough for me. If I can't go to South America, if I can't help the poor, what am I left with? You can't imagine what I'm left with."

"You're left with me," he said softly.

"You don't understand."

"No, I don't," he said. "Because I'm selfish and greedy and afraid and you're the only person I want to take care of. That's who I am. That's me. I can't be someone else."

She had no reply. Finally, what felt like hours later, she asked: "When did you find out? About the Peace Corps? When did the letter come?"

"December," he said. "Or late November."

"Tomorrow is March eighth."

"Actually," he said, looking down at his watch — it was two in the morning — "today is March eighth."

"Go to hell." She walked away from him, and into the bedroom, slamming the door behind her.

THEY STAYED AWAY FROM each other all day Sunday; she went shopping and he went to Alston to watch a basketball game at the home of a bartender he knew from work. He came home late, and drunk, and slept on the couch. She was angry, and he was afraid of her anger because he had never really seen it. On Monday she was gone all day, and he stayed home, his day off. But when she didn't come home by midnight, he became concerned. The doorman, Tommy, had not seen her in days. There was no one to call — Bruno had no phone. He checked the listings for Jerry Stiles but found only a Millicent Stiles, an old woman who barked that it was late and she'd never heard of the man, then hung up. He hardly slept that night and was out of the apartment early. Robert walked the streets of Cambridge in the timid March sunshine, going down alleys, searching in the co-op and the cafés, and then in other shops around the Square. When he got to the bookstore, at 10:00 a.m., the owner had not yet unlocked the door and Robert had to pound on the glass and yell until the man finally undid the bolts. Bruno wouldn't be in all week, and the man hadn't seen Gwendolyn — she had missed work the day before. Anyway, she wasn't on the schedule today. "I'm not responsible, you know," he said, as if Robert had said he was. "Not for any of them."

"That's a fine way to talk about your employees," Robert replied.

"Hey, I do more than my share!" he yelled, as Robert left the shop.

He went to the church in Arlington and found a bunch of girls making phone calls, and another working a mimeograph machine. A little boy played with blocks on the floor. No one there had seen her in weeks. "We figured she just got tired, needed a break," said the girl at the machine. "The war will still be here when she gets back."

Not knowing where else to try, he took the T to Boston University, where he wandered the campus, such as it was, a conglomeration of shops and buildings along the northern end of Commonwealth Avenue, full of students and student housing, and he asked random men and women if they knew her, but none of them did. He looked futilely around in the library and finally went to the admissions office, where he was directed down a hall, and he charmed a young girl into checking on which classes were currently in session and who had signed up for them. If Gwen was in class, he might wait outside and grab her when it was over. The girl worked hard for him, smiling and assuring him all along that she could help. But after much checking of files and a few phone calls, she called over an older man, conferred with him, and informed Robert that there was no foreign student named Gwendolyn Smythe enrolled at Boston University. In fact, there was no Gwendolyn Smythe attending the university, not even the night school, not even as an auditor.

When he got home from work that night, she was in bed and

offered no explanation of where she'd been. He was so relieved that he didn't ask, only stripped off his clothes and got in next to her, pulling her toward him. She didn't smell like herself, needed a shower, and when he tried to kiss her she pulled away. "I don't want to make love, Robbie. I want to die." And then she rolled over and went to sleep.

CHAPTER EIGHTEEN

Cambodia

For the rest of March she remained in bed. He got a coworker to cover his shifts for a week and stayed home, trying to get her to eat something, making her tea, spoon-feeding her chicken broth. But he was an impatient nurse and soon grew frustrated, demanding that she get up, and then apologizing for demanding. Whenever he asked her what she wanted to eat, or if he might get her a book from the library, she had the same refrain: "Leave me alone. I want to die."

"Well you're not dying, not on my watch," he said finally. The dark bedroom smelled stale, like a sickroom. He needed to change the sheets. "It's almost spring. Don't you want me to open the shades? Don't you want to walk in the park? Or by the water?"

"No," she replied, turning her back on him. The next day he called the maid, Dana, and asked her to sit with Gwendolyn while he went to work. Dana agreed, continuing the cleaning that she'd always done, and at his request she cooked, too, and he paid extra for all these things, so that she was nurse and housekeeper all in one. If she had other customers' houses to clean, she did so in her off hours. She was a hard worker, a strong, broad-backed woman of fifty with wide-set watery blue eyes and chiseled cheekbones, pale brown hair that was graying, and an immigrant's stoicism. She was not taken aback by Gwendolyn's sudden lethargy. "Happens all the time in my country," she told him after the first day. "People go to bed. They do not get up. Here everyone tries to be happy, happy, happy." She pulled her lips apart comically but he didn't laugh.

Dana made Gwendolyn soups and fancy cakes, squeezed orange juice for her every morning, and read to her from magazines and novels. Still, Gwendolyn didn't get out of bed. In April, Dana mentioned to Robert that a doctor had called the house several times.

"What kind of doctor?"

"Gwendolyn said he's a chiropractor," Dana replied. "Dr. Moses. Wants to come to the house."

"Get a phone number and I'll call him back." Robert was not letting a stranger in just because he said he was her doctor. Where was Bruno? Why had he not visited? Where were her parents? Why had she come to Boston? He felt as if he were losing his mind.

And then on the last night in April, a Thursday, Robert was sitting in the living room watching the news on television when Gwendolyn appeared, still in her pajamas.

"What is it, sweetheart?" he asked. She sat down next to him on the couch just as President Nixon came on to announce that he'd be sending troops into Cambodia. Robert put his arm around her protectively, wondering if she should even be watching this, but he could not be her censor, was relieved, too, that something had finally gotten her out of bed. More troops to Cambodia would mean more numbers called up. How many numbers? By summer he could be on the move. What would happen to her then?

On Friday morning she got up early, taking a shower for the first time in almost two months. She asked him to cut her hair, which was long and dead at the ends, and he trimmed it in the bathroom with newspaper under her chair to catch the pieces that fell away. They made eggs and sat at the table eating together. "Why don't we go on a vacation this summer?" he asked, taking her hand. "I have some savings and Hank could cover my shifts; he's always looking for more work. We could go to the beach. Or rent a car and drive across country? You haven't seen much of the United States, and neither have I, really." He'd leaned on her too much, he thought, and she'd broken. They were coming through a terrible struggle that he didn't fully understand, the same one she'd had before he took her to his parents. It was connected to the news, somehow, or brought on by it. She was sensitive. But she had healed a year ago and would do so again.

Despite his feelings about the news, he could not dissuade her from watching the television on Monday night. Four students had been shot dead at a college in Ohio. The networks replayed the blurry images over and over again. A boy hit by a bullet crumpled to the ground; phalanxes of troops holding rifles marched across the campus as if it were a battlefield; a girl knelt by her dead friend, screaming. The high-pitched sound of girls screaming, that's what he would always remember.

"I can't take the screaming," Gwendolyn said. "I wish it would go away."

"Please, let's turn off the TV," he said gently, getting up to do just that.

"I'm not talking about the television," she said, staring at him oddly. "Let's go to bed."

He followed her into the bedroom. The windows were open, and the place smelled of Dana's special cleaners, as if it, too, had come out of a long, musty siege. The bed was made, and they stripped off their clothes, got under the cold sheets, pulled the blanket around themselves. He held her and she took his hand and told him that she loved him. She had not said that to him in so very long. "I love you too, baby," he said, his heart lifting in the darkness.

"I was thinking about that time when I fell on you at the concert."

"That was the best afternoon of my life, Gwendolyn."

"Me too. Me too," she said. "I think you're right about going away."

"Anyplace you like. I can arrange everything. We need to enjoy ourselves." He buried his face in her hair. "We're young and it's been so long since we enjoyed ourselves." He kissed her and kissed her, pausing only to say that when all this was over, they'd get married. After August, he would know. In August the last numbers of the year would be released. Maybe he'd be free. Thinking about a future for them beyond the draft and the war made him feel wonderful, if only in the moment. He kissed her again, running his hand up her side, feeling the slight curve of her hip. They hadn't touched each other like this in months. He heard her respond, and he kissed her again, cupped her breast in his hand, his mouth moving down her body, taking the hard nipple in his mouth, hearing her moan. They made love slowly, and he stopped periodically, pulled out to prolong the pleasure. When he came deep inside her, heard her scream in climax, he thought, in a split second, of the young girl on the television, screaming as she knelt over the body of the dead young man. The two sounds were remarkably similar, as if Gwendolyn were unburdening herself of some mysterious terror. Laying back on the blankets, his arms around her in the darkness, he felt afraid again.

The next day, at four, Dana came to stay with Gwendolyn as usual. She had to leave a little early, she said; her husband couldn't pick her up and he didn't like her getting on the trains so late. "Sure," Robert said casually, grabbing his keys. "Leave whenever." The patient was out of bed, dressed. Dana and Gwendolyn were going to bake some brownies that afternoon. He'd have a treat, Dana said, when he returned from work. "What would we have done these weeks without you?" Robert asked, and shoved some money into her hand, extra on top of her salary. He was in such a good mood that he'd have given money to strangers on the street if he could. Dana smiled and told him to have a good night.

He got home at eleven. The television was on in the empty

living room. The bed was made, the kitchen spotless. He smelled chocolate — the brownies. He called out her name over and over, getting no response, but she was there. In the hour between when Dana had left and Robert had come home, Gwendolyn had hanged herself from an overhead pipe in the bathroom.

CHAPTER NINETEEN

Aftermath

She had showered beforehand, and when he cut down her body, removed the drapery cord from around her neck, her hair was still damp, and he could smell the lavender scent of her shampoo. The body felt warm to him, and there was still color in her cheeks, though she had no pulse. Robert had seen a demonstration of mouth-to-mouth breathing on a local TV channel, and he pinched her nose and put his lips to her mouth, trying to imitate what he'd seen, but he didn't have much lung capacity and soon began to cough, then feared he was wasting time when the emergency workers might be able to do more. He carried her into the bedroom, laid her on the bed and called the operator, who connected him to emergency services. He gave the information and hung up, then sat in the dark bedroom, stroking her dark hair, willing the ambulance to come faster.

When the emergency workers arrived, two guys around his same age, they took her pulse and shook their heads. But Robert yelled at them, pacing the room, his eyes wild as he insisted that her body had felt warm to him just moments earlier. He could see that the two young men were shaken — they rarely saw someone this young, unless it was an overdose, and never this beautiful. And because of this, because they felt sorry for him, they, too, breathed into her mouth, their actions a kind of performance that all involved understood, until finally they looked at him pleadingly and said that she was dead, had been dead for some time, and it was undignified to go on. The warmth he'd felt from her flesh, the pinkness of her cheeks, one of the men told him, was likely from the steam of the shower.

He had been just that close. Had he come home minutes earlier, he might have found a pulse, called faster, saved her. After the workers removed her body, he wandered into the kitchen, not sure what to do with himself. The floor lamp in the living room shed a weak, orangey glare into the back of the apartment, and he sat at the kitchen table bathed in that eerie semidarkness, mentally retracing his steps home. Where had he been when she stopped breathing? In the lobby, where he'd paused to chat with Tommy about the Red Sox? Helping that old lady down from the T? What could he remove from his day that would get him home in time? He would torture himself with that thought for years.

On the table was a bottle of whiskey and a shot glass with a bit still left at the bottom. She had needed courage; the thought was almost too much for him, but then he heard a sound, the opening of the door. Who had a key? Someone else was in the apartment. He was shaking, and now Tommy came up behind him, put a blanket around his shoulders. Doormen knew everything that happened in a building, didn't they? An older neighbor came in, too — she'd heard the commotion — but Tommy told her to go home. It was just past 1:00 a.m., Tommy said. He'd have come up sooner but he had to wait for his shift to end and lock up for the night.

"She liked you," Robert said.

"Who didn't she like, exactly?" Tommy replied. He had found a can of coffee above the sink, and now he was filling the bottom of the percolator with water.

"She liked how you turned your head to listen to her. She said you listened very intently."

"Actually, I'm deaf in one ear," he said. "Got me out of the draft."

Soon the pot was hissing a comforting hiss. She had never liked coffee—the electric percolator was his, one of the few things he owned here—and so he did not associate that smell or sound with her so much as with his parents, Barry, Disston Street. When the coffee was done, Tommy poured him a cup and added some of the whiskey, then did the same for himself. They sat in the darkness and said nothing, drinking their coffee and whiskey, listening to the clock tick. At 6:00 a.m., as the apartment began to lighten, Tommy lit a cigarette. Then he made some toast, which Robert quietly refused. Tommy, his doorman, had stayed up with him all night, giving up sleep and precious hours off. Robert wanted to thank him, but he couldn't seem to find words. He could only sit at the kitchen table and try to keep breathing, taking the occasional sip of coffee, aware that he was still alive, and that with living came responsibilities to the dead that he neither wanted nor could bear.

Others did for him what he could not do himself; it was that kind of building. The management company had a PO box and the name of a lawyer on file, and two days later the lawyer called Robert to collect the details. Three days after that, Robert went to meet Gerald and Alice Smythe, Gwendolyn's parents, at the Ritz-Carlton on the Common.

They had flown in from London to have the body cremated and would return home with the ashes, which now sat in an urn in their hotel suite. The idea made him feel vaguely sick. His own family did not cremate; it was against the religion. But when he saw Gwendolyn's father, he immediately knew that he was Jewish, in the way that Jews recognize each other, as if with a sixth sense. Mr. Smythe was olive skinned, balding, trim; his eyes were honey colored like Gwendolyn's, and his hair, what there was of it, was dark like hers, too. He wore an expensive-looking suit, but then his father had been a tailor (Gwendolyn had once mentioned this), and so he would care about his clothes. His accent was hard to discern; Robert imagined he had altered it. The mother was certainly born in England; she sounded like one of the announcers on the BBC, was tiny, wore a beige dress, and her blond hair was short and stylishly cut. Her eyes were ice blue.

No wonder Gwendolyn had loved his parents so. Compared to these two, Stacia was a slobbering cocker spaniel. They did not move a muscle, or seem even to blink as they told him that Gwendolyn was no student and never had been. She was not twenty-three, but rather past thirty, though young-looking for her age, naïve like a child. She was a graduate, not of an American university or a Swiss boarding school, but rather of several of the world's most sophisticated and forward-thinking asylums, starting at age fifteen, when the troubles, as they called them, had begun. Robert met her after she'd done two years of inpatient at McLean, Harvard Medical School's booby hatch for the rich and famous, and "they'd handled her well," was how the father put it, so well that she was able, for the first time ever, to do outpatient therapy, to hold down a job and live on her own. "A little bookstore. Several other patients worked there as well. A charitable owner, I suppose," the mother said.

How had he not seen that part? The first time he laid eyes on Bruno?

The mother cleared her throat. "She got awfully caught up with American politics," she said. "It wasn't good for her." She looked him over, from head to toe: his hair needed to be cut, his clothes were wrinkled — he'd slept in them, or rather, tried to sleep — and he had the beginnings of a beard. "I warned her father, when we saw all those children on the news, screaming and carrying on. 'This,' I said, 'will be our undoing.' "

Had they known of his existence? He had barely known of theirs.

"We knew of you from her letters," the father said. "They were more rational than in years. She said she was in love. She said she was happy. At first we wondered if she hadn't made you up." She withheld things, he said, from her parents, from her psychiatrists. These doctors in Boston had been better at getting her to keep appointments. "She was prone to embellish," he added. "She was charming. She was beautiful. People believe those who are beautiful. They credit them with all sorts of qualities."

"She may have been unbalanced," the mother said, "but she was clever. And she could be devious." Then she added, "Her IQ was quite high, you know."

Robert could tell by her tone that she'd clung to that piece of information all her daughter's life. At least if she'd given birth to a mental case, Gwendolyn wasn't a stupid one. "I don't give a shit about her IQ," he said.

"Mind your tone," Mr. Smythe said calmly. "She assured us you were taking care of her."

Robert felt as if he'd been slapped. "Her fiancé would have taken care of her," he added, his voice high, in danger any moment of breaking, "if he'd known what, exactly, he was supposed to take care of. If anyone, say her parents, or her doctor, had picked up the goddamned phone, just once, and clued him in —"

He wished that they'd break down. He'd have been happy with even the smallest show of emotion. They'd left their only child in the hands of psychiatrists and barely participated in her life at all. The father said that Robert didn't understand how trying, how frustrating it could be, to have a daughter with such problems. Long periods of depression, she'd been that way for much of her teens, and then long stretches of mania in her twenties. There had been periodic suicide attempts. One doctor had thrown in schizophrenia, too, but there was never a consensus on that diagnosis. No medication under the sun did a thing.

Her money had to be handled; an employee dealt with Gwendolyn's finances and bills in America; the girl could not be trusted with a nickel, was known for wild spending sprees, for writing huge checks to scam artists, or giving away hundred-dollar bills to beggars on the street. "She gave herself," the mother said, looking him in the eye, "to all kinds of horrid people."

The father, suddenly more accommodating, putting his hand on Robert's shoulder, said, "One can feel so very alone with it all."

What kind of parents, with all the money in the world, did not insist on visiting? Or were they just so happy to get her off their hands? Yes, they had done with her long ago, did their duty but nothing more. He would not let them off so easily. They would damn well *feel* something. He stood up, shook his fist like some street-corner evangelist and told them not to put this on him, because he could see it coming. "I loved her!" he said. "I was *there*, which is more than I can say for either of you!"

They rose to leave, saying not a word as they walked toward the elevators.

CHAPTER TWENTY

Chelsea

B y now it was the middle of May. Men came to pack up her belongings and take out the furniture. The lease, conveniently, was up in
June. The letter had come to him from the management company,
asking if he would be renewing. But he could not afford this apartment, and wouldn't have stayed even if he could. For two weeks after
her death, he slept on the floor, in a sleeping bag that had belonged
to her and been left behind. At the restaurant, people were covering
for him. He'd told his boss that he needed two weeks, but he knew
that when the time was over, he wouldn't return.

For the past two years, he'd holed up with his beautiful Gwendolyn on this top floor of this luxury building and shut the world
out; consequently, the world was not there for him. He still had his
family, his brother, but he could not disappoint them with this news,
not when they'd loved and valued her so much. In the beginning, his
and Gwendolyn's isolation had been about the selfishness of love,
but then it had turned into something else—he'd become afraid.
Certainly there were details that did not match up. But he could
not have admitted that such details pointed to a desperate situation,

and so, to protect them, and because it was easier, he became like her, like a rich person, depending on strangers to provide services that he had always gotten from friends and family, isolating himself until he had no one to ask the favor of a couch to sleep on until he got himself together, no one who might steer him toward a cheap sublet. He was utterly alone.

It was Tommy who offered him a place to live in East Boston, really just a room, on the top floor of a building owned by his brother. The room had its own bathroom but no kitchen, just a refrigerator and a hot plate. The rent was only eighty-five dollars a month. Tommy had stayed there before he got married, and still did occasionally, when he and Esme had a fight. Robert had not even known Tommy was married. He'd walked past him so many times in the lobby, exchanging meaningless chatter, and never asked the man a single personal detail, hardly imagining he had a personal life. Another sin he'd committed, one more on the endless pile for which he must atone.

Tommy took out his wallet and proudly showed him a picture of a round-faced young woman with black hair, pale skin, and small, dark eyes that were ever-so-slightly crossed. A man his own age, married and saving for a home, working full-time and going to school part-time to become an accountant. He'd be taking the CPA exam in a few weeks, and then it was no more holding doors for him. Robert had forgotten, somehow, that the country was filled with such men, a parallel universe of the useful. The times did not rile them, the draft did not change them; even the president, to them, was trying his best. Tommy would have gone to Vietnam, he said, had it not been for his hearing, though he was relieved that he had an out. Robert took the apartment, gratefully, and sight unseen.

"John has to live in Chelsea," Tommy explained, "because he's the alderman."

"What's an alderman?" Robert asked.

"Hell if I know," Tommy said, smiling. "But a lot of cops hang out at his place; safest building in town."

"How do I get there?" Robert asked.

"Take the Blue Line to the end, to Wonderland. Then you get on a bus."

"Wonderland?" Robert asked. Why not? Had he not fallen down the rabbit hole?

"Yeah," Tommy said, smirking, "but there's nothing wonderful about it."

AND SO ON THE FIRST of June he moved again, carrying only his duffel, now significantly lighter. All he had from Gwendolyn was the leather jacket she'd given him, and a few affectionate notes she'd left for him on the refrigerator, which he saved in the pages of her Spanish-English dictionary; he was desperate, somehow, to remember her sloppy, sprawling handwriting. Someday, he knew, he would forget the sound of her voice, and so he listened for it in his head every day, to check, as if pressing a wound, then feeling oddly relieved that the pain was still there.

He followed Tommy's instructions, taking the Blue Line all the way and then transferring to a bus, getting off in a tree-lined neighborhood with a main street of stores: a coffee shop, a small grocery, a Salvation Army, a bar, and a Laundromat. Older women in housedresses walked with their bags and carts, children played on cement as they had where he grew up, only here the lawns were even smaller. The houses and apartment buildings were boxy, close together, made of siding or clapboard with flat roofs. His own building was yellow with tiny windows, high steps, and an iron railing. It was the tallest building for blocks except for the housing project across the street, where just then a buxom blond woman sat outside, braless, wearing a stained orange T-shirt and smoking a cigarette. She waved at him like an old friend.

He now had an unkempt beard, and his hair was longer than usual, hanging in his face so that to anyone who'd known him even three months earlier he was almost unrecognizable. His jeans were falling apart and his shirt, one of Tracey's shirts, was faded after so many washes, the cuffs fraying; his sandals had so many holes in them that he could feel the hot pavement under his feet. He still had another man's initials on his pocket, but other than that he fit in well here with the poor, the lost, the angry. The neighborhood of Italians and Irish was giving way reluctantly to incoming Dominicans and Puerto Ricans. People stared at him, trying to place his background. He shouldered the duffel and walked up the steps. Inside, he shook hands with his new landlord, Tommy's brother, John, a beefy, affable man with a round face, who directed him to the top floor and offered assistance, which he declined.

His room was in the back of the building, and from one of two windows he could see the roofs for several blocks, with their clotheslines and pipes. From the day he arrived, he gave in to his desire to sleep, sleeping through John's late-night parties and the hum of a loud television downstairs, the occasional scream of fury at a Red Sox game lost, or a poker hand poorly wagered. There were always men crowding into John's apartment, or sitting out on the stoop. Cops mostly, as Tommy had said. Tommy was the serious one in the family; John was more of a partier. Of the new tenant, John would tell Tommy that he'd never imagined a man could be so quiet. Most of the time, he forgot anyone was up there at all.

Tommy came to visit every few weeks, carrying a pizza and a six-pack of beer. When Robert refused the beer, he drank it all himself, his pale skin blooming into a healthy pink. Usually, after attempting to get Robert to eat some pizza, he'd give up and go down to spend most of the evening with his brother. Robert was invited along but always declined. When Robert commented once that Tommy and John were close, Tommy mentioned a third brother, in the middle between them, no longer living. And Robert wondered if perhaps this was the reason a stranger had grasped so quickly his helplessness and come to his aid. But he did not ask.

Robert wasn't trying to starve, but he wasn't ever hungry. He drank water and juice, and sometimes, when Tommy yelled at him enough, he choked down a milk shake with a raw egg in it. But by mid-July Tommy couldn't take being around Robert so much, and Robert couldn't blame him. If depression is contagious, he had caught it — the bathroom was filthy, food rotted in the tiny refrigerator, and dust clumps rolled like tumbleweeds across the floor. When Robert thought of cleaning, or leaving the house, he felt so very tired. One minute he was paralyzed by remorse at all the ways he'd failed her, then the next he'd become furious, up all night yelling at her in his head: She had deserted him for whatever foul plans barked at her. She had not loved him enough to stay alive. She would not live for him, and she had left him to this.

August came, and though he didn't read the paper or watch the news, he heard from John, who came up the steps to tell him: the Defense Department had asked for the last of this year's troops, and the final number called up was 195. He had come within two digits of being drafted, but now he was safe forever. No amendments, nothing to be done. In six months, they'd pick the next year's victims. His life had been returned to him, only he had no life left and no energy to live it. He thanked John for the news, declining an invitation to come down into the air-conditioning and have a cold beer. Then he got back in bed and went to sleep.

THREE WEEKS LATER, at ten in the morning, a man knocked loudly and repeatedly on Robert's door, getting him out of bed. Robert put the chain on the door and looked at him through the crack. A tall, sandy-haired cop. "You have the wrong apartment," Robert said. "You want John Connaghan. He's downstairs."

"Vishniak?" he asked. "Robert Vishniak?"

Robert opened the door. "Yeah, I'm him. But I'm number 197. You can't take me."

The man looked around at the room and shook his head. "I don't give a damn what number you are," he said. "People are looking for you, son. How'd you disappear like that? Call your parents."

"I don't have a phone."

"Connaghan has one downstairs," he said. "Hurry up."

"What's the problem?"

"Just come with me!" he barked. "They need you at home."

CHAPTER TWENTY-ONE

Homecoming

Robert did not call. Instead, he packed his bag, left a month's rent for John, extra money to hire a cleaning service, and a note explaining the situation. Seven hours later, he was coughed up on the shores of his childhood home, clutching his tattered duffel. The train from Boston had deposited him at the 30th Street Station, and he'd taken the SEPTA rail line to Holmesburg Junction, the stop that bordered the Holmesburg Prison, its impenetrable walls visible in the near distance. Then he'd taken the bus that let him off a block from the house, walking as if in a trance, relying on the instincts of a homing pigeon.

A group of teenagers wearing bell-bottoms and macramé headbands walked in twos and fours up the sidewalk, laughing and shouting amused threats to each other. They stopped at the corner, then shuffled up the walk to a mother who held the doors open and asked, loudly, what they wanted to eat. A mailman, shoulders slumped, finished his rounds. A truck with an image of a giant stork painted on the side pulled up across the street, and a man began unloading piles of diapers wrapped in plastic. A neighbor, spotting Robert shuffling up the walk with his bag, called his mother——*Stacia, there's a filthy vagrant outside your house*——so that now, as he reached the steps, Stacia stood at the door yelling that she didn't have any money to spare.

"It's me, Ma," he said. "It's Robert."

She did not reply, only stared, her expression oddly slack. And then she embraced him, her arms awkwardly around his neck. She was not a hugger or a crier, yet he could feel her terror in that embrace, and her relief.

Entering the living room, he found Vishniak sitting in his usual chair wearing his Sunday uniform of shorts and an undershirt. Only this wasn't Sunday. Robert stared at his father's legs. One was its usual ghostly white, but the other was a stump ending just above the knee.

"We called your apartment but the number was disconnected," his mother said. "And we wrote, but you never replied, and the letters were returned. Nobody at the university knew anything, nobody at her building either. Then I couldn't be bothered anymore; your father was in the hospital, and I said, 'If he wants to be lost, or is lying in a ditch, nothing I can do.'"

"I moved," Robert said. The stump of his father's leg was pink with a dark scar across it.

"Your brother left for college last month. When your father got sick, he was a help, surprised us all. His idea to call the police."

"Nothing you could have done," his father interrupted, looking up into his face and seeing his expression. "Bad circulation. Gangrene set in." Then he added, "Eventually they'll want the left leg too, I bet, and then they'll take my prick, and soon I'll be nothing but a head."

"Will the head know when to shut up?" his mother snapped, moving toward the kitchen.

"I'd have come home," Robert said softly. "If I'd known."

"You're home now, that's all that matters," Vishniak said and took Robert's hand, pressed it to his lips. Robert could hear his mother removing things from the refrigerator.

"I'm not hungry," he called. She would make him sit down anyway and try. And he would leave the table gagging from food he had loved all his life.

VERY QUICKLY, THEY DIDN'T know what to do with him. Each morning he got up to help his father out of bed and down the stairs, then went back to his room, dozing all day until it was time to get Vishniak back to the second floor. Several afternoons a week a short young man named Igor, with bulging muscles and a heavy accent, came to help his father do exercises to strengthen his upper body and arms, paid for by the Postal Service health plan. For once, Stacia was happy about the help, and relieved that the postal workers finally had insurance. Igor had worked with Vishniak during his stay at rehab, and after Robert heard about him for a few days, he crept down the stairs, curious, only to observe his sixty-year-old father crawling along the floor like an infant. He retreated quickly back to his room. Sleep, he plunged into sleep, resting there as if on the bottom of a vast ocean, wanting only the sweet oblivion of unconsciousness.

Meanwhile Stacia cooked everything she could think of to tempt him, and Aunt Lolly and his grandmother contributed, too. A child who wouldn't eat was a child in crisis, Cece proclaimed, though she added that she couldn't really see what he looked like, not with her bad eyes and all that hair covering his face. The cakes piled up in the kitchen and dining room, each more tempting than the next, though none more so than Aunt Lolly's coconut-raisin-cinnamon-carrot cake with chocolate bits and cream cheese frosting, which he'd never been able to refuse before, but stared at now as if it were a piece of art.

One morning in late October, his mother stood at the foot of his bed. "When are you going to——?" The words were on the tip of her tongue——*get a job, make money, pay us rent*——but she looked at his face and stopped herself. They had asked him about Gwendolyn once, and he shook his head, as if to say *Do not enter*, and they obeyed, afraid to ask more.

And then there were the nightmares. He hadn't had them in Chelsea; there, he'd slept like a dead man, but here, in his childhood home, his subconscious roamed free. In one dream, he was back in Boston, coming home from work, knowing what Gwendolyn was going to do, only the elevator was broken and he had to take the steps, but his legs got so heavy, as if his pants were filled with cement, and Tommy would be there at the top of the steps shouting at him, *Faster, faster, man!* and he'd try and try, panicked, hysterical. In another, he made it into the apartment and there she was, standing in front of him, asking for one good reason why she shouldn't do it. He'd rush at her, but no words would come out of his mouth, and then he'd realize that it wasn't her at all, but an impostor, and she was already in the bathroom, dead.

He woke up from these dreams coughing so hard that he could not catch his breath, and then the wheezing began. When it got bad enough, he ran to the bathroom, throwing up what little was in his stomach. That saved him, and then he could gasp and cough and get enough breath back to feel that the crisis had passed. By then it would be almost morning and, too frightened to go back to sleep, he would lie in his too-small bed in the dark, curled up like a child.

He tried to be helpful with his father, but could not seem to hit the right note, sensed that Vishniak just wanted to be left alone with his own pain, as Robert himself did. Only for the physical therapist did Vishniak perk up, as the two talked about the Eagles' losing season, and the exploits of the team's high-living owner, Leonard Tose, and his hapless coach, Jerry Williams.

He missed Barry. Barry had always been closer to their father, the two of them so alike, their conversations effortless—Barry would know how to act around Vishniak, how to kid him and make him laugh. Robert was closer to his mother, though he didn't like to admit it. She watched him now in a way that she never did when he was a child, hovering, asking if he wanted something to eat, and straightening up his room as he yelled at her to leave. She was stuck between the two of them, father and son, each wanting to be left alone yet still needing her for their most basic survival. After she left for work they'd stare at each other, not knowing what to do with themselves. Eventually, doing all her usual routine week after week while they lay around the house, and having failed to get Robert to eat or Vishniak to cut back on his eating, Stacia fell into her own black mood, snapping and barking, threatening that Robert had to start thinking about a job. At least this version of his mother was comforting, familiar.

And then one night, hearing first the endless coughing and then a loud thud, Stacia came into the hall and found Robert sprawled on the pale pink shag of the bathroom floor, passed out, having hit his head on the toilet bowl on the way down. She helped him up, brought him ice for his head and ginger ale for his stomach. For the first time in weeks, he fell back to sleep, only to be roused from bed by Stacia at seven. She gave him a cup of tea and some crackers and told him to get dressed. When he refused, she began to strip off his T-shirt as if he were a child, so that he agreed to do as she asked just to get rid of her. But she stood outside his room, waiting. Seeing him emerge, in an old pair of trousers, a shirt, and a sweater from high school that now fit him again, the only decent clothes he had left, she took him by the arm and marched him out of the house and up the street, as she had when he was nine and had lifted a pack of gum from Rapoport Pharmacy. She stopped on the corner, at the house with an office where just a year and a half ago Robert had been turned away by the ancient Dr. Oppenheim.

The office had been redone, painted bright colors with royal blue carpeting and hip plastic furniture. He had no appointment, but the young receptionist welcomed them as if she were a hostess in a restaurant — they were the only patients in the room. She told his mother to wait, and only when he saw his mother sit down and pick up a copy of *Good Housekeeping* did it occur to him — he was in a doctor's office with Stacia. She was just that worried. Either that or Vishniak's situation had improved her opinion of the profession.

The doctor was only six years older than Robert. His name was Schwartzman, and he'd grown up in the neighborhood and come back. He examined Robert so thoroughly that it took hours — was he bored? — then gave him a B_{12} shot and sent him to Nazareth Hospital, on the other side of the Boulevard, to get a chest X-ray and see a specialist.

A week later, in late November, he wandered the quiet hallways of the hospital, clutching a folder. When he finally found the waiting room, it was crowded with coughing, gray-looking adults and skinny children who breathed like old men. He took his place among them and waited until he was ushered in to see a nurse, who administered a scratch test on his naked back. An hour later, he met Dr. Kryzchek, a middle-aged man with an officious manner who rattled off a long list of irritants that he was allergic to and suggested shots, which Robert still had no intention of taking. Then the doctor made him breathe into a machine and looked at his chest X-ray. "You have asthma," he said. "It's severe enough to get you out of the draft, if that's an issue."

Dr. Kryzchek prescribed a medication that was to be inhaled three times a day, and another one that he was to use only in absolute emergencies, if the other wasn't helping. "You're very lucky. There've been big breakthroughs. We can control it now."

"Oh, I'm lucky, all right," Robert replied.

"This is serious," the doctor said, not appreciative of Robert's tone. "If you don't treat this, you could die. People have died from asthma attacks."

Robert thought of his grandfather, how his breathing problems made his life a daily battle for decades, aggravated by a windowless factory where he worked with chemicals all day. Leukemia had finally killed him; the workers tanned leather without gloves back then, the dyes seeping into their skin. Vishniak would be the next to go. A severe diabetic should never have worked two jobs in the first place.

"Are you all right, son?" the doctor asked, putting his hand on Robert's shoulder.

"Would you mind telling me how two different doctors found me perfectly fit?"

"The condition can change over time," he said, writing the prescriptions on a pad. "Especially if you've been exposed to extreme temperatures, poor diet, stress." He looked up, frowned. "Have you been under a lot of stress?"

Robert could hear his father in his head—*They all stick together, Robert. You think he's going to point a finger at one of his own?*

"It wouldn't hurt you to gain some weight," Kryzchek said. "There's information downstairs on a food bank the hospital runs, if that's needed."

"I got food, Doctor," Robert replied, taking the prescription slips in his hand. "I got enough food to run my own food bank."

On the way out, he passed a mirrored wall in the waiting room, and for the first time since coming home he looked at himself. His beard had taken over the lower half of his face; his hair, parted on the side, hung to his shoulders and fell partially in his eyes, which were bloodshot with dark shadows under them. On his forehead were smudges of purple bruise from when he'd fallen and hit his head. No wonder the doctor thought he couldn't afford food.

As he waited for the bus, his thoughts raced. If only he'd gotten to *this* doctor before; he'd have been safe. She'd never have latched onto the Peace Corps. He could have looked for a real job and moved them to a place he could pay for. He'd have taken better care of her, been less distracted. They might have *lived* instead of waiting and waiting. Surely, he could conjure another life to escape to, another past that spared everything and kept her alive.

An old woman walking by shoved a dollar into his hand. He had to get out of Oxford Circle.

He found his father alone in the living room, listening to a radio call-in show and dialing a number over and over. "Keep trying," Robert said, patting Vishniak's shoulder. In his current condition, Vishniak's one remaining passion was radio call-in shows. Stuck at home, unable to hunt for scarves or umbrellas, he spent each afternoon trying to get on the air to give his political opinions. Larry from Kensington was on the air now, saying how Nixon would end the war in a dignified way. Cambodia was necessary; they had to help the Cambodians, or who were they?

"Sheep! Sheep!" Vishniak screamed. "Nixon feeds them, *You have to stay in to withdraw. You have to fight to have peace!* — Tricky Dicky could sell ice to Eskimos . . . !"

"I know, Pop, I know."

"You know what I wish on him? Sons! Instead of those two daughters of his. And let him watch them . . . !!" His voice trailed off, anguished.

He was only making his parents miserable. And they were treating him too well. He didn't know who he was anymore or what he wanted, but he sure didn't want to be cooked for and worried over. He could suffer for his mistakes just about anywhere except in front of them.

His father continued ranting. His fury gave him focus, a reason to live. If Nixon didn't exist, Robert and his mother would have had to invent him. Robert wished he had someone like that, someone he could hate as he'd once loved, totally and completely, so that his rage was all that mattered, an all-consuming, cleansing fury.

THE NEXT DAY HE CALLED his father's sister, Henry, and her husband, Danny, now living in Queens. Plenty of college graduates were driving cabs these days, they told him; there was no shame in it. Danny owned his own medallion now, and Robert could work for him if he was willing to drive off-hours. Robert wanted to leave for New York as soon as possible, but Danny told him to wait. The cabbies were about to go on strike, and rumor had it that the police would follow right behind them, in January. Then it took Robert awhile to get used to the asthma medication, and for a few weeks he was sicker, but finally, in March of 1971, he said good-bye to Stacia and Vishniak again, hardly knowing what he was doing—only knowing that he needed to do it on his own.

CHAPTER TWENTY-TWO

Eighty-fifth Street

All the way to Midtown, the couple argued about the baby who now lay stretched out across the woman's lap, half covered by a pink blanket. It was almost midnight, and the man thought they should have taken the kid to his mother's.

"You're a lousy father, you know that," the woman spat, then lit a cigarette. The light turned red, and Robert caught a glimpse of her in his rearview mirror. A pretty peaches-and-cream blonde in a short skirt and long leather jacket. "You never want to spend any time with her."

"You're lucky I don't call social services on your ass, what with you and the guy upstairs and the—"

Robert cracked the window, feeling a cold breeze and the occasional drop of rain on his face. They were yelling now. The man, tall and lanky, had so much bushy brown hair that his head appeared smashed down by the cab roof.

"She needs to be fed!" the woman shouted, though the baby had not made a sound.

"That's not how you do it; she'll get gas. You tilt the damn bottle too high!"

"Like you ever feed her!"

"Shut the fuck up!"

Luckily, the woman announced to the man that she wasn't speaking to him, and they were silent until Times Square, where the man directed Robert to a storefront. Two fat guys in jeans, cowboy hats, and sheepskin jackets barked at each other like cheerleaders for opposing football teams: "Naked naked naked!" yelled one. "Nude nude nude!" replied the other.

"That's two seventy-five," Robert said, turning off the meter.

"You want a free pass," the man whispered by his ear.

"No, just the two seventy-five."

"Suit yourself," he said, handing Robert three crumpled dollars. The couple got out and walked toward the door. The woman now dragged the pale infant by its feet, the blanket falling away, skimming the sidewalk. Only then did Robert realize that the child was made of plastic.

After that, he picked up a small, silent man who needed to get to Riverside Church in Harlem. On his way back down Broadway, at 110th he spotted a young guy in nothing but slacks and a sweater jumping from foot to foot in the cold rain. Next to him a small girl stood doubled over, clutching her stomach, with an oversized jacket over her shoulders. The guy asked for Columbia-Presbyterian, said it was something she ate.

"She gonna retch in my cab?" Robert asked. He cleaned up enough shit back there as it was. The girl was shaking now; he didn't think it was from something she ate.

"Come on!" the guy pleaded, helping the girl in, then getting in himself and slamming the door. "Get going!" The girl lay across the seat, her head in his lap as he stroked her hair.

"St. Luke's is just a few blocks away," Robert offered, "if she's that sick."

But he insisted on Columbia, and Robert wasn't going to argue with driving an additional fifty blocks. He turned onto 110th and then got on the Henry Hudson going north. As they were pulling up to the entrance, an ambulance sped ahead of them and workers quickly pulled a patient out of the back. Robert's young passenger flagged someone down, but they pushed him away, and he returned, saying that he had to get her in there himself.

"Good luck," Robert said. "That's five dollars."

"You're not gonna help me?"

"Five dollars," Robert said. "I can't leave the cab, and they got a hospital full of people."

"But she's heavy!" he pleaded.

"Five dollars!" Robert repeated as the girl opened the door and vomited. "Make sure she aims at the sidewalk!"

The boy threw the money onto the front seat, no tip—and then he and the girl limped together toward the double doors. Robert drove back down the driveway; the cold February rain had turned to sleet. He would continue driving until morning, 5:00 a.m., when he'd drive to Forest Hills, drop the cab at his uncle's spot, and then take the subway back to the Upper West Side, making two transfers. He'd be lucky to get home by seven.

ELEVEN MONTHS EARLIER, during Robert's first weeks on the job, Danny, older now and with a baby daughter, had sat him down, this time at a bigger kitchen table, and told Robert *not* to carry a weapon—too many drivers were having their guns turned on them. He and his friends issued warnings—the Caribbean drivers told Robert not to pick up blacks, the Puerto Ricans said to stay away from Spanish Harlem, and the public-school teachers, moonlighting to make extra money, warned against picking up anyone under twenty-five.

Robert paid no attention; he went wherever he wanted, picked up anyone and everyone. And perhaps because he cared so little about his own safety, no one held him up. He worked 9:00 p.m.

to 5:00 a.m. except for every other Saturday night, leaving the morning rush and the after-work crowd for Danny. But he picked up other shifts, too, from friends of Danny's looking to sublease to someone reliable. He drove and drove and drove, the nights blending endlessly into days.

His main expense was $167 a month for rent, which he paid in cash. He did just about everything in cash, small bills. After two months on Danny and Henry's couch, he had gotten his own apartment on a tip from one of the other drivers. The one-bedroom on West Eighty-fifth Street, between Columbus and Central Park West, was rent stabilized and, as instructed, Robert had bribed the super, a guy named Ramon Arzuega, with $500.

Arzuega said it was a good block, one with a block association, where a combination of neighbors and police had gotten rid of the rooming-house types, kicked the junkies off the corner.

At that end of the block were small prewar walk-ups in limestone and sandstone, and a few intact brownstones. But closer to Columbus, three brick boxes stood with prominent fire escapes in front. They'd been renovated in the 1960s, and Robert's was the easiest to spot — the other two had been painted neutral colors, but Robert's building marked the halfway point in the street, standing like a beacon of bad taste, in a lurid blue the color of a robin's egg.

He could hear his neighbors doing just about everything — frying food, sneezing, making love — and could tell what footwear the woman upstairs wore by the variations in sound her feet made clomping overhead. Many of the tenants worked nights and slept days, as he did. When he returned from work, the streetlamps turning off one by one, the first bits of grayish light visible on the horizon, he sometimes ran into a few of his neighbors; most kept to themselves, nodding hello but rarely speaking, perhaps because they already knew too much about each other.

That morning, as usual, Robert went upstairs and put his tips away in a padlocked box he kept in the back of the closet. He took a shower, then wrapped himself in a towel, drank some water, and took a sleeping pill. He no longer had many nightmares, but then, he hardly slept. He still didn't eat much, either, nor did he have any desire for women. He had long ago stopped looking in the mirror because the gaunt face that stared back at him, half-hidden by brittle, dry hair, with only the black eyes staring out like some crazed monk, was surely not his own. This was why people joined religious orders, took up robes and vows: this desire for nothingness, the eradication of want, which in itself was addictive.

He lay down on the floor on his mattress, an old one donated by his aunt and uncle that was his only furniture along with a beat-up bridge table and two chairs in the living room. He watched a mouse scurry hypnotically back and forth in the hallway outside his bedroom, then listened for a while to a fight going on next door. She didn't like how he dressed—his shirts were too loud! He looked like a clown! He said nothing, but then she was crying. Had he whispered something cruel? And then Robert dozed off, awakened a few hours later by shouting. He rolled over and put the pillow over his head, but that didn't help. Now there was talking out in the hall; an angry neighbor, the same one who hated her boyfriend's clownish shirts, was out in the hallway screaming: "*People are trying to sleep* around here!"

The knocking grew louder, and Robert, now hearing his own name, pulled on his pants and went to the door, putting the chain on the lock and peering into the hallway. Standing there in hiking boots, jeans, a gray sweater, and an anorak, and carrying a beat-up leather backpack over one shoulder, was his brother.

"Why aren't you at school?" Robert asked, as he unchained the door and opened it.

"I dropped out," Barry replied. "Man, you look lousy."

"You want to kill them?" Robert asked. "You give up your scholarship and everything?"

Barry stepped inside and surveyed the apartment. "This should be big enough."

"Big enough for what?" Robert asked. "Am I dreaming? I just got up."

"I'm going to sleep on your couch."

"I don't have a couch."

"So we'll buy one," Barry said.

"No way in hell are you moving in here," Robert said, watching Barry set his backpack on the floor. "It's a terrible idea."

CHAPTER TWENTY-THREE

The blind lead the deaf

You didn't get some girl pregnant, did you?" Robert asked. They were sitting at the small table, on his only chairs.

"What are you, my father?" Barry replied. "I just came from there, and believe me, I heard enough lectures; I don't need another."

"No one ever knows what cockeyed thing you're going to do next," Robert said.

"I could say the same about you," Barry mumbled.

"What about all your ambition? And you have a low number, don't you?"

"I still have lots of ambition; I'm just relocating it. As for the draft, I got a doctor to say I have a heart murmur. Actually, I have a real honest-to-God heart murmur. Who knew? But it's not the kind that kills a person or anything."

"So that's why you left school?"

"I left school because I hated that damned place," he said. "I'm not dropping out, really. Technically I'm transferring."

"Transferring where?"

"I haven't decided yet."

"And how do you intend to pay for two more years of college?"

"I'll manage," Barry said. "I can always earn a living."

To Robert, Barry did not look like someone who had been unhappy at school. He'd lost some weight, but it did not make him gaunt; rather, he looked good. His hair, like Robert's, hung to his shoulders and, like Robert, he had a beard, but his hair was curly and somehow the look suited him. He removed a package of M&M's from his pocket and offered some to Robert.

"No thanks," Robert said. "I don't eat much during the day."

"What are you, a bat?" Barry asked. "Take one, it won't kill you."

Robert took a yellow M&M, put it in his mouth, and began to chew slowly. The M&M tasted suddenly sour to him, like bile. "Stop studying me!" Robert said to Barry, who'd been watching him chew. Then he began to cough. He took a Kleenex out of his pocket and spit out the glob of chocolate and yellow shell. Barry went to the kitchen and found the one glass Robert owned, which was in the sink. He rinsed it out, filled it with water, and brought it back. Robert took a sip of water, then removed a plastic inhaler from his back pocket, put it over his mouth, and took two slow breaths.

"You want to smoke something?" Barry asked. "That might calm you down." He sat down again and began searching through his backpack.

"No, grass doesn't really help me anymore, if it ever did."

"How about Valium? You drop one or two in some methadone, and then—"

"And then when I wake up from my coma, will you leave me the fuck alone?!" Robert snapped. "I'm on a reality trip these days."

"And how's that going?"

Barry put a hand on Robert's shoulder and the two began to laugh. They had always been able to make each other laugh.

"I'm sorry about what happened in Boston," Barry said. "I mean, I have no idea what happened, Stacia doesn't tell me a damned thing, but I can see that something sure did. And then Gwendolyn—"

"What the hell do you know about Gwendolyn?"

"I know she's not here," Barry said. "And that's not good."

"She's dead," Robert said. He had never said it out loud before.

"Oh, man." Barry cleared his throat several times, staring intensely at the bare floor. "We don't have to talk about it now, if you don't want to."

"I don't ever want to talk about it," Robert said softly, and Barry nodded.

THEY BOUGHT A FOLDOUT couch. Barry, rarely bothering to put a sheet down over the couch cushions, slept in the nude. The apartment was not visibly cleaner — clothing now collected in heaps in the corners, the shower curtain developed a larger pattern of black mold — but Barry did attack the roach problem, spreading boric acid around the tiny kitchen and, each morning, sweeping the tiny corpses into a dustpan. The refrigerator amassed, slowly and then all at once, a collection of Chinese take-out boxes, a dozen eggs, containers of orange juice, bottles of Coke and black cherry soda. The freezer was no longer empty — now there was ice cream, a freezer bag of marijuana, a bottle of vodka; the ice cube trays, once frozen cavities of plastic, now contained cubes. On the counter in the tiny kitchen sat a beige plastic percolator.

Barry surprised Robert by getting up early each morning to make him breakfast when he came off his shift. He had not known that Barry was capable of getting up at seven, let alone shopping and cooking. On one such morning, Robert arrived home to find Barry scrambling eggs and frying bacon, the smell so seductive that he had to come closer. On the counter was a paper bag from the supermarket on the corner — inside was an Entenmann's crumb cake, the only kind of store-bought cake his mother ever allowed into the house, and then only under duress. It was Robert's favorite. As Barry scraped the eggs from the side of the pan with a spatula, he informed Robert that he'd enrolled in City College on 138th Street.

"Don't you know what's going on up there? They're rioting in the streets," Robert said.

"That was last year," Barry replied. "With the open admissions, now it's perfectly calm. And tuition is cheap."

"You don't live in New York."

"I do now; I used your address," Barry said. "Make some coffee."

"None left."

"Check the bag."

Robert obeyed, and a few minutes later they heard the slow squeaking and thumping of the percolator. "City College is nothing more than an experiment now. Anyone off the street can walk in there."

"Exactly. It's fair, it's equal. So by definition it's not a racket and people won't have an attitude," Barry said, scooping up the eggs and placing them on a plate, "like they did at Syracuse."

"What kind of attitude?" Robert asked, pouring himself a cup of coffee. For weeks he'd been trying to get out of his brother exactly why he'd left school.

"I don't mean to smear our people, but honestly, sometimes I thought the Jews were the worst. Not all, but you know the ones I'm talking about—they weren't like the kids in Oxford Circle, that's for sure. You sent me off totally fucking unprepared, brother. Not a word of warning. Their doctor and dentist parents worked their way through school, but now they want their babies to go in style. They send them with stereos and cars and blank checks. And those were the hippies! Running around in their flowing clothes, their noses surgically tilted in the air! Talking about oppression and the common man, and running off to volunteer at some job, calling it righteous because they don't have to earn money. Or my favorite, going to summer camp until they're like forty-five. You're not a socialist because you sleep in a log cabin and dance in a circle! And who are they angry at, really angry at? Not the Man—they wouldn't know the Man if he froze their Bloomingdale's charge cards. No, they're angry at their parents! The people who fund all this in the first place. If they don't want their parents, send them my way. I've been looking all my life for someone to wipe my ass and pay my bills."

"You sound like an anti-Semite," Robert said. "And what was I supposed to say to you? You adapt. You try to give people a chance, and you adapt."

"I don't look like you," Barry said, placing the last of the bacon on a paper towel to drain off the grease. "Or I don't look like you used to look, before you became Casper the Hairy Ghost. People don't line up to be my friend like they do to be yours."

"You always had more friends than I did."

"Yeah, but you had *quality* friends." Barry began taking the food to the table. "I always admired that about you. *I* had to offer people incentives."

"What did you ever offer Victor Lampshade?"

"I'm talking women. The first girl who slept with me, it was for the weed, I'm sure. Look at the first girl you brought home. Perfect. I never saw another one like that, not before or since."

Robert looked away, and Barry bowed his head. "Sorry," he said. "Eat your eggs. That was insensitive of me."

The bacon burned his fingers. As soon as they were old enough, the brothers had snuck off to Mayfair, to a diner where they feasted on salty, crunchy bacon and ham and every other food their mother didn't let in the house. Their kitchen was not kosher, but she would only go so far, and pork was too far. Which was more forbidden to them—eating bacon or paying for a meal? He hadn't known, but he'd loved both.

They ate their breakfast now on newly acquired plastic dishes in bright, children's-birthday-party colors. Where had Barry gotten these?

"I was up at City College yesterday. So much energy. And every-body works and goes to school. It's a place to regroup and prepare for my big moment."

"Your big moment?"

"When I show up everyone and become a huge success," Barry said. "On my own terms. I got some ideas, and I do have one big advantage over you, you know. People underestimate me."

"Yeah, clearly my reputation for competency has paved the way for all this," Robert said, gesturing around the room.

"Anyway, this was the right move. Manhattan is my place. Filthy, broke, corrupt, yes, but does anyplace reward elbow grease and a little ingenuity more than this one?" Barry asked. "And somebody has to look after you. I swear, Robert, you scare small children." He cut Robert another piece of cake. "Another piece won't hurt you." He scooped out the cake with a spatula, holding it out for Robert to take. Barry's large brown eyes pleaded with his brother to eat. "Think about how good life can be sometimes," he said. "It can be, you know? It really can be." And Robert took the sticky piece of cake in his hand and placed it on his plate.

CHAPTER TWENTY-FOUR

Nixon

Barry diligently attended City College, and got As in everything; he'd always been effortlessly, frustratingly smart. But he couldn't settle into a major because everything interested and excited him. While Robert had spent college searching for the singular passion that would carry him into a career, Barry was as passionate about Biology as he was about Nineteenth-Century Romantic Poetry or Economics or History of Art.

"When I die," Barry told Robert, "I want my tombstone to say, 'Here lies Barry Vishniak. He knew what was good.' And how am I going to know what's good if I don't try everything?"

"You can't try everything."

"Says who?" he asked. There weren't many jobs, anyway, and no particular urgency to his degree. He enjoyed school while making a tidy living in the one business that was inflation proof. The apartment had been abuzz since his brother moved in — doorbell and phone ringing while endless varieties of people paced the halls, clutching their cash. One day Barry came home with a large machine that took over the table where the phone stood. "The Phone-Mate," he said. "It answers the telephone for you and takes a message. How about that?"

"No one calls me."

"Well, people call *me*," Barry said. "And it's important that I know about it. Anyway, it wouldn't kill you to extend yourself a bit. There's a whole city of people out there."

"I've seen them. They stand in our hallway and shake," Robert said. "And no thank you."

After that, the small red light on the machine seemed always to be blinking: Janice, Rashid, Allison, Chester. Endless first names, no message. Barry would have to call them back.

"Why not major in business?" Robert asked. "You seem good at that, in your way."

"Maybe I will," Barry said. "But that shouldn't stop me from taking anthropology if I feel like it. Or physics, for that matter. This system is flawed. A college education is too narrow."

"And if you had an estate, an income, and an inherited seat in the House of Lords, then your argument would have merit. But Renaissance men went out of fashion in —"

"— the fucking Renaissance?" Barry asked, cutting him off.

Who was he to lecture? With the gas crunch taking a bite out of his profits and Barry prompting him endlessly to live a little, to try to put his sorrow behind him, he was no longer satisfied driving all night and getting nowhere; but he wasn't ready to change, either. Meanwhile, Barry received a beat-up used car in a barter and the two brothers drove home to see their parents.

NIXON WAS SCHEDULED TO make a television address on the Paris Peace Accords. Their mother was in the kitchen cleaning up from dinner. Robert and Barry, having helped their father into his old recliner by the door, sat on the couch. Barry egged Vishniak on, ranting about how he couldn't believe it would be this asshole and the turncoat Kissinger who'd get the credit for ending the war, and then he went upstairs to use the bathroom before the broadcast. Vishniak turned toward Robert and said in a low voice: "This cab-driving, Robert. It's gone on too long."

"What do you mean, Pop?" Robert asked. It was a strange non sequitur from talk of the president, usually a foolproof topic.

"You driving a cab, it's too close to home. Do I have to spell it out for you?"

Robert stared at his father's face, illuminated by the table lamp. Barry looked more like Vishniak, with his pudgy cheeks and smaller nose, but both sons had their mother's brown-black eyes, whereas Vishniak's eyes were a washed-out blue. He was back at the PO now, working part-time at a desk job, and he looked tired again, though not as tired as he'd looked when Robert was a child.

"Don't be a failure like your father, Robert," he said. "You think I wanted to end up working at the post office?"

"You're not a failure, Pop," Robert said, patting his father's shoulder.

"A monkey could do my job."

"Jesus, Pop, have a little mercy!" Robert pleaded. Then Barry returned—Barry, who, according to their parents, was a full-time student, though a slow one. No questions would be asked of Barry unless he requested money, which he wouldn't. Only Robert, the oldest child, had to shoulder their hopes and expectations. Stacia came in then and turned on the television. There was black-and-white static at first, and then slowly the president's face came into focus, his receding hairline forming a dark point in the center of his forehead. Robert stared at the screen, stricken by what his father had said.

BACK IN NEW YORK, there was talk of another taxi strike, and his uncle took him out for a beer and announced that he was getting out of the business, would be going to school part-time to get a teaching degree. Robert could now have the cab more during the day, and during rush hour. That spring, he spent more time in the world of the daytime people — well-dressed, educated, mostly sweet-smelling professionals trying to escape the filthy subway cars covered in the endless hieroglyphics of the poor. Even in a recession, Robert delivered them to upscale restaurants where well-dressed couples sat by the windows toasting each other. For the first time in years, Robert thought of Tracey. He'd done this to himself, placed himself on the outside looking in, when his degree should have put affluence and ease more within his reach than ever.

And then his uncle would want the car again for a random day, and he'd be thrust back into the late-night crowd — women fleeing bad dates; parents with a sick child, unable to get an ambulance to come to their neighborhoods; men, and they were mostly men, who did their business under cover of darkness. So many of them desperate, hopeless, lost. And Robert heard the voice again in his head, the one that had been silent for so long — *get out of here, save yourself, make money, make money, make money.*

He heard the voice and realized how, after two years, he was so tired of fingers permanently black with ink from handling cash, of crazy hours and cleaning crusted bodily fluids off vinyl. He wanted to work when other people worked, go out to dinner at restaurants that proclaimed their names in fancy gold script above the entrance and used starched white tablecloths and heavy silverware; he wanted to go to the theater and he wanted to ride in cabs as a passenger. Most of all he wanted to go to bed when it was actually dark outside, and make love to a beautiful woman, more than one even, who wouldn't put up with a man that arrived at seven in the morning and slept until one.

But what, exactly, would get him from where he was to where he wanted to be? In the end, the person most helpful in guiding him to his future was someone who, over the years, Robert, Barry, and their mother had come to know almost as a family member: Richard Nixon. The end of 1973 brought Watergate, the hearings, the articles, the public knowledge of what the two young journalists, men not so much older than Robert, had uncovered.

Robert had been stuck in rush-hour traffic with a mother and her screaming toddler when news came over the radio that Haldeman and Ehrlichman had resigned, and even the child had gone silent, sensing that something unusual was happening. Driving an elderly couple to one of the big apartment buildings on Fordham Road, he'd listened to John Dean III tell Samuel Dash about the official enemies list, could picture the committee leaning forward, trying not to breathe into their microphones. And when Nixon gave his "I am not a crook" speech, Robert had just cashed out for the night, but continued driving with his cab light off so he could hear the words for himself, the bathos of them, the insistence.

Nixon had been a litigator, and most of them were lawyers—Dean, Ehrlichman, Haldeman, Mitchell. Robert's customers aimed their anger and betrayal at the profession, telling endless lawyer jokes: "Did you hear the tragedy about the bus full of lawyers that went over a cliff? There was an empty seat." "What's five hundred lawyers at the bottom of the ocean? A start."

Robert would always laugh, because you laughed at customers' jokes, but he found himself strangely uplifted by the questions of the Senate Watergate Committee and their chief counsels. As 1973 turned to 1974, and Nixon still would not turn over the tapes, it was the Supreme Court that stepped in, insisting. And the House Judiciary Committee—again, lawyers—passed the articles of impeachment. The checks and balances had gotten the nation somewhere. The president announced he would resign, the Plumbers were in jail, and America was still intact. The scandal hadn't culminated in a revolution, only a television broadcast.

*　　*　　*

THEY COULD HEAR THE NOISE halfway up the walk. Robert and Barry found the screen door unlocked and, entering the house, were not greeted by the usual kisses and enthusiasm but rather by grunted hellos as the crowd stayed in their seats, focused on the screen. The children had lined up Indian style on the floor. His mother passed around buttered popcorn and glasses of seltzer and black cherry soda. Uncle Frank continued adjusting the large V of the antennae, and Aunt Lolly and Uncle Fred moved over to make room for Robert on the couch. Barry sat on the floor with the children. When the man himself appeared, Vishniak, from his recliner, announced proudly that with this new television, they could see every pore on his nose.

"That's the Japanese for you," Uncle Frank interjected, and was immediately shushed.

In the end, the speaker was subdued as he met the eyes of the nation. He spoke in a calm, unreadable monotone and the audience on Disston Street, waiting for something ironic or angry or apologetic to react to, began, slowly, to deflate.

"—as president, I must put the interest of America first," he said, and now, tired of waiting, the children threw popcorn at the screen. The president told the nation that leaving was abhorrent to every instinct in his body. The adults fidgeted, wanting him to say the words, already, that he was in fact a crook and that he was sorry. They wanted him to cry and beg forgiveness. Instead, he talked about his accomplishments, about China and the Middle East and the Soviet Union, and about having brought the troops back from Vietnam. Finally, just when they were ready to give up, he said that he was resigning, that he hoped to speed the process of healing, and ended with "may God's grace be with you in all the days ahead."

When the scene abruptly changed to Gerald Ford standing in front of a large suburban mansion in Virginia, they all looked at each other as if unsure what had just happened.

"He barely admitted to doing anything," Uncle Fred announced.

"He was angrier when he lost to Kennedy," Stacia said. "At least then he had spunk."

"Don't you see?" Robert asked, and all eyes turned to him. If the pronouncements of a cabdriver were little regarded outside these walls, here, as the only person in the room with a college degree, his opinion still meant something. "He's beaten down like a dog. They've taken everything from him. Now he'll go home and cry with his wife."

"And a lot of comfort *she'll* be," Aunt Lolly remarked.

His analysis cheered them a bit, and halfway through Ford's speech the men turned the volume down while the women went into the kitchen to get more cake. The handful of children danced around the table, waiting as if at a birthday party.

Robert felt celebratory, too. For the first time in almost four years, he had plans. He would tell his parents after everyone left: he was applying to law school. What else could a boy do who had ambition but no specific passion, intelligence but no concrete skills? Where could he use a liberal-arts degree and a tendency to see the worst in every situation? How had he not realized this before? Journalism degrees were fashionable that year, inspired by the profession's finest hour, but Robert still didn't want to save the world. He only wanted to save himself.

The Vishniaks and Kupferbergs might have been disappointed at the tenor of the speech, but within moments they'd bounced back, and the room was filled with laughter. Robert's father moved slowly, using a cane — he was wearing the prosthesis, so that to the careful observer his pants fit oddly, the material strangely looser on the synthetic leg — but he managed, with surprising deftness, to pour cherry brandy into shot glasses, which then made their way around the room. He was not supposed to drink it, but he snuck in thimblefuls. No one was going to stop him.

"How do they drink that cheap shit?" Barry said to Robert, refusing a glass that came to him. "Hey, Pop!" he yelled out over the din. "You got any slivovitz?"

A roar of approval went up from the crowd.

Robert watched them with a strange sense that all, for once, was as it should be. They were a family built for the 1970s. His parents and their siblings, alumni of the Great Depression, understood recession, unemployment, and high gas prices. They mostly held government jobs for low but secure salaries — drove public buses, delivered mail, read meters. Stacia, calling them into the dining room to eat, was, Robert noted, as close to cheerful as he'd ever seen her. She hadn't voted for the bum either time, nor had anyone in her family. She didn't own a car! Even her stove was electric! It was as if she had always known.

CHAPTER TWENTY-FIVE

Law school

The air conditioner trilled loudly in the shop on Sixth Avenue just off Twelfth Street, as the elderly man with a twirled mustache, in a shirt and bow tie, cut Robert's facial hair with a scissors, getting it short enough to shave. The shaving cream he used smelled of lime. Robert enjoyed being shaved and washed and taken care of more than he'd expected — for the last three years, he had wanted just the opposite, but now he remembered how people lived, could live.

In a few weeks, he would start law school at New York University. He'd chosen it over Columbia because it was cheaper but still highly rated, and the class hours would allow him to catch a few nights driving the cab for extra money, if needed; the three thousand dollars he'd saved from driving would not get him through three years of school, and he still had undergraduate loans. He associated Columbia University and the Upper West Side with the last few years, and though he would continue to live there — his rent was too cheap to pass up, especially with Barry as his roommate — he was ready now to invest his hopes in a new neighborhood, a new identity, a new slice of Manhattan.

When the barber was done, he dusted the back of Robert's neck with powder, tickling his skin with a horsehair brush. Robert's face tingled, and he felt the coolness from the air-conditioning on his neck. In the mirror, he saw a version of his face that had not been visible for almost four years: a dramatic face with a strong jaw and neatly trimmed eyebrows arching over dark eyes that stared back at him with even more determination than he remembered. There were a few lines in the corners of his eyes that had not been there before, and a few gray hairs, too. In short, this was the face of a full-grown man, and the small touches of age, the hollows of his longer, more angular face, suited him. "There you go," the barber said. "From Sasquatch to Cary Grant in under an hour. What a transformation." Then the barber went to a drawer, took out a boxy Polaroid camera, and snapped Robert's picture. While waiting for it to develop, the barber undercharged him — the longhair fad was killing business and Robert would be a good advertisement, he said, to the younger people. "Tell your friends," he added, as Robert stumbled out into the hot summer street, shorn and vulnerable. A woman came toward him, her clogs making an odd clomping on the sidewalk; she was an attractive blonde in jean shorts and a red tank top, and she asked him if he had the time. He told her it was 3:00 p.m., and she lingered for a moment, as if expecting something, then she pointed to the barber's window. "Hey, you know, that guy's putting your picture up in his window."

"I know," Robert said, smiling. "I'm wanted in three states."

"Wanna make it four?" she asked, then offered her name and number, which he took, because why not? It had been offered.

He smiled, watching her walk away, remembering that strange feeling of not so very long ago when people gave him things based solely on what he looked like. He was healthy again, had put on enough weight to look merely slim instead of gaunt. His face was exposed to the world, and it was a world that offered the children of Stacia and Vishniak precious few natural advantages by which to distinguish themselves — and in a city the size of New York, he had to use what he could and not think too much about it.

HE WAS OLDER THAN many of his fellow law students, though not all, because the draft, avoiding it or going to Vietnam, had taken up at least a few years of most everyone's time. In his section, he could spot the vets, the GI Billers, not just by the signs of neighborhood and origin, but by an aura that hung around them: of disappointment, a heaviness that they pulled behind them, despite their superior posture. There had been no need for Robert to cut his hair, though, not ideologically, at least; NYU law students wore sandals, tie-dyed T-shirts, and jean jackets, and many of the men had beards and long hair. In the fall of 1975, they talked of white-shoe firms like Sullivan and Cromwell, and Latham and Watkins, but dressed more like Fidel Castro and Che Guevara.

There were courses, like Contracts and Torts and Procedure, and then there were electives. The professors taught in a combination of lecture and Socratic method, liking the occasional surprise attack, but mostly you had to have your hand up to be called on. In college, if you hadn't done the reading but were a relatively intelligent person, you could often guess at some interesting if not perfectly correct answer, but not in law school. Stanley Dunphy, a third-year around Robert's age, gave him some advice one afternoon as they sat in the park eating hot dogs from a nearby stand. "In the first semester, if you read the cases, you're mostly fucked," Stanley said, "but if you haven't read them, well, you're totally fucked."

College had not really prepared him for any of this, not even the writing, because lawyers did not write like regular people. He had to throw away everything he'd ever learned about writing, actually, and he'd considered himself a good writer, as had his teachers. His legal analysis class was for the fewest number of credits, yet it took up the most time. This was not just because of the amount of work, but because learning to write in a way that was acceptable to the powers that be was the key, along with grades, to earning a coveted spot on the *Law Review*, an important stop on the road to the best jobs.

As he read the examples of actual legal analysis from his text-books—memoranda, motions and appeals, briefs and summa-ries—he could see that lawyers, the ultimate advocates for their clients, never acknowledged that a client might have done something wrong or illegal. Lawyers were paid to be aggressive, but they wrote in the passive voice, the voice of the unfairly victimized. He and Barry had assumed that Nixon, in leaving office, had said "mistakes were made" and not "I made mistakes" because he was an asshole—but by the end of his first term, Robert understood that the former presi-dent chose those words because he'd gone to law school.

NEW YORK CITY'S ECONOMY WAS still in tatters. If he wanted to gain some needed experience as a first-year, he'd have to work for free, at least during the school term. Such largesse went against his principles—he'd never worked for free in his life—but then, this was an investment in his future. A flyer had been posted outside one of his classrooms advertising for law-student volunteers who spoke Spanish. Robert's Spanish was high school and college Spanish, but he'd gotten real practice as a cabdriver who often went into the Puerto Rican and Dominican neighborhoods of Spanish Harlem and the Bronx when others wouldn't. What he spoke, or had picked up, was more a hybrid of the Spanish and English spoken on the street by those groups, more Spanglish than Spanish, but perhaps that would help him, too. He called the number and ended up spending three afternoons a week at the Patricia Friesèe Alexander Law Clinic.

The clinic was in one large and unadorned room in a nondescript brick building off Union Square that housed, among other things, a talent agency specializing in circus performers, a design magazine, and, on the ground floor, the Clifford Odets Memorial Theater (and dry cleaner). He worked in a cubicle, surrounded by high-strung first-year law students masquerading as lawyers. There were two actual lawyers on staff: a recent Yale grad named George Raft (before Robert could ask, he was assured that this truly was the man's name), and an NYU alum named Stella Depillis, a redhead in her late thirties, married and with a six-year-old daughter—with the appropriate desk photo of happy family to prove it—even as almost everyone in the office openly acknowledged that she was having an affair with George Raft. This resulted in a very flexible idea of time at the office—lunch was as long as you liked it, hours were set in advance but could be changed, and the two third-years who still volunteered three afternoons a week provided the most consistent, if not always the most reliable, direction and advice. The first day Robert walked in he was directed to a bridge chair and a tiny desk, then put to work doing intake. The desk, recovered from a local high school library, was covered in obscenities.

His first real assignment involved a group of mostly Puerto Rican tenants in low-income housing in the South Bronx. The tenants, now part of a tenants association, had filed endless complaints about the conditions in their apartments and hallways. They knew, vaguely, what a class-action suit was, and they were not dissuaded when Robert pointed out that no one had ever successfully sued the Department of Housing and Urban Development, and that the best they might get, if they all filed complaints, was some fresh paint, a few repaired steps, maybe a maintenance man who wasn't high all the time. As instructed by George Raft, Robert interviewed them and wrote down summaries of the complaints: children damaged by eating peeling paint; old ladies with broken bones from tripping on upended floor tiles, or pneumonia blamed on the lack of heat and a roof that leaked all winter. If there were doctors involved, Robert contacted them when he needed more specific details, and made endless calls, with little success, to the building superintendent and various bureaucrats who were supposed to have inspected the place.

Clients came for more mundane reasons, too. Their food stamps had been mysteriously cut off, or a relative working under their Social Security number had used it to get a credit card and then left the country without paying the bills, leaving them to deal with furious creditors.

Robert had expected all of these people to be beaten down, tired, hopeless — their lives were an endless series of small hurdles that they could not clear; a circumscribed life was how Robert thought of it. Yet most of the poor people he saw each week were, if not cheerful, then certainly more optimistic than he'd have been, more patient. They waited in endless lines, laughed at each other's jokes, told their stories with surprising humor. And then one day he realized: they were being listened to. In each and every cubicle, the law students listened with rapt attention, and wrote down their stories carefully. How often did a person, any person, get another human being to really listen to them? It seemed that in New York, in late 1975, even the poorest people wanted, and were beginning to expect, that it was their right to be heard. If he could do nothing else, he could listen. And if they were hungry, and some were, he gave them a few cereal bars from his desk and emergency food stamps. He was authorized to do that, and when he did they looked at him with an expression of such awe and relief that for a little while afterward the city was beautiful to Robert, strangely bright.

He also saw a lot of artists that year. Artists had been living illegally in SoHo for decades, taking over the lofts that had been used for industry but were then abandoned as blue-collar jobs fled Manhattan. The zoning changes of 1971 had made it possible for these artists to form co-ops and buy their places, or rent legally, so long as the loft was under 3,600 square feet, but they had to prove that they both lived and worked in the space, and also that the building had become obsolete for manufacturing purposes. All this took paperwork; they were supposed to register with the Department of Buildings, and become certified. This could take years, and they often needed help. So they showed up at the law center.

Weren't people who lived outside mainstream culture supposed to be nicer, if not to others then to each other? Wasn't that what the 1960s had been about, or claimed to be? But these musicians and painters, playwrights and sculptors, were often the most difficult of the people he met with. Though generally better off financially than the genuine poor—some were buying their own lofts for five thousand dollars or more, and many had college or even graduate arts degrees and had clearly chosen the lives they lived—they liked to whine. About the speculators making enormous profits selling unregistered properties, about the other artists who'd gotten better deals, about the developers trolling the neighborhood for properties that could become discos or department stores. He heard over and over the same mantra from these people—that artists made a place nice, put their sweat and blood into fixing it up, just so the bankers and lawyers and developers could come in, hike the prices, and sell to the bourgeoisie. And it occurred to him, as person after person made this pronouncement, that they assumed he, Robert Vishniak of the 2100 block of Disston Street—driver of a taxicab and packer, daily, of a bag lunch, with five thousand dollars still to be paid on his undergraduate student loans and thousands more he would incur in law school—was that bourgeoisie.

"Hey, it's not your job to like your clients," Barry often reminded him. But somehow, in the face of their righteous anger, the loud speeches as they shook their paint-stained fists in his face, he often became tongue-tied. There was power in being so sure of who you were and what you wanted, and these artists had that power, even as they insisted on their powerlessness. He began to do more research on the loft laws, and to think about what they meant to New York, so that at least he could look his most annoying clients in the eye and know more than they did.

One twilight afternoon in December, with a silent, chilly feeling in the air that portended snow, Robert took the number 1 train all the way to Houston Street and walked south down Broadway, looking at the dirty windows of the enormous half-abandoned factories and tiny coffee bars, a bookstore, and the occasional gallery existing here and there on a ground floor, behind barred windows. On Prince Street, two men played the guitar — the sign said "playing to put ourselves through school" — and almost every passerby tossed in some change. A woman in a lime green dress with a bull's-eye over the stomach tossed in a five. Two guys stood on the corner smoking a joint, with no fear of the cops. *It's still 1967 here,* Robert thought, as a pack of kids brushed past him, their black clothing smelling of cloves. They all filed into a record store, or at least he assumed that was what it was from the album cover in the window.

You could still see plenty of the ugly bits, reminders of how industrial and bleak the area had been before the artists came in. Some of his clients at the law center had scars and poorly healed fractures from the work they'd done erecting walls, installing plumbing and wiring. To live illegally in a large work space was to do everything for yourself, including toting your own garbage to the dump. In these buildings, tenants made collages all day long that few people bought, or created a giant swimming pool in the living room where they could float wax carvings. What an odd, self-absorbed existence, Robert thought; they lived like children. Yet he understood now what he hated about the artists who came to his office to champion their cause — their insistence that this place belonged to them. They had made a home, surrounded by other people who cared about the same activities and shared their fury at anyone who threatened their way of life. He envied them this sense of community. In a city so huge and demanding, he knew, when you found a place to make your own, you held on for dear life.

From there, he walked over to the wasteland of long, half-empty streets, boarded-up buildings, and broken glass that City Hall referred to as Washington Market but the artists called TriBeCa, the triangle below Canal Street. The Office of Lower Manhattan Development was studying this area — City Hall would have a hearing in a month. Hundreds were living here illegally as they had once lived in SoHo, and for once developers and artists were on the same side, though neither would admit it — both wanted to ease restrictions so that TriBeCa could be zoned residential.

Off Canal, on Walker Street, he saw a fat little man leaving a graffiti-covered door. Looking up into a lighted window next door, he could see several women still at their sewing machines. There was writing on the doorway the man had left, but Robert couldn't read it — the street was too dark, illuminated only by a single lamp and the light from the women working in that window. He imagined the man to be a machinist or warehouse worker. He walked slowly, the way a man walks after a too-long day at a physical job. As he passed by, Robert could hear the squeaking of his shoes, a familiar sound, momentarily touching, for it reminded him of his father and uncle, who wore a certain work shoe with a thick rubber sole shaped like jagged spikes, a sole designed to absorb shock and last for years, bought by men who stood up all day.

Manufacturing was disappearing from New York. Why had the owners and workers been so quiet about the taking over of their business district? In 1971, when SoHo was rezoned, there were twenty thousand blue-collar workers employed there, yet even the unions had hardly made a peep, seeming to accept the inevitable. His properties professor had once remarked that no place abhorred a vacuum like Manhattan. Nowhere did New York's identity seem more in flux, more confused, than in its building codes, its attitudes toward preservation and destruction. A student of history, Robert thought about neighborhoods, about their rules and regulations, and how a place to live could shelter and nurture you like a lover's arms, then turn on you one day and leave you out in the cold for reasons you barely understood.

Those were the very words he'd use when he wrote the essay that was part of his application for the *Law Review*, which he applied for even though his grades were not as high as they should have been, in the hopes that admission would help get him a job after graduation.

Even if he failed, he knew that it was time to compete again, to put himself on the line. And in the end, he was lucky — the fictionalized court case that he was to write on called into question the Landmark Preservation Act, the 1965 law that forbade the destruction of buildings that for reasons of history and/or aesthetics contributed to the character and economy of the city. Robert had become fascinated by landmark preservation law — what else could salvage the past, the most beautiful and valuable buildings so often destroyed by the wrecking ball?

People, he insisted, had a right to live with beauty, to touch their own history. He had grown up in a place that smelled bad, where everyone lived in a carbon copy of the house on either side of it and no one had a yard big enough to throw a football in. What relief he'd gotten had been in the form of public works — the two public pools where he swam for free; the Max Myers Playground, where he learned to play baseball; the Cobbs Creek Park, where, rarely, his father took him to commune with nature (even if nature was sometimes mixed with snack-food wrappers and empty beer cans), and the magnet high school, with its superior facilities and sense of mission, built to attract the city's brightest regardless of income.

Those who believed in preservation often cited economics to justify New York's landmark law — beautiful buildings attracted tourism and business. But the law needed to be about neighborhoods and the people who lived in them. Landmarking was concerned with a specific building, but zoning was about entire districts conforming to a plan that, ideally, benefited the public. The two kinds of laws needed to work together better. He advocated the rewriting of the 1965 law with stricter adherence to the demands of neighborhoods.

And when he'd finished his brief and wrote the five-hundred-word personal statement to which he gave scant attention, he suddenly felt that without realizing it he had learned something from his first year of school. And he knew something else, as well—he wanted to be a real estate lawyer.

CHAPTER TWENTY-SIX

Barry to the rescue

That summer, he continued to work mornings in the law center — they paid a small wage to students who worked over the vacation, but it was more of a stipend than anything like real money. He drove his cab from 4:00 p.m. to midnight and on weekends, though business was slow, even with the Bicentennial. On his lunch break he combed through ads at the career center, hoping for a job, any job, that might help his legal résumé or give him an idea of what his future held, but there were few such jobs to be had — and what positions there were went to students entering their third year.

New York was especially hot and humid that July, and for the first time in a while he had trouble with his asthma. One evening at work, he had to pull over for fear of driving off the road. The customer, an elderly man, had seemed sympathetic at the time, talking of a granddaughter with the same problem and insisting on paying the full fare. But the man filed a complaint with the review board — such complaints, in a year of falling ridership, were taken seriously, plus the man, it turned out, was a retired judge, and Robert feared having to go to a hearing. Was driving a cab even worth the hassle anymore? Yet how many other jobs fit his limited hours?

Nights were the worst. When he did sleep, his nightmares returned, perhaps brought on by the frequent use of his asthma inhaler. He had recently bought a proper mattress and box spring because sleeping on the floor was bad for his asthma. He had a small air conditioner in his bedroom, too, bought used, and it helped cool the place down, but never so much that he needed even a top sheet. One morning, at four, he awoke from a nightmare unable to breathe. He grabbed for his emergency inhaler, knocking over a lamp, and put the thing to his lips. The mist hit his throat, and he waited, seconds passing — nothing happened. He pushed the release button again, wheezing now. Barry entered the room and turned on the light.

"What's wrong?" He looked at Robert, pale and panicked. "The stuff's not helping?"

Robert felt light-headed and pointed to the bathroom. There was some cheap stuff from the drugstore; sometimes it worked when the prescription didn't. Barry went to find it as Robert passed out. When he woke up, Barry was ripping the device from its plastic casing, holding it over Robert's mouth. "You want to go to the hospital?"

Not waiting for Robert to answer, he went to the phone and dialed 911, then quickly cleared the apartment of any offensive matter. They arrived fifteen minutes later, just as Barry was finishing up, and by then Robert seemed to be breathing just fine.

"Who knew you guys actually came when called?" Barry said to the attendant, who insisted on strapping Robert onto a gurney and carrying him out reclining like a pasha.

"Could this be any more embarrassing?" Robert asked Barry, as the attendants took him out to the elevator. Barry turned down the chance to ride along; he would follow in his car.

Robert expected to be taken to Harlem Hospital, which was

public, or to NYU, which, though on the other side of the city, and private, might cut him a break because he was a student. Instead he was taken to St. Luke's, closest to his house. In the ER, patients were not curled up on tables, or moaning in pain for all the world to see. Instead, they had spaces curtained off where you could be examined and suffer in private. The floors were spotless, and every few minutes a nurse arrived to see how he was, assuring him that the doctor would arrive any moment. How was he going to afford this?

Half an hour later, Barry arrived and found Robert behind his curtain. "I fucking hate hospitals," Barry said. "They just remind me of when Pop was sick."

"Before I woke up, I was dreaming about him," Robert said. He had seen his father swimming in the ocean, like he used to, with his uncles Frank and Fred, and his grandfather, all of them, swimming one minute, then belly-up, like dead fish, the next. And Robert stood onshore watching them, one after another, float to the surface.

"Robert," Barry said, "you gotta calm down, man."

"It's you that's making me nervous," Robert said, watching Barry pace in the small, curtained-off space, too small for such movements, so his elbows kept jostling the curtain.

"You ever wonder why no one in our family ever did what they set out to do?"

"What did they set out to do?" Barry asked. "Besides keep a job and pay the mortgage? I never really noticed the agenda beyond that—"

"Could you put it in neutral for a minute?" Robert said, his voice raspy and strained, as it always was after a bad attack. He wanted, more than anything, to sleep, but the medicine kept him up. It was a kind of purgatory, added to by his brother's refusal to stand still or stop talking.

Barry took out a silver flask from his jacket and had a drink.

"It's not even five in the morning."

"You want me to come down?" Barry whispered. "It's this or smoke a joint, and I don't think I can do that here."

"What are you doing with that flask?" Robert asked. Barry passed it to him, and he took a sip, then wiped off the excess with the back of his sleeve. The liquid felt good going down, warm. "There was a guy I knew in college had one of these."

"It was payment," Barry snapped. "On a debt."

"I was trying to say before that they had dreams, you know. Pop owned that candy store before we were born. And Uncle Frank with the repair shop."

"For like five minutes."

"But he still owned it."

"And Uncle Izzy Vishniak, with the lightbulb that never burned out."

"Did he ever get a patent?"

"Whadda you think? And then Uncle Georgie, with the night school classes?"

"Yeah, but he never got a diploma."

"My point exactly. They all wanted things and they all ended up at the post office."

The doctor arrived and began to examine him. Barry talked the whole time, so that the doctor, who was around his own age, asked Robert if his brother needed assistance, then placed a mask attached to a nebulizer over Robert's mouth and told him to breathe. Barry stepped away for a few minutes, and when he came back the doctor was writing a prescription for a new pill, telling Robert that something even better would be approved soon, was already used in Europe and Canada. Barry asked the doctor what he'd prescribed — steroid? Tranquilizer? Upper? Downer?

Robert took the nebulizer off his face. "Shut up already! Could you do that for me?"

The doctor smiled, then told Robert to keep the mask on and left.

"Why don't you go call Stacia?" Robert asked.

"You want me to tell them you're here? What are you, crazy?"

"No, just call," Robert said. "See if Pop's okay."

"I'll scare them half to death at this hour. And keep that damn thing over your face."

Robert did as he was told.

An hour later, at seven, having signed all the necessary paperwork, he stood in front of the hospital, watching an ambulance roar down 113th. Barry pulled the car around. "Maybe I should drive," Robert said.

"I'm in better shape than you are."

"No you're not." They argued and then flipped a coin, and Barry won. He drove down Broadway, past the bookshops and bars and restaurants, the pharmacy and bodegas, a strange mixture of high and low, stores that served both Harlem and the university. Store owners were coming out to unlock the metal gratings on their establishments; a garbage truck stopped in front of a bar. Two women, dressed as if it were still night, walked arm in arm toward the Barnard dorms. Barry halted at a red light and asked Robert what was wrong.

"I wonder how much that stay is going to cost, is all," he said. For years he had spent very little and now, all at once, his whole life was bills. "Not much coming in these days."

"Don't worry about it," Barry said.

"Easy for you to say," Robert replied, as the light turned green.

"I mean, I paid it. I was the one that called the ambulance, and I had a good month."

"When don't you have a good month?" Robert asked, but then thanked him. He never knew how to take a spontaneous act of generosity from Barry.

"At least they tried," Barry said. "You could be from a family where nobody even tried."

"True," Robert said. He leaned his elbow out the open window. Already he could feel the beginnings of the heat of the day. By noon it would be unbearable. "You remember what Uncle Frank always said?"

"Nice guys finish last?"

"Uh-huh."

"Think of it this way," Barry replied. "Frank is a hell of a lot nicer than you'll ever be."

"Thank you."

"You're welcome," Barry replied, shifting the clutch as they turned down Eighty-sixth Street and sped toward home.

CHAPTER TWENTY-SEVEN

Robert makes the grade

Perhaps his brother was right, because a week later Robert found out that he'd made *Law Review*. The news came in a phone call from the editor in chief, a third-year named Nan. Robert asked if it was his comments on the landmark preservation case that had made the difference. "No," she said, chomping on some gum as she spoke, "your summary read like notes to the gardening-club set." What had impressed the staff was his personal statement, an essay to which he had given all of fifteen minutes of his time, about his work at the law center.

Making *Law Review* bestowed a kind of importance on Robert—his classmates, Nan told him, would know who he was now; his professors would, too. He felt as if he'd been rescued from some terrible future by a lucky fluke. *Lucky.* He rolled the word around in his mind. Probably there was another word for this.

On the first day of his second year, Robert awoke elated. Drinking his early-morning coffee, he felt as if the world were his. Barry, seeing him rushing back and forth in the kitchen, gathering his things and whistling, asked what he was on. "I'm high on life," he replied.

"You're a fucking psycho is what you are," Barry yelled after Robert, who was now waiting for the elevator. "All summer you brood like Hamlet. I can't say a word without you snapping at me!"

Robert decided to walk the three flights down. Barry went to the top of the stairs and yelled after him, "These moods of yours, Robert! Get yourself a shrink!"

THE GETTING OF THE THING proved more exciting than the reality. Soliciting, fact-checking, and proofreading articles was hard, detail-oriented work under the best of circumstances, but he now worked in an overheated, moldy basement office with a group of younger, tightly wound perfectionists who labored for the glory of faculty members and the hope of publishing the occasional note or lending a suggestion. He enjoyed the articles on legal history — was allowed, even, to write a short piece on how the zoning changes in lower Manhattan were affecting the shape of the city. But theory and its obtuse, endlessly circular language bored him to tears. The same people proofed and reproofed each other's work again and again — the point being to catch even the tiniest human error, then champion oneself for having caught what one's colleagues were too stupid to catch — a process guaranteed to create screaming matches over minutiae.

They worked particularly hard in the week before one of the *Review*'s bimonthly issues went to press, and during those times he was often thrown in with the sloppily attractive but annoying Nan, the editor who'd said such critical things about his application. Nan worked harder than any of the men she managed and did not wear her position with any particular modesty. By winter she had secured a clerkship after graduation with an appellate judge, and she took particular relish in bossing everyone around. Her clothing was wrinkled because she often slept on the battered conference table instead of going home. Her curly brown hair half-covered her face, the occasional loose strand winding up stuck to a galley, or in his coffee cup or someone's lunch; her presence was said to be just that ubiquitous.

The stress of the place when they were on deadline, the backaches and headaches from leaning over long strips of type, the manner in which Nan, chewing vigorously on endless sticks of wintergreen gum, stood over his shoulder pointing out problems that it was generally too late to fix, made him tense and horny. He supposed it did the same thing to her, because after these late-night deadlines they often went back to her studio on West Tenth Street and, before they could even get the key in the door, were undressing each other on the stairway. There was no question of their relationship being more than physical. In the light of day they couldn't stand each other, fought often, and were considered, in the politics of the *Review*, to be mortal enemies, a fact that made their rendezvous even more intoxicating and ultimately, disposable.

The *Law Review* made a whole new level of job possible for Robert, and this was doubly so after his first midterms went well. Among the many places he interviewed for summer work was Alexander, Lenox and Wardell, a midsize firm known for its real estate department. The firm's cofounder, Jack Alexander, was just then in the news as one of the lawyers who'd presented friend-of-the-court briefs supporting the preservation of Grand Central Station.

His advisor, an alum who was married to a lawyer at a very large first-tier firm, said that Alexander, Lenox and Wardell had just started recruiting at NYU—in the past, she said, they generally got their people from Columbia and Yale—and the place was known to be formal in its style, kind of stodgy. "I could stand a little bit of formality," Robert replied, "a little stodginess." Though this firm did not pay as well as some of the larger ones, to him the summer money was enormous—four hundred dollars a week, over twice what his father made per week after thirty years of service.

His first interview, just before Christmas, involved facing four lawyers, all overly serious young associates. The three men and one woman wore black suits and white shirts—one man had a royal blue tie, but the others stuck to neutrals. They sat in a row, looking to Robert like a firing squad that also provided funeral services, and their questions focused on the basics: what courses he enjoyed most, why he'd gotten mostly Bs his first year when clearly he was capable of better—were there mitigating circumstances? Robert wondered when a B had ceased to be respectable, but pointed out that it had taken him awhile to get the hang of things, which was probably the wrong answer. He was also asked many questions about his work at the Patricia Friesèe Alexander clinic—which was funded by, among other people, Jack Alexander. The late Patricia was his wife—Robert's work at the clinic was part of why he got the interview, though his enthusiasm for the place did not get him any smiles. What, he wondered, might have made these people smile? The woman on the panel talked mostly about what they might offer him, and this made him relax a bit more and finally sit back in his chair.

By the second interview, a month later, he was less frightened of the place, which took up two floors of a glass-and-chrome office building on Sixtieth, close to Lexington. The firm had been around since the war, but the decor was strangely modern, even futuristic. The walls were white, the stairs up to the second floor metal. Behind them hung an enormous silk weaving in swirling colors of black and white and gold. Walking behind the secretary to the office of the partner who interviewed him took concentration—he wanted to examine the cream-colored walls with their assortment of abstract art, paintings so spare that a child might have done them in art class. Certainly the place did not feel stuffy, but he did not understand then that a decorator's taste and a firm's philosophy could be two different things.

He met with Phillip Healey, a freckled blond who dealt with the summer associates. He was young for a partner, or at least youthful-looking, and had a cultivated but friendly manner.

"Is there a lot of public-interest law done here?" Robert asked, thinking of the firm's connection to the law clinic.

"A certain amount," Healey said, enunciating his words with care. "Summer associates particularly, but if you're looking for a major commitment to the public sector—"

"I want to make money," Robert said.

The man smiled. "That's honest," he said. "Perhaps too honest."

So what was the right note? he wondered, beginning to panic. He wanted to make money and, when possible, he wanted to do right. Were the two incompatible? Did he sound naïve? Robert felt that the interview was not going well, but then Healey gave him a hand.

"You mentioned that you were interested in landmark preservation. Can you elaborate?"

"Yes. I think it's only a matter of time before more of lower Manhattan goes the way of SoHo, especially now, with so many tax incentives for development and conversion."

Healey smiled and leaned forward, and Robert continued talking, feeling encouraged. "But with opportunity, I think, comes responsibility—and the tension between a livable city and a profitable city excites me."

"We represent several big and many smaller developers," Healey said. "If you know at this stage of the game that real estate is your passion, even better. There are other practice groups here, but real estate is a big focus."

"So I'll be working mostly for real estate lawyers?" Robert asked.

Healey assured him that he would get plenty of experience, but he didn't answer Robert's question. "It's a tough time, as you say, but there are opportunities," he continued, "public-private partnerships, and a renewed interest in preservation even, assuming such interests can be made profitable. At A, L and W, we've managed to stay in the game."

"I think I'd be able to learn a lot here," Robert said, taking the man's cue.

"You will indeed," Phillip Healey said. He tipped his chair back and smiled at Robert in a way that reminded him of one of his favorite high school English teachers.

After the interview, Robert floated out as if on a cloud, feeling that he had a good chance of being hired. Healey had told him that if he wanted real estate law, this was the place to be. Certainly there were other places, but they were larger, and he liked the idea of being in a firm with fifty-five lawyers, big enough to show strength but small enough that he might distinguish himself. A bigger firm might try to persuade him to specialize in something else, or he could get lost in the crowd.

He walked past the two secretaries, who smiled at him, then down a long hallway lined with black-and-white photos of children playing on the streets of Harlem and back into the lobby, with its pale, armless couches and black-and-white rug, all seemingly guarded by the portraits of three men, the founding partners. The red-haired Jack Alexander, youngest of the three, seemed to be scowling at him, as if to caution that he didn't have the job yet. Alexander, Lenox and Wardell was written in dignified silver script over the entrance. As Robert pressed the button for the elevator, he was only half aware of the distant, discordant slamming of a door, and the sound of heels clicking angrily against wood flooring, the rapid pace advancing in his direction as, alone, he got into the elevator.

His new black penny loafers pinched his feet. Dressed for the part, he decided to treat himself to a taxi. He was off until seven the next morning, when he'd change identities, turning from a passenger in a cab to a cabbie. But it was already the beginning of rush hour, and a cold, windy evening, too. Half of Midtown was trying to hail a taxi and Robert, who as a driver had a map of the city streets imprinted on his brain, was suddenly less savvy on foot. The thick froth of bodies carried him along, and before he knew it he was on Fifth Avenue at Fifty-ninth Street, across from Central Park and in front of the Sherry-Netherland Hotel, perhaps the worst corner in the entire city for hailing a cab at rush hour. He was thinking about the bus when he saw, miraculously, a cab approaching Sixtieth, trying to get itself from the center lane over to the curb to deposit passengers. Robert raced up Fifth, then darted across on a diagonal, dodging the parking lot of cars and yelling to the driver, who was now dropping off a woman with a baby and a cumbersome stroller. As he ran, he became aware of someone just behind him. *No way am I giving up this cab,* he thought, grabbing for the door handle, just as a woman grabbed for the same handle, their hands brushing abruptly against each other. She removed hers quickly and he opened the door.

"You together?" the driver asked. A car honked behind him.

"In this traffic, we'd better be," the woman said. She got in and slid over to make room for him to follow, which he did, shutting the door behind him. She had long, reddish blond hair and small, close-set, green eyes that turned upward at the edges, pale skin, a narrow nose, and dangerously long legs in high-heeled brown boots. She unbuttoned her tan suede jacket, revealing a pale yellow dress, the kind that wrapped around a woman, showed the curve of her hips and just a little cleavage. A silk scarf of navy, yellow, and gold was tied intricately around her neck, one end dangling just over her left breast. Carefully packaged, he thought, as she slowly removed a leather glove, then put out her manicured hand. "My name is Crea, by the way," she said.

"Robert," he said. "Crea is an unusual name."

"Have you never heard it before?"

"Actually, I think I have, but I don't know where."

Crea reached into her purse for a cigarette, tapped the pack, and put one in her mouth, a feminine extrathin cigarette, the kind that he'd seen on a television commercial trumpeting the arrival of the liberated woman. She tilted her head toward him, seeming to need a light, but then revealed the tiny silver lighter in her hand; she lit the cigarette and took a long inhale, blowing the smoke slowly out her nostrils.

"A direction would be nice," the driver snapped, as the traffic inched forward again. "Not that I wanna interrupt you people's getting acquainted."

Robert leaned forward, speaking close to the driver's ear. "In this traffic, chief, where you gonna go? Huh?" He was paying for this ride and he deserved all the niceties he had coming to him. "Take a right here and go around the park to Central Park West. I'll direct you from there. If you can't manage that, then cut over now and go east, turn up Park Avenue, stay on it until Eighty-first, then go west and cut across the park, but for Christ's sake don't stay on Fifth Avenue. All right?"

Crea turned from the window. "For a man in an expensive suit, you can be, uh, very down with the people," she said.

He had no intention of telling her that he had only one suit, which happened to be from Brooks Brothers, or that he'd gone there on the recommendation of another law student, having never spent so much on himself in his life. She looked him in the eye now, smiling, and he decided that though she was not beautiful, she was striking, sleek. With those upturned green eyes, that thick, reddish hair, she looked almost feline. He rolled down his window, then reached over and took the cigarette from between her fingers, threw it out the window, and kissed her, lightly, on the lips. "I have asthma," he said. "Don't smoke."

"If you don't smoke, do you at least drink?" she asked. "We might get out here and walk to the St. Regis for a cocktail? I've always loved that Maxfield Parrish mural." She must have noticed that he looked puzzled, because she added, "You know, *Old King Cole?*"

"Old King Cole, the Merry Old Soul?" Robert asked. "Can't say I've seen it."

"And you live in New York? Well, that settles it."

The driver sighed. He was about to make the turn. "Wadda you want?" he asked.

They had gone just one block.

"Let us out," Robert said, and threw the man a five.

Much later, after they'd each had a martini at the bar, decided to stay for dinner, ordered two steak frites, and drank two bottles of wine that she picked, they decided, stumbling arm in arm down the elaborate marble halls and past a private dining room, to take a room. "You sit over there," he said, not wanting her to hear how much it would cost. She found the gesture charmingly old-fashioned and positioned herself by the uniformed bellhop who stood at attention near the stairway. Initially the man at the desk said they didn't have a room, but then Crea came over to inquire, and another employee took the guy aside. When he returned, something had materialized. Was she a hooker? Robert wondered. A really high-priced one who often stayed here? He was too anxious to get upstairs, too tipsy to think much about it or about the bill, which would set him back considerably — the dinner alone had cost him almost a month's rent.

In the enormous room with the pink-and-gold-striped wallpaper, elaborate windows, and heavy brocade curtains, he stripped off her dress, unwrapping her body like a package. As he kissed her, he was aware of her quickened breathing, of the tiny line of sweat on her upper lip, and of the straight-backed way that she held herself, like some kind of queen, even as she took his hand and put it between her legs, asking him, over and over, to touch her, to please touch her.

"Move closer," she whispered, as they tossed right and then left, clinging to each other.

"If I were any closer, I'd be behind you," he replied. "That's not original, it's Groucho." She laughed as he turned her over and mounted her from the back. Even then, even on all fours, she had that straight back, like a dancer, or a horseback rider, with a high behind. She was not what he'd expected, hours earlier, when he observed her posture in the bar and judged her rigid, unyielding. She didn't make love like a woman with perfect posture; she made love like a woman who hadn't been touched in months, though if he read the right pages of the papers, he'd have known that for the past year she'd been dating a local sportscaster, and before that a professor of art history at Columbia University who was also titled Italian royalty.

Afterward they lay on the bed, her head on his shoulder. "You're a very fast walker," she said, "so I'm awfully glad you take your time in other areas."

"How carefully did you observe my, uh, walking?" he asked, twirling a piece of her hair around his finger.

"Didn't you notice? I chased you all the way from Alexander, Lenox and Wardell."

"Really?" he asked, recalling the sound of heels clicking behind him. "You a lawyer?"

"God, no," she replied. "I was there to speak to my father. It's impossible to have a constructive discussion with a lawyer, you know? You're all terrible at conceding anything."

Robert took a moment to realize that she was including him in this comment. That he was, in fact, a lawyer, or almost one. That interview had felt like years ago.

"He was treating me, as usual, like an infant. We argued over money—what else do parents and children argue over? Only it's my very own money that he's keeping from me."

"You could sue," Robert said, stroking her hair.

"You be my lawyer." She pressed close to him in the dark and ran her big toe up and down his calf. "I left without saying good-bye, left my father halfway through his sentence, slammed the door, and told myself that I was going to get the first plane out of New York, going anywhere, so long as it was as far away from him as possible."

"So why didn't you?" Robert asked.

"It was pure instinct, actually. I didn't think at all."

"I don't understand," he said.

She rolled on top of him and placed her finger across his lips, moved it along his chin, her nail scratching lightly at the cleft, then traced her way along his Adam's apple and down to his clavicle, ran her finger down his arm to his side and then to his outer thigh, until softly, ever so softly, she traced inward along his groin.

"As I walked down the hall, I saw this man heading for the elevators, the handsomest man I'd ever seen," she said, as Robert groaned softly under her touch. "Everything else went out of my head — my father, the argument, where I was. All I knew was that I had to have him."

A few hours later Robert got out of bed, leaving Crea asleep in the enormous, far-too-comfortable hotel bed. In only his boxers, he sat down at the desk by the window, wondering what excuse he might give for rushing off so early. He wrote her a quick note on hotel stationery: "Meeting at school. Must run. Love, R." He added a PS with his phone number, realizing that he'd forgotten to get hers, that she might not be listed, and wondering, as he dressed, if he even wanted this to be more than a one-nighter. In the light of day, she struck him as an expensive, aggressively self-confident girl. She knew exactly what she wanted, that was clear, but he wasn't sure he was up for the task. He was still discovering his future, and the city was full of women. One thing for sure, he thought as he closed the door softly behind him, even if he hadn't left his number, Crea would likely track him down. Either way, he'd have to deal with her.

There were three uniformed men on duty downstairs, two behind the desk and another at attention by the landing. The guy by the stairs tipped his hat to the tall, handsome, but bedraggled young man in the rumpled navy suit, a powder blue patterned tie hanging undone around his neck. As Robert walked out into the eerie quiet of Midtown, the streets shockingly empty save for the

occasional cab or waitress leaving after the night shift, he thought
of the portraits of the founding partners in the lobby at A, L and
W, and Jack Alexander with his reddish hair, small green eyes, and
narrow nose. He had not even gotten a summer job yet and already,
he was almost certain, he'd had sex three times with the founding
partner's daughter. He shook his head in wonder, trying to sort out
if this was a good thing or a bad thing. Descending into the empty
subway, he decided that perhaps it was neither; perhaps it was simply an opportunity.

CHAPTER TWENTY-EIGHT

Robert learns about beauty and its opposite

No woman had ever been quite so curious about Robert. Crea asked him questions about his upbringing, his parents, his brother. He answered her, sometimes honestly, as when he regaled her with stories of his father's collection of scarves and umbrellas, or the enormous amount of food consumed by his brother's friend Victor Lampshade. She thought that he was talking about himself in very honest terms and thanked him for it, finding his honesty alluring. But in reality, by then Robert had the telling of his own story down to a science. The ways he had learned to bluff and evade in college had been further developed since Gwendolyn's death, which he still could not, would not, talk about with a single soul. He could tell funny stories and amuse, occasionally even holding his parents and his brother up for her enjoyment, though mostly he stuck to the oddities of his Oxford Circle neighbors for entertainment value; but when it came to the real details of his past he gave Crea a sanitized outline.

Of course she also held back her own family details more than he liked, saying little about the subject that fascinated him most—her relationship with her father. Perhaps he was better off not knowing. Jack, after all, was technically his boss, though as a summer associate, he'd been welcomed by the man on the first day, as the others had—a few words to rally the troops—before they were sent on their way, and he never saw him again. Robert had asked for real estate work, but found himself first doing tasks for the corporate department. The woman who gave out the assignments to the summer associates simply said, "You all rotate. Your preference has been duly noted." He was then directed to an associate who gave him a pile of documents and told him to write a case summary. "In the law library, red books are the cases and black books are the statutes. Now get moving."

In the decades to come the firm would woo its summer employees with dinners and booze cruises, baseball tickets and shortened hours, but not in 1977; he got little direction and less encouragement; jobs were in short supply, and this was clearly a test. The first time he had to do a contract, for a company that supplied artificial hair to doll manufacturers, he asked a young associate for help, and the man shrugged and told him he was too busy. What on earth was he supposed to *do*? The lawyer who'd given him the assignment was not even in that day. On the way back to his cubicle, he saw a man leaving his office and figured he'd have to try again. "I'm new," he said in a low voice, "and I'm trying to figure out this contract. Can you help me out?"

The man smiled, and even if it was a condescending smile, it was the first Robert had received in two weeks. He motioned Robert into his office. "I was about to leave for a fast lunch, but I can give you a minute," he said. "I know what the first weeks are like." He had only the vaguest trace of a foreign accent that Robert couldn't place, and he wore a winter-white suit, a pale blue shirt with a yellow silk tie and pocket square, and brown and white wing-tipped shoes. Everything about him was so neat and pressed as to be either intimidating or just plain strange. His broad shoulders looked, under his suit, as if they'd been drawn artificially wide with a ruler. Maybe this was what a certain kind of European called fashion. He was from somewhere else, all right. What American had the nerve to dress like that for the office? But Robert was desperate. He explained his situation.

"You'd be better off asking someone in corporate, my friend. I'm real estate."

"Oh," Robert said, brightening. "That's what I'd really like to work on."

"I came last year from another firm."

"You must be very good," Robert said, "if they took you in this market."

The man shrugged.

"What firm?" Robert asked.

"Bernicker and Carlysle."

Robert whistled. "That's impressive. Why on earth did you leave?"

"It wasn't my cup of tea," he said, making it clear by his tone and the pursing of his lips that Robert had asked one question too many.

"So any suggestions about this contract? I've tried people in corporate; they don't seem to have any time for me."

He smiled. "Check the files. There could be a contract done for those two companies with regularity. Just find the old one and change the quantities and the dates. At least, try that first."

"Could it really be that simple?"

"If it was complicated, they would not give it to you. No offense."

"No offense taken. I readily admit my own ignorance."

"Sometimes you're better off asking one of the older secretaries. They know a lot and they're more forgiving than the lawyers."

"I'll try your suggestion. Nothing to lose. My name's Robert Vishniak, by the way."

"Mario Saldana," he said, shaking Robert's hand with a firm, almost crushing grip.

"Spain?" Robert asked hesitantly.

"Caracas, Venezuela," he corrected. "Tell me, Roberto, do you play rugby?"

"No. Are you working on a lawsuit or something?"

"You're quite funny. How about soccer? Tennis? I want to organize a team at the firm."

"I don't know how athletic these guys are as a group."

"All this sitting at a desk is not natural. Human beings need to move around."

"I'm only a summer associate. You may not see me again after August."

"We can always hope, yes?" he said, smiling. "And now, I must get some lunch."

Robert thanked him again and went right to a secretary in corporate. As Mario had said he would, Robert found the contract from the year before. Crisis averted.

NO MATTER HOW UNCOMFORTABLE he sometimes felt at Alexander, Lenox and Wardell, Robert knew he was lucky. He didn't work on class-action suits — friends had gone to firms where endlessly complicated torts kept them going through boxes of documents day after day, doing little more than clerical work — plus he was encouraged to continue working one day a week at the law clinic. He found himself looking forward to that time; what a relief to know what he was doing.

There was not so much work that he had to go in on weekends, and he spent his free time with Crea. She knew more about beauty than anyone he'd ever met, and also about its visual opposite, which was a kind of beauty, too. This was her gift to him, to teach him about what people bought when their only considerations were aesthetic or emotional, never financial or practical. She had helped her father and almost everyone she knew decorate their offices — though it never occurred to her to charge for these services. She was generous with advice and with pieces that she often bought for people, sometimes giving away valuable modern art and sculpture as gifts. "It's not really generosity," she said. "I just can't stand bad taste." But he knew that this was modesty — she was generous in a graceful, self-effacing way.

Slowly, over time, she changed the way he saw things. She took him to galleries, holding his hand and whispering to him about the materials the painters used, and how to approach the work. Some of it, for Robert's taste, was hopelessly abstract. Yet she seemed to understand all the layers of thought and technique that the artist had stripped away to get three perfectly blurred lines that formed a sort of primitive horizon. He began, through her, to understand negative space, to perceive how the taking away of something could be more powerful than any amount of excess.

Mostly she liked to venture below Fourteenth Street. The first time they went to SoHo, he felt nothing but dread. One of his artist clients at the law center had told him that when she saw well-dressed corporate types wandering through her neighborhood, she wanted to pelt them with rotten tomatoes. But Crea was welcomed in the galleries; she had both taste and money, was an ideal customer who both collected and promoted art.

That summer, she was already obsessed with photography, considered a brand-new art form — the art form, she said, of their generation, of the revolution. Hearing her use such words made him laugh; she was no rebel, but he loved her passion. She collected the documentary work of W. Eugene Smith, including his famous photos of coal miners, and Berenice Abbott's shots of New York in the 1930s — a series of her photos taken from underneath the Brooklyn Bridge hung in Crea's study. Robert was shocked to realize that one of them was a version of the same photo that hung as a poster in his bedroom as a child. But hers was no poster.

Her particular interest was in street photographers, people

like Diane Arbus, who was on Crea's radar before anyone else he knew had ever heard of her. She took him to exhibits, showing him Larry Chatman's photographs of black men and women in urban bars; Roy Colmer's focus on the lonely office worker in the crowd, and John Milisenda's photos of his family posing over and over again with his retarded brother. What, he wondered, did these portraits do for her? Why was she drawn to portraits of the ordinary, the poor and disenfranchised, to photographs that intruded on people's privacy, caught them in moments of sadness and vulnerability? Was this what she wanted to do to him, too? Dig for such moments? She told him that she found a photograph most effective if she had to fight the need to look away. Robert felt that need often, but the faces stayed with him all day, reminded him of his father, now sitting in his wheelchair, or of the friends he'd left behind in Oxford Circle who didn't return from Vietnam, or the faces that showed up daily on the other side of his door, looking for Barry — their expressions haunted, hollow-eyed, hooked. There was so much sorrow and poverty in the world — why stare at it for hours? In those moments, he feared her voyeurism was heartless and empty.

He preferred when she talked about architecture. Wherever they went, she had her favorite buildings, like the Italian Renaissance–styled University Club in Midtown, or the Neo-classical Washington Square Arch — which Robert had walked by countless times without really noticing. Six weeks into their relationship, she took him to the apartment where she had grown up, assuring him before they went that her father was at his summer place in Orange County; he wanted her to look in on things. The summer before, the family below had insisted that a pipe from the kitchen was leaking into their child's bedroom; several nasty exchanges followed, and though no actual leak was found, her father could not sleep easily unless she checked in weekly.

The apartment was on Park Avenue, one in a long row of tall, smooth white buildings in the East Seventies. They got out of the cab. Robert paid the fare, then remained on the sidewalk for a moment, his head craning skyward to take in rows and rows of perfectly spaced windows, some with interesting architectural detailing—pedestals and tiny faces of angels with wings popping up here and there, then the tall limestone base at the bottom and the ornate gold filigree front door with its intricate intertwining vines and leaves. There was a time when someone thought of all these details, and craftsmen made those leaves, or carved those angels' wings, meticulously and by hand. At the very top, the high floors were stacked from widest to smallest, like the layers in a giant cake. Robert knew these were called setbacks, had studied some air-rights cases from the 1920s where the term was employed. They were used before the war, invented out of necessity by a brilliant architect named Rosario Candela at a time when no one apartment building was allowed to hog too much of the view. Manhattan zoning had strayed far from there since.

"Hello, George," Crea said to the doorman, who held the door and asked how she was, clearly not expecting an answer. George continued holding the door, staring straight ahead, waiting silently until Robert ended his mysterious revelry by the curb and came inside.

A young porter stood at attention behind a small desk. As they proceeded to the back elevators, he came out from behind his perch and asked who they were. "You must be new," Crea said, walking back toward him, her voice edged with impatience. "Alexander, we're in—" George stuck his head in just then, interrupting her to say that this was Jack Alexander's daughter. The porter immediately apologized.

"What's your name?" Crea asked the now-flustered porter.

"Mohamed. Call me Mo," the man said. "So sorry. I've only been on the job a week."

She waited longer than she should have to respond and the man stood at attention, looking half terrified. The moment felt important to Robert. A test.

"No apologies necessary," Crea finally said. She glanced over at Robert, who had moved closer to her so that his shoulder grazed hers. "I'd rather this than that you just waved us through." Robert exhaled—he'd been holding his breath—and they walked quickly to a narrow elevator, one in a long line. Crea pushed a button and they waited.

"This is a Candela building, isn't it?" Robert asked, feeling proud of himself.

"Yes," she said abruptly, as the elevator doors opened to reveal yet another uniformed man. This one she greeted with some genuine enthusiasm, but after asking him a few cursory questions about his wife's health, she was again silent.

"There are only what, ten, twelve of his buildings in the whole city?" Robert asked.

"I wouldn't know," she replied. Usually she would talk endlessly with him about architects and architecture, but he could tell by her tone that she was done. From the length of the elevator ride, they were going to one of those upper floors. Finally, the doors opened onto a private vestibule with a white and black marble floor, a brass umbrella stand, and a small wooden bench. The front door was painted red. The color of luck, and caution.

Letting them into the apartment, she told him to look around if he liked, but this was no architectural tour—she had a checklist and was off to her tasks. A dog yapped in what sounded like a distant country, but was actually the maids' rooms upstairs—two employees, a couple, had remained in residence. Walking through a pair of French doors into a long sitting room, Robert went over to the wall and opened the heavy brocade drapery to reveal a panoramic view that stretched across the park. The windows were set deeply so that when he took a few steps backward, it was like looking at a picture within a picture. Long beams of sunshine streamed across the Persian rug and across the furniture covered in white sheets.

He did not see most of the duplex—many of the rooms were

closed off, and he wasn't going to tag along behind Crea like a child. He walked through a wide entranceway, past a group of pictures covered by cloth. Only one painting remained visible — a favorite of the help? — of a voluptuous nude woman reclining on an unmade bed. The frame was gold and ornate. Walking closer, Robert saw that it was a Bonnard.

He walked from there into an enormous room with a grand piano and walls the color of the whipped lime in key lime pie. On one side of the room six hollows had been carved into the wall, the tops scalloped like giant seashells. Inside each one was a small, perfect white vase. On the ceiling, the molding formed intricate circles around two opposing glass chandeliers. He walked through an archway, surveying the dining room with its enormous oval table and chairs with backs upholstered in a striped silk fabric — at least thirty people could sit down to dinner, but he couldn't imagine three or four ever doing so. Returning to the room where he'd started, he approached the fireplace, where a wide marble mantel was crowded with photos, mostly of Crea.

In one photo, she was a redheaded baby resting on her father's wide shoulders; in another, a toddler leaning against her mother; and in a third, she wore a school uniform and held her father's hand. Then a girl of ten or eleven riding a pony, her chin tilted defiantly in the air, her expression surprisingly serious. The rest were older and more giddy: Crea attempting to blow out the candles on a sixteenth-birthday cake; Crea throwing a square cap up in the air; Crea in what he assumed was her early twenties, water-skiing in a bikini top and tiny shorts. Robert felt somehow disappointed; it might have been nice to see her with braces, or something, anything, to mar the smooth surface of a girl who appeared to have been born attractive, smart, and pampered, and remained that way, growing into a glamorous woman without so much as a bruise. But there were no photos of her in adolescence, few of her as a teenager, really.

When Crea came downstairs a few minutes later, she found him staring at a wedding photo of a very young Jack Alexander with his thin, dark-eyed, black-haired bride, her skin porcelain, her expression so serious next to Jack's boyish grin. Crea's mother was a classic beauty, prettier than Crea, though he felt guilty for thinking it. Crea looked more like her father. In the photo, her mother wore a lace dress with an enormous train that spun out airily around her feet in a wide circle.

"My parents," Crea announced, coming up behind him. "Totally different temperaments, as you can see."

"I can't imagine growing up here," Robert said, turning around. "I can't get a foothold on imagining it. Who are you?"

"What a strange question."

"Have you seen how most people live in this city?"

"It's just an apartment," she replied. "We moved here when I was seven. My mother had always wanted to live in this building, grew up just down the block. I don't know why Dad agreed to buy it, probably because it's a hard building to get into, very exclusive, and he likes to prove himself in that way, but then he disliked the place from the minute we got here. He likes contemporary architecture and decor. I always thought he developed that aesthetic in reaction to my mother, who loved all things old-fashioned—her greatest desire was to create a place stuck in time, whereas my father is all about what's coming next." As she said this, she took up two fingers of his right hand, and he turned around and looked at her. "They fought a lot, though you'd never know it when they entertained. That was really their best time, and Dad still likes entertaining here—these big old places were meant for parties." She dropped his fingers and walked over to the couch, adjusting the cloth cover on it, and then moved toward the window, drawing closed the heavy draperies, so that they stood in semidarkness. "I wish he'd sell it. The apartment is too big for him, and he hates the furniture. I never understood why he didn't redecorate after she died, though there's only so much variation you can force without ruining all the details. Anyway, the market is horrid."

"Why the gap in pictures?" he asked, smiling. "Where is the Crea in braces and pigtails?"

She frowned.

"I meant it affectionately, darling."

"I had a back brace," she said. "Curvature of the spine, diagnosed at twelve and a half. Because of it, I couldn't go away to school. I associate the brace with living here, to be honest, and it's probably why I don't like this place much. I hated that brace, like wearing a giant cage, a big contraption with a chin rest. The first time I had to put it on, my mother wept. Appearances were very important to her. You probably noticed how beautiful she was."

"No more beautiful than you," he said, aware that there were times when a man must lie, and this was one of them.

"My father never changed when he saw me in the brace," she said softly. "He loved me the same, looked at me the same." She was standing now, in the dim light, on the other side of the room, and he could barely see her, only hear her words. "Sometimes I think he saved me, Robert. That impartial, paternal love. People looked away, honestly, but Dad smiled at me, always, like I was the most beautiful girl in the world. He was working long hours at the firm then, building it, and still he found time for me. He took me to Broadway shows and art exhibitions, knew that I needed him more because my mother was so clearly unable to handle the whole thing. He knew I'd try to get out of wearing the brace, so he was very strict. Anytime I'd cry and whine and my mother would want to let me slide, he'd be very strong and tell me that someday I'd be happy I wore it. And he was right. Once I got the thing off, everything changed."

"How do you mean?"

She moved closer, came and stood by him in front of the fireplace. She was nervous; he'd never seen her fidgety. "That summer, the summer I turned sixteen, I worked part-time at my old camp as a water-skiing instructor. It was a bogus job, really, an excuse to have fun, but for the first time boys noticed me. I went with the other girls to a Sears in town and bought a tiny yellow bikini, went from wearing all this fabric and metal to wearing almost nothing at all. It felt wonderful, powerful." She pointed to the photo of herself on water skis in that same bikini. "All I wanted was be touched and looked at. A lot of boys fell in love with me that summer, I think; I was in love with life. And maybe I still am, maybe it comes from that awful time. Once I was out of the brace, my mother forgave me for being ugly those three years and bought me lots of clothes, but I never forgave her. We were not close, even when she became ill. There was a difference, I realized, between how Jack loved me and how she did, and I'd seen it up close. By senior year, I'd come into myself, more than that, even. I was a hellion, sneaking out of school, meeting older boys, constantly in New York, running around the Village."

"And you still like to be touched," he said, taking her in his arms.

"Being caged like that, you appreciate the feeling of skin against skin. I always told myself that I'd know the man for me by his touch." She looked into his eyes, and he kissed her.

"I don't like to talk about this," she said, "so let's not again, if that's okay."

"Sure, of course," he said. She was not a complicated person so much as a person with a story. Everyone came with a story. People revealed themselves as an act of intimacy; women did so to make sure that men felt protective and fell in love with them, or so he'd always thought. So why, after such a story, did he not feel more for her?

A WEEK LATER, on the Friday after the blackout that had paralyzed the city for twenty-five hours and kept them, mostly, in Crea's bed, they were finishing up dinner in a small French restaurant off Gramercy Park, when Crea put down the dessert menu and announced that he had to come to Tuxedo Park to meet her father. "Soon he'll think that I'm making you up."

"I could almost say the same thing about him," Robert replied. "Other than when he welcomed us on the first day, I've hardly laid eyes on him."

"He's not in the office as much in summer," she said.

"Yes, well, he rules by reputation, and the occasional appearance when we least expect it," Robert replied. On the few summer days that Jack was in the office, everyone knew it. The buzzing, from associates and partners alike: *Jack's in. Let me tell you what Jack said to me in the men's room. Have you seen Jack?* It was code to not linger in the halls, to keep your door open, to be on your toes. A, L and W's staff and colleagues endlessly ran after him. And yet, the few times he'd observed Crea's father in conversation in a hallway, he seemed always to be looking over his companion's shoulder, as if waiting for someone better to come along. His patrician manner of speaking was legendary, but only in the worst of dive bars far from the office — where summer associates and the occasional first-years sometimes congregated — were imitations ever attempted. His fellow summer associate, Wilton Henry, was the best at these, although he, like the rest of them, had heard Jack speak only a few times. Henry, a former child prodigy on the violin, had an ear for sound, and an eye on the real estate department, and Robert considered him his stiffest competition. He didn't know if he even wanted to spend his career at A, L and W, but he certainly wanted the offer, wanted the option to decide.

"And it would be good for your career," she added, "to spend a weekend with Jack."

"For him to know I'm having sex with his daughter would be good for my career?" he whispered. "How, exactly?"

"Oh, he doesn't care about that."

"I've never heard of a father who didn't care about that."

"He long ago gave up trying to control me."

"When we met, you said he did nothing but try to control you. I think your words were, 'treats me like an infant.'"

"Can't you be like other men and ignore most of what I say?"

"Great," he said, smiling. "We can spend the weekend in the city." He slowly finished off what was left in his wineglass, saying nothing more.

"That's all you have to say for yourself?"

"You just told me to ignore you."

"I'm not that easily deterred, smart aleck," she replied.

No, he thought, easily deterred was not how he would describe her. Though she got what she wanted so sweetly, and with such good humor, that he wondered if she'd ever been refused by anyone. She leaned closer. "You need to come out to the house. I'm tired of arguing with Dad about why I can't be there, or going alone and missing you all weekend." She paused, twisting a curl fetchingly around her finger. "You said you like to swim. Or we could take the boat out. And some of my friends come up to see their families, so it's not just old people. Like I said, it could be good for your career—don't you want them to offer you a job after graduation?"

He was ambitious, and she knew it. Amazing that she was willing to extend herself that way, dangling the advantages of her situation in front of him, as if he hadn't already thought about it.

"You make a very good case," he said. It was not that he didn't want to go—he did. She was right; this could be a chance to distinguish himself, assuming he made a decent impression. But there was a big risk. He had no choice but to be honest with her. To do otherwise, in his situation, was to court disaster. He took her hand. "We haven't actually been seeing each other for that long, you know? And meeting a woman's family, well, it's a statement of serious intent, at least I think it is."

He could see the flicker of recognition, as if a light went out in her eyes, if just for a moment. And then she regained her composure so instantaneously that had he not been studying her face carefully, he'd have missed it completely. "I've brought plenty of men to Tuxedo, Robert. And I haven't married a single one of them. No one will regard you as more than one in a long line unless I say that they should." She pushed a stray hair behind her ear and regarded the dessert menu with great interest.

"Crea, look at me," he said. "This is the best summer I've had in a very long time. I adore you. But maybe I'm just more cautious by nature."

"Men fall in love with me," she said, looking him in the eye and smiling. "They always have, since I was seventeen. And you will, too." Her voice lifted suddenly, as if she'd already put the whole conversation behind her. "That settles it, then; I can tell Jack that you're coming?" She squeezed Robert's knee under the table, not knowing how ticklish he was there, so that he gave out a high-pitched, helpless yelp, a sound somewhere between laughter and pain, prompting a passing waiter to stop and ask if he was feeling all right.

CHAPTER TWENTY-NINE

Tuxedo Park

Tuxedo Park, forty miles northwest of Manhattan, was developed in 1886 by tobacco baron Pierre Lorillard as a private lakefront resort where he and his friends could spend their time reveling in the outdoors before the start of the Newport season. When Lorillard's grandson Griswold decided to copy the Prince of Wales, wearing a short dinner jacket and black tie to a ball, he simultaneously gave the tuxedo its American debut and gave his grandfather the name he'd use for his new community. The etiquette authority Emily Post grew up in Tuxedo Park. Her grandfather built some of the original cottages.

All of this history Robert read in a book he found in the New York Public Library — if he was going to spend a weekend with Crea's father in a place called Tuxedo, then he would at least be prepared. On microfiche, he read old articles about the various debutantes who continued to bow at the town's famous Autumn Ball. Looking at articles from the 1960s, he searched anxiously for Crea's name, but was relieved to find no mention of her.

Tuxedo Park was a gated community. Within the Park's confines was a private lake, eleven hundred acres of parkland, and the country's second-oldest golf course, but the difference between being inside the Park and out was not money—many of the surrounding residents were heads of major corporations—but birth and background. Crea tried to assure Robert, on the ride from Manhattan, that Tuxedo Park residents were misunderstood. She insisted that they had a sense of humor about themselves.

Robert had rented a convertible, refusing to be picked up by Jack's driver and wanting the freedom to come and go as he liked. They were there in an hour, though as they drove through the village, he wondered if his anticipation of Tuxedo would utterly overshadow the reality. The homes he saw, built into surrounding slopes overlooking a distant river, might have had remarkable views, but they were nothing thrilling—boxy suburban ranches and shingled faux Colonials. But then they passed through the guarded entrance to the Park—Crea smiled at the guard, who waved jovially—and the houses instantly transformed.

On West Lake Road, the lawns were as big as public gardens, with curving driveways the length of country roads. The structures themselves were mostly Tudor and Gothic revival style with turrets and domed rotundas like castles out of a children's story, where some poor princess was imprisoned for having selected the wrong man to love. *If these are the carved-up mansions of the original families,* he wondered, *my God, what did the originals look like?* Many of the homes were carefully camouflaged by shrubbery and tall trees, difficult to see in their entirety, but the Alexander house came quickly and luridly into view—a two-story wooden structure with windows all around, so many windows that the house itself appeared almost to be made of glass. True, Crea had said that her father hated the Park Avenue apartment, but Robert wondered how it was possible that the same man lived in both residences.

In the open entrance hall, a large gush of water spewed endlessly from a block of marble. So much midafternoon light came through so much glass that he was glad he'd kept on his sunglasses. "I suppose your family never had to worry about throwing stones," Robert said.

"Uh-uh," Crea replied, "and you're the first person ever to make that joke."

On the pale green wall behind the fountain was a lithograph, on an enormous canvas, that had been divided in four: all four images were of Crea in her late teens, with a smudge of pink across her lips, comically orange hair, and emerald green eyes. Crea had told him that the only way to understand art or photography was to look at it as carefully as possible, that there was no mystery; you simply had to invest in that care. He looked clockwise, trying to figure out which Crea he had come to know: in one she was half-smiling at the viewer, as if she had a secret; in another, she looked off to her left, seeming distracted; in a third, she pushed her hair behind her ear and looked down, and in the fourth, she bit her lip seductively.

"I hate how he has that out in front," she said. "So embarrassing."

"How old were you?"

"Not quite eighteen," she said.

"This house," he whispered. "Not exactly what I expected."

"Le Corbusier wanted to rip out the center of Paris and replace it with a dozen towers in a park," Crea said. "Daddy loves Le Corbusier."

"So he wanted to rip out the center of Tuxedo Park and replace it with a medical building?"

"I wouldn't say that too loudly. It was hard enough for him to buy here. He wanted to make a statement."

Somehow Robert had assumed her family to be original, but before he could say another word, a woman in a plaid housedress rushed at them, arms outstretched. He wasn't sure where she came from — three hallways met where they stood — and she embraced Crea extravagantly. "You've brought him, good," she said, and smiled at Robert. She had short gray hair and deep blue eyes that stood out all the more from a sallow face full of expression lines.

"Robert, this is the most important person in the house, Eleanor Dawes. And if she doesn't like you, you're in trouble. She practically raised me."

"Then I owe her a thank-you," Robert said, and held out his hand.

"Well done, Crea," Eleanor said, and kissed him instead. "They're out back. Everyone's in a jolly mood. A lot more gin than tonic today."

Eleanor Dawes would not be a problem. Such women were always on his side. She'd put him, she said, in a bedroom next to Crea's. How discreet, Robert would think later when he saw the adjoining door, how liberated and yet proper. Crea told him to leave his bags in the hall and he obeyed, walking behind her into a long, rectangular kitchen. On the far right, two black women in polyester uniforms sat around a table, alternately smoking and peeling potatoes. They smiled and waved at Crea, who took Robert's hand firmly as the two passed through the sliding glass doors onto a large patio. Now Robert understood why Jack might have wanted to live in a glass house — he looked out on a panoramic view of green hills that sloped toward a lake.

"Beautiful," Robert said, half to himself.

"Here we are," Crea announced, then kissed her father on the cheek. "Daddy, this is Robert Vishniak."

Jack Alexander, tall, heavily built, with pale skin and red hair now diluted by gray, was a man who took up more room than Robert remembered from his occasional sightings at the firm. Taller than Robert, and much wider, he wore a tan golf shirt and green-and-white-plaid golf pants that might have made Robert laugh had Alexander's grip not been so tight. "A pleasure to meet you," he said. "Do you go by Robert or Rob?"

Robert, intensely focused on his host, was about to speak, when someone cut him off.

"He goes by Robert, and Robert only. Whatever you do, don't call him Bobby."

Coming toward him, smirking as if involved in a private joke that only Robert could understand, was Tracey. His smile seemed to say that the past was forgiven, even irrelevant. "Vishniak," Tracey said, clasping Robert on the shoulder as the two shook hands enthusiastically. "You're a damned sight for sore eyes."

They sat around the table, Robert between them, and ate tuna and pimiento sandwiches on warm white bread, and cucumber slices and potato chips—there was something of a summer camp for adults about Tuxedo. To their left, Crea's father lay on a lounge chair that barely contained him, flipping through a golfing catalog and injecting a comment into the conversation when it suited him, or looking over just long enough to notice if anyone needed a refill on their drinks. When he did, Crea thanked him, calling him "dear." He'd never heard a daughter call her father dear, but then expressions came out of her mouth that no other person could get away with, except perhaps the man who now sat on Robert's other side.

All through lunch they went back in time, connecting the dots to the moment when Robert had truly first met Crea, a high school senior in a green dress whom Tracey had been dragging around the Village in the summer after their first year of college. Now it made sense why her name, so unusual, had sounded familiar to him. He could recall everything, though much of it he kept to himself—he had come very close to losing his life that night, only to emerge from the subway and be mortified all over again. Hard to believe now—looking out at the view, drink in hand, sophisticated girlfriend beaming at him as if he were all that existed for her—that the evening had somehow played a role in getting him here.

"Amazing—that boy was you! You were Tracey's roommate! I remember it all now," Crea said. "I thought you were good-looking, at least what I could see of you in that light, but kind of rude. It was hot and I was worried about sweating in that taffeta dress. When Tracey introduced us I couldn't get you to look at me."

"She's not used to men ignoring her. Are you, darling?" Jack interrupted.

"But Cre, when were we ever in the Village together?" Tracey asked. "When did I ever run into Robert in the city? I think you two must be making this up."

"Mark Pascal was supposed to take me, but he canceled, probably for a family event. You know how tight-knit they get at Christmas time. Anyway, he palmed me off on you."

"You have some memory," Tracey said.

"Yours is a bit fuzzier," Crea replied, reaching over and patting him on the hand. "I just can't get over this! I don't know why we didn't make the connection sooner."

"So you know Mark Pascal, too?" Robert asked.

"Look to your right, over there, that's the Pascals' house," she replied, pointing off in the distance; any house that would be close would still be very far away.

She was practically giddy. Relieved, perhaps. Had she worried, too, that he might not fit in? "We haven't talked much about college," he said. "I'm too caught up with law school."

Crea's father got up and announced that he was leaving them, off to his golf game. "Do you golf, Mr. Vishniak?"

"No, but I'm learning."

"Play tennis?" he asked.

"Yes, but not well." He'd never had a lesson, had just picked it up, badly, in college, assuming that his childhood love of handball would transfer to a game with a racquet. It didn't.

"Vishniak's worst quality is his honesty," Tracey interjected.

"I'm sure you'll find plenty to amuse yourself with," Jack said distractedly, and walked quickly toward the house. For a big man, Robert observed, he walked with a light step.

Tracey looked much the same as he had in college—his hair

was a little shorter and bleached even blonder by the sun, and his ruddy face already showed some of the lines that would mark him as an outdoorsman and a heavy drinker, but the basic man was the same as he remembered. Even his clothes were back to what they had been freshman year — shorts and cotton tennis sweater, small round sunglasses, sneakers so white that they sparkled in the sun.

On the other hand, Mark Pascal, when he arrived about twenty minutes later, having been hastened by an excited call from Crea, was almost unrecognizable. He had lost all his hair, was thin and haggard-looking, and seemed, if anything, to have shrunk. He was in jeans and riding boots — he'd ridden his horse over and walked up from the stables, and he was sweating considerably, so much so that before shaking Robert's hand, he took a handkerchief from his pocket and mopped his forehead. "Vishniak, I knew you'd pop up again one of these days," he said. "You always liked to be in the thick of things."

"No, that was you," Robert replied. "How's the newspaper business?"

"I'm not in the newspaper business," Pascal said, kicking at a stone with his boot. "I'm working for my father now."

"Real estate, wasn't it?"

"Residential development. Amazing what you remember," Pascal mumbled.

"Robert and Crea seem to have much better memories than we do," Tracey pointed out.

Robert remembered it so well, how Pascal had announced to him, the first time they ever met, that he would never work for his father, that it was all a trap that only he and Tracey were aware of. Why, at age twenty-nine, did Pascal look so old and disappointed? So silent and uncomfortable? And Tracey, once so reticent in public, talked and commented much more than Robert remembered. Or perhaps Tracey knew things that Robert couldn't see and was anxious to smooth the way for his friend, as he always had.

"If we're going to ride," Mark said, "you'd better all get changed."

Robert had been on a horse exactly once, if he counted the old nags you could rent by the hour to plod through Fairmount Park. It was ninety degrees outside, and this was hay-fever season. He could not take the risk. "I thought riding was for the mornings," he said, "before the high heat of the day."

"Oh, Crea's oblivious to heat," Mark said.

"I figured we'd go out on the boat," Crea said, turning to Robert. "You'd like that, wouldn't you?" She wore a short green cotton shift and flat sandals, and her hair was up. Robert thought she looked especially flushed and pretty. She had two selves, really. She could be remarkably sensitive, like so many women, to the needs of the group, aware of the tiniest calibrations in the surrounding mood—yet at other times she was oblivious to the desires of others, anxious to get her way. Today she was gracious, the first self and not the second.

"I've got my heart set on riding," Pascal replied. "We can all take the boat out later."

"I'll tell you what," Tracey said. "You two go riding, and I'll take Robert to the pool. We can take a dip and then go out on our boat, if you like. Robert should see the club, and they, of course, should see him. Then you can join us there later and cool off. What do you think?"

"Anything you arrange is fine with me," Robert said. "I'm already wearing my trunks."

"You are?" Crea asked. "All this time?"

What had he been thinking? It was a reflex, a holdover from childhood that he hadn't thought much about until this moment. The rooming houses with their terrible accommodations, the family anxious to get right to the beach, or the smelly changing rooms of the public pools. When going anyplace to swim, you wore your suit under your shorts for convenience and expediency. But in Tuxedo, expediency was not the order of the day. These people *lived* here.

"If you're that anxious to swim, then by all means," Crea said. She gave Robert a passionate, but quick, kiss on the lips and walked off to change into her riding clothes.

"Good, then," Pascal said, mopping his head again with the cloth. "Who says you can't please everyone?"

CHAPTER THIRTY

Welcome to the club

Getting into the Tuxedo Club for the day required being with a member, and even then he had to sign a form. But once he passed the checkpoint, he could not help but admire the place. The main clubhouse was a one-story U-shaped building of wood and stone, with a low slate roof and intricate window designs running along both sides. On one side of the building, Tuxedo Lake stretched out underneath a series of wooded hills. Many of the members' boats were docked here. Around the outdoor pool, with its enormous veranda, waiters dressed in white jackets and dark pants served drinks and snacks. That day the whole place was decorated in red, white, and blue streamers, as if they were still recovering from the Bicentennial or were, more likely, terminally patriotic.

The air smelled of coconut suntan oil and French fries mixed with a faint aroma of seawater. Tracey informed him that you couldn't actually swim in the lake, or at least it wasn't recommended. The children there that day took advantage of the pool, playing by themselves in the shallow end, left to their water toys and private disputes. A handful of tall, glossy, gorgeously tanned teenagers stood by the diving board, flirting and posing, while their elders smoked and got slowly and reliably tipsy under large umbrellas, or left to go sailing. Most of the adult crowd looked more like grandparents.

Tracey had said that the club was aging. Adult children didn't want to come up here and be with their parents, wanted to go to hipper places.

"What about you and Mark?" Robert asked. "And Crea loves coming here."

"We have happy memories of childhood here. We were all a pack, at least until we went off to school, and then we were together in summers. But we don't have children, so we're out of the social whirl for our age-group. Anyway, I like it up here. The house would sit empty if it weren't for me. Despite all the rebellion and posing of my college years, I've become as conventional as the next guy."

Robert found that hard to believe. They claimed two chairs close to the pool and had barely sat down when Tracey suggested a race, just up and back. Robert agreed, realizing that it had been ages since he'd swam. "The most exercise I get these days is walking to the subway."

"Even better," Tracey said, getting up, "you won't feel as lousy when I beat you to a pulp."

"Don't underestimate me," Robert said, walking quickly to the edge and diving in, giving himself a few seconds of advantage. It felt good to move, to feel the power in his body, to blot out everything but each stroke as he moved toward the opposite edge.

Even with his head start, it was not even close. "Don't worry about it, Vishniak," Tracey said. "I swim every day. And play tennis."

"Best of three?" Robert asked.

"A glutton for punishment, as always."

*   *   *

FOUR RACES LATER, Robert dragged himself, panting, out of the pool to lie on his back, arms splayed. "That's it," he said. "I'm having a heart attack."

Tracey kicked him lightly in the side. "Get up," he said, "or the decorum police will have us arrested." He stared down at Robert, who was unaware, as always, of what he looked like, his skin the deeper brown that it became in summer without his even trying, his hair saturated with water, so shiny black that it was almost blue, and his long legs still muscular despite so many years of sitting in a cab. Tracey reached for his sunglasses, left nearby on a table, but he dropped them and they hit the cement, landing just a few inches from Robert's shoulder. Tracey bent over to get the glasses as Robert also reached for them, so that their fingers met for a moment. Robert pulled away abruptly, seeing Tracey's expression, remembering that stare of Tracey's like a familiar, vaguely unpleasant adversary. He stood up, walking a few steps to the dry spot where he'd placed the enormous bath towel provided by the club, and wrapped it around his waist. The two padded back to their seats as Tracey hailed the waiter and ordered a gin and tonic. Robert ordered club soda.

"I feel like an old man," Robert said.

"You don't swim like one. You did beat me twice. Where'd you learn to swim? Camp?"

"Boulevard Pools," Robert said. "Olympic-size swimming pool with diving boards, plus vending machines with all the soda you could beg your mother to let you buy. All thanks to the largesse of the city of Philadelphia."

"You won't exactly see a representative sampling here, I'm afraid," Tracey said. "No huddled masses yearning to breathe free."

"No drunken Frankfurt boys looking for a fight either," Robert said. "That was more my brother's province than mine; he'd egg on the nerdy neighborhood Jews to take back the deep end from the football players from Archbishop Ryan, then sneak away when the sparks flew. You think the way I grew up wasn't exclusive and gated in its own way?" He thought then about the pair of black kids, twin boys who'd come up from God knows where—North Philly, maybe? They left quickly. If not overtly kept out, blacks were not welcomed; they were ignored, or worse, depending on which side of the Boulevard dominated the pool that day. He was not going to be bitter on behalf of his people, or anyone else's for that matter. He was a guest; he was with Tracey. "I'm having a very nice time."

Tracey nodded, raising his glass in Robert's direction. "To our squandered youth," he said, "and to your romance."

"It's bad luck to toast with water," Robert said. "Didn't you tell me that once?"

"Glad you've remained such a stickler, Vishniak. Anyway, countless men would sacrifice life and limb to be in your situation. She's mad for you."

"Did she tell you that?"

"Anyone can see it."

"We're trying to take things slowly," he said. "Or at least I am."

Tracey laughed. "Good luck."

"Yes, Crea is a very determined sort of person, isn't she? Almost a force of nature. I've never known anyone so self-confident—not even you."

"It's all done with mirrors, in my case."

"I can't make the father out at all, though."

"Don't even try," Tracey said. "The only thing you can count on is that he'll be as protective as possible. Crea's the original Daddy's little girl."

"Yeah, I get that impression," Robert replied. "She told me about the brace."

"I don't know much about that. I was away at school, and my parents didn't socialize much with the Alexanders; it was Mark's parents who brought them around. But I do remember when they first started coming to Tuxedo. Crea was maybe ten, and Jack would come with her to the pool and spend all kinds of time coaching her on her swimming. Sometimes I'd see them walking hand in hand. I was terribly jealous. People didn't do that back then, show their children such blatant affection, let alone spend time with them, especially fathers."

"No," Robert said, "fathers were at work."

"Or off doing mysterious manly things," Tracey said. "Ours couldn't stand us. Anyway, you should ask Crea about it yourself. I feel like a gossipy old woman talking this way."

"Stay a gossip for a little longer," Robert replied, glad for the opening. "Tell me what's happened to the others. Cates? Van Dorn? They're not going to pop up when I least expect it?"

"Cates moved to France, to be near his mother. Married a French girl. He works in the diplomatic service."

"Perfect for him!" Robert said. "We'll be at war with the French in no time. Van Dorn? Was it the National Guard?"

"Spent a lot of time in Virginia then decided to stay there. Doing some kind of gentleman farming, not what you'd expect. Special cows or something, maybe they produce chocolate milk, who the hell knows? He sends one of those interminable Christmas letters every year, or his wife does, going on and on about which of their stock has calved. I hope they have children soon, for all our sakes."

"And Mark," Robert said, "what happened to Mark Pascal?" It was safer to talk about Mark's life, about the others, than to ask Tracey about his own, or to try to explain all that had happened to him, or even to continue their conversation about Crea, especially about Crea. Robert wasn't sure he was ready to live up to the assumptions people were making—it was why he had been reluctant to come in the first place. Maybe Tracey was relieved, too, to talk about others. Something had opened him up, or at least had made him more communicative. *Maybe,* Robert thought, *he's lonely.* Whatever it was, Robert found this new loquacity a relief. "For years all Mark talked about was journalism," he continued. "He was always at the *Crimson.* All he wanted, I remember, was to go to Vietnam and write about the war."

"He got a job at the *Globe* after college," Tracey said. "Started out as someone's researcher, I think, then graduated to captions or punctuation, I don't remember the details. But we were all relieved when they gave him Obituaries and let him write whole paragraphs."

"Probably everyone starts out that way," Robert said.

"I teased him as much as anyone — you know, obituary writer, graveyard shift, starting at the bottom, the *way* bottom; too many jokes came very easily. Perhaps we were all to blame, maybe even we were jealous that he'd stuck so thoroughly to his early ambition, or that he'd even had one. I was always on him for his grind of a job that kept him locked in the office late at night doing menial work, or got him sent to God knows what horrid Boston neighborhood at whatever hour because someone's grandfather choked on a bone in his chicken sandwich, when the rest of us were up here together or out somewhere having fun. Did you know that newspapers write obituaries in advance for certain people, to be prepared?"

"I didn't."

"That's what a man gets for a life of accomplishment — a prewritten obituary. Pretty sorry stuff if you ask me. They've got one on file for each of the former presidents, major artists, celebrities. They probably had one on file for my father before he kicked. He got a long tribute in the *Times*."

"I'm sorry," Robert said. "I didn't know. When did it happen?" There were years when he didn't read a paper. It was Watergate that had brought him back to the news.

"In 'seventy. Heart attack. Just past his fifty-eighth birthday. We Traces are not known for our longevity. Don't look so sad, really, no love lost here. Like a weight was lifted, actually. He died before I could disappoint him any further."

"Are you in the business, too?" It was an odd way to refer to what Robert knew to be a kind of dynasty. There were office buildings in the city named Trace, and a cruise line. His question sounded like something Vishniak would ask about a cousin's dry-cleaning business.

But he'd never quite known how to talk about what Tracey's family did — *work* did not seem the right word, or *business*. Those terms were too small, too simple.

"My little brother graduated last year from Harvard, and I suppose he'll step in eventually. He was too smart to look up to me, and he's done well at school. There are very competent people running things anyway, though of course I'm involved when needed — mostly to attend very dull stockholder meetings. On the whole, though, I do exactly what is expected of me up here and that is, blessedly, not very much at all. I read a lot; I'm in the Tuxedo Park Association, which lately has been more trouble than I ever wanted. I dabble in the market. This is what I was meant for, Vishniak. Nothing in particular. Public intellectual, in a private sort of way."

Robert wondered how someone so young could live here full-time. Tuxedo was beautiful, but it was not dynamic or exciting. Tracey had retired from the world before he'd really begun. Certainly he looked relaxed, content, but that was no guarantee with Tracey; he was good at faking it, better than Robert. Tracey put his hand into a dish of peanuts on a table to his right and tossed them, one by one, into his mouth. No, Robert thought, there was no way he had changed that much, but still it was easier to talk about Mark. "Did Pascal ever actually cover the war?"

"I gather a reporter has to work his way up to that. They're not going to send some kid out of Harvard with a few clips. Well, maybe they would have if someone had put in a word, though the *Globe* was always a liberal institution, and a Catholic one; maybe that's why Mark chose it, you know, outside anyone's sphere of influence. And Mark's father was against his taking the job in the first place, so he let him experience what it was to persevere without help."

"But Mark was getting what he wanted, I mean, he was writing, and he might have advanced further." Robert still didn't understand. Why did they all insist on making a tragedy, or a cautionary tale, out of what was just a first job?

"There's wanting and then there's wanting," Tracey continued. "Pascal, like me, has a low humiliation threshold. He made a few mistakes, had a few tongue-lashings from editors. Probably standard fare. It sounds like there are a lot of tempers in a newsroom, everyone thrown into those nasty little cubicles. I visited him once. The reporters were like rats in a maze."

"That's how entry-level people work," Robert said. "That's *life*."

"That's *your* life. You have a reason to want to *get* somewhere, and if need be, in the interim, or if your plans somehow fail, you can live on very little because you're used to it."

Robert felt Tracey's comment like a slap. He knew Tracey had not meant to offend him, but his words seemed to imply that by virtue of what Robert was used to, he would get less from the world and be contented with it. He signaled for the waiter; he would have a gin and tonic after all.

"Who knows if Pascal would even have been a good foreign correspondent," Tracey continued. "I can't see him in a tent in the mud. He has position and respect now that might have taken him decades to build as a journalist. Not to mention the potential to make real money. Plus his father's happy."

"But *Mark* doesn't look very happy," Robert replied. "And I doubt he needs the money. When did making his father happy factor in?"

"You know, they get older, or they get sick. It starts to matter. I never gave a damn about my father, but I worry about my mother now in a way I never did before. Though the woman still has more energy than both of us combined."

"How is your mother doing?" Robert asked, remembering that awkward lunch.

"Right now she's at a spa in Cap d'Ail with Cates's mother."

"My God, it's a small world you live in," Robert said. He was now back in it, like it or not, he thought, as if all roads led in this direction. Unfinished business, that's what it was. He was not so different from Barry — he still had things to prove.

"I'm lazy about making new friends. Real friends, anyway," Tracey said. "Which is why your arrival is a godsend, Vishniak."

The waiter arrived with his gin and tonic, and Robert wondered if he was supposed to tip him. He doubted it. Not in this place.

"Poor Mark," Tracey added.

"You just said that he's got it so good."

"The rest of us, me and Cates and Van Dorn, we didn't set out with such lofty ambitions. Less far to fall."

"You used to say things like that in college, about the uselessness of pinning your hopes on a goal. And I didn't think you really meant it. But I suppose you do."

"More than ever."

The waiter returned with a fresh drink for Tracey and more peanuts. Nearby, a child cannonballed into the water, and cold drops hit the bottoms of both men's legs. The water felt good, though moments later the child was screaming as a woman came and removed him, forcibly, from the pool.

"And then you show up with Crea. That can't be easy for Mark. He set out to get Crea years ago." Tracey paused. "I think he imagines that if he hangs around long enough, he'll wear her down. Or grow on her, like moss."

"In college, he was after Cates's sister—salivated over her for years, I thought."

Tracey glanced behind him cautiously. "Crea was always the one, since she was in high school. But he got crushes on lots of girls, I think. The man is hopeless with women."

"Practically every guy was gaga for Cates's sister, me included," Robert said, conjuring now the memory of her at that dance, the way her legs looked in those lace tights, the point of her chin, her enormous eyes. "But she was off the market, if I remember."

"Married Charlie Webb. Those two were so madly in love it was almost sickening. He didn't go to school with us, but we all knew him. Stupid tradition in his family, the oldest sons going off to West Point. Died in Vietnam, you know."

"That's lousy," Robert replied, though his mind was still in the past, at Smith College. "We had a little tussle once, Claudia and I. Some mixed signals there; maybe I deserved it, but she humiliated the hell out of me, like no other girl I'd ever met."

"Yes, Claudia's quite good at that," Tracey said.

"So she's around, too?" Robert asked, sitting up ever so slightly.

Tracey nodded, then took another sip from his drink.

"Did she remarry?" Robert asked.

"You might say that," Tracey replied. "She's my wife."

CHAPTER THIRTY-ONE

Outdoor grilling

At dinner that night they sat outside, surrounded by glowing yellow candles perched on tilted spears and stuck into the ground. The guest list had expanded since that afternoon. Now Tracey and Claudia were included, and Mark's father, Trenton Pascal, as well as Mark's younger sister, a surprisingly plain, tired-looking young woman named Mignonne — Robert could just hear Vishniak saying, *Leave it to the rich to name a kid after a steak.* Trenton Pascal was short and bald, with a strong resemblance between father and both siblings — Robert remembered him only vaguely from the time he'd taken all Mark's friends to dinner. He shook Robert's hand enthusiastically, and his manner and easy way of chatting reminded Robert of the way Mark had been in college, making him wonder if son and father had switched roles.

Crea's father and Mark's father manned the barbecue grill, an ornate contraption at the end of the patio. A black woman in a dark dress and white apron, one of the two women who had been sitting in the kitchen when Robert arrived, moved back and forth between the barbecue grill and the table, then the table and the kitchen. Crea's father called her Dinah, and Robert imagined that she must have been very warm—it was a hot evening and she was wearing stockings and polyester, and the barbecue gave off visible clouds of heat.

Crea stood over in a corner talking with Tracey and Claudia, her face flushed with sun, while Mignonne Pascal remained on her own at the other end of the vast yard, throwing a stick with one of the dogs. Tuxedo was known as a community hospitable to wildlife. As Robert stood by the table, he noticed a possum limping along by a bush, and a wild rabbit, not four feet from the barbecue. Just an hour or so before, Robert and Crea, taking a walk, had seen three cars sitting in the middle of the road, waiting for a doe and her fawn to cross.

Robert heard Crea laugh, a low, throaty laugh he liked, not too melodious, not too ladylike. She wore a white T-shirt and white jeans, flat sandals. Her muscled thighs looked good in the jeans, and the thin T-shirt was tucked in and clingy, making Robert aware of the contours of her body. Earlier that day, after riding for over an hour, she had shown up at the pool, Mark in tow, and quickly removed her shift to reveal a black bikini. She, too, had wanted to race him. Was everything a race with these people? Did they ever just get in and splash around? They worked awfully hard at their leisure. Tracey and he had just had a rematch—again Tracey beat him two to one—and he was tired of racing. So Crea suggested that they play volleyball; there was a floating net and balls available for this purpose, but Robert wanted to relax. She had pushed him playfully. So antisocial. Then she snapped her towel at him, and he picked her up and dumped her in the deep end. As she fell, she pulled his foot and threw him off balance, so both of them ended up in the pool. They trod water and she kissed him, pressing her body against his. "Let's go home," she said.

They got out of the pool and walked toward the others, shaking off water. Crea sounded defiant, almost arrogant, as she told them that they were going home to take a nap.

"Weren't we going out on the boat?" Mark said. "Wasn't that the plan?"

"We're going off plan," Crea said gently. "We'll sail tomorrow. Have a drink, Mark."

Now, four hours later, Robert looked back on his day. Having swam for miles then made love twice to his girlfriend, somehow he had allowed himself to be dragged off for a before-dinner "walk" with Crea that turned into a two-hour hike in the woods, which forced them to half-walk, half-jog back, shower together not half as quickly as they should have, and rush down, both with damp hair and flushed faces, just as her father was firing up the barbecue. Everyone looked a little drowsy except Crea. On their walk, she had told him, "I'm always happiest in Tuxedo; it's such a peaceful place, isn't it?"

Robert wasn't sure if *peaceful* was exactly the word he would have used—*active*, perhaps, or *civilized*—but he replied that she was lucky to feel that way about a place, and left it at that.

Mark Pascal, who was manning the bar, came over to where Robert stood by the table and asked him if he wanted a drink. "Maybe later," Robert replied. What he needed right now was coffee, but he settled for iced tea. He poured a glass, drank it down and, though it was a little sweet for his taste, poured another.

When Jack had decided that the steaks and corn were done, and the salad and fresh tomatoes from the garden had arrived along with giant bowls of potato salad, the older men joined the others around the table. Crea's father's face was shiny pink from the heat. He and Mark's father sat at either end like the heads of a corporation. Robert sat between Mignonne Pascal and Claudia Trace, and, across from him, Crea sat between Mark and Tracey.

He didn't know how to talk to Claudia. Sitting next to him, she hardly said a word. Still beautiful, with large hazel eyes and the same sleek black bangs, she was much thinner than he remembered. Her short red dress came up high at the neck, but it had no sleeves and her arms were thin as twigs. She reminded him now of Audrey Hepburn, a good actress to be sure, but he'd never fantasized about bedding Audrey Hepburn and he didn't know a man who had. He asked Claudia to pass the salad, wondering if she could lift the bowl, and when she turned toward him, he blurted out, "Claudia, I remember dancing with you to 'The Shoop Shoop Song.' "

When she smiled, he noticed a furrow between her eyes. "I danced with a lot of boys to 'The Shoop Shoop Song,' " she said softly.

She didn't remember him. What a relief. Not knowing what else to talk about other than the past—her brother? her marriage? all minefields of their own—and still somehow unable to let go of the fact that she had once rejected him, the only woman to do so, he pressed on.

"I don't think I treated you very nicely," he said, a statement he only half-believed. Really, he thought it was she who'd led him on.

She shrugged, as if to ask why he bothered. "I had just gotten engaged, hadn't I? Now I remember." She toyed with her food, and then motioned to Tracey, who, though seemingly involved in conversation with Crea's father, passed her a package of cigarettes and a lighter. Robert picked up her lighter and lit her cigarette for her.

"I'm sorry about your fiancé," he began, wondering why on earth he had chosen this line of conversation. Yet he had begun, and how to switch directions?

"First husband," she corrected. "Charlie and I were married before he shipped out."

She stared into her plate and he tried finally to talk about the quotidian—the beautiful weather, the coincidence of Crea bringing him here. "I missed Tracey, you know?"

"Yes, Tracey is a good friend," she replied, smiling so sadly that he knew, in that moment at least, she had decided to show him something of her real feelings. Tracey would have been a safe choice, an accommodation.

They'd reached an impasse—for him to acknowledge that he understood that look, and why, would have been impossible here or, perhaps, anywhere. He had to settle for communicating to her, somehow, his sympathy. Quickly, furtively, he squeezed her hand. She remained silent, still as a statue, and now, awkwardly, he searched for another topic, feeling as if he were drowning. "So," he said, taking a sip of tea, "what's it like living up here full-time?"

"I'm glad you and Tracey are in touch again," she said, pushing some potato salad around with her fork. "So many of his friends have moved away. He only lives up here because of me, really. I can't take crowds. And I need the fresh air, and my garden."

"Tuxedo isn't much of a sacrifice," Robert said, suddenly aware that the others around the table were involved in another conversation. He and Claudia, relieved, turned their attention outward. They were all talking about real estate.

Tracey had been made vice president of the Tuxedo Park Association, which represented the home owners within the Park. Tracey, Jack, Mark, and Trenton talked about land development—the village of Tuxedo was one of the last places in Orange County with so much untrammeled space, not to mention two forests, but some of that space was owned by a corporation that was anxious to develop, and there was litigation going on around some of the town's restrictive zoning. Strangely, it was the people in the Park, the old families, who were for the development, while those outside the Park, the younger and more upwardly middle class, fought it—probably because it was their view and quality of life that would be affected.

"I wouldn't have expected you to be for development," Robert said to Tracey. "I mean, I just assumed that you'd want to keep this all as it is."

"We're not *for* development, exactly, so much as we know it's inevitable and we want to try to control it," Tracey said. "The people who want to stop the corporation from developing land that they own already have their heads in the clouds. Change is inevitable."

"Taxes will go down with development," Robert said. "Property values will go up."

"Money isn't the issue," Crea's father snapped. "Maybe for some, but for those of us at this table, a larger issue is the future of this place. There's not enough young blood coming in, so we need a younger tax base. Will my grandchildren still want to come here?"

"What grandchildren?" Crea asked, with excellent comic timing.

Jack clearly did not like to be interrupted—but Crea could do anything, Robert supposed, because he laughed like the rest of them, then continued: "Can we exert some influence in how the area will look? Look at that night sky, Robert. Have you ever seen so many stars? No skyscrapers to interfere. This is about more than money!"

He sounded angry; Robert wondered why.

"Our taxes are astronomical," Claudia whispered, patting Robert's arm sympathetically.

Had Robert touched a nerve? He rather enjoyed it, actually. As Dinah cleared the plates away, Robert addressed his next comment to Tracey, from whom he could, at least, depend on a dispassionate reply. "Isn't it a terrible time to build?"

Pascal answered instead. "The corporation's doing a joint venture. Believe me, they'll make money. Too many incentives these days not to pounce. But a lawsuit's pending. The situation is more complicated than we're going into—"

Robert doubted the situation really was so complicated. They just weren't going to discuss it in front of him anymore. Crea, sensing that he was getting annoyed, said she was finding all this real estate talk dull. Then Dinah came back carrying a big strawberry shortcake decorated with gobs of fresh cream. All conversation stopped as the guests broke into applause. Jack praised Dinah's desserts to Robert, who nodded and pretended to be pleased, when his mind was elsewhere, trying to translate what had just happened.

He had assumed them a closed community, insular. And perhaps they still were, at least in their club memberships, but they were practical, too. The world was changing, had changed already, and old money acknowledged this when new money somehow could not. Maybe it *was* possible to learn from the past. He wanted to be optimistic, wanted to believe that this world, like Crea herself, was easily comprehensible. It had not been to him in college, but in dating Crea, Robert stood even closer, had lived through more in the interim, and told himself that now he might finally learn to feel at home.

CHAPTER THIRTY-TWO

Robert discovers a few more things about Crea

After returning from Tuxedo, Robert was busy at work, had finally been given something interesting to do: research for a partner who specialized in air rights—and air rights fascinated him. Only in New York was the air over buildings literally for sale, used endlessly as a negotiating tool. The associate who'd given Robert the task had assured him that his memo would only go into another memo that would then go to a partner. It wasn't much, but it was better than combing through tax filings. Coming on the heels of his trip upstate, Robert wondered if this sudden change wasn't in some way due to Crea's father. Likely Jack had far too much to do to be bothered, but what if Crea had been right and the trip had improved his profile? More likely Phillip Healey had seen how dour Robert looked in the halls and asked someone to toss him a bone. Robert stayed late, typing the memo himself.

He got out of the office at just past ten and did not want to go to Crea's—rather, he wanted to, but at the end of the day she wanted conversation from him and he wasn't in the mood. He ate dinner at his desk and declined the firm car home, hoping a walk in the evening air would clear his mind. He walked west to Fifth Avenue, then continued on Central Park South, staying on the park side, past the men offering carriage rides and the vague odor of horse manure. Then he crossed Columbus Circle, bought a newspaper, and walked up Broadway, turning onto Columbus. He was approaching Eighty-first Street when he saw Tracey coming toward him, accompanied by another man.

"What are you doing on the West Side?" Robert asked, shaking his hand.

"On my way to dinner with Juan Carlos," Tracey said, as if that were explanation enough. He introduced Robert to the short, dark-haired man, who smiled vaguely in response. "I'm in the city until Friday," Tracey continued. "Come for dinner tomorrow?"

Robert agreed and Tracey gave him the address, in the East Fifties, near the Museum of Modern Art. "Tomorrow at nine, then? Must run..."

Robert watched them turn onto Eighty-first, heading toward the park. That block, he knew, had no restaurants. The enormous Beresford apartments took up most of it, with its long stretch of office space and endless side doors, and then a small tourist hotel attached only to a coffee shop.

THE NEXT NIGHT ROBERT ARRIVED at Tracey's while his host was still preparing dinner — meaning a waiter from a nearby restaurant was arranging two serving dishes of pasta and several sides on the table. "I remember that you liked Italian. I hope that's okay," Tracey said.

"I'm starving," Robert said. "I'm not sure I even need a plate."

"Use one anyway," Tracey said.

The man who'd brought the food bowed and left. Robert noted how Tracey, being Tracey, had paid and tipped him when he got there, so no money had to change hands in front of a guest. He told Robert to help himself, and Robert heaped Pasta Bolognese onto his plate. The smell was heavenly. As Tracey poured the wine, Robert reflected for a moment on how wonderful it was to be back in his friend's good graces, how comfortable he now felt with him.

"So will we see you next weekend in Tuxedo?" Tracey asked.

"I'm still recovering from my last visit. Not to mention my trip to Jack's place in the city."

Tracey took a sip of wine. "Claudia and I were hoping you and Crea would be regular weekenders in Tuxedo. You're one of my few old friends whom Claudia actually likes talking to. You'd do me a favor if you made a point of drawing her out a bit. You're good at that."

"When I'm up there, if I'm up there again, I'm happy to talk to Claudia for as long as she likes," Robert said, thinking this an odd conversation.

Tracey smiled. "You'll be back sooner than you think, I'd wager." He took a sip of his drink. "You remember Claudia in college, how she never shut up? Now she's quiet. I find her silence very companionable, actually — part of what attracted me in the first place. But sometimes I think she spends too much time alone or with just me."

"I think they call that marriage," Robert said, shoveling a big forkful of pasta into his mouth. He hadn't eaten since noon, was so hungry that it was hard to remember his manners. "Does Claudia eat? She's much thinner than I remember."

"I like them on the thin side, Vishniak," Tracey said. "Thin women look better in clothes."

Robert wiped his mouth. "Women with a little meat on them look better out of clothes."

Tracey put down his fork — he had hardly touched his

food—and sat back in his chair. "As you know," he said, "I prefer my women dressed."

"So nothing's changed there?" Robert asked, staring into his plate.

"Most of the time, no," Tracey said. "But things are good between us. I love her, Vishniak. Maybe not the way you love Crea, but I love her."

At the mention of his love for Crea, Robert was anxious to change the subject. "You own this place?" he asked. The apartment was smaller than he'd expected, cozy, with bright area rugs and Dutch Modern furniture. The view stretched so far down to the east that he could see a narrow slice of the river.

"Bought it after college. We're all called 'Penthouse' up here, all three upper floors. Marketing." Tracey shrugged. "It's my private retreat. I'm particular about who I invite."

"I'm honored," Robert replied. "Looks pretty exclusive."

"People mind their business, which I like. It's not so hard to get into a building like this really, if you have the right name, know the right people. Which is of course my specialty."

"But Crea knows the right people, and she made a point of saying how hard it was for her father to get into Tuxedo, said the same thing about the apartment where she grew up. Pascal, too, made some comment to me about his father and Crea's being so close, and Trenton having a hand in helping Jack Alexander get into Tuxedo. What do they put you through?"

"You're considering a place on Park Avenue?"

"God, no, I just—they seem to assume that I know what they're talking about."

"Don't you?"

"Is it about money? Because I sure have noticed how no one talks about that."

"For the Alexanders it would be a little harder."

"How so?" Robert asked through a mouthful of pasta.

"I don't need to explain it to you of all people. What do you care about people's silly prejudices?"

"What prejudices?"

"I assumed that was part of your appeal to Crea."

"What appeal?!" Why was Tracey being so obtuse?

"I mean the fact that you're both Jewish," Tracey said, shaking his head and pouring his now-silent friend more wine.

CHAPTER THIRTY-THREE

First fight

All week, Robert felt annoyed with Crea, but he couldn't articulate exactly why. Finally they were lounging in bed that Friday, watching Johnny Carson, when she asked him how dinner had been with Tracey.

"Fine," he replied, as she picked up the remote and lowered the volume on the television.

"I wish we could see the two of them in the city," Crea replied. "It drives me crazy how that woman won't leave her house. She was such fun when we were younger. I looked up to her. Now she's, well, maudlin."

"She's had a hard time."

Crea rolled her eyes in response.

"Not everyone is as strong as you are, Crea."

"I'm not talking about me!" she snapped. "She acts like she's the only person who's suffered. Thousands of Americans lost loved ones in Vietnam. Thank God Nixon got us out."

"It may be about the only thing he did right."

"History will be kinder to him."

"Did you read that somewhere?" Robert asked. "Because no matter what, Nixon is still going to hell when he dies."

"I don't want to fight about Richard Nixon," she said, trying to take the remote from his hand. She looked at him. "You've been picking fights with me all week. What's wrong?"

"Why didn't you tell me you were Jewish?"

"Why would you care?"

"I don't," he said, but as he said it, he knew that, in fact, he did. Had she been Christian or Buddhist or anything else, her religion would make little difference. Barry had made a point, while visiting California the year before, of going to Disneyland on Yom Kippur. Much shorter lines, he said. But if his family's Judaism — with the exception of his mother's occasional Saturday synagogue attendance — was more culinary than scriptural, and if they didn't always exactly pay attention to what they were, well, they certainly knew what they *weren't*, and that was Jews who bought Christmas trees, changed their surnames, and attempted to pass for Episcopalian. He was somehow bothered by the "help" that the Pascals and Traces had given to the Alexanders to get them into the Jewish apartment — there was one, he knew, one Jewish apartment in most of the exclusive places on Park or Fifth, reserved for Jews who didn't look or act too Jewish, who kept a low profile and were just as anxious not to live around their own kind — and this disgusted him in a way he could not explain. Meanwhile, he stuttered on, oddly inarticulate, then began to cough.

"It never mattered to me," she said. "I wasn't bar mitzvahed like you."

"Bat mitzvah," he said. "If you're a girl. And how do you know I even was?"

"Because I just know, that's all. We didn't look Jewish, and my father said, 'Why create problems?' Mother was from a Spanish background, they lived in Paris until the war, and her parents were dead by the time I was born. My father's parents were Germans, they came in the early eighteen hundreds—I could have come out at the Autumn Ball if I'd wanted, could even join the DAR! Jack wanted it, but I refused. We fit in Tuxedo in most ways, and anyway, why bring it all up? The Jews were chased from England, then Spain and Portugal, and the places that haven't chased them out have butchered them. Is it any wonder that many who could join just don't want to belong to the club?"

"It isn't a club," he said. "Not everything is a club! That's the whole damned point." He could feel it now, the thinning of the air, the need to take shallower and shallower breaths. He stumbled out of bed and went for his suit jacket, but he couldn't find it, couldn't get to his inhaler. Crea got calmly out of bed and began to look, finally locating it as Robert had begun to wheeze. He was a portrait of confusion, an unsightly mess in the midst of her sangfroid.

When he'd recovered, and she'd made him a cup of tea, assuring him that she could, at least, boil water, they decided to stop fighting. Neither of them wanted to argue over religion—something that wouldn't really be relevant to their daily lives. But was this about religion? He could not describe what, exactly, made him feel a divide between them, when their shared, if distant, heritage should have brought them together. *Heritage*, that was her word. So neat and compact, ignoring the sloppy crossover from blood to culture to religion and back again.

As Robert sipped his tea, he thought of Gwendolyn. Such memories always cost him—he tried hard to avoid thinking of her most of the time, but now he could not help it. He had not known her background until she came for Thanksgiving, and his family had insisted that something was there—he'd seen later, of course, that her father was a Jew, an English Jew with a *goyishe* name, but none of it had mattered to Robert. So why did Crea's situation bother him? He could not figure it out. Unless the answer was simply that he did not love her, and he'd loved Gwendolyn, and so had been willing to accept anything that came along. Of course by the time he'd found out anything definitive about Gwendolyn's origins she was gone. Maybe if he were not Stacia's son, if he didn't look the way he did, or have the last name and nose he did, or fight that twang of Jewish Northeast that came, occasionally and without his consent, into his vowels, maybe if he didn't have all that which marked him so clearly as who he was, then he, too, would choose to leave well enough alone.

TWO WEEKS LATER, Robert's summer internship at A, L and W ended, and he was called into Phillip Healey's office. Thus far, only seven associates had received offers, less than half of the summer help, and only one offer in real estate — to Wilton Henry, whose mimicry had clearly done him no harm. The losers moped around the office, regaining face after several profligate long-distance phone calls at the firm's expense, then picked up their final checks and left early.

Robert stood stiffly in front of Phillip Healey's desk, his hands grasped together to keep them from shaking. Phillip put Robert quickly out of his misery. "We want you to come on board. In real estate." Healey grinned, then stepped forward, enormous palm out-stretched, adding that he was happy for him. "We had to make some tough decisions. In this climate, an offer is an act of faith."

"I'm honored," Robert said. What had been the criteria? He was never sure. But he had done his best. His personal life, he hoped, had not been a consideration. If anything, it would probably be a negative. But as Crea told him, he was one in a long line of boy-friends. For all Jack knew, he'd be gone from her life in a month or two. He had to treat this offer as separate from her, separate from Tuxedo and all of that. Otherwise, what had he gotten himself into? And yet, it was a job, a good job, in a time when jobs were damned hard to come by. As Healey's expression implied, he was lucky to have this chance. Robert waited for further instructions, but none came. "When do I need to tell you?" he finally asked.

"Tell me what?" Healey replied.

"If I accept?"

"November, in writing," he said. "This year all our offers have been accepted on the spot." He paused. "We all, that is the hiring committee, assumed your experience was positive?"

"Oh, yes," Robert replied. "I certainly learned a great deal."

CHAPTER THIRTY-FOUR

Down the shore

Robert's last year of law school would start in three weeks, but in the interim he had meetings at the *Law Review*; Nan was gone, off to her clerkship, and though he hadn't made editor, hadn't even tried, his class would be in charge now, ordering around the underlings. He was back to his schizophrenic lifestyle, so familiar now as to be almost comforting: power and prestige at *Law Review* meetings by day, cabdriving by night. He had spent more than he'd intended that summer, and he would have to make it up. If he'd been more careful, if he had not tried so hard to keep up with Crea, he could have taken these last few weeks of summer off, but there was nothing he could do about that now. At least he'd used his salary to enjoy himself.

Not ready to give up his claim on the Upper West Side apartment, he would spend the next few weeks sleeping in his bedroom on Eighty-fifth Street, no matter how proprietary Barry had become about the place. Robert's name was still on the lease — not that he intended to throw his brother out in the cold; rather, he just wanted to reclaim a little bit of what was his, mark his space again.

This was easier said than done, as now there was a third occupant of the apartment who was also marking his territory: Barry had gotten a dog, an English bull with a smashed-in face, enormous shoulders, and the breathing of a prizefighter. The dog was neurotic, having been rescued from starvation and God knows what else on the streets of Brooklyn, and he comforted himself by dragging his enormous balls across the wooden floors of the living room. But the dog was good-natured, despite what he'd suffered, and so Barry had named him Vishniak, after their father — a dubious honor, at best. Robert was determined not to let the presence of the slobbering, farting dog get in the way of his plans.

And with that, he would take a little break from Crea. He looked forward to the time away from her with a sense of relief. He was not always relaxed in her presence; then again, he was not a relaxed sort of person, not like Barry. If asked to choose between a night in his underwear watching TV and eating chips with his brother, or a night out with Crea, well, each had different attractions. But with Barry, Robert could be fully himself.

Robert had not yet told Crea of his job offer, though he suspected that she knew or, worse, that she'd had a hand in it. She always spent the last two weeks of August in Tuxedo. If Robert could, he might join her for a weekend at some point, as a sign of goodwill, but he did not communicate this intention. There had been no fight, no breach, only a strange feeling on his side that he needed time to regroup, and so he made no promises, gave no excuses as to why most of his August would be so full — too full for him to commit himself just yet.

Meanwhile, on that first weekend, he decided to go to Philadelphia. He had not seen his parents since Christmastime. Barry offered his car, and then himself as travel companion; Stacia and Vishniak would be pleased to see both sons at once. But then their mother had an idea — Cece was staying in Atlantic City all week, at the Deauville Hotel, and why didn't they drive down and see her?

Robert was suspicious. The Vishniak family, and specifically their mother, did not go in for spontaneity. Spontaneity implied the last-minute, the emotional and frivolous, and, hence, the expensive. Yet here she was, on a Wednesday, suggesting a jaunty adventure for the weekend.

"Good idea," he said cautiously. "I'll make reservations at the Deauville for two more rooms."

"We're not staying there. Cece can stay there; she got fancy in her old age. I'll call one of the rooming houses."

"Those days are over, Stacia. Are there even any rooming houses left? Let me pick up a couple of extra rooms at the Deauville for all of us, on my dime." On his credit card, but it was the same thing. He would not go back to one of those places, if they even existed anymore.

"I'm not sleeping in a seventy-dollar-a-night hotel room when there's no need. Forget it, mister."

"Then you sleep on Virginia Avenue, or better yet, go to Oriental with the needle freaks and the whores, I don't give a shit!" Robert yelled. "But Barry and I are staying at the Deauville." He hung up the phone, and the situation remained unresolved.

AND SO IT WAS that on the first Friday in August 1977, the brothers Vishniak and the dog Vishniak set off in Barry's old VW Bug, the front a different shade of blue than the back. In the trunk were two small overnight bags, one flannel dog bed, a box of doggy treats, three cans of beef-flavored Chuck Wagon, and a can opener. Vishniak the dog lay stretched out across the backseat on a towel, eating pieces of pastrami and coleslaw that Barry fed to him from his sandwich, until the animal passed out just as they were entering the New Jersey Turnpike.

Months before, Atlantic City had accepted gambling. The shore of their childhood, the brothers knew, was coming to an end—or at least the outlines of what was left of that shore. Could that be the reason for their mother's suggestion? Was Stacia getting sentimental on them? It seemed hardly possible. No, Barry said, their parents went to Atlantic City like homing pigeons because they didn't know where else to go, because Atlantic City was the only place they'd ever gone when they wanted to get away.

They had to make one stop just outside Trenton. Once off the exit, Barry directed Robert along a series of narrow streets and past a junkyard, which dead-ended at a tiny, aluminum-sided single house with several old tires and some discarded baby furniture out front—the kind of place, Barry said, where the pervs on TV cop shows always took their underage hostages. This was where Victor Lampshade now lived, alone, editing pornography and the occasional barely B movie, when he could get any editing work at all.

In his sunny kitchen with its friendly layer of filth, Victor served the two old friends a beer, and they caught up briefly. Then they went back out to the driveway, where Barry and Robert traded their small car for Victor's 1970 Buick station wagon and transferred dog, dog bed, and various bags into the larger vehicle. Then back onto the New Jersey Turnpike. Victor's car made a series of squeaking and heaving noises as if it were alive, as if it could breathe and might expire on them at any moment. When they finally reached Disston Street, they double-parked and added to the car: one father, with foldable wheelchair and surprisingly lifelike prosthesis wearing a black shoe and white sock; one mother, with battered faux leather suitcase with duct-taped handle and bottom; a plastic Korvette's shopping bag full of sandwiches and paper napkins; a warming tray; some plastic dishes; metal forks, spoons, and knives; an angel food cake; and two frying pans, which Robert did not argue over, despite the fact that he was not *under any circumstances* staying in a place with a kitchenette but would sleep in a regular hotel with clean towels supplied, where he could order off a menu and swim laps in a normal-size pool that did not border a major artery. All this he would have, he told himself, as he shoved a bag of bathing suits under a space in the front seat, if he had to kill her and climb over her dead body to get it. And then, slamming all doors, they got onto I-95, then across the Walt Whitman Bridge and into New Jersey again, heading for the Atlantic City Expressway.

In the glove compartment was Barry's freezer bag of various concoctions, everything from Percoset and lorazepam to a high-test mixture of hash and marijuana — plus Victor, in addition to his generosity with the car, had left Barry a few quaaludes, either knowingly or by mistake. Robert did not question the need for such supplies, even with their parents in the car, even with the cops stationed notoriously along that particular stretch of the Garden State Parkway, for he knew that a man had to do what he had to do to get through a weekend with his aging parents.

And so they were off, but to where? Their poor father stretched across a rather narrow, bunklike back section, forced there by a need to elevate the bad leg, which was now the one that had not been amputated. He did not complain, even as Stacia, up front with Robert, argued the whole way, with Barry occasionally called on to chime in — Barry, who was getting more and more calm with each mile, so calm that Robert wondered if he'd be able to walk when they got there. Somewhere before the Atlantic City exit everyone took a break, and all that could be heard was the sound of Vishniak the man's exhausted snoring, and then an attack of flatulence from Vishniak the dog, who, Robert snapped at his brother, really should not be fed any more goddamned pastrami, no matter how lean the deli guy sliced it.

THE DEAUVILLE HOTEL WAS then in its third reincarnation as a Sheraton, but before that it had been, going back as early as the turn of the nineteenth century, the Chelsea Hotel, then the Deauville Hotel-Motel, then the Deauville East, and the Deauville West, as well as the Deauville Motor Inn. Now it stretched out over both sides of Brighton Avenue, a machine with many parts, few of them built in the same year. In the front was an Olympic-size pool, and there was a dining hall and, Robert had heard, a skating rink. Only Cece ever stayed here, and then only in her later years, because her older sister Rachel stayed there. Rachel's bill was paid for by her children — the infamous rich cousins — so it was important to Cece's children and grandchildren that in old age she could enjoy some equally small comfort, although Stacia, for one, was loath to understand her mother's need for such showy accommodations.

Through the summers of the 1940s and 1950s, and into the early 1960s, Robert's family had occupied one of the numerous three-story kosher rooming houses with a large basement that stretched between Atlantic and Pacific avenues, just blocks from the Board-walk. Their place was called the Zelmar, a name with a very romantic ring to Robert at age eight or nine, sounding like a movie studio, or a nightclub, when really it was just the combined names of the owners, Zelda and Marvin. The place was divided up into tiny bedroomlike compartments along narrow hallways, with shared toilet facilities on each floor and a shared kitchen on the first floor with tables, all of them occupied by separate clans. Each summer, one woman or another would insult the group by claiming that food meant for her family had been stolen out of the communal refrigerator, or a pot now had to be rekoshered because someone, some mysterious ghost in the night, had taken liberties with a fry pan. The resulting feuds often lasted for decades.

In the midst of such chaos, only the children were content, as children will almost always be at the seashore. The women were so occupied by their squabbles that Robert and Barry and their many cousins could run around as they pleased, at least during the week. On weekends the men came down, exhausted, wanting only to sleep late, play poker in the basement or, alternately, lie on the beach in the sun, their faces covered by wet towels. Visitors, too, arrived on the weekends, and more people used the bathroom. Sometimes on Saturdays the bathrooms were so crowded that the boys had to pee into a plastic bucket or, once, in a hole in the floor, an innovation that caused more trouble than it was worth. Only on the weekends did Robert and his cousins sniff reluctantly at their limitations, aware that way too many people stayed here, that these people left strange clumps of hair in the shower drain and shiny rows of teeth on the sink, and that the hallways sometimes stank of adult decay, that bodies together tended to rot, and that this inconvenience, this communal bad mood, meant something, though they didn't yet know the word for it, didn't know that it meant they were poor.

When the Zelmar was sold, in the mid-1960s, Robert asked Cece about it, expecting lamentations and beating of her breast, but instead she'd told him that it was about time, that the Zelmar was a rattrap, and it had been no fun to go on vacation with all her pots, pans, dishes, and sacks of flour and sugar, chained to the stove while others frolicked on the beach. Into her eighties now, Cece Kupferberg, almost blind and often confused, was liberated in a way her daughter Stacia would never be. The rooming house had been fine for Stacia then, more than fine with her mother doing much of the cooking and child care, and it was fine for Stacia now.

As a child, Robert had seen the Deauville as a signpost of luxury, a symbol devoid of symbolism to him then, a place where patrons could be at the ocean in only a few steps with a front-row seat to the goings-on of the Boardwalk and Convention Hall, and most of all, a place his large family could not afford to stay. Now, at almost thirty years of age, he knew that the Deauville was not just a Sheraton in New Jersey but the name of a resort in Northwest France, a once-posh place not far from Normandy. No, it was the place that Daisy and Tom Buchanan honeymooned; no, it was the basis, along with neighboring Trouville, for the mythical resort in Proust's *In Search of Lost Time*, the series of books that Tracey had first told him to read back in freshman year, the translation of which he'd only had time to attempt with any energy as a cabdriver. He was not an invalid taking a bite of a tea cake, but the whole damned Boardwalk — the beach, with its Kohr's ice cream stand, giant Mr. Peanut, and Fralinger's saltwater taffy — all of it was his Madeleine.

After they parked the car, helped their mother out, then woke up their father and lowered him slowly and carefully into his wheelchair, Robert whispered to Barry to go and check them in, quickly and without ceremony, before their mother could make a fuss. Then he stood in silence with his parents in the parking lot of the Atlantic City Deauville, a funny-looking hybrid of too many renovations, encompassing far too many architectural styles, so many as to be not much of anything, just a nondescript, enormous Sheraton. No one said anything for several minutes; they still had no idea where they were sleeping. Then, anxious to get into the shade, Robert finally pulled out his last card. Lowering his voice, because his father sat in his wheelchair a few feet away, Robert asked Stacia how on earth she could do this to their father. "You can't let him sleep in a decent bed, in a nice hotel, for maybe the first and last time?" He paused. "And what about Cece? How many more weekends do I have with her? Come on, let's all stay together in style for once; let me do this. The old days are over. The Zelmar is gone."

Using her hand as a sun visor, she squinted up at him, her expression unreadable; just as she seemed on the verge of a ruling on the situation, Barry returned, dragging an overheated bulldog behind him.

"The Deauville," he said loudly, "does not accept dogs. Under any circumstances. So fuck 'em, I'm not staying there."

Robert sighed. Why oh why was it all so complicated? His family, a simple weekend trip to the beach, the money, the hurt feelings, the constant intimations of mortality, the memories? Why couldn't it be simple, an established routine, a friendly, familial dignity — like in Tuxedo? And as that thought went through his head, he turned and walked away, walked away from all of them, and the bags, and the hideous embarrassment of a car, only apparent now next to so many shiny new Cadillacs and Buicks and even the occasional Mercedes. Then he took the handles of his father's wheelchair—his father's good leg raised forward at a slight angle, like some strange human compass—and began to wheel him out of the parking lot and toward the entrance. "You figure it out and let me know!" Robert called over his shoulder. "I'm hungry and Pop's thirsty, and we want to see the ocean and walk on the boards."

His mother yelled after him, "Why didn't you eat when we stopped on the road?" and he let her words echo behind him, as the two men rolled away toward the Orange Julius stand. He'd read in the paper that there was scaffolding on the Chalfonte-Haddon Hotel, but the state had been slow, very slow, to issue casino licenses, and the hotels were getting impatient. Robert was glad about one thing—the Boardwalk was not yet dug up or cut into, at least from what he could see, and the skyline more or less remained. For a few more months, anyway. For himself, he could cope, but he knew his father needed it to be the same.

After their hot dogs and orange drinks, Robert and Vishniak rolled along in the salty sunshine, the wheels of Vishniak's chair making a *clomp clomp* sound on the wooden boards. They said little even as they got to Convention Hall. It had been the family's custom, and the custom of many they knew, to drive to Atlantic City at Easter, watch the parade, and pose for pictures in front of the neo-Grecian hall with its tall columns. Why this tradition had started among the Jews of Philadelphia, no one quite knew, but it had ended with his parents' generation.

"You don't see the crowd that used to come," Vishniak said. "The place is full of schleppers now. And you hardly hear a word of English."

"Some of it is the same," Robert said, pointing out that the old men were still lined up under the candy-striped canopies reading the newspapers by the band shell, and the yellow motorized trams

315

still beeped to get you out of the way. Up above, a small plane flew slowly over the ocean. A streamer blowing out behind it read: Come to Benny's, Steel Pier, kids eat ½ price.

Robert wheeled his father toward the rows of seats that looked out on the water. Up above, the seagulls dove low and occasionally swooped down to pick up some trash, or a peanut shell. He took wonderfully deep breaths, simultaneously unwrapping the wax paper from piece after piece of bright pink, sea foam green, and red-and-white-striped saltwater taffy, as he had always wanted to do as a child, when he was never allowed to eat the whole box but had to ration it, one candy a day. For once, father and son were at ease, their faces turned toward the sun. His father, so tired from the beginning, now dozed under the wide straw hat that kept the heat off his pale face. Robert could escape a decision no longer. They needed a place to sleep.

Robert put his hand on his father's shoulder and shook him lightly awake. "Pop?" he asked. "Where do you want to stay?"

"I don't give a rat's ass," he replied, patting Robert's hand. "Just stop the screaming with your mother. Stop it. I want to sit by the water, and I want some peace and quiet. Understand?"

They found a motor inn closer to Brigantine, a little too far out for convenience, but good enough, clean enough, Robert supposed. Stacia unpacked her pots and pans, which she didn't use at all except for breakfast, but that was enough to satisfy her. She slept in the same room with the kitchenette and her husband while Barry and his dog slept next door, their combined snoring a cacophonous symphony of mouth breathers. Robert stayed in his own room at the Deauville. It was a small room, which was what you got at the last minute in the height of the season in a hotel that was still, it turned out, doing a decent business. There was no view; the air-conditioning came out in alternating arctic and tepid blasts, and the bathroom smelled of disinfectant, but the floors were marble, the soaps, conditioners, and shampoo were provided daily, wrapped in pink tissue paper, and the towels were soft and thick. All in all, he had what he'd wanted: a sad, barely middle-class comfort, that much less lofty for all that he'd gone through to get it.

They had an easier Saturday. His mother spent the morning around the pool at the Deauville with Cece, while Robert and Barry took turns wheeling their father on the Boardwalk. Just after lunch, while Vishniak napped in Robert's room, the two brothers went to the beach, set up their towels and cooler of soda, and marked their territory. After they were settled, Robert signaled to the ice cream boy, who brought over his selection of ice cream sandwiches, chocolate-dipped cones, frozen rocket ships made of red, white, and blue ice, and orange creamsicles. Robert bought cones for himself and Barry, telling the boy to keep the change on a five. At the start of the trip, Robert had so much he'd wanted to talk about with his brother—the job offer, his relationship with Crea, their father, their shared apartment, even his wish that Barry, once and for all, would finish the degree and get a straight job—but now, as they unwrapped their melting cones, he wondered where, after all, to begin. Could Barry even understand his life anymore?

Easier to enjoy the hot sun, taking a break now and then, when the heat became deliciously unbearable, to go and ride the waves, swimming out into the cold, salty water, dunking his head as he had in childhood, allowing himself to be towed back, over and over, to the shore, with its blowing trash and strange, otherworldly piles of seaweed, and treacherous shards of broken shells. Each time he returned, sopping wet and coated with sand and salt, to lie once again on the towel and bake, numb and relaxed, it would be Barry's turn to swim or take the dog for a walk. And before he knew it, the sun was dropping lower in the sky, the air cooling off; the brothers, exhausted and exhilarated by the salt air and the short swims, dragged their stuff slowly back to the hotel. Tomorrow would be a short day, full of logistics and driving home. He had missed his chance.

That Saturday night, no longer able to bear his own guilt, Robert moved himself to the motor inn. He knew that sleeping in a room with Barry and the dog would not be sleeping much at all, and the mattress would be hard as a rock by comparison, and the place smelled of mold, and the pipes moaned and groaned, but he gave in so that for one night they might all be together in the same place, a family, if only for a little while, even as he told himself that this was the last time, the very last time, that he would make such a compromise.

DANNY, WHO LONG AGO gave up on Atlantic City, had taken the cab for a family trip to Long Beach, so when Robert got back he drove the cab of a friend of his uncle's, Lou Stein, who was away, too, but had left his car behind. Like most of the newer cabs in New York that year, this one had a lockbox. The driver was encased behind a bulletproof Plexiglas wall, could see the patrons only in slices, and often only the tops of their heads. The air-conditioning in the cab was sketchy — no wonder its owner took off part of August. Some days the cold air blasted in the back and hardly at all up front, and other days, for no apparent reason, the reverse was true, and he wore a sweatshirt while his passengers mopped their brows, complained, and tipped more poorly than usual. He felt the familiar sticking of his fingers to the coating on the steering wheel, the scent of his own sweat inside the box that now contained him. At the end of his first week, he counted his money and realized that after paying Lou, he'd made all of fifty-two dollars.

The next day, his day off, he typed up a letter to Phillip Healey and accepted the job. And the following weekend he went to Tuxedo. He'd missed Crea more than he'd expected to, and perhaps she could feel this from him because they had a wonderful time together, full of small jokes and subtle affection, helped along by Mark Pascal's absence and Jack's good mood. Robert had missed her body, especially, and her smell, which he identified with the grassy-sweet scent of Tuxedo. They had been apart for only two weeks, but Robert could not remember a time that felt longer. He had even missed the huge glass house in the middle of the grove of trees, missed how smoothly everything flowed there, how rarely people yelled, how little he felt about much of anything as he stared out at the view that stretched for miles and miles, the endless green of the property and two neighboring estates, with their hedges and peaked roofs and landscaped flower gardens nestled in deep valleys, and watched over by distant mountains.

The first night, Tracey and Claudia came to dinner. They sat outside, the patio illuminated by giant citronella candles that cast shadows on the flagstones, and ate barbecued chicken and corn on the cob, washing it down with beer, licking their fingers. Even Jack seemed young for those few hours — for once, he made eye contact with Robert instead of looking over his shoulder. This had to be progress, Robert thought, as they all joked and teased each other, debating the question of modernism. Did the Beaux-Arts qualify, as in the controversial exhibit at the Modern? Or had it begun in Germany between the wars, with the designs of Josef Hoffmann? What was the difference between the modernism of America and that of Europe?

"Can someone tell me what postmodernism is?" Claudia asked, taking a sip of beer. "Am I a fool for asking that question? It's taken me this long to figure out abstract expressionism. You know, de Kooning and Pollock and that lot. Is that postmodern?"

Tracey took her other hand and kissed it.

"There's overlap," Crea said, taking her seriously. "If you put the beginnings of modernism between the wars, but then some people claim it started earlier, which throws everything off if you ask me. Most people say this is the era of postmodernism, right now."

"I declare myself a neomodernist. Art is about the moment we haven't experienced yet," Jack proclaimed, interrupting her, and raised his glass. "Does anyone want to challenge that?"

"I'm not sure we could, dear," said Crea, patting her father's hand indulgently, "as none of us has any idea what you're talking about."

"Are we still talking art? Or have we moved on to the realm of personality?" Tracey added.

Crea and Robert and Tracey and Claudia laughed and laughed. They hardly knew why, but everything brought on a fit of giggles. Jack was talking about the future, what was next, in the space beyond the stripped away, the streamlined? What was next?

Yes, what *was* next? Robert wondered. Was a path not set out for him? And yet he'd refused it, run from it, and why? He looked around at the faces of his companions, alternately flattered and then made ghoulish by fluttering candlelight. Food flowed from kitchen to table to kitchen, as if on a timer. Crea squeezed Robert's hand under the table.

"To your future and to all of ours," Tracey said, holding up his glass. "I know Claudia and I are a damn sight happier when you're both up here."

Robert raised his glass. *Surely this is where I belong, because I have made it so. Surely this is where I belong.* So much was being offered to him, the whole world, practically, or the Alexanders' large piece of it, with the sky full of stars so visible from the backyard, and all the rooms in that glass house. He would appreciate the beauty in front of him and not spend so much time looking back.

That night he made no show of staying in his own room, or crossing through the discreet door that joined their rooms, but simply entered her room with her, then pulled her white T-shirt over her head and kissed the side of her neck. He took her small, perfect breasts in his hands, not caring if his desire made him weak, or greedy; all his life he had needed women, it was simply who he was, he liked to touch them and talk to them and make love to them, at times clinging to those small moments of sweetness as all that grounded him to the earth.

After they'd made love, they lay side by side, staring into the darkness. Robert felt sweaty and exposed, happy for the night breezes from a series of open windows; the Alexanders were not big on air-conditioning. All day long he'd expected questions from her about the time he'd been gone, but she'd said nothing, only reached over and ran her fingers through his hair, massaging his scalp, lulling him almost into unconsciousness.

"You know," she said, "I have so much room in the city." That was all she said, and he answered that yes, her place on Gramercy Park was the biggest one-bedroom he'd ever seen.

"What does your father think?" he asked.

"He thinks I should please myself, or rather, he knows that I always do."

"I don't think I should move in unless we're married," he said. "It wouldn't be proper."

"Proper? Robert, it's nineteen seventy-seven."

"I want to do things right for once, from the beginning."

"What's that supposed to mean, 'for once'?" she asked. But he was not going to explain his past to her, not then, and probably not ever. She was his fresh start; a fresh start and a strange nod to the past. He could begin again and also settle old scores.

"I ask a woman to marry me and she gives me an argument."

"Are you sure? Back in June you said—"

"I didn't know what I wanted then," he said. "Now I do."

She laughed and hugged him, kissing his neck. "Really?! Do you mean it?"

"Yes, my love," he said. She leaned over and kissed him on the lips, and he turned over and began to kiss her back, marveling that her skin was, always, so soft.

He never said to himself: I will marry this woman for her money, her position, her family. Later, others would think that. But the decision was so easy that night, so evident. He enjoyed her company, cared for her, admired her confidence and grace, much the way his younger self had admired these qualities in Tracey. That he did not love her the way he had once loved Gwendolyn did not matter — he no longer had such expectations; indeed, they seemed naïve to him. He would be practical, for once, and take the deal that was offered.

CHAPTER THIRTY-FIVE

The period of trials

The announcement went into the papers in September, and Crea and her secretary set to work. It was unorthodox, but her mother had passed away years ago and she wanted to make the decisions about what would be the most important day of her life. He hated when she referred to their wedding that way; surely they would have other important days? To her, walking down the aisle was like graduation, an accomplishment that deserved public recognition. To him, it was merely a ceremony.

Most nights that fall the couple went out. Robert was a new face on the social scene, and their picture appeared in society pages from New York to Palm Springs. Crea did not work for money, but her charitable activities amounted, some months, to more than a full-time job. She was on the board of several museums and seemed to be involved in everything from cancer research to Architects for the Preservation of Cast Iron. When they were out in public, and even as he stood at her side chatting and shaking hands, Robert observed Crea's talent in a crowd. Going from politician to heiress to artist, she always remembered the names of people's children, where they'd spent their last vacation, even what style their houses were decorated in. Did she write these things down? She never stayed too long in each group, and by the end of the evening, it was inevitable that she'd gotten someone important to give money to something else.

Once he'd overheard Crea asking a tight little clump of women, "Have you ever seen a man look better in a tux than Robert?" And he wondered then, as if overhearing an insult, if he'd proposed or been cast in the role. Crea's friends — young matrons in patterned dresses that swept gracefully to the floor — did not, like so many women he knew in law school, talk of careers or a male-dominated world from which they needed liberation. Liberation from what? The freedom to do as they pleased? But, excepting the occasional awkward moment, most of the time he enjoyed the glamour, the beautiful surfaces, and the easy sociability of this world. Crea introduced him to important people — real estate developers, heads of companies, philanthropists with political connections — and he was surprised by their friendliness toward him. He understood that were he to meet them on his own terms, he would likely not receive a second look. But wasn't everyone like that, and didn't most opportunities come from who you knew? In the worst of times, he reasoned, with New York still climbing out of bankruptcy and humiliation, this small group of revelers with their charities and expensive clothes were actually admirable. They not only kept the city's cultural institutions going, but without them who would even believe in gay old New York anymore?

These days, his schedule was flexible, and even with putting in hours at the *Law Review* office, he did not start classes until noon. He might at one time have given those early-morning hours to the law clinic, but these days he needed the sleep. In falling in love with the woman who funded the place, he no longer had time or the desire to volunteer there.

By the end of September, he had settled into this life. No longer driving his cab, he once again walked each morning and evening through a door that was held by a smiling doorman. Comfort had never been hard for him to adjust to, and for a little while he forgot that he'd ever lived any other way. And then he got a late-night call from Barry: Vishniak was in the hospital again. Gangrene in the other leg. The doctors would have to amputate, but first they'd have to stabilize his sugar level. His father was gravely ill.

He and Barry left the next morning, taking up residence in their old bedrooms. The harkening back to an earlier time felt bittersweet because it highlighted so starkly the absence of their father. Then they drove their mother to the hospital, getting there each day by nine. His father would have no legs — Vishniak's worst fear, the first thing he had said when Robert walked into the house that day after returning from Boston. His heart was their next worry. His father's body was slowly self-destructing, from the ground up.

At the end of the first week, they finally performed the surgery. Days later, Robert watched a male nurse roll his helpless father over like a sack of flour so that he and an orderly could make the bed. Eventually, after rehab, he might be strong enough to do things for himself, but now he was as helpless as a strangely proportioned child. Robert looked away from the exposed stump of one leg, the bandages of another, and Barry got up and walked out of the room.

Robert concentrated on the practical. This was what he'd been taught to do in law school; emotion was endlessly subjective, malleable, and abstract; best to stick with facts and actions. He bought a secondhand chairlift, hired a contractor to install additional railings and a removable ramp out front. At first he asked Stacia for the money, and seeing her confusion, as if he were speaking a foreign tongue, he got a check from Barry and put the rest on a credit card.

The Post Office dragged its feet paying the disability. Robert spent hours on the phone with union officials who directed him to government administrators, the slowest voices, humans drained of all life force, endlessly shifting him down the food chain until he became furious and threatened a lawsuit. "I'm just a clerk," a voice replied. "All things in good time."

But Stacia Vishniak did not know from good or bad time; she knew only that there was no money coming in, except the $120 a week she would collect for another month while she used up her back sick time, years of it—had she ever taken a sick day in twenty years as a crossing guard?—and then there would be nothing coming in. "Robert," his mother said, grasping at his arm in a hospital hallway, her fingers digging into his flesh, "there'll be no money coming in."

"You have savings, don't you?"

"Not enough. Not enough for no money coming in."

"I'll fix it, Ma."

"You're not working. Why aren't you working?"

Because I'm here with you. Because I couldn't drive a cab all day and come home to Crea on Gramercy Park East. And because in the fall I'll make more than twice what Vishniak made in his best year. But he said none of this, only repeated, "Barry has money. We'll fix it."

He muttered the same staccato attempts at comfort to her day after day as his father slowly got better and his mother grew more hysterical. Not outwardly hysterical, inwardly so, which was harder to watch. She paced at night, up and back, up and back, footsteps so heavy on the carpeting that the wooden floors squeaked underneath; she could not eat or sleep, her eyes blazed black as two coals. She snapped at them if they left a light on, or put too much toothpaste on the brush. "Don't waste that bread. Scrape the mold off" was printed in letters now, over the bread box. How much his mother had in the bank, and the thick roll of bills Barry took out of his pocket to show her—"See, see, Ma. I got money"—none of it mattered. She had gone somewhere else, to another time, even before they knew her.

Then one day the first disability check arrived. The payment was almost as much of a relief to the brothers as the news that Vishniak could start rehab and might be home in as little as six weeks. There was money coming in, and his mother returned to them.

BY NOVEMBER, ROBERT WAS back in New York, driving to Philadelphia for weekends. On one such drive, Barry informed him that he was, in fact, finally graduating from college, had smashed all his disparate credits together to get a degree in general studies. This would surely make their father happy, and in the nick of time. Robert asked if this meant Barry would get out of his current business, but Barry would give no further details, replying only that he had a plan.

Robert had never let Crea come with them to see his father. He should have, but he put her off, saying that Vishniak didn't want her to meet him in this condition, though that was a lie. When Vishniak had come out of the anesthesia, one of the first things he said was, "Am I ever going to meet her? You think I have so much time left?"

Now Crea lay next to him in bed, her head on his shoulder, her body curled around his, and he felt distant from her. She had no idea what he'd gone through and he wanted to punish her for that, when he was the one who'd insisted she stay home.

"Sweetheart," she whispered. "This is so awful. The timing couldn't be worse."

"Yeah, so inconvenient of my father to need an amputation just before our engagement party."

"That's not what I mean. How dare you twist my words! Do you think I'm a monster?"

"Of course not, I'm just tired. I'm sorry, darling. It *is* awful." That was when he asked her if they could possibly put off the party.

She had already thought of that and agreed completely. "We'll put it off until your father's better," she said, kissing his cheek. "We can't think of having the party without them."

His family would have to come to New York. Why did this only now occur to him? His family in Tuxedo. How would they handle it? How would Jack handle them?

Crea told him to get some rest, but he could not sleep. Why was it so hard for him to imagine a happy ending? He had expected the worst with Gwendolyn, and she had seen all their secret and not-so-secret merits, even the ones he couldn't see, and insisted he be proud of them. In the end, she'd fit in better than he had. Why not imagine a similar ending here? Had he learned nothing?

CHAPTER THIRTY-SIX

Meet Barry Vishniak

Barry Vishniak stood in the center of a tight group, and Robert—curious as to what had drawn Tracey, Claudia, Mark Pascal, and several others around his brother—took a step closer, but all he could hear in the crowded living room was the echo of Barry's raucous laughter. Then his words soared above the din of low conversation. "I'm not kidding, Tracey. Someday, everyone will have one. It'll drive your car for you, write your checks, dictate your letters—"

Robert caught a glimpse of Barry's face, cheeks flushed with excitement and alcohol.

"—no one will need their secretary, or their brain for that matter. The machine will do the thinking for us, the tedious thinking, that is. Leaving us free to, you know, contemplate."

"Who wants to contemplate?" Pascal asked loudly. "I'd rather just look at naked people."

Robert heard a high-pitched giggle. Claudia. It was so rare to hear her laugh. She'd had a lot to drink, they all had, though no one could compete with Mark Pascal, who'd begun with cocktails hours before the party started.

"I can get you into that," Barry continued, lowering his voice. "The soft kind. Totally legal, cheap to produce. Plenty of big entertainment companies have quiet subsidiaries. The markup is like a thousand percent. Guaranteed return. The hard stuff, on the other hand..."

Barry's voice faded to a whisper and Robert couldn't hear the rest. Jack Alexander tapped him on the shoulder. "What field is your brother in, again?" he asked.

"Stock brokerage," Robert replied. "Prudence Brothers." Just after Christmas, Barry had announced to Robert that he was working as a cold caller for a brokerage firm, sitting at a low desk all day and making endless phone calls from names he got off lead cards or out of the phone book. It was humiliating work, but Barry informed Robert that he had to start somewhere. Was this sudden industriousness purely the result of Vishniak's second amputation? A reaction to Robert's imminent job at A, L and W? Or had his recent holdup, by a regular customer wielding a knife, been more distressing to him than he admitted? Maybe all three, but here he was, six months later, having passed the Series Seven in record time and able to make his professional debut at Robert's much-postponed engagement party.

Jack pulled Robert gently in the direction of more guests who wanted to congratulate him as Stacia and Aunt Lolly approached. Robert had asked his brother to keep an eye on the family, but Barry was too busy, it seemed, to be bothered. His mother stared blankly at Robert; since entering the Tuxedo house, her expression had gone slack. Lolly, fashionably stuffed into a pink silk dress, smiled gamely. Like Cece, she had always cared more about clothes, whereas Stacia wore a black short-sleeved wool dress, stockings, practical shoes — she had wide feet and bunions, so all her footwear looked military. The house was warm, even for those wearing summer clothes; he felt for his mother in that wool dress. The front and back doors were open, and a few ceiling fans buzzed fifteen feet overhead. One of the few things Stacia had in common with the Alexanders was that neither household used air-conditioning, only Stacia's choice was about the electric bill, whereas Jack's reasons were harder to discern. The house would cool off in an hour or so when the sun set. Robert put his hand sympathetically on his mother's shoulder, but she shook him away.

"Is it all right to take a few photographs?" Lolly asked.

"Of course," Jack said genially, "but we have two photographers." He pointed them out in the sea of women in patterned maxidresses and sheaths and the men in cotton sweaters, bow ties, and khaki pants. "I'll mail you the proofs and you can choose what you like."

"I don't mean of the people," Aunt Lolly said, taking a small Polaroid out of her purse. "I mean of the house. To show to our family back home?"

"If you like," he mumbled. Then, changing his tone, aware of his role as host, he added: "If they come out well, I may ask you for copies for the insurance adjuster!" He laughed at his own joke, and Stacia and Lolly thanked him politely and walked off with their cameras. "I think things are going well, Robert, don't you?"

Robert nodded, following behind his future father-in-law. A few hours earlier, when Stacia had arrived in the hall with Barry, Crea rushed at her with the full confidence of one who is always liked, but seeing Stacia's expression, she'd stopped in her tracks. The black dress and severe hair did not help. Stacia, too, remained in place, her neck craned heavenward. "Some place to keep clean," she'd remarked. "All these windows. Shows all the dust."

"I suppose," Crea replied. She wanted a word of praise, some assurance. But Stacia only pointed at the painting on the wall.

"That you?" Stacia asked.

"Guilty."

"A cartoon? I mean, is it meant as a joke?"

"A Warhol lithograph, but some people would say that's the same thing."

Stacia had not responded. Aunt Lolly and Uncle Fred arrived then, bustling into the hall with arms outstretched, and then more guests behind them. His family should have come earlier, but they'd gotten lost on the way. They might have stayed over at the house the night before—the invitation had been extended more than once—but they'd declined, sure they'd be putting Crea's father out, and so Robert had found them a bed-and-breakfast nearby. Walking in, seeing the house, they must have realized that Robert was not lying when he'd said Jack would hardly know they were there. But by then they'd already checked into the B-and-B, leaving their bags behind, and Robert knew that this was for the best. They could use the privacy, and he would sleep better with them staying somewhere else, guilty as he was to admit it. As always with his family and hotels, with his mother and leaving Oxford Circle, arrangement led to headaches. He wanted to show them the wider world, to do for them while simultaneously wanting them to go away. These impulses warred with each other, but never more than they were doing that day.

Jack stopped to introduce him to an ancient friend, then to two Tuxedo neighbors. Every few feet they stopped to chat with someone, Jack's hand resting paternally on Robert's shoulder. "Yes, this is him, the man who makes my daughter so happy. Yes, hello there! Good to see you!" And then to Robert, "He doesn't smile because he's having trouble with his teeth. Don't take it personally." He found Jack's sudden attentions, his private whisperings, intoxicating. Jack had always seemed oddly neutral about the engagement, neither thrilled nor horrified. Robert understood why people at the firm ran after him—he bestowed his attention so reluctantly, so rarely, that it felt irresistible when he suddenly focused on you. Robert thought of poor Vishniak, at home with a nurse and his two brothers; Stacia had not wanted him to travel yet, and the doctor concurred. He *had* a father, one who had always loved and cared for him. Why, then, was he so grateful for the smallest attention, the slightest hint of approval, from Crea's? Because he did not have *this* father, a man who might initiate him into the world, a successful man whom people ran after, who did not ask for power but took it for himself.

In the backyard, the grass was so green and even that he felt as if he were in a painting. A string quartet to his left played Vivaldi. Waiters circulated with glasses of wine and champagne. He scanned the horizon for his family and saw that Barry, his mother, and his aunt had gotten into the buffet line. Two partners from the firm joined Robert and Jack: one was a litigator, the other in corporate. Robert had never met them before. "Yes, this is my future son-in-law," Jack announced in a theatrical tone, as each man shook his hand. "I had to promise him my daughter to get him to sign with us!" He made a few jokes about the ever-expanding size of the wedding guest list—last anyone had heard, it was up to four hundred. Then an elderly man with a cane teetered by, and Jack followed him with his glance. The two partners did the same. "Excuse me, gentlemen. I see Schoenberg from the Real Estate Board," Jack said, and was gone, and then the two others followed suit, so that now Tracey was at Robert's side.

"Robert, I'm investing some money with your brother. He's quite the salesman."

"Are you crazy?"

Tracey looked at him. "I thought you'd be pleased."

"He's had his license for about five minutes."

"I'm only giving him a little bit to start with. Nothing I'd miss one way or the other."

"It's your money," Robert said, shrugging. He would not be so small as to step on Barry's chance. "I'm sure he's appreciative."

"He's amusing and he's smart, if a bit rough at the edges—and I'm curious to see what he'll do. He makes Claudia laugh, always a plus—and he's related to you, after all."

"Jesus, I hope he hasn't approached Jack," Robert said. "That would be a disaster."

"Jack Alexander can take care of himself. You shouldn't be so servile — it's a strong word but I'm sorry, it fits. Hang back and he'll respect you more."

"Does he not respect me now?"

"Don't care so damned much," Tracey said, taking a drink from a passing waiter and leading Robert away from the music and the crowds and toward the hedges. "He had you investigated, you know."

"Investigated?" Robert asked. "By whom?"

"It's standard procedure when no one really knows the groom or his family, and in your case it's been, what, eight months before the families met?"

"My father was sick." Though they might have met months ago; Robert had fielded offers from both sides that he somehow forgot to deliver. This was partly his fault, wanting to spare his family and himself. Still, a detective?

"I'm only saying that no one knew much about you."

"You did."

"I tried," Tracey replied. "But what do I know? I'd never met your parents or your brother. I don't even know what you did after graduation."

"Does Crea know? And for that matter, how do you know? Maybe you misunderstood."

"Association meeting. I heard Trenton Pascal recommend this guy to Jack. Seems Trenton used him when some musician came sniffing around Mignonne."

"So all of Tuxedo knows I've been vetted by a detective?"

"I'm sure no one heard but me. And Crea doesn't know. She'd have a fit if she did. She's madly in love — and she's loyal."

What secrets did he have? Drugs when he was young — like his whole generation. A dealer in his family, at least up until two months ago. And Gwendolyn. Even if they could find anything on her, nothing he'd done was illegal, only stupid and naïve. "Anything turn up?" Robert asked, trying to sound casual.

"You think we'd be here if it did? Jack's going to be protective, I told you that."

"I wish you hadn't mentioned it at all." He took out his inhaler, gave himself another preventative blast. Once more and he'd start to shake.

"So do I," Tracey snapped. "I thought I was doing you a favor. Silly me."

They stood side by side, not sure what to say next. Neither one wanted to walk away on an angry note, and so they silently stared out at the view until Tracey had found something else to remark upon. "How does that man get away with that blue? I've never seen a suit that color."

"Mario Saldana," Robert said, "from Caracas. Works in real estate. Nice guy, if you like to talk about sports."

"Does he sail?" Tracey asked. "I'm putting a crew together and a man dropped out."

"Let's go ask him," Robert said. "They say he's a shoo-in for partner."

But the two of them had only taken a few steps when they collided with Mark Pascal, who seemed to need help standing upright.

"Crea Alexander and Robert Vishniak!" he called out loudly. "Crazy! But then, you're a lucky bastard, you always were."

"I think I'll go talk to that man about sailing," Tracey said. "I'm not good with affairs of the heart." He clasped Pascal on the shoulder sympathetically, then disappeared.

"The world is full of women, Mark," Robert said. "You're rich, young. Go enjoy yourself."

"Haven't you figured it out already?" Pascal asked. "I don't really know *how* to enjoy myself."

It was true, Robert thought; he'd always been old, even in college. Pascal had relinquished his dream of journalism without much of a fight, and now Robert was taking away the last of his youthful fantasies. But even Mark's fantasies were somehow old and practical—he'd dreamt of the only writing job that provided a regular paycheck, and of a woman he'd grown up with, of whom his family approved.

"I was too serious for her," he said, lowering his voice. "She slept with me once, you know. She was seventeen and I was nineteen; she and my sister were counselors at that damned camp and I came up for visiting day—"

"Mark, shut up." Robert took Pascal firmly by the arm, trying to lead him out of the crowded room but not getting very far.

"Afterward, she pretended like it never happened. Tortured by that for years—just once, and never again. She wouldn't tell me what I did wrong—" He shook Robert off, grabbed two glasses of champagne, and careened off in another direction. With uncanny timing, Mark's father found him, and the two disappeared down a hallway. Of course Trenton Pascal had recommended the detective. It was his last-gasp attempt to get his son what he wanted. Robert spotted his own family, sitting not far from the buffet, and felt strangely relieved to join them.

Having finished their dinner, his mother and aunt and uncle sat staring out at the view. Barry was gone again. His father's cousin Miriam, the only Vishniak relative who had made the trip with them, sat in his place. The group was whispering in Yiddish. Always a bad sign.

"What do you think of the house?" Robert asked, sitting down.

"She grew up here?"

"No, this is where they came on the weekend."

"Ooooh," Aunt Lolly said, with a slow outlay of breath.

"You like the food?" Robert asked.

"Very fancy-shmancy," Fred replied. Aunt Lolly added that the meat was done just right and that the guy serving it said they used beer in the marinade.

Crea came over. Robert jumped up to give her his chair, then grabbed a passing waiter and asked for another one. The waiter obliged quickly and Robert sat down again. "I've hardly spoken to you all day," she said, taking his hand. "I don't know if Robert told you, but we're definitely having the wedding at the Plaza. My father was against it. Too showy, not modern enough. He wanted it here, but I thought we could have a dinner here Friday night, for the out-of-town guests, and that seemed to satisfy him. I loved the Plaza as a child, and so did my mother, and you only get married once."

Robert doubted his aunt or any of them knew what the Plaza was, but everyone nodded. Crea began to talk rapidly, uncomfortably, about the wedding. Stacia, waiting until a pause, leaned over and said she had something for Crea. Then she removed from her purse a stack of three-by-five cards fastened with a rubber band.

"We put these together for you," Stacia continued. The relatives smiled, and Crea looked to Robert, confused. "Me and his grandmother and his aunt. All Robert's favorite recipes. We always did things from memory. Cece can't write English. But we sat down together and wrote them out." Triumphantly she held the stack out, and Crea took it. Robert looked out at the sky fading to a pale pink, the endless waiters and scurrying caterers and servers, plus Dinah and the uniformed help pitching in, grabbing what they could to take into the kitchen for washing.

"So nice of you," Crea said, still holding the cards out in front of her. "The thing is, though, I don't cook."

The table went silent. Uncle Fred raised an eyebrow, and Lolly looked into her lap.

"You don't cook?" Stacia repeated loudly. "You mean it's like this all the time?"

"No," Crea said, smiling. "Not like this, no caterers or waiters. Not for our little apartment. But I'll hire a housekeeper who cooks." And then she added nervously, "Someone very good. She won't sleep in or anything."

"Is this one of those feminist things?" Stacia asked.

Crea handed her back the cards, shaking her head.

"No, you keep them. Give them to your cook. Maybe she can use them."

No one said a word and then, to Robert's relief, Dinah came over and said that an old friend of Crea's was about to leave. Crea excused herself, asking Robert to join her.

Not long after, his family thanked Jack Alexander in a flurry of words and then came at Robert and Crea with the traditional white envelopes, stuffing them in their hands and pockets, wishing them mazel tov and finally departing en masse.

"What are these for exactly?" Crea asked, holding three enve- lopes together in her hand.

"Cash," he said. "They always give cash. No cards."

"Why no cards?"

"They don't like them," he said. Just names and "with love" scrawled on envelopes. His mother believed cards were a waste of money, especially if they could not be reused. But he could not say that, not then. A handful of guests still lingered in the yard, but he and Crea took a few minutes for themselves in the back hall. Sud- denly she bombarded him with questions. Why had his family left so soon? Why didn't his mother smile? Why did she wear black; was she in mourning for his choice of wife? Was this about the cooking? And why had they shown no enthusiasm about the Plaza? Did they think it too extravagant?

Robert cringed, hearing in her tone that they would not be asked to pay anything, so the least they could be was enthusiastic.

"Why did she dwell on the Warhol, Robert? Does she think I'm not pretty enough for you?"

On that last one, Robert laughed out loud. "She doesn't care what anyone looks like."

That had come out wrong and now Crea began to cry. He took

her in his arms. "She has Bell's palsy, I told you, her face is frozen like that. And that's her only good dress."

Crea stared at him, incredulous. His excuse sounded flimsy, even to his own ears. Her son was engaged. For once she could buy a new dress. But knowing Stacia, she was saving her money for the wedding weekend, which would require two dresses and a very nice gift. That would be enough of a shock to her system.

But how to explain his mother? How to explain that when she asked questions, sometimes with a negative inflection, it was because she did not know something and wanted to understand, and not because she was discounting the information? When she stood at attention, not coming forward to kiss Crea, it was because, well, she had not come forward to kiss Robert, either. Kisses and hugs were distributed with extreme discretion. When her face occasionally went slack, showing neither the smile nor the frown — as it had when she walked into the house and met Crea — that was a rare expression. He'd seen his mother like that only a few times in his life — eight months before, when his father entered the hospital and the doctors were reluctant to operate; seven years before that, when Robert showed up on her doorstep looking like a scarecrow; and the day he left for college. "That's terror," he said. "She's terrified."

"Of what?" Crea said. "Weren't we as kind to her as we could be? I don't know how I'm supposed to act with them."

He could not explain anymore, he was tired, and suddenly it felt useless to even try.

CHAPTER THIRTY-SEVEN

Prenuptus interruptus

Weeks went by, and then months. Robert passed the bar — he'd had so much else to worry about that it did not even occur to him he wouldn't pass, and perhaps because of that attitude he succeeded on the first try, while some of his more focused colleagues were stuck taking it again.

The winter holidays had ended and the wedding date drew perilously close, but for Robert and Crea the social hubbub never seemed to end. The night before, a Thursday, they'd been out at a benefit for the restoration of the Old Merchant's House on East Fourth — she was a donor on the project. As Crea's evening plans went, this one was on the quieter side, but then they'd stopped in SoHo at a gallery opening and weren't home until almost 1:00 a.m. Her public self at these parties now stood out to him in bold contrast to the awkwardness and insecurity he'd seen when she met his family. How was she able to exist so easily in this intimidating world, yet go to pieces when confronted with the terrified Vishniaks?

He was having trouble sleeping through the night. In a distant corner of the living room was a wall clock that chimed on the hour and half hour. It was something called a Jugendstil Regulator made by Gustav Becker. Admittedly, the clock was beautiful, with an austere walnut cabinet, and the bobs and weights inside were ornately engraved. Though the apartment was large and the walls thick, late into the night he found himself listening for that soft chiming, which sounded to his ears like *Bonn-Bonn-Bonn,* as if the clock were homesick for its country of origin. She said he would get used to the sound over time, and he didn't have the heart to tell her to get rid of it. The clock served a purpose, too; his alarm, with its cheap drugstore beep, went off at a quarter to seven, and if he was not out of bed, then the wall clock took over on the hour.

When Crea heard Robert's alarm that morning, she rolled over and groaned, though in minutes, he knew, she'd be asleep again, getting up around ten. Robert made his way quietly to the bathroom, feeling hungover and anxious, not unusual after one of their late evenings. The alcohol, the lack of sleep, the powerful new asthma medication—his system was a test-tube experiment gone awry. This uneasiness would stay with him until he bought a giant cup of coffee on the way to work and forced himself to eat a muffin at his desk. But the first hour was always hell. He looked at his face in the mirror, wishing that he didn't have to shave. Days like this, with his hands shaking, he feared cutting his own throat. Could a man who billed in fifteen-minute increments really keep up with a woman who had nothing but time? Sometimes he wondered.

He dressed quickly and rushed out the door before the clock hit seven fifteen, then hailed a cab at Park Avenue. Falling asleep in the backseat, he was awakened at his destination by the driver—the fare was high but he paid it, glad for the extra sleep, though he now had less than twenty dollars to get him through the week. The day before, the arrival of a notice from his bank had alerted him to a bounced check. This year's Christmas bonus of five hundred dollars had gone toward the engagement ring. They were having her mother's ring reset, adding an extra diamond. The rest of the money came from what he could pull together from his paychecks and the very last of what he had left of the money he'd saved from driving a cab. Her engagement ring was long overdue.

Living at her apartment, he had not, this time, made more than the cursory attempt to talk about what he should pay in rent. Seeing her disinterest, he'd dropped the subject. She owned the place and paid the bills, not her father, and if she didn't want to talk about money, then he wouldn't, either. Instead, he simply paid bills as he saw fit — leaving her checks for the phone or utilities, leaving cash for the maid when he remembered, picking up groceries when he was home early enough to go shopping. Unlike Gwendolyn, Crea accepted his money with a smile and a nod, or the money simply disappeared from the perch where he'd left it. And he always paid when they were out in public. For once, he had hit the right note. But even paying for a portion of Crea's lifestyle was pricey.

At 8:00 a.m. he found the usual assemblage of associates gathered around the coffeepot. Jack's secretary was not in yet. Secretaries generally made the coffee at A, L and W, but the first young associates in the office were always desperate — a small crowd now waited for the water to percolate through the filter. Their shoulders slumped, their skin sallow and dry from lack of sleep and sunlight, they grunted hello or nodded at him; an attractive brunette from litigation complimented his overcoat. But unlike when he was part of the summer program and no one knew he was dating Crea, now real conversation always stopped as he drew near. It was the same in the men's room, used exclusively by associates, where surprisingly long conversations went on, but not in front of Robert. Everyone assumed him to have Jack's ear, which showed that they were not very observant. After the engagement party, and from the day Robert started at the firm, Jack had been as oblivious to him as he was to every other first-year associate.

Wilton Henry, real estate wunderkind, walked with him to his office. The two were neighbors. "Off to fill in loan applications,"

Henry declared. "I'm so damn bored." He loved to laud it over everyone that he worked three times as fast and was always out the door by six, while the rest were still struggling.

"Saldana has me working on a few things," Robert said. "Not too bad."

"The Latin Beau Brummell?"

"You're so hip with those nineteenth-century references," Robert replied. "Reading Lord Byron again?"

"I'd be a lot more interesting if I were," he replied. "Didn't he sleep with his sister?"

"Have we uncovered some dark childhood fantasy?" Robert asked, stroking his chin as if it were a beard.

"All I'm saying," Henry asserted, and then waited to continue until Robert had taken some papers from Lola, the secretary they shared. "All I'm saying is that there's something strange about that guy."

If there was anything strange about Saldana, it was that he bothered to explain assignments and treated Robert like a person, not an idiotic underling or Jack's privileged son-in-law. Robert felt grateful to him.

"Saldana's not in yet, by the way," Henry added over his shoulder, as he and Robert went to their own doors.

In Robert's windowless room, so small that the desk had to be placed perpendicular to the entrance, he took off his trench and hung it on the hanger behind his door, then ripped the month of March off the calendar. In two weeks the invitations to the wedding would go out. Somewhere in Chinatown, a group of women sat at a long table writing names on the thick, cream-colored envelopes using an ornate calligraphy. Soon they'd be assembling the pieces for the two-day event. In TriBeCa, a similarly strange ritual went on around the lace on Crea's gown. His wedding was a cottage industry from another time, employing workers by the hundreds.

Robert's secretary arrived at eight forty-five, and by then he was on his third cup of coffee and a shot from his inhaler, nervous energy and adrenaline pushing him along. He'd spent the past month doing nothing but preparing ancillary closing documents, reviewing title reports and surveys, reading and rereading tiny print until his eyes ached. But Mario, recognizing his frustration, and knowing his interest in landmark preservation, had just asked him to do some research for a client who had bought a run-down hotel that he planned to demolish, not realizing that it shared a party wall with a building that was up for landmark status. Robert was in the firm library all morning. When Lola knocked, he was sitting behind a stack of books and his notes, surprised to discover that it was past noon. "Are you going to lunch now?" he asked.

"Not yet," Lola said. "Selene called. Mr. Alexander wants a few minutes of your time."

"He does?"

"Yes."

"When?"

"Now," she said, smiling encouragingly.

"Any idea why?"

She shook her head. "Comb your hair."

Though Robert had worked at the firm for a little more than seven months, he'd never before been invited into Jack's office. Was this a lunch invitation? An assignment? Work filtered down through the food chain. He received it from higher-level associates, not partners.

Jack's secretary, Selene, was not what he'd expected. Each time he saw her, he was reminded all over again of his future father-in-law's inscrutability. No longer young, Selene dressed like a floozy. Women in the office were not even allowed to wear pants, but there was no caveat on miniskirts or see-through blouses, at least for Jack's assistant. Whenever he passed Selene in the hall, Robert wondered what exactly went on, or had gone on, between those two. There was never any gossip about Crea's father's personal life, not at the firm or in the news. But Jack had been single a long time, and before that unhappily married. Was Selene the answer? Or did he put up with her cheap taste only because she was good at her job?

"Go right in, Robert." Selene's hair was done up in a high, lacquered style, her freckled cleavage pushed up above the deep V in her sweater. "He's expecting you."

Jack, seated at his desk, got up and shook his hand. Robert looked around at the enormous rectangular office with its low white couches, white carpeting, and three white walls. The fourth wall, a blue-gray color, was lined with white paintings in narrow chrome frames. Thin lines of red or black zigzagged and danced across the white canvases. Between the two couches was a round glass coffee table with an enormous blue marble on top. On the other side of the room was Jack's glass desk, held up by legs so narrow that it seemed to hang magically in the air.

Jack motioned for Robert to sit down on the couch, though he remained standing. "How are your parents?" he asked.

"Fine, sir, looking forward to the wedding." They exchanged small talk about Jack's favorite topic — Crea. She looked tired, she thrived on busyness, all the usual, until Robert began to wonder why he'd been summoned. Then Jack walked to his desk, returning with a thick manila envelope. Was Jack giving him work? Was this the beginning of some new professional confidence between them? Jack, holding the envelope, now walked back over to Robert and lowered himself, awkwardly, onto the couch. "I need you to look this over," he said, sliding the envelope across the table. "Consult someone if you like and get it back to me."

"How long do I have?"

"I'd suggest you deal with it right away."

Robert picked up the envelope. It was heavy. He was a first-year associate, just getting good at the most basic of tasks — what could he possibly do for a founding partner? A, L and W was big on the pecking order — none of this made sense, yet he wanted badly to be favored.

"And who is the client, exactly?" Robert asked.

"Excuse me?"

Robert opened the envelope. The edges were sharp and he got a small paper cut, watched the tip of his finger as the blood slowly came to the surface and he placed the finger, momentarily, in his mouth, switching hands so as not to dirty the papers.

"I asked Crea to talk to you months ago," Jack said, "but she keeps putting it off. So I've decided to deal with this myself. You've always struck me as a levelheaded young man."

Pulling out the papers and looking through them quickly, Robert realized that this was not a piece of work to be completed and billed for. This was a prenuptial agreement. He cleared his throat and pushed the papers back down into the envelope. It wasn't that he hadn't expected it—he was a lawyer, knew what a prenuptial was, understood that one applied to his situation, if to any, but a person can understand the logic of something and still feel shocked by its arrival. Before this, the only prenuptials he'd seen had been the long-outmoded ones used as examples in his matrimonial-law class. He stood up, uneasily, while Jack remained seated.

"You look that over carefully," Jack said. "On your own time, of course."

"Of course," Robert said. *Of course I won't take a moment away from your precious billable hours, you son of a bitch.* He could not help but feel that he'd been sucker punched. For the second time. First the detective and now this—what else had to happen before he realized that this man would not be his friend, let alone his family? He was going to make Jack extract himself from that low, awkward couch and he was going to watch. No matter how long it took, no matter how difficult it was for him to get up. And indeed it was difficult; Jack huffed and puffed, and Robert stood, smiling slightly, with his arms folded over his chest. Just as Crea's father finally heaved himself up with a slight groan and was standing erect, Robert thanked him and walked to the door. "No need to walk me out," he said, and left.

As soon as he got back to his office he closed the door and spent the rest of the afternoon studying the information inside, billable hours be damned. He tried to look at the papers as he might have for a client, but could not. This was why lawyers could not be their own advocates; staring at the lists of assets, he could hardly think straight, had to stop to use his inhaler again, which gave him, for some time afterward, a slight tremor. Who on earth was this person he was about to marry? It was one thing to be rich, but Crea Alexander's level of wealth was stupefying. There was the apartment in New York, a winter place in Aspen, and a beach house on the North Carolina coast. There was a property in France, but that had been occupied by some cousins for generations. Still, the rent went into a trust and she could take possession of the place at any time. She owned a townhouse, too, on the East Side, which had been her grandmother's and was rented to an art gallery. Her Gramercy apartment had a large mortgage, but this was likely for tax purposes. There were stock portfolios and endless investments in the U.S. and abroad, plus art, so much art, paintings and sculptures on loan to museums and universities. She had art in storage, photographs at galleries, drawings on her walls, totaling millions of dollars. Technically Crea owned much of the art in Jack's Manhattan place. Though successful in his own right, he was not half so wealthy as his daughter, who had inherited a fortune from her mother.

Robert already knew that Jack had come to the marriage with less. His father had been a doctor, a GP in Rye, New York, who put three sons through Columbia and then retired to Florida to flyfish and die in his sleep. Crea told Robert this information early on in their courtship, as if to imply almost a tradition of women in her family marrying men with less money, who then went on to make their fortunes. She had no doubt Robert would be equally successful.

When Crea had first brought up the subject of her father's middle-class background, his humbler beginnings, Robert had wanted to say, but did not, that the son of a doctor in Westchester County was very different from the son of a mailman in Oxford Circle. Perhaps, having met his parents, she understood this now, but he doubted it. His level of debt was higher, his obligation to his parents in old age larger; the family capital did not get passed on but rather was eaten up by living. But just as she lumped together all people in the center, he had lumped together those on top. He saw now how naïve he'd been, or maybe just deluded. Why was she at so many parties with the very rich or famous, and how could she write so many checks? He was a man with nothing marrying a woman with far too much. Some part of this must have bothered her, too—having him see all this, acknowledging the vast gulf between their resources—because she had given the task over to her father. Or had she? The act was uncharacteristic, cowardly. Or maybe this was who she really was. The contract protected her completely and ceded virtually nothing to him. Even gifts, if they divorced, were to be returned.

He called Stanley Dunphy, his pal from law school who'd gone into a matrimonial-law practice with his father. Divorce, an inflation-proof industry, was always booming. In fact, his friend was so busy that it took some time for Robert to get him on the phone, and when he did, Stanley apologized—he had back-to-back appointments. Robert explained a few things over the phone.

"To start with, we're going to ask for a lump-sum payment up front," Stanley said, unable to keep the excitement out of his voice. The man loved his job.

Robert told him that he didn't want such a payment—the idea was humiliating.

"You believe you're being noble, but really you're being impractical," Stanley replied, as a series of beeps sounded and someone called his name over an intercom. "They expect us to negotiate. Bring in the contract tomorrow morning. I'm here at seven a.m." And then he hung up.

*　　*　　*

UNABLE TO CONCENTRATE, Robert left work early and went to the law library at NYU to research recent precedent on antenuptial agreements. Generally, it was the woman who came in with lower assets, and then the contract involved just what Stanley mentioned—cash up front, property in some cases, plus additional money after each child. But he was a man, and to accept money for marrying Crea felt degrading, unmanly. Not that anyone was offering. He felt like he was back at college. Back to Gwendolyn and, before her, Tracey. How had he gotten here again?

Being in the endless corridors with their smell of ancient books, disinfectant, and anxious graduate students, he was reminded of his last three years of training, of all he'd been through. Law school did nothing if not discipline the mind—certainly it didn't prepare you for practice; that much he'd learned already—but in the library he calmed down, got hold of himself. This was a contract. He knew how to approach a contract. If Crea wanted a nineteenth-century marriage, one founded on property mergers and dowries, then why shouldn't he play the game? His heart was not truly at stake, not as it once had been. He could admit that to himself. What he felt for her was as much as he expected to feel for any woman who was not Gwendolyn, but it had never, ever, been enough to make him lose control.

Her father had set him up. If he asked for too much—asked for anything, for that matter—then Jack could point out the obvious to Crea and Pascal, and God only knows who else: Robert was a social climber, a gold digger, a money-hungry Jew. If he asked for nothing, then he'd be endlessly beholden to his wife. He had seen what she was used to—she was not going to turn around and live on his salary.

Hours later he left the library, aware that he had not called Crea, as he usually did when he was going to be home after eight. He took a cab and then walked up the steps, plugged in the alarm code, and entered the apartment he'd lived in now for over a year. The walls were white with dramatic overhead lighting. Crea's collection of photographs was scarce here; instead, the place was decorated with bodies. In the center of the hall stood a somewhat emaciated female body in bronze on a pedestal, a late work of Wilhelm Lehmbruck. In the living room hung an oil painting by Oskar Kokoschka — a nude woman with long hair sat on the ground, legs bent in front of her, hands grasping her head in distress. Crea had told him it was a portrait of the artist's great love, and muse, Alma Mahler, and that she broke his heart. Over their bed hung a series of drawings of another somber nude, early work of Gustav Klimt. He understood why a home decor magazine wanted to do a profile; he lived in a museum. Then there was that damned clock, chiming now for nine long counts.

She loved the German and Viennese secessionists and the bridge they formed into expressionism. Her cultural history, she'd told him. But all the artists went insane, didn't they? Killed themselves or went into exile? There was something sad in these faces around him. Their eyes looked into a tragic future that they could not see . . . or could they?

He thought again about Gwendolyn, of how little she cared for decoration, how carefully she'd arranged his books on her empty shelves because it had meant something to him — for herself, she needed almost nothing. He knew it was not fair to contrast the two women so starkly. Crea would always come up wanting. No one could compete with a ghost, or a saint. And Gwendolyn did not have the luxury of romanticizing pain; she had lived it, at the mercy of her brain chemistry. He poured himself a scotch and sat down at the dining room table. On it was a note telling him that Crea had gone to a restaurant nearby, the romantic site of some of their early dinners. He changed and left the apartment quickly, as if it were haunted.

The restaurant was close enough for him to walk. He passed the Players Club on the corner, lit by streetlamps, though he could still make out its ornate Victorian Gothic molding — the dripping gewgaws, she called it. Crea had taught him how to classify and categorize beauty, and how to see. There was much he did not want to lose, yet he would if need be. She loved him, he knew, more than he loved her.

The streets were crowded along Lexington, the restaurants full — people wandered aimlessly in pairs. A mother walked in front of him, wheeling a stroller toward the supermarket as if it were three o'clock in the afternoon, except that it wasn't; it was past nine in a city that lived in the eternal present, while Robert still wrestled with the past. As he entered the restaurant, the staff greeted him warmly — everyone knew them here — and then he was taken to the back, where Crea smiled at him as if he were all that she needed. Women had always responded to him, but no woman had ever looked at him the way she did. She had called him at the office but he was gone. Yet she did not scold. Perhaps she'd wanted to, but when she saw him all was forgiven. Maybe she was used to waiting for men; her father had come home late all her life.

They ordered and ate quickly. He was silent, biding his time, and then he paid and they decided to walk home; it was still warm out, felt almost like spring. On the way, she asked him more than once if anything was wrong and he said no. As they stood in the doorway of the apartment, she pointed out, gently, that he had not set the alarm before he left. He did that too regularly, and it was not a good idea.

She put down her purse in the hall and walked into the bedroom, where he was already yanking at his tie. She came over and asked him for help undoing her outfit, a kind of one-piece jumpsuit with a halter top that tied at the nape of her long white neck, which she offered him, while he stood behind her, his fingers fumbling. "I'm going to leave the firm," he said.

She turned around, so he had to let go of the fabric. "After eight months?"

"I want more independence." He took off his jacket, hung it in the closet.

"Why?" she asked casually, reaching behind to her zipper and finishing the job, making him wonder why she'd asked him for help in the first place.

"Your father called me into his office today," he said, unbuttoning his shirt. "I thought he was giving me work, but instead he slid a prenuptial agreement at me and told me not to waste company time reading it. He also said he'd been waiting for you to do it, but you took too long."

"The subject," she said, turning around, pink-faced. "I knew it would be hard for you."

"So you sent Jack to do your dirty work?"

"He's done this all my life, interfered. I told him to let me talk to you first."

"I have an appointment with a lawyer in the morning."

"You're seeing a lawyer?"

"No, of course not," he replied. "I'll just sign on the dotted line."

"Don't take this out on me, Robert. I don't read contracts. I don't know anything."

Anyone with assets like hers knew more than a little. She was not a fool; she used her father to divorce herself from any unpleasantness or responsibility. That was how she played it. "My lawyer will reject the prenup as it is now. If I sign, I'll be a virtual guest in your house."

"We can sell this apartment, find our own place. You'll be my husband, not my guest."

"First, it will be years before I can put a down payment on an apartment comparable to this, or whatever it is you want to live in next, which I assume will be larger. Those are my means — are you prepared to live on them? I suspect not. Second, I'll never sign that contract as it is. Stan Dunphy will draw up something else, your father's lawyer will respond, and on and on it goes." He said all this casually, calmly, as he'd prepared himself to do. "It's nothing personal, right? Our lives are now in the hands of lawyers."

She'd been standing there in only her underwear and now went to the closet and put on a silk robe, a beautiful one in a pinkish peach. She was not wearing it for warmth — Crea never got cold. He imagined she wanted something around her, some bit of beauty as ballast against all this ugly conversation. "This isn't what I wanted," she said softly.

"What *did* you want?" he asked.

"I'm not sure," she said. "I guess I figured we'd talk about things just between us."

"Then you shouldn't have brought in a contract like that," Robert said. "The list of assets alone goes on for ten pages. I appreciate your being so honest about what you have. So I'll be honest, too. I have nothing. Only debt. That's what I bring to this marriage. The potential to make money. But only potential. Now, what are we going to do about that?"

"You really have nothing?"

Had she not met his parents? Had she thought, when they began dating, that he'd refused to bring her to his place because it was just too sublime? "I could get the contract right now," he said. "We could burn it in the fireplace and pretend this never happened. We don't have to marry at all; we could live together. I know I said I wanted to do things right, but maybe doing things right in this case is *not* getting married. Free love. Emphasis on the word *free*."

"But I want to be married. I'm almost thirty and I want a family." She sat down in the corner, curled up in a chair like a little girl. "Explain it to me again. Why can't you sign?"

It was alternately charming and exasperating, her ability to squint at him as if she'd just arrived out of nowhere and then ask what exactly they'd been arguing about all along. "The issue is that I have no money," he said, "and you have piles of money, and no matter how much I make, even if I make partner, we'll never ever be equal in this marriage."

"Sure we will," she said. "What does money have to do with equality in a marriage?"

"Everything," he said, unbuttoning and removing his shirt, then throwing it over a chair. She got up and began to smooth it out. She had taken him to get that Charvet shirt, custom-made to his proportions, the cotton so fine it felt like silk. A perfect shirt. "If we divorce and that family you want so much falls apart, how will I keep our children, even for weekend visitation, in the style to which they'll become accustomed?"

"We haven't gotten married yet and you have us separated with custody problems!"

"Lawyers, Crea, we're trained to look at every contingency. Every miserable, rotten, horrid possibility. We'll likely have children and we could divorce."

She walked into the living room, expecting him to follow. He found her pouring herself a drink, another for him. "Money is our only problem, it seems to me," she said. "And that's easy. If you're so self-conscious about your situation, I'll simply give you some."

He had not expected this. She was endlessly surprising, had taken the argument to its logical conclusion without even the slightest prompting. She did the hardest work for him.

"Father never has to know," she continued, "better if he doesn't. And it's my money. Serves him right, surprising you at the office like that. He needs to learn to keep his nose out of things." She took a sip from her drink and her voice grew stronger. "You could pay your debts, and we'd consider it an engagement gift. I was going to buy you a Cartier watch, you know, from Father, it's tradition, but—"

"I don't need an eight-thousand-dollar watch, Crea."

"How much debt do you have, exactly?"

"About fifteen thousand, give or take a thousand."

"Well, you lawyers like to be so specific, so I'll give you a hundred thousand. How is that?"

"Half a million," he said.

She laughed, though he wasn't sure why. Nervousness? Or was she somehow enjoying herself? "One hundred and fifty thousand," she countered.

"Four hundred and fifty thousand," he said.

"Two hundred."

They haggled on like merchant and customer, finally settling on $275,000. "That wasn't so bad, was it?" she asked, yawning audibly. "Is that what you lawyers do all day? You could have asked me for what you wanted in the first place. That was what you wanted, wasn't it?"

Endlessly surprising. For so many years, he had wanted to talk about money in the open, to not hide behind code, or legal negotiations, or his own shame. Now, with Crea, he'd finally had that conversation, and he felt a little sick. Maybe it wasn't Tracey or Gwendolyn or any of them who had the problem. Maybe it was him.

"I do have one condition," she replied, her face looking up at his. "Don't leave the firm. A, L and W is right for you, for us. And my father wants you there."

"He barely notices me."

"He doesn't want to show favoritism, but believe me, he wants you there. I wouldn't oblige him by going to law school. Who else does he have? Make partner, and then if you're still unhappy, you can make a lateral move and I won't say a word. Or maybe you'll retire early and we'll travel. Who knows? It's all ahead. Marriage is supposed to be an exciting adventure."

"If it's half as exciting as engagement, maybe we should stick to being just friends."

She laughed. The crisis had passed, though not completely. The hardest thing he had to ask her for was yet to come. "All right," he said. "I'll stay at the firm. I don't want to, but I will." He walked over to the bar and put a melting cube in what was left of his drink. "But I have a condition, too."

"I thought we just made a deal," she said. "One condition for another. You have two?"

Money she had to spare, and giving it had seemed almost easy for her. He had not counted on that, but then, giving money was almost always easier for the rich, wasn't it? Easier than giving their time or ceding their way. "I'll sign the prenup as it is," he said, "but you'll give me the money. And I'll stay at A, L and W, and work for Jack. But I don't want a Plaza wedding for four hundred people. I want to elope, just us."

"What if we did it in Tuxedo, like we originally planned, instead of at the Plaza? I can cut down the list if you hate it so much. You might have said something earlier."

"You don't understand. This isn't about the Plaza. I want to elope."

"Give up my wedding? Robert, how can you ask that of me?"

"Tomorrow I'll call in sick and we'll drive to Maryland where we don't need a blood test." Random members of his family—knocked-up brides, couples too young or too poor to afford the simplest of parties—had been eloping to Maryland for generations. "I've said what I want and you can refuse. But then I'll refuse and we're back where we started."

His family. He would spare them. He did not say this was about his family, but she had to know that they were part of it. He could not put them through the reporters and black-tie-optional, the congressman, the mayor, the shrimp forks—could not put himself through it, either. But there was a delicious bonus, too. No one would be more upset by this than Jack Alexander. She was his only child. And no man wanted inclusion in his daughter's decisions more. After all his meddling and checking up, he would be shut out completely. The thought of such a triumph made Robert feel almost gleeful.

On the wall behind them, the wall clock chimed *Bonn-Bonn-Bonn*. She was right that he might, eventually, get used to it; through the last hours he'd not even noticed the sound but now it intruded, insistent, *Bonn-Bonn-Bonn*. "This is the only way," he said over the noise.

She stood just a few feet from him, her face illuminated by the one lamp that was on in the room. Her eyes were puffy from lack of sleep, and he could see two thin lines running along the side of her mouth, lines that had not been there before. Then she nodded — that was the only answer she gave, a nod — as she pulled her robe around herself and walked back into the bedroom, leaving him there alone with the chiming, so loud and urgent now that the room seemed hardly able to contain it.

PART III

CHAPTER THIRTY-EIGHT

Of trading floors and shoe shines

The spring rains came, first in a pitter-patter and then a steady drumming, assaulting the windshield of the pale yellow Mercedes that made its way along Water Street. In the backseat, Robert Vishniak had long ago given up looking through a thick stack of papers that lay in front of him on a small pull-down table, and was instead taking in the buildings rising along the southern tip of the East River. These included a three-story mall designed to look like a ship in dry dock, plus outdoor restaurants and retail stores, all on an open promenade of remarkably clean cobblestones. A tall ship from another era was docked permanently in port for tourists who wanted to go onboard.

A, L and W had little to do with the fifteen years of political and legal fights, or the architectural compromises, that created the Seaport—other law firms had reaped those rewards—and Robert felt privately pleased by this. He'd been down here with Crea early in their courtship to look at the crumbling nineteenth-century Federalist townhouses and old maritime warehouses, and he had to admit, if only to himself, that he had liked the area better when it smelled of fish from the market and feral cats prowled the streets, nestling in the doorways of pubs that sold cheap beer to dockworkers. The place had been a neighborhood then. Now, he wasn't sure what it was. He still loved old buildings, lived with his wife and daughter in a landmark Beaux-Arts townhouse on the Upper East Side, but this love was a guilty pleasure, played out more in theory than practice. In daily life he was paid, and paid well, to justify new construction.

The car approached its destination, a fifty-story skyscraper that stood out conspicuously among the low-rise architecture. Robert watched men and women in dark suits emerge from the revolving doors, their golf umbrellas blooming like enormous striped flowers on the wet streets.

"At least there's parking down here," mumbled Robert's chauffeur, Troy Gibbons. "Even if we've about fallen off the edge of the earth."

Robert gathered up the papers, stuffing them back in his briefcase and snapping it shut as the car pulled up to the curb. "I'll need you back at two," he said.

"Will do," replied Troy, a burly man with a blond crew cut, as he got out and opened the passenger door, then held an umbrella over Robert's head as he exited the car. Robert thanked him and walked quickly to the entrance and through the revolving doors.

Two men, both in uniform, sat at a large marble desk in the cavernous lobby.

"Prudence Brothers, thirty-seventh floor," Robert said, and was waved through.

The receptionist had a dark tan, white teeth, and long, permed blond hair that had been teased high. She wore an ivory-colored silk blouse and a dark blazer that made her shoulders as broad as a linebacker's. "Mr. Vishniak, Hilary just buzzed," she said, leaning toward him with what appeared to be great interest, "he's on his way." Then she slid something across the top of her desk. He was meant to take it and he obliged — picking up her business card with the company logo. At the bottom, in a scrawling hand, she'd written her name and phone number.

"For a rainy day, Jennifer," he said, putting the card in his pocket.

"It's raining right now, from what I've heard." She licked her lips and was about to say something else when Barry Vishniak rounded the corner, stomach first; prosperity hung on him like a pregnancy. Robert still felt a small shock of recognition every time he saw his brother these days. It was like looking back in time, to what their father had looked like in Robert's clearest memories, with the potbelly and the mostly gray mop of curly hair. Their father had died the year before. Vishniak had been dying for so long, and in such complicated ways, that when he finally went they were surprised at the simplicity of it — a quick heart attack, in bed with the television going.

"Come on back," Barry said. "I'll show you my new office."

Robert followed him through a series of glass doorways that led to an enormous open room where rows of men held phones to their ears, all talking at once.

"Pussssssy!" The word pierced the air like a battle cry.

"If you can afford ten thousand shares, then you can probably afford fifteen —"

"What do you mean, you have to ask your *wife?!*"

"*Yes, ma'am. A very safe investment for anyone on a fixed income —*"

One by one the men hung up their phones, scribbling furiously, then waved pieces of paper in the air that were quickly whisked away by a variety of young female assistants. Barry paused to light a cigar. "Bull pen," he said loudly. "We call them the great unwashed." Then he led Robert to a glass office in the corner.

"Congratulations," Robert said, as he walked inside. "A corner office." The office was not large, nor did it have a window to the street, but it announced to the world that Barry was an earner worthy of separation from the pack. At a smaller lower desk sat a boy; he appeared to be little more than a boy, with his own phone and a stack of cards.

"This is Justin, my cold caller," Barry said, and Robert shook the boy's hand. "Go get yourself some lunch, kid." Barry put his hand into his pocket and took out a roll of bills so thick that Robert wondered if it had been assembled for his benefit. He peeled off a twenty and sent the kid away, telling him to keep the change.

"Empty walls," Robert said. "Put up some pictures and your diploma, at least."

"I just got here," Barry said. "How long have you owned that apartment that doesn't have a stick of furniture?"

"About three months," Robert said. It was his first real estate purchase, a one-bedroom co-op on Ninetieth Street, close to Broadway. "Trying to decide if I'm going to rent out the place, sit on it for a year or two and flip it, or what. Boy, has that neighborhood come up since I lived there."

"Crea going to decorate it for you?"

"She doesn't know I bought it," Robert said.

"I figured," Barry replied. He threw his head back and laughed, drawing out his amusement for an extra few moments.

"Finished yet?" Robert asked, folding his arms in front of him. "You make me sound very sinister, when I'm faithful as a monk." As if to prove his point, he removed Jennifer's card from his pocket and ripped it into little pieces, letting them fall like snow into the waste can.

"You seen your statement lately?" Barry added. "You can afford to buy *three* apartments with what I'm making you."

Robert considered himself partially responsible for his brother's success. Were it not for him, Barry would never have met Tracey and Claudia and connected to a certain high-end client base. Even if Tracey's account wasn't big, it had established Barry's reputation. Robert had been nervous about Barry's new role at first, but he couldn't resist the easy profit. Initially he'd given Barry a cautious five thousand and then, seeing a big return, more after that. By now, most of what was left of Crea's prenuptial gift was invested with Barry, as was much of his savings. He tried never to touch the principal, as he had done early in his marriage, dazed by possessing actual wealth and spending down almost a third of it. And though he was loath to admit it — hated that he, the older brother, now needed the younger — without Barry, he'd be struggling, and failing, to keep up with his own lifestyle.

Most of Robert's profession disdained Wall Street, even as they invested with them. Wall Street played games for a living and were out the door by six, whereas lawyers, the straight-A students with more schooling behind them, slaved away until all hours for a lower payback. Barry now had a better office than Robert, and a bigger salary, while working fewer hours. Robert loved his brother and tried not to be envious. But Barry had always been given so much more leeway by their parents; he'd always taken more chances, doing whatever he felt like doing while Robert, the oldest son, agonized and tried to please. And once again, Barry had ended up just fine. More than fine. "That cigar is killing me," Robert snapped. "Put it out. Where do you want to go for lunch?"

"First we'll go upstairs and you can meet one of the traders. May need a lawyer for some crap with his co-op board. I'm always looking out for you."

"Sure, thanks," Robert said. "Invite him to lunch."

"Traders don't leave the Quotron this time of day," Barry replied, putting out the cigar. He added something that Robert did not hear on account of the sudden whistling and hollering coming from the floor. The door to the office had been left slightly ajar when the cold caller exited, and as the noise got louder, Barry walked over and shut it.

"What the hell is that?" Robert asked. Most of the men in the bull pen were standing now, and those who weren't had their hands in the air. "Did something just happen in the market?"

"Boner Thursdays," Barry replied. "That's what the boys call it."

"Excuse me?"

"Look up there," he said, pointing toward the trading floor.

"I don't see anything," Robert replied and, just as he said the words, he did, in fact, see her: a blonde in tight jeans and a thin blue T-shirt that pulled across her ample chest. She was unusually tall, all T and A and long legs, and she carried a large, rectangular box on a strap around her shoulder. Despite the encumbrance that hung by her hip, she walked with theatrical poise, as if aware of being watched. She reminded him of a woman from another era, a statuesque Rockette or a Ziegfeld girl. As she approached the man on the end of the first row, he nodded, pivoting in such a way that his leg jutted out from his desk, and then he went back to his call.

"What the hell is she going to do to him?" Robert asked.

Barry did not reply. The girl had put the box down on the floor and was now bending over, giving Robert and Barry a clear view of a magnificent, heart-shaped behind. The box, which was about fifteen inches high, had a red leather seat that she straddled and slowly lowered herself onto. Then she opened up a trapdoor that flipped outward at an angle, with a piece of metal on top. From inside the box she removed a checkered cloth, which she spread on the floor around her, then two large wire brushes, a bottle of white liquid, and, finally, a metal can. Across her thigh she folded two pieces of dirty-looking flannel, then she reached out and took the man's loafer in her hands, placing it in the metal toepiece so that he sat with his foot elevated. Then she set to work, first cleaning his shoe with the white liquid and a brush, then wiping it off with the rags. She placed a scrap of cloth on her finger, then took some polish from a can and, bending over the shoe, began to spread it on the leather in a slow, circular motion. The man slid back in his seat and hung up the phone, watching the girl beat on his foot with two bristled brushes, first slowly, and then very fast, so that her body bounced up and down ever so slightly with the effort.

"Who is she?" Robert asked.

"Sally Johannson," Barry replied. "Our shoe-shine girl. She's early today. Still in a hurry to eat? Or you want a shine first?" Not waiting for an answer, he went out and spoke to the girl, who nodded, then went back to her current customer, finishing off the first shoe with a fast snapping of the flannel rags. Then she put the foot back on the floor and took up the other. When she was done, the broker reached up and placed his money in the wide front pocket of her apron. She smiled and stepped across the aisle to Barry's office, pulling open the heavy glass door.

"Sally, this is my brother, Robert Vishniak."

"Nice to meet you," she said, looking him in the eye — the two of them were about the same height. Robert extended his hand. "You don't want me to shake that hand," she added, showing him her own, fingers black with embedded polish. "I don't like gloves — they make my palms sweat." She took the box off her shoulder and placed it in front of his chair. "Gucci loafers, very impressive; they're the best. But you have to use water-based polish on leather this thin. Somebody's been using wax."

"That would be me."

"You shine your own?" she asked, lowering herself onto the red seat.

"When the need arises," he replied, unable to take his eyes off her.

Barry, who had returned to his chair by now, continued talking, but Robert hardly heard. Usually he liked subtlety, liked girls that were more natural, less obvious. He didn't much go for pale blondes, either, at least not those so obviously bleached, or for women so generous in their proportions. Her face was not particularly beautiful, though she had lovely, wide-set blue eyes with long, dark lashes, but her nose was wide and her mouth large with too many teeth. Still, there was a quality about her. And what was happening to his foot? The thought had not occurred to him when he got his shoes shined by one of the old black men in Grand Central, but now he realized that a shoe shine, if the worker applied enough pressure, was a kind of foot massage.

As she slid the flannel rags fast and light over the leather, he noticed a bit of sweat that had come out on her upper lip. She wore gloss on her lips — the lower one was noticeably fuller, shiny and pink, and he wanted to take it in his mouth. When she was done, she placed all her equipment back inside the box and moved over to Barry. Sitting on the floor behind the enormous desk, with her head bent toward the shoe, she all but disappeared. Robert went over to stand in the corner and watch her from behind.

"Sally, you shine shoes at law firms?" he asked.

"All the time."

"Ever go to Alexander, Lenox and Wardell? On Sixtieth?"

"We have to have a contract with the firm," she said, still absorbed in her work. Barry was now making a low, contented purring sound. "That place has a reputation."

"As what?" Robert said, taking a few steps closer.

"They hate shoe shiners."

"You talked to the office manager?"

"I don't know," she said. "My boss is the one who signs up new business."

"You have a boss?" he asked, as Barry switched feet.

"Yeah, we're a real company. A Shining Star."

"Don't tell me," Robert said. "Actresses?"

"And musicians, yeah."

"You definitely have stage presence."

"Really?" she asked, turning then to look up at him, and he caught in her voice a sudden girlish insecurity that he found touching.

"Yes, really. So I can't get you to just show up and take care of my shoes?"

"Only one way," she said. "If your brother sends you a shine as a gift. But you have to warn the receptionist or she won't let me in."

She stopped talking, giving Barry's shoe her full attention. Robert now sat on the corner of Barry's desk watching and waiting.

When she was done, had packed up her stuff and stood to leave, Robert took out his wallet and asked her how much she charged.

"Two dollars for a shine, and then you can tip if you like," she said, smiling. "Most of the guys tip a dollar."

He walked closer, so close that he could smell the oily scent of polish on her skin, and the candy-sweet scent of watermelon from her lip gloss. "Here, for the two shines." He wrapped a twenty around his business card and slipped it into her apron pocket.

"Thanks," she said. "Wow, that's generous." She stared back at him, but he could not tell what she was thinking — she was, after all, paid to be friendly.

"I want to send a shine to Wilton Henry at A, L and W," he said. "And to Mario Saldana. And Barry here is going to send one to me."

Barry opened his eyes as if awaking from a trance. "Yeah, yeah, how much?"

"It's mine," Robert said.

"You can't pay for your own gift shine," Sally said.

"Sure you can," he replied, leaning closer, slipping another twenty into her apron. "Haven't you ever heard of giving a gift to yourself?"

CHAPTER THIRTY-NINE

Everybody into the water

Sweetheart, don't do that," Crea said, jumping up to pull the little girl back as she put her two small palms on the instrument panel. "Come down here on the bench with Mommy."

"She's not bothering me," Tracey replied, "a regular little captain." He had taken off his Yankees cap and put it on Gwen Vishniak's head. The child, five years old, sat on a small seat near him in the cockpit, pulling the hat down lower. Then she waved to her father, yelling, "Look at me, Daddy! Look at me!"

Robert waved from the opposite end of the deck. "Ahoy there, first mate Vishniak," he called back. He was sitting on the generously apportioned bench of Tracey's new sailboat. Tracey jokingly referred to the area as the "lux salon"—that had been the phrase employed by the salesman who persuaded him to buy the fifty-footer. Mark Pascal's new wife, a former Texas deb and Dallas Cowboys cheerleader who went by the unfortunate moniker of Biscuit, sat to Robert's right, between himself and Crea. Mark was on Crea's right, with Claudia next to him.

"What a magnificent child!" Biscuit announced.

Robert smiled at her. He thought Mark's wife a fool — Pascal could have done better — but he never tired of hearing his daughter complimented.

"That hair!" she added.

The drama of the child's hair elicited endless comment, even from strangers. The black locks tumbled to her shoulders and framed her face in Pre-Raphaelite curls that now peeked out from the red and white cap tilted on her head.

"I only worry," Crea said, lowering her voice, "about the — " She pointed to her nose, though it was not her own that worried her. "We may have a candidate someday for Dr. Green."

"He did my cousin's lips," Biscuit replied.

"Her nose looks just lovely to me," Claudia Trace mumbled. She stood up and lit a cigarette, then left their group to stand on the starboard side and smoke.

In the cockpit of the boat Gwen grew bored with talk of tacking and wind velocity, and jumped off her perch, then ran down the three steps to the group of adults. Around her middle she wore a harness that had been tied to a railing on the deck; like a leash, it allowed her only so much slack, but she took every inch, straining on her tether. Now standing in the center of their circle, she used her hand as a microphone, sticking her butt out and shimmying back and forth as she sang, "I'm so excited, and I just can't hide it / Umabout to lose control and I think I . . . !"

"She's got a thing for the Pointer Sisters," Robert said, and shrugged. "The nanny's taste."

"Gwen Vishniak!" Crea yelled, just as the boat lurched and the child fell on her behind. "What did Mommy say? About sitting down or standing still?!" She went over and picked up her daughter, but Gwen screamed for her father. Robert, right behind Crea, swept Gwen up in his arms and carried her a few steps to his seat. "She didn't sleep well last night," he said. Gwen, entering kindergarten in the fall, had figured out early how to spell *N-A-P*, a word they now conspicuously avoided. "Gwen-Gwenny-Gwendolyn, you want to take a snooze? Down below?"

Her response was a loud wail. "I thought not," Robert said. "If I unhook you from this thing, you have to stay with Daddy. Will you do that?"

She nodded, taking a piece of hair and curling it again and again around her finger, the usual sign that she was tired. Having gotten her out of the harness, he lifted her back into his lap. Soon, he knew, Gwen would be too big to sit with him like this. She leaned back against him and he hoped she might nod off, worn out by the sea air and the lulling movements of the boat, though this afternoon cruise had turned out to be more turbulent than expected. He put his face to her hair and inhaled the smell of salt and baby shampoo.

"I told you this was a bad idea," Crea whispered.

"She'll be fine," Robert replied, then raised his voice. "Our captain is a highly competent sailor with an excellent assistant. You need any help over there, Captain Queeg?"

"No, I wouldn't want to bother you!" Tracey replied, and then quickly gave Robert the finger, violating his own rules about this being a G-rated cruise. They were practically a Memorial Day traveling circus, that was what Tracey had said when they started out, complete with a child in harness and a dog off leash and now seasick down below. Mario Saldana moved around the upper deck, checking the tension on the ropes. He was a semiregular weekend visitor at the Traces and had been for years. He kept Tracey occupied, as Claudia so often put it. The two raced together in local regattas, and the year before they'd trained for the New York Marathon. When Mario was not in residence, the Traces hosted one of several young tennis or sailing partners of Tracey's. The week before they'd all been forced to endure the company of a nineteen-year-old ranked tennis player who used the word *like* so often that he seemed to be speaking a foreign language. Mario's appearance was always a welcomed relief.

Gwen squirmed in Robert's lap, but he bounced her up and

down as if she were a baby, and she giggled, then settled herself, finally nodding off. Behind him, Robert heard heavy footsteps clomping up from below.

"Finally!" Pascal said loudly, then lowered his voice as Crea pointed to the child, whose eyes were now closed. "We were about to send a search party for those beers —"

"Hold your fucking horses!" said Barry Vishniak, emerging with four Coronas that he held by their necks. "My dog was sick down there." Mark took a beer, as did Robert, who handed it to Mario and took another for himself. Everyone else drank gin and tonics.

"I'm not going to warn you again to watch the language," Robert said softly.

"She's asleep," Barry replied. "And she's smart enough to know I'm not a role model."

Claudia, silent all this time, suddenly laughed, then threw the rest of her cigarette overboard and returned to her spot on the bench.

"You should consider a Portuguese spaniel," Mario said from the cockpit. "We had them growing up. They love the water."

"I'll never switch breeds," Barry replied. "Nothing better than the English bull. His problem is that he's old now and low to the ground."

"I know how he feels," Pascal said.

"Speak for yourself, honey." Biscuit looked into a small compact, redoing her lipstick.

"Anyway, I gave the dog some Valium. He'll be out for a while," Barry said, as the boat suddenly lurched with the swell.

Crea put her hand on Robert's arm. "When the sea calms, you should put her downstairs," she said. "But do be careful."

"I'm always careful," Robert replied, whispering over their daughter's soft mass of hair. "A person would think you'd never been on a boat before."

"Don't start with me, Robert. I didn't think we should go out today at all."

"That was something else entirely." Crea was no fan of Barry's; she didn't trust his success and resulting social ascent. It made her feel, she said, as if the world had gone haywire.

When the wind calmed, Robert stood up, holding Gwen in his arms, ignoring Crea's obvious anxiety. Down below, the accommodations were as spacious as many people's New York apartments. There was one round double bed blocked off by a screen, and one small single across the room. On the floor next to the single bed was a towel on which Vishniak the dog lay snoring like a motor. The room had an antiseptic smell — Barry had obviously given some elbow grease to cleaning up after the animal. Robert laid Gwen on the bed. She opened her eyes momentarily. "Ahoy there, Daddy," she mumbled. He smiled, kissed her forehead, then drew a curtain around her to give the illusion of privacy.

Robert had not expected Crea to get pregnant within their first year of marriage. She had never actually consulted him, and at the time he felt betrayed, taken by surprise. But from the moment he'd laid eyes on his tiny daughter he'd been besotted, his emotions so powerful that they almost knocked him over. From then on, he'd been a goner. His daughter held his heart in the palm of her small hand, and she knew it — and so, unfortunately, did her mother.

He went to the kitchen and got himself a glass of water as Claudia came down the steps, Barry following behind her. Robert put his pointer finger over his lips to remind them to be quiet, but they barely seemed to notice him. Barry went into the tiny bathroom and Claudia waited outside, pacing back and forth. The bathroom was compact, with only enough space for one person at a time. Claudia was thinner than average, but Barry more than made up for it. He emerged a few minutes later. "All ready for you, kiddo," he said.

"And to think," she said, laughing, "a few months ago I didn't even like it when water went up my nose at the pool."

As Barry walked by, Robert grabbed him by the arm. "You only have to look at her to see she's fragile."

"Calm down, Nancy Reagan," Barry said, shaking him off. "Everyone here, last I looked, knows how to 'just say no.'" And then he was gone.

When Claudia finally emerged, she found Robert bent over, searching through the small refrigerator to see just how many brands of beer the Traces kept on hand.

"Hey, handsome," Claudia said, and made an unladylike sniffling sound. "Stand up."

Robert turned around, holding a cold Corona.

"Want some?" She motioned with her head toward the bathroom.

Robert declined. As if on cue, Mario Saldana came down the steps, nodded to both of them, then crossed the room and entered the bathroom.

"Gwen asleep?" Claudia asked. Robert nodded. Claudia leaned across a small counter in front of Robert, lifted herself up and momentarily swung her legs, then dropped to the floor.

"Take a load off," he said, pointing to a chair that, like everything in the room, was bolted down. "You want a beer?"

She shook her head. Robert took a cup and filled it with water, then handed it to her. "You'll be happier later if you drink some water."

"I'm darned happy right now," she said, as Mario left the bathroom mumbling something under his breath.

"You didn't leave much for anyone else, my dear," he said, as he passed by.

"Then go ask him for more!" Claudia snapped, and Mario walked silently up the stairs.

A few minutes later, Biscuit came down, her flip-flops slapping the teak wood. Mark followed behind. She waved and he nodded as they made for the open bathroom door. Robert wondered how on earth they would both fit in there, but somehow they managed.

Claudia, in white jeans and a roomy blue-and-white-striped T-shirt, once again bent over the counter, supporting herself on her elbows. Robert could see the deep tributaries of her collarbones. Her hazel eyes blazed green with intensity. "You know what I thought of the other day?" she asked. "I thought of that time when we were kids and you tried to stick your hand up my dress."

He nodded, and then took a long swallow of his beer, avoiding her glance.

Through the wall, they could hear a low moaning, and then a loud intake of breath. Claudia rolled her eyes. "They only have like ten bedrooms onshore."

"Mark just wants to show us that he finally got the girl."

"Biscuit looks like Crea, don't you think?" Claudia asked. "The red hair, the eyes?"

"I hadn't really thought about it. You want to go up on deck, avoid the theatrics?"

"No," she said, coming around the counter to stand with him, almost toe-to-toe in the narrow alcove. "Maybe I'll learn something."

"You don't need to learn anything from them."

"I wish you'd screw me now," she whispered, "like you wanted to then." She began to kiss him, placing his hand firmly between her legs, but he shook her off, holding her by the shoulders. She smelled strangely, overly sweet, but her breath was acrid.

"I worry about you, Claudia."

"Well, don't!" She shook him off, then walked back around the bar, doing a graceful ballet turn as she went. When she stopped, she began to pull her shirt over her head, revealing her belly button and narrow waist, and the first few jutting bones of her rib cage.

He came over quickly and pulled the shirt down. "You really think I would start something with Tracey's wife? With my daughter asleep five feet away and Crea upstairs? Sit down." He motioned to a chair. "We've always been able to talk. Let's talk."

"Nothing to talk about. Crea's not coming down here. She has that wonderful self-protective quality, you know, like those monkeys? See no evil, hear no evil?"

"People could say the same thing about you."

"Oh, I see. I hear. And I don't buy for a minute that Tracey would care if we went to bed. In fact, he'd like nothing better. As long as he could watch."

The sounds from the bathroom got louder. Robert felt trapped in the relative smallness of the space and the smallness of his own circle. He knew too much about these people. He glanced anxiously to the back, where his daughter slept behind the curtain. "Tracey would be very angry and you know it," he said. "Not to mention jealous."

"Maybe he'd be jealous," Claudia said, "but it wouldn't be of you, Robert, it would be of me." She stared at him, fidgeting from one foot to the other, hands now in her pockets, with the self-satisfied look of a child who had blurted out a truth that none of the grown-ups would say aloud. She began to walk the perimeter of the room, putting heel to toe as if measuring it, all the while staring at her feet. "Why do you think he married me in the first place? Because he knew something had happened between you and me. He asked me about it once, when we first started dating. And back then it struck me as so very strange that he'd care, such ancient history. But I get it now. If he had me, it would be the closest he could get to — well, you understand the transitive property."

"Claud, I hardly remember what I had for breakfast, let alone that many years —"

"Sure you do," she interrupted. "You never forget anything. You think women fall for you because you're so handsome, but the world is full of handsome men, and anyway, I've seen better-looking than you. The truth is we like you because you listen; you pay attention." She walked the other way now, her back to him. "You think all the girls at Gardner House were downstairs that night? You had a whole upper floor of wallflowers waiting for the party to end. All it took was one whisper and it spread, like wildfire." Claudia, too, seemed on fire, enthralled with her own story. She came up close to him again, wrapped her arms around him, pressed her narrow body against his. "He tried in the beginning, you know?" she whispered. "About the only time we ever really had a sex life were those first weekends when Crea started bringing you around. That's when I started to make the connection."

She began to kiss him again, and Robert gently unwrapped her arms. "Very dramatic," he said, sitting down, trying to pretend he was not unsettled by what she'd said. "But if you're so unhappy, leave quietly and be done with it. Stop bad-mouthing your husband."

"You have it all wrong," she said. "I adore Tracey! And leave him for what, exactly?"

"Another life. A man who loves you the way you want to be loved."

"What way is that?" she asked. "I did the great, complicated romance — once was enough. Anyway, I'm lazy. Tracey lets me do what I want and I extend him the same courtesy."

"You don't have to be married for that."

"But marriage has such benefits!" she said. "The magic 'Mr. and Mrs.' keeps the neighbors from talking and other women from guarding their husbands. And then there's all that wonderful public approval."

"We eloped," Robert said. "I don't remember much public approval."

She ignored him, talking faster now, back to walking around the room. "Tuxedo is a small, gossipy village. I'm past forty and have no plans to leave it, or Tracey. Being married is the best way in the world to get people to leave you the hell alone."

"That's a bumper sticker if I ever heard one," he said. Then all further conversation was cut off by the noise on the other side of the wall — Biscuit called out Mark's name in a rhythmic sort of chanting. Robert stood up, more than ready to go up on deck.

"You had enough yet?" he asked.

"This room is exactly twenty feet wide," she said. "Does that sound right? Twenty of my feet, I suppose. I take rejection well, don't I, Robert?"

"Is that what it was? You've been talking so long, I'd forgotten," he said. She kicked him in the rear then rushed up the steps. Robert let out a long breath and started climbing, happy as he'd ever been to see the light of day.

On deck, everyone was restless, ready to go back. Crea went below to wake Gwen, and a few minutes later Mark and Biscuit came back up, looking a little too pleased with themselves. Tracey steered while directing his crew to slowly let the sails out. "Try to keep them at a ninety-degree angle," Mario said, as Robert pulled harder on the sheets. "Barry, stay out of the way of the boom," Tracey yelled, "or you'll get hit in the head!"

"Might do him some good," Robert mumbled. He'd been sailing with Tracey many times, but he still watched in wonder as the wind filled up the main sail, bright red under the aquamarine sky, and the boat began to turn. Suddenly, the image of the shoe-shine girl passed before him — the way the hair arched over her eyes as she worked; the sound of her voice when she'd asked him if she really did have stage presence; the roundness of her ass when she bent over — and he lost himself in revelry, interrupted only by the voice of his brother, which now rose above the wind.

"You just take it once in the morning, like vitamin C. Changes your whole outlook. Cures depression, alcoholism, obsessive-compulsive disorder. Makes fat people thin and thin people sleep better. No side effects, either. Gonna overhaul the whole mental health industry."

"How is that possible?" Biscuit asked, pushing the hair out of her eyes.

"No more need for therapy," Barry said. "They just write you a prescription. It's going to revolutionize life as we know it. And make anyone with stock in the company very rich."

"I'm already very rich," Claudia said, staring off at the water.

"Pills that make people happy," Mark Pascal said. "Don't we have those already?"

"You got a point there," Barry said, squinting into the sun. "But none of those businesses are registered on NASDAQ."

CHAPTER FORTY

Of deals and dames

The smell is a mixture of certain streets in Calcutta and the men's restroom at the Port Authority," said Mark Pascal.

"When were you in Calcutta?" Robert asked.

"Or the men's restroom at the Port Authority?" added Elaine Norton, a pretty second-year associate who was in the room for reasons Robert didn't completely fathom. Pascal liked an audience. Elaine, at least, added a good pair of legs to stare at under the long glass table.

"What we need is damage control, emphasize the massive cleanup under way," Mario Saldana said, playing idly with the stem of a small bunch of grapes. In the center of the table sat a tower of untouched sandwiches and a half-eaten tray of fresh fruit.

"There is no such thing as damage control in Connecticut!" Pascal snapped. "People hear environmental cleanup, they panic." He wanted to scrap the project, a condominium development in an area just off Long Island Sound where raw sewage, escaping into the water from a nearby treatment facility, had washed into people's backyards during a heavy rain.

Robert sensed that Pascal was in one of his moods. When the market was lousy in the 1970s, his father had expanded the business tremendously. Now the market was booming, yet Pascal, Inc., under the son's direction, could not seem to catch a break. Mark's plan to spread his seed, in the form of condominium complexes all over the tristate area, did not seem as realistic as it had been even a year ago. Recently Tracey had said to Robert of Mark Pascal, "Finally lucky in love and, well, you know the second part."

"All that time and energy invested in blueprints and building permits and goddamned attorneys' fees, but it's nothing compared to what I'll lose in the long run if we stick with this."

"You're losing your nerve," Saldana said. "You had the same response to Carroll Gardens, and you'll make money there if you can just wait—"

"I'm not in a patient business!" Mark interrupted. "Developers put up buildings, sell them off, and move on. I'm not a landlord."

"All right," Mario said softly. "So what, exactly, is your plan B?"

"We're going to sell off what we can of Connecticut and stake a bigger claim in lower Manhattan," Pascal announced. Then he directed the conversation to Chip, a Harvard MBA with close-cropped blond hair who looked to be no more than twenty, though Robert knew that was hardly possible. Chip had been mostly silent, but now he cleared his throat and began to talk rapidly and with great enthusiasm about the Battery Park City — TriBeCa—SoHo residential corridor. "We're going to rehab old lofts not far from the new investment banking center on Water Street, create luxury apartments with artistic flare," he said, "giant picture windows, exposed pipes, distressed beams. Bankers eat that artist's-loft shit right up."

"Zoning is like a checkerboard below Canal," Mario Saldana said. "Have you talked to Carpenter? If I'd have known this was where we were going, I'd have gotten him back here from the bloody Hamptons."

Carpenter was their land-use specialist. He had a degree in civil engineering and they'd paid a lot of money to lure him from another firm. Like the tax guys, who knew they were in demand, Carpenter walked around in a strange state of either arrogance or oblivion, Robert wasn't sure which, but he never seemed to be where you needed him. Then again, they had all assumed that the reason for this meeting was sewage in Connecticut, not building in TriBeCa.

"Right now we're only putting feelers out. Anyway, I had lunch with Carpenter last week," Pascal said.

"I wish someone had bothered to tell me that!" Saldana snapped.

Robert had never heard the restrained Saldana snap at anyone in his life.

"We're making overtures to the owners of an old button-and-fastenings factory on Hudson," Pascal continued. "Owned by one family for generations. They're cagey; the space has sentimental value, et cetera. I'm having lunch with the grandfather and two grandsons on Saturday."

"Family businesses are tough," Robert said.

"We have a few other possibilities, but I like this one. The adjacent loading dock gives us a large envelope," Pascal added. "I'd like you to come with me to the lunch on Saturday."

Robert knew what that meant. The owners were regular people who didn't go to college, people with regional accents. He was known for being good with such people, had been called in more than once by Pascal, Inc., to advise them in disputes with construction companies. He had no labor background—only the experience of being on the other side of management, as a cabbie. "Sure," Robert said. "If you want me there, I'll be there." *You say how high,* he thought, *and I'll jump. At least this year I will.*

In the next six months, Robert, Wilton Henry, and a third lawyer, a woman named Liesel MacDuff, would all be officially in competition for partner, a process that could keep them in suspense for another full year. There were three other men being considered, as well — though Robert didn't think that any of the three had strong backing. There'd be pressure to make the first female real estate partner, and though Wilton Henry had not brought in much business, he was an excellent craftsman with a head for complex transactions, and he had supporters. Robert had brought in business — much of it came from Barry and his contacts, the new banking money — but the big, long-term money was in developers, large construction issues, and there he had been less successful.

Mario was talking now about financing. Which banks was he talking to? "Local this time," Mario said. "No more of those German banks. It looks bad."

"I thought you South Americans liked the Germans," Pascal replied.

Robert looked over at Saldana, waiting for a reaction, and found himself focusing on something he could hardly believe: a stain on the ridiculously fastidious man's collar, tiny, brown, and circular, perhaps a bit of dried blood from shaving. If a small colony of tiny humans had appeared on Saldana's collar, Robert could not have been more surprised.

A knock at the door interrupted his thoughts. Assuming it to be someone who would clear away the food, Mark told them to come in, adding, "Let's get some of this shit off the table."

But it was not a waiter. It was Sally Johannson.

"There was nobody at reception to help me," she said. "And I — I saw you through the glass — you told me to come today, and —" She looked at Robert, as if for help.

He stood up, aware that not one of them was looking at him. All eyes were on Sally. "I'm sorry. This is a little poorly timed surprise of mine. Sally is a shoe-shine girl, and an excellent one. Your shoes will stay shiny for days afterward. And I've bought you all a shoe shine. As a gift. She'll come back, though, won't you, when we're finished? We should be done here in about, well, when do you think, Mark?"

"I think we've said everything that we need to say for today," Mark replied, still staring at Sally. "Can I go first?"

Robert never did figure out how she'd walked all that way without being stopped by reception, or one of the secretaries, but it was late in the day, not quite five, and likely the receptionist had left early. By late June the partners had already begun their three- and four-day weekends—many of them did so in lieu of actual vacations, which were becoming more difficult for anyone to take as business grew and took on computerized urgency; and men who might have cut back, as partners had always done in years past, now found themselves working as hard as ever, or retiring. But even A, L and W did not ignore summer altogether, or the way in which businesses in the city adopted their own schedule from June to August so that Mondays and Fridays always held out the cruel hope that freedom was possible.

When Sally had finished in the conference room she went to look for Elaine, who was still owed a shine. As she passed from office to office, lawyers looked up from their work, got out of their chairs and walked to their doorways, watching as she moved down the hall. Those who understood her purpose asked for a shoe shine, others who did not found her later in the offices of their colleagues and did the same. People bought each other shines. There was chatting and laughing in the hallways in a way rarely heard. Two hours after she'd arrived, Sally showed up in Robert's doorway to thank him, and to be paid for all the conference room shoe shines.

"You won't believe how much business I got today!" she said breathlessly.

"I thought you didn't get business. I thought that was your boss," he said, sitting down and lifting his pants leg to show his shoe. "Don't forget your benefactor."

She put her box down at his feet. "No, I mean, I gave out our card all over the place. Everyone wants me to come back."

"Then you'll have to come back," he said. "This is a democracy."

"Not if the receptionists won't let me through, or one of the partners goes ballistic."

"Have your boss call me," he said. "I take full responsibility. I've never seen so many unhappy people smile in my life."

She had his shoe up on the footrest and now squirted white liquid all over it. "Mark Pascal wants me to come there, too. Wow, I'm going to rake it in."

"How much *do* you make?" he asked.

"A lot," she said, then lowered her voice. "Twenty dollars an hour minimum, with tips. That's under the table. Plus I don't have to work with food, or deal with drunks."

She scrubbed his shoe with a narrow toothbrushlike instrument, bending over it with concentration. The room was over-air-conditioned, but she looked disheveled and flushed from exertion. "You should ask your boss for a cut, you know, like a finder's fee on new business."

"I don't want to get involved in the business end," she said. "I only work four days a week and I have auditions. These are English shoes, right?"

Robert nodded. Her nipples were visible through the thin fabric of her pink T-shirt. "When do you go out?" he asked.

"Hardly at all," she replied. "I'm in a play now, and rehearsals take up a lot of time." She stopped what she was doing just then and lowered her brush, looked up at him. "I know how this goes. At this point you ask me out. I have a boyfriend. He's on the road now in *A Chorus Line*."

"What about your show?" he asked.

"Oh, the usual," she said, finishing off with a quick back-and-forth of the flannel rag. "A young playwright, a director right out of NYU, make lemonade."

"The play is about lemonade?"

She told him to switch feet. "I mean take lemons and make lemonade. In this case the lousy part and wooden dialogue are the lemons. And when you do that for enough years, maybe, maybe someone will spot you doing something great in a bad part in a terrible play."

"Sounds awful."

"Actually," she said, raising her head from her work, "it's the best thing in the world. You think anyone would live like this otherwise?"

"I'll have to come see for myself. When's the performance?"

She paused to pull a polish-stained piece of paper out of her apron. "Here's a flyer," she said. The play was called *Bus Sickness*, five performances at a theater off Union Square.

"This is soon."

"In two weeks; and in three weeks I have to move out of my apartment—my boyfriend's apartment, actually, because the subletter is coming back. And don't offer to buy me an apartment. I've had that offer from clients. Plenty."

He laughed. "Sally, you assume nothing but ulterior motives from people."

"Don't you?" she asked. "Have those? Because that's all I deal with all day long. Like I'm for sale. Let me make it clear right now: I'm *not* for sale."

"I didn't think that you were!" This was going to be difficult. "Sally, look at me. Do you think I hurt for women?"

She stopped again to scrutinize him. "Probably not," she said, and went back to her work.

"And I'm married."

She snorted. "Yeah, whatever."

"I do, however, own an apartment that you could rent. You'd have to pay, of course."

"How much?"

"It's empty now. Three and a half rooms on the Upper West Side."

"How much?"

"If I break even on the mortgage, that'll be enough. Say six hundred dollars."

"No way your mortgage is six hundred." She took a brush out of a bottle of what appeared to be black ink, and the strong scent of chemicals filled the air. Then she ran the brush around the edge of his sole to make it darker.

"Don't you want to come see it?" he asked. "Prewar, great light."

She sat up and brushed the hair out of her eyes. "I guess I don't see the point of going to see an apartment I can't afford because your mortgage sure as hell is more than six hundred dollars. I'm not for owing anyone anything. People have a way of demanding payment, men particularly." She placed his other foot back on the cloth, and then began to put her belongings back in the box. "Look, you got me some business, which I appreciate. I had a good day. Let's leave it at that."

"Okay," he said, sighing. Was he getting older, or was she anticipating every line before he could say it? She was right about the apartment, but he was suddenly willing to take a loss, all previous plans disregarded. "But I know how hard housing is in this city."

"Tell me about it!" She stood and picked up her box. "I counted the other day. You know that I've been in nine different apartments since I left Philly? That was six years ago."

"Philadelphia? As in Pennsylvania?"

"Not Mississippi. Oh, you owe me eight bucks for the shines in the conference room. What's the matter, you never met anyone from Philadelphia before?"

"I'm from Philadelphia." He handed her a twenty and told her to keep it.

She took the bill and thanked him. "Don't tell me, you're from the Main Line, right?"

He shook his head. "You?"

"The Northeast," she said. "Oxford Circle. You even know where that is?"

"I grew up on Disston Street."

"Harbison."

"My grandmother lived on Harbison," he said. "The garden apartments." The coincidence struck them both with the same force, as if they had come from a distant country known only to its inhabitants. Neither said anything for what felt like a long time.

"Three years, I've never met a single person from home in New York."

"That's because they don't leave."

"I guess maybe that makes things a little different," she said, and put her hand on her hip, studying him again. She would tell him later that she didn't see her customers most of the time; she'd trained herself that way. Even walking down the street, people were a blur to her. She moved impervious to men's catcalls and women's patronizing questions, safe in her own little world. She was an actress. And maybe, he thought, all attractive young women had to be actresses, to survive the probing eyes of the world, and the curiosity and aggression of men.

"Sally, I'll give you that apartment for whatever you want to pay," he said. "My intentions are honorable. I won't bother you or expect anything. I swear. Scout's honor. Just take it; make your life a little easier."

He meant it, at least in the moment that he said it. When he stopped trying, dropped the flirtation and games that had worked so well all his life, then and only then did he pull her in.

"Okay, Robert Vishniak," she said. "When can I see the place?"

CHAPTER FORTY-ONE

Empty house

Robert had entered his marriage intending to be faithful. His parents had been faithful for forty years, and so had all his aunts and uncles. In fact, until he got to college he'd never met anyone whose parents were divorced. He didn't think it even occurred to Stacia or Vishniak to cheat; marriage was a legal and religious contract, a binding condition, and besides, neither one of them had such a high opinion of their own charms, nor did they seek out people outside their own families. Yet among their children, his generation of cousins, many were already divorced. Barry was almost thirty-five and no closer to marriage than he'd been twenty years ago. When Robert asked Stacia what happened, why there was suddenly so much divorce in the family, she'd replied, "The sixties happened, that's what. Everyone thinks they have all the choices in the world now. Well guess what, mister, you don't."

But the problem was that Robert, in fact, did. He was aware of this privilege and appreciated it. Appreciated, for instance, having a driver, though he'd initially fought the hire until he realized that if he picked the man himself and paid his salary then he might have the best of both worlds—freedom and privacy. He appreciated that he and Crea never had to worry about babysitters or radically change their lifestyle, because their nanny lived in. She was a homely Hunter graduate student in linguistics who could speak to his daughter in several languages and kept to herself when not working. Crea hired her. He enjoyed the luxury of their homes, the liberty of so many choices. No purchase was prohibitive, no vacation too extravagant, if they could only schedule the time. Crea was still a profligate gift giver, which created a problem because he felt the burden to reciprocate but could not always afford it. And there was nothing he loved more, no moment that gave him a bigger thrill, than picking up the check. He did it whenever possible.

His personal finances and those of his wife (the "family" finances) were two separate but interconnected things, yet he denied that separateness to himself. Trying to keep up with his own wife meant that out of nowhere, the arrival of certain bank statements could make him feel as if he'd laid his hand on an electric fence. Easier not to look too closely at such mail. Still, he benefited from Crea's generosity. Recently, she had bought him a Patek Philippe watch, waterproof, and platinum, with a large blue face. When he was concentrating on a problem at work, he would sometimes take it off and hold it in one hand and then the other, shuffling the object back and forth, feeling the heavy weight of its worth. In the first few months of ownership, when he'd taken the $25,000 watch, warm from his own touch, and slipped it back on, he felt a pleasure that was almost erotic. But that feeling didn't last long and only left him empty and restless for something else.

Life with Crea might be equated exactly with that watch. The novelty, the heft, while still impressive, had worn off more quickly than he'd expected. He was left with the satisfactions, some of them quite substantial, of work and family life, of caring for his daughter and watching her grow up. This, and the rare moments of peace between himself and his wife, would have to suffice. The lives of other married associates sounded dull in the extreme: the concerns of private school tuition and repaving the driveway; the striving to get invited to the lowest-level parties and find a sitter, the desire, unfulfilled, for a second home. He was grateful that his marriage, at least, existed above *that* fray.

In his twenties and thirties, he'd believed that he was jaded, and what had made him so was the loss of his young love, but now he understood that losing Gwendolyn had not jaded him — any relationship mourned for so long did not jade a man, only made him more aware of the potential depth and vulnerability of his own feelings, if they could only be touched. Marriage had jaded him and done it quickly. Being married, he was let in on the secrets of other people's unions, either overtly, because sometimes after work and a few drinks married men talked to other married men, or through observation, at the coupled parties and fund-raisers he and Crea attended. And what he'd determined was that his marriage was no better or worse than most.

Marriage was marriage, except for a certain type of rare couple who existed among them as if they were a separate species. At parties, a husband or wife of this type watched the door, not because they feared being caught by their spouse while flirting with someone else, but because they awaited their spouse's arrival with genuine anticipation. It did not matter that they saw each other at home or had known each other for many years — still they watched the door. A couple of this type meeting for dinner in a restaurant would begin talking before they'd even sat down, burdening everyone around them with their passion to share, as if life did not actually happen until one told the other about it. They mystified him, even infuriated him, because they threw a wrench in his theories. He was big, now, on theories. And his most beloved theory was that starting out with a grand passion was no recipe for success in marriage, just as starting out with not much more than warm respect was no guarantee of disaster. And all things being equal, he would rather be in his

392

situation than most. Except when, once in a great while, he saw one of those damned couples at a party.

His wife believed in servants and specialists and now he did, too. A woman had come to arrange his closet, creating special nooks and instruments to keep everything spotless and easily coordinated. All forty pairs of his shoes were similarly arranged. This was how the men in his social milieu always looked so neat, in one sense hardly like men at all, devoid of stains and five o'clock shadow and wrinkles and dull shoes. Expensive clothing in natural fibers had to be steamed and dry-cleaned, wrapped in tissue, arranged and taken care of; luckily other people did this for him. The result being that in summer his linen or cotton suits moved with his body as unobtrusively as a whisper; in winter, fine Italian wool was unusually warm but not bulky. Both were as foreign as possible from the scratchy blue polyester uniform that his father wore to work, with the name embroidered on the pocket, the white undershirt underneath with the collar peeking through, and the crepe shoes with the squeaks that announced him anywhere he went. Getting dressed for work each morning, Robert could feel the art and craft of his clothing.

Despite wearing these things, he still fought personal vanity as he always had, despising men who used hair gel or stared at themselves for too long while shaving — he occasionally cut himself working not to fall into the trap. Gyms with their weights and steam rooms, once the training places of dancers and professional athletes or the social outlet of homosexuals, now dotted every block in the city. He found the concept humiliating. To ride a bike or jog around the park in old clothes, panting and sweating, was one thing, but wearing spandex and jumping up and down, staring at oneself in the mirror, this he could not abide. Perhaps it was all he could do, with so much care going into his wardrobe, to carve out a little niche of self-abrogation for himself, to continue his own personal battle against narcissism.

It was an uphill fight. Almost forty, he now had his asthma more under control—age had reduced its severity—so that, still lean, he looked healthy from the outdoor exercise he was now able to enjoy. His posture was still excellent, but the tragedies of his early twenties, and his natural intensity, had taken their toll on his physiognomy: there were frown lines etched lightly around his mouth and across his forehead; a pronounced furrow was visible above his nose, and the gray was quickly overtaking the black in his hair. But when he smiled and the dimple flared on his cheek, there was still that about him which was boyish.

There was nothing that New York women of all ages, and men, too, liked more than a handsome man of a certain age who dressed meticulously and reeked of affluence. Young women, and some men, too, stared at him on the street, in movie lines, or while waiting for the elevator. They offered him their phone numbers, or looked right at his wedding ring and invited him to dinner. And it was even easier to say yes now, because the women had changed. They didn't care so much, did not hang on a man the way they used to—they now had their time, the way men had always had time, to enjoy themselves. Oh, his generation had it, too, but the women of his youth were absorbed in their own novelty and its challenges. Their energy went into the making of the thing, the opening of heavy doors that had once been bolted shut. But for the young women coming of age in this decade, there was little sense of breaking down anything, only the desire to live and enjoy being young and single before, someday, in some distant future, settling down.

In short, to be Robert Vishniak in New York City in the summer of 1986 was to be faced with endless temptation—beautiful women were everywhere and they wanted him, often without strings, and he had only to stretch out his hand and take. Much of the time he said no, was proud of himself for that, perhaps too proud; his wife was so focused on him that he didn't have the heart. Were she to discover an affair, he feared it might kill her. Most certainly it would end life as he knew it.

Having set his boundaries so deliberately, so painstakingly, he could not help but wonder, as he sat in the backseat of his car and waited to be delivered home in the bright light of an early summer evening, why had he taken so many stupid chances with Sally Johannson? Why *her*? She was sexy and young, but no younger or sexier than so many of the others who'd offered themselves so freely to him. Yet he had brought her into his workplace, a place where right now he had to be at his most careful, had offered her his apartment, an apartment he had intended for a wholly other purpose, and now all he could think of was being alone with her there. This was about something more than being from the same neighborhood, it had to be. From the moment he'd seen her shining that first pair of shoes, he'd felt powerless to resist.

Punching in the alarm code, Robert could hear his daughter chanting, "Dad-dy! Dad-dy!" on the other side of the door. He hadn't expected to find anyone home. Since Gwen was born, she and Crea spent Memorial Day through Fourth of July in Tuxedo, and Robert came up on the weekends. Then for July through Labor Day they moved on to Bridgehampton because Crea liked to be there for the polo competitions and the horse show, and because her younger friends preferred the newly chic Hamptons to Tuxedo. They had bought the cottage several years ago. Unable to bear the idea of his wife owning yet another piece of real estate without him, he'd put in some of the down payment. The mortgage was a small one, but even so, with his new Upper West Side apartment, he found two mortgage payments a strain on $75,000 a year. He had other expenses as well, including Troy's salary, which he alone took responsibility for, because he got most of the benefit, and he wanted his chauffeur's loyalty and also, somehow, his respect. Was it possible to be a kept man while drowning at the same time? That was his problem — he was neither fully kept nor fully independent — but he had made this deal and had no one to blame but himself.

His daughter was jumping up and down, and he picked her up

and kissed her. "I'm so glad to see you, Gwen-Gwenny-Gwendolyn! What are you doing here?" He carried her, his arms gripped lightly around her behind, her legs wrapped around his chest like a monkey, into the living room where his wife sat reading a magazine.

"Surprise," she said languidly. "We had to come home." She paused as if for effect. "The pills the allergist gave her are just not working."

His daughter had not only inherited his face, she had inherited his allergies.

Robert sat down with Gwendolyn in his lap. "Honey, go ask May when dinner is going to be ready," Robert said. "Maybe she'll let you help."

Gwen, smart enough to sense where the action was, hung on him until he forcefully sent her on her way. Once his daughter entered the kitchen, she'd become entranced. She was fascinated by the processes of heat — blending, baking, melting — wanted nothing more than to watch the alchemy of ingredients all day long.

"I don't like to do that to May," Crea said. "She's a cook, not a babysitter. And we have an extra tonight for dinner."

"Oh?"

"My father came back with us for the appointment. He's coming by for dinner — don't look like that. He's staying in the city overnight, so I invited him."

"You see him every night in Tuxedo. You can't take a night off?" Robert got up and went to the stairs, then yelled up to the nanny, whose name was Karen; she had her own studio and bathroom on the third floor.

"Must you yell?" Crea asked. "Use the intercom."

"I hate the intercom," he said. "It makes me feel like I'm at work. Anyway, she's in there with her music on."

Karen called down to him, and he asked if she could go watch Gwen in the kitchen. The nanny ducked out of her room, closed her door, and came charging down the steps. She had a heavy footfall.

"Problem solved. Why was she up there, anyway?" he asked, sitting next to Crea on the couch.

"Because Gwen was with us and Karen needs some time to herself."

"She gets awfully absorbed in her reading."

"It's better than getting awfully absorbed in the wine cellar," Crea said, lowering her voice. "You need to be more consistent with the staff. Either you ask nothing of them, or you expect them to read your mind and be at your beck and call."

"I know. You're right. Even after all this time, well, it still feels odd having so many strangers in the house. Don't get me wrong, I enjoy the convenience, but I feel like we're never alone. Not to mention the 'guests' who stop by for dinner."

"My father is not a guest. Anyway, when we're alone lately all we do is fight," she said, and moved her hand closer to his.

"Tell me what the doctor said." He lifted up her hand and kissed it. The slightest show of affection by him made his wife sit up straighter, her face lit with a sudden and frightening hope. Each night, he came home determined to be kind but broke his resolution within moments. His parents had bickered all his life, but they had money and health problems to worry about; he and Crea bickered over stupid things.

They went on to discuss Gwendolyn's allergies, and the change of medication that was supposed to keep her up less at night and make her less drowsy during the day. In a few years she would likely need shots. Robert heard accusation in Crea's every word—his genetics had given her this. "She seems fine now," he said.

"Well, she's always worse in the country."

"Then maybe you shouldn't take her there so much."

"That's just what you want, isn't it? Any excuse not to go to Tuxedo."

"Our daughter's health is not an excuse."

"She has to be in the world, Robert. We can't keep her locked in a box. She has to be able to run and play and be outside with other children."

"It's not that I don't like Tuxedo or even think it's so bad for her," he said. "I just don't see why we have to always stay with your father. Instead of buying in the Hamptons, we should have bought in the Park years ago. Tracey and Claudia were dying to sell us that lot."

"Jack has seven bedrooms. It's not like he crowds us. And he likes seeing Gwen."

"My mother likes seeing her, too, but I don't see us running there every weekend."

"I never keep you from going," she said. "But I don't think I'm welcome."

"That's ridiculous. You don't want to go and so you blame it on my mother. Anyway, we're not talking about Philadelphia, we're talking about Tuxedo. Honestly." He stood up. "I feel like I can never breathe. I've got your father and his people looking me over at the office, and then there he is on my weekends. And Mario, too, another member of the partnership committee."

"You said that Mario has helped you a great deal."

"That doesn't mean I want to see him on weekends!" As soon as the words were out, Robert knew he was being ridiculous. It wasn't Mario he was annoyed about. "Jack stays out of my way at the office, too, yet still manages to make his presence known. And what's that I hear? Oh, he's right on cue."

The buzzer rang, and Karen and Gwen rushed to open it. His daughter was chanting, "Gram-pa, Gram-pa," and for the second time that day the child was lifted high into the air and then dropped gently to the ground. Robert went over and welcomed his father-in-law as if the past ten minutes of conversation had never occurred, a smile plastered on his face. Jack looked around at the Arts and Crafts–style furniture, the stained-glass window in the entrance, the early-twentieth-century feeling of the house, and frowned. "What is that over there?" he asked Crea.

"It's a clock," Robert said. "Erhard and Söhne," he added. "Silver on wood." This one, which did not chime, had replaced the larger, louder clock from her Gramercy place. He pointed to the intricate carving of the two knights jousting on the bottom.

"What did she do with that Chuck Close portrait I gave her?" Jack asked. "When I give a gift, I like to see it on the wall."

"Why don't we sit down?" Robert said. "May just gave us the signal."

During dinner, Robert was forced to summarize that day's meeting with Mark Pascal for his father-in-law, though he tried to avoid too much detail about the sewage problems.

"Perhaps I need to go back to sitting in on those meetings," Jack said.

"Talk to Mario," Robert mumbled. At almost seventy, Jack was backing away from the practice of law in favor of the management of the firm. There was hope among some of the younger partners that this signaled his move toward retirement, but Robert knew that his father-in-law would hold on to his firm — his baby — for dear life, just as he held on to his daughter.

"That was a solid business five years ago," Jack replied. "Now Mark's making all kinds of crazy decisions."

The unspoken message being: when the older generation managed things, all was well. Robert did not reply.

"Gwen, eat like a big girl. Don't use your fingers," Crea said. "Must you two talk about the office at dinner? I feel completely left out."

"All right, dear, let's talk about Gwen's allergies," Jack said. "She looks much better. This morning she gave us quite a scare with that coughing."

Robert looked at Crea, but she changed the subject. "Here's something Gwen will like," Crea said. "We're invited to a pool party at the Evanses' on Saturday."

"Can I use my new wings?" Gwen asked.

Robert, who had not planned to tell her so far in advance, so as to avoid argument, now had to announce that he would stay in the city this weekend for a meeting with Mark Pascal.

"Is that really necessary?" she asked. "On a Saturday? In June?"

Jack continued eating in silence.

"You can ask Mark if you don't believe me."

"Why wouldn't I *believe* you? Gwen, eat some of that sautéed spinach, it's very good. What about Saturday night?"

"I think I'll need the whole weekend," Robert said, "to catch up on some work."

"I assume you'll be up for the Fourth," she said. "You wouldn't miss the Traces' barbecue?"

"I will if there are no crises at the office," he said, glancing at his father-in-law, who did not raise his eyes from his plate. "Barry will be at the Fourth this year, too."

"You're lucky that your brother is in the city," Jack said wistfully. His one remaining brother had recently retired to Palm Springs.

"Yes," Crea said, picking up the decanter and pouring herself some more wine, "how lucky for all of us." She let the decanter drop to the table with a disapproving thud.

"Crea, be careful with that!" Jack said. "It was your grand-mother's."

AFTER DINNER, ROBERT AND JACK sat in silence reading the newspaper. Upstairs, Crea was in the middle of giving Gwendolyn a bath when the screaming began, echoing throughout the house.

"That doesn't sound good," Jack said.

"No," Robert replied. "I'd better get up there."

"Can't you send the girl?"

"No, she's screaming for me."

Jack only shook his head, as if to ponder the mysteries of modern parenting, and went back to his reading.

Gwen did this whenever her father was at home. She claimed that Crea got soap in her eyes, but she was perfectly happy to let her mother bathe her and wash her hair when he wasn't around. Robert felt for his wife in these moments. She looked so rejected. "Look at her arm," Crea said, as soon as he entered the bathroom. Gwendolyn sat in the tub, her face blotchy and red from crying. Her arm, held aloft by Crea, was dotted with a large round rash.

"She's allergic to tomatoes," Robert said.

"Don't tell me," Crea replied. "You had that, too."

"Barry, Barry had it," he said. "Well, who knows what it was because we never saw doctors. But he got rashes like that when he was small, and he wasn't allowed to eat tomatoes."

"What about spaghetti sauce?" Gwen asked.

"That's tomatoes, too, kitten," he said.

"Soap my hair, Daddy." She took his hand and put it on her head. Crea dropped the washcloth and left the bathroom.

"Okay, Gwen-Gwenny-Gwendolyn, now let's get down to business here," he said, rolling up his sleeves, then hiking up his trousers and kneeling beside the tub. He reached for the baby shampoo, taking a small puddle into his hand. "Close your eyes."

"It's just the two of us now, right, Dad?" she asked from behind her closed eyes, her voice merry with satisfaction. "Just Daddy and his Gwenny."

CHAPTER FORTY-TWO

Sally will not give in

For the record, I'm not going to sleep with you. I don't care how nice your place is."

"I haven't even shaken your hand yet," he said, standing close to her in the long hallway. He put his hand carefully on her lower back as if to lead her around the place. "I can control myself." He had been late, coming from his business lunch with Pascal and the owners of the button factory. The meeting went well; the family was more open to selling than Mark had implied, albeit for the right price. Mark, elated, took Robert to his club afterward to have a drink and discuss a few things. He kept him there for too long, but then, any wait might have felt like forever with Sally at the end of it.

"You said this place was unfurnished," Sally said, peeking into the bedroom, "so why is there furniture here?"

"I ordered a few things this week. Just a few chairs, a couch, a bed."

"If it's furnished, does the price go up?"

"Sure," he said. "Let's say six hundred and fifty dollars."

"What's the actual mortgage? I won't do this if you don't tell me."

"Fifteen hundred, plus three hundred a month maintenance."

She frowned. "Can't pay more than eight hundred. For a little while. Until I find something else."

"I'd have given it to you for six fifty. Negotiation is not supposed to mean that the buyer hikes up the price. That's highly unorthodox."

"You could get anyone in here, for full price or more," she said. They were standing in the living room that looked out onto a courtyard and got the midday sun. Sally wore a short summer dress and flat red sandals, her hair held back by a clip. She looked more proper than at the office, but he could see her legs better this way. They seemed to go on forever, and then there was the line of her panties, visible under the thin skirt.

She plopped herself down on the couch, which still had on the plastic cover it had been delivered with. "Plastic," she said, and looked up at him, "just like home."

"You had to have been the only Johannson in Oxford Circle," he said.

"Who says that's my real name?"

He sat down next to her on the couch. "You're something else."

"A lotta tricks up these sleeves," she said, gesturing to her naked arms.

He put his hand on her bicep and ran his finger down her soft, pale skin.

"I told you," she said, standing up, "it's not happening. Not even because you're cutting me a break with the rent. I'm only doing this because I'm desperate. I'll be out in a month or two." She walked over to the windowsill, then stared up at the molding. "How many friends from Philly do you have in New York?"

"Just my brother."

"Barry Vishniak?" she asked sarcastically. "You and me could be friends. I bet that would break a pattern for you. Friends with a woman? Try something new for a change."

"I have a woman friend," he said. "Claudia."

Sally sighed. "What is Claudia, like, a friend of your wife's or something?"

"She is, among other things."

"Doesn't count. I'm not talking about someone who's your friend because sleeping with her would destroy your life. I mean someone who's your friend because, you know, you have stuff in common, or you get a beer after work, or whatever."

"What do we have in common?"

"Lots of stuff."

"I can't be friends with you. Not when I want to see you naked," he said. "I'm trying to be honest here."

"You're honest, all right," she said, walking back into the hallway. "Why'd you buy this place, anyway? Is it an investment or something?"

"Something like that," he called from the couch, then got up and followed.

"Your wife know about it?"

"Absolutely."

"Should I, like, call her and ask how she feels about your renting under market value?" she asked. "Damn, this kitchen is small."

"All kitchens in New York are small."

"This one is for some chick who weighs ninety pounds. So what is this? Your love den? What kind of place do you live in with your wife?"

"Beaux-Arts townhouse, circa nineteen twenty-one, East Seventy-third Street."

She whistled. "And you bought *this*? What, three floors wasn't enough space for you?"

"You probably won't believe this, but I wanted a place where I could be alone and think."

"That I *do* believe," she said. She now stood uncomfortably close to him. He could smell the watermelon lip gloss and a faint odor of bubble gum from a piece cradled in the back of her mouth. "You have it all, don't you, Robert?"

"Pretty much, yup."

"The saddest people in the world, if you ask me."

"Who is?"

"People who have it all."

CHAPTER FORTY-THREE

Independence Day

The last week in June, Robert went to see Sally in her show, a horrid mess about a group of soldiers, a nurse, and a drug-addicted doctor in Vietnam. The dialogue barely got above the level of bad television, but he saw something in her performance, some spark beyond mere physical charisma, and he found himself relieved. She was not a fraud. She could act. It would have been awful, somehow, if she were just kidding herself. She had a monologue toward the end, about a boyfriend she'd left behind, whom she knew she'd have to leave as soon as she returned because he'd never understand what she'd been through, had never experienced *this*, but she'd hold on to him for now, no matter how selfish, because she needed his letters. Needed someone, anyone, to speak words of love to her. As she spoke the lines, she seemed to look right at Robert—the only one in the audience, from the looks of things, who'd actually come of age in the era that these actors in their early twenties now gamely tried to reconstruct. Or maybe it was just that the house was small—only about fifteen people in a place with easily three times that many seats — and he wanted that longing of hers to be specific, to be for him.

Afterward, going backstage, he had asked if she wanted to get a drink and celebrate, but she was going out with the cast, a scruffy bunch of young men from the show. They had taken up a certain dirty, hippie-ish style that made him uncomfortable in his Italian suit and, feeling old and separate, he left quickly, wondering why he could not get this girl out of his system.

EVEN IN TUXEDO THAT WEEKEND, he thought of her. It was Fourth of July, a time of parades, evening fireworks, and the Traces' annual barbecue, held, as always, in their enormous backyard over-looking the lake and distant hills. The Traces' home was a castle, enormous and Gothic, complete with rounded turrets and a large, pointed corner tower with a window seat on the tippy top. If you dared attempt to sit on it, it rewarded you with a view that stretched across the Park, the river, and into the next county. Robert always enjoyed the extent to which Tracey's house dwarfed Jack's. The only time he ever saw his father-in-law look uncertain was when he was surveying the Traces' property, perhaps reflecting on what it might be like to have a place preserved through the generations, as opposed to one that had swept the past so utterly clean.

Robert still thought it the most wholly romantic house in the Park, at least from the outside. Claudia had long ago taken over the grounds work — it was her one true pleasure, working outside with the gardener. In front was an extensive flower garden, and around each side were herbs and vegetables. Guests often asked: how could one woman do so much with only an elderly man to help? She was always out there weeding and pruning. Except today, when she came toward Robert in tiny white shorts and a black sleeveless turtleneck, so that from far away, and even more up close, what he noticed were her long legs, so strikingly, luridly lean, her thighs the width of an adolescent's, and the narrow but shapely arms, muscular from so much weeding and work outdoors. As she moved, he could almost see the bone and tissue and muscle all working together under her skin. "Isn't Gwen getting big?" Claudia kissed Crea and smiled at him, then made quickly for Barry, who had just pulled up in his new Audi convertible. "Finally — I'd almost despaired! You're going to be bored out of your head, you know?"

Barry, getting out of the car, looked pleased with himself. "I'm a one-man band, kiddo. When I'm here it's never boring."

Claudia grabbed his hand and ran with him toward the house.

"Can I go with them?" Gwen asked.

"No, sweetheart, let's go see the juggler," Robert said.

"What on earth do those two say to each other?" Crea asked.

"He can be charming sometimes," Robert replied, as they walked toward the back patio.

Tracey played lord of the manor, shaking hands, hurrying along waiters, holding babies, and directing people to a croquet game set up on the lawn. When the food was almost cooked, Tracey stepped in, taking the tongs from the caterers to turn over the bratwurst and flip a few burgers, so that, just as in college, he had taken the credit for the thing without actually having to do the work. The children, off together on the other side of the house, were now being rounded up for the food, which would be served to them separately. Crea stood with her head thrown back, laughing, her hand on Mark Pascal's shoulder. Robert rarely heard her laugh like that anywhere but in Tuxedo. Around her stood several childhood friends and a few elderly neighbors, people who'd known her for so long that they might as well have been family.

Robert remembered what she told him on his first visit — there was no place in the world she felt more at peace. Tuxedo was her history. But what of his? He rarely saw the familiar faces of his childhood — the young cousins he'd run with or the girls with whom he'd first had sex. Stacia was a voice on the telephone, or the guilty pull of a fast visit, made alone or occasionally with Gwen for an afternoon. He had done what he was raised to do, moving beyond Oxford Circle — and he had made money. Yet, witnessing Crea's comfort, as if Tuxedo were an old sweater she put on for warmth, he felt adrift.

As the afternoon wore on, he chatted with a successful contractor, then shook hands with a developer who had claimed for the last twenty years to be "considering" A, L and W to represent him. Robert made another lunch date with the man, hoping he'd keep this one, but had low hopes — even Jack had failed to reel him in, after many tries. Then he talked to an "independent financial advisor," which was a nice way of saying that the man invested his family's money. Tracey's group of friends was virtually unchanging, and they had long ago been squeezed for business, where possible. For Robert, there was no more juice to be had.

For Barry, on the other hand, the day was filled with possibilities. Robert could hear him on the other side of the lawn talking with a few members of the local bridge club about limited-liability partnerships. He sounded certain, trustworthy, sober even, as he described low-risk investments in oil and natural gas. Where had he gotten that tone? Not at home, that was for sure. Someone asked him about junk bonds — Boesky was still in the news, and now there were murmurings about Milken. "Junk bonds are not for you, Cathleen; they're for billionaires, and pension and insurance funds. Not for your average investor," Barry said. "Let's talk about what's *secure* —"

Barry had already caught on to what it took Robert years to realize — that the rich liked to consider themselves middle-class. The idea comforted them in some strange way, and was about the only thing that they shared in common with the poor. Robert walked off alone to stare at the view. Just then, Sally was back in New York, moving her stuff up into his apartment with two male friends — it was so humid today, would be especially so in the city, and he could imagine her drenched in sweat, the rings under her arms, the beads of moisture collecting on her upper lip as they hoisted her furniture and dragged up boxes and trash bags of possessions—in his imagination, somehow, Sally had endless possessions, as many as he had, though he knew that this was unlikely. Afterward the three would probably go out to dinner in the neighborhood, someplace cheap. He wondered if she was sleeping with either boy . . . or was she loyal to the boyfriend? And when would he be back to claim her?

HOURS LATER, THE SUN SLIPPED below the horizon, and Robert could hear the futile pops of the first few impotent fireworks set off in a field behind the club. The adults sat on folding chairs while the children were on blankets on the lawn, staring up at the dark sky dotted with stars, waiting for the festivities to begin. He had hardly seen Barry all day, saw no sign of him now.

Crea sat behind him in a folding chair, while Robert sat on the blanket with Gwen. She'd had a hard day—the ragweed was early that year. Even with taking her medicine in the morning, Gwen still had to have an antihistamine before dinner. He felt her forehead—it was warm, but she had insisted on staying to see the fireworks; still, as she settled down, he felt her dozing against his shoulder. He put his arm around her. "Dad," she whispered, opening her eyes abruptly, "did I miss anything?"

"You won't sleep through the fireworks, baby, it's not possible."

"I decided that I don't like jugglers," she said. "Bo-ring."

"And how do you feel about sack races? Or running with an egg on a spoon?"

"Nope," she said. "People fall down and cry."

"When I was little," he said, "I didn't like most of the activities grown-ups dreamed up to amuse children, either." Stacia had drained all that out of him. But what was Gwen's excuse? He stroked her hair. Maybe she'd been born that way, his chip off the block. From earliest memory, he'd doubted magic, was bored but didn't

410

have the heart to say so the one time Uncle Frank took him to the circus; and he liked few board games except Monopoly, the child's game that he knew now was no game at all.

"You know what, Dad?"

"What, my love?"

"I wish we could be joined together forever, like those twins we saw on the news."

"But they were joined at the head, and remember how uncomfortable they looked? You asked me if each one got to have her own thoughts, remember?"

"I don't need my own thoughts," she said. "I could have yours. We could share."

"No, baby," he said. "Have your own." He hugged her closer. This child was his family, his past and his future. Had his parents felt this rush of emotion when they looked at him? No, they had not been so in need of grounding, surrounded as they were by relations, entrenched in all that was familiar and continuous. They could not have felt this alone.

A loud pop became an explosion of magenta in front of them, followed by green and then gold, and then white. His daughter, finally, finally, struck with the awe of childhood, her mouth hanging open, was so absorbed that she hardly noticed him get up. He felt restless. The sky was not completely dark yet but would be any minute, and as he walked toward the house he saw, in the shadows under the empty, shaded patio, Tracey leaning against a wall next to a tall waiter, the two of them jostling and laughing softly, trying to throw each other off balance.

Robert entered the house from the side, walking through a bustling kitchen with the sound of dishes being stacked, the clink of silverware, and voices barking orders. He came out into a long hallway as lights flickered in front of his eyes, twinkling in the hollowed spaces of walls. Candles—placed there, no doubt, to create this mood, romantic in principle but eerie now—cast long shadows on the floor. Not knowing what he was looking for, he followed the light.

Approaching a collection of doors, he heard a familiar male laugh and then some giggling. Robert opened the door just a crack and peered through — illuminated by a corner lamp, his brother stood with his back to Robert while Claudia knelt in front of him. At first Robert imagined the most obvious, and the idea was so shocking that he almost looked away until he realized, relieved, that it was an optical illusion — she was bending over a table as Barry watched her. Robert knocked softly. Barry rushed over and, seeing who it was, told him to come in.

"At least lock the door, for God's sake," Robert said, closing it behind him.

Claudia looked up and in one fast and efficient motion sucked up what was in front of her. He noticed the perspiration on her forehead and upper lip, and when she stood up, shakily, and came toward the two brothers, Robert took out a handkerchief and wiped her face.

"Come on Robert," she said, taking his hand. "Join me."

"Claudia, I don't do that stuff, not since Gwen was born."

"Suit yourself! Little Gwen, so pretty, I don't care what Crea says about her nose —" She went back to the table, where the LP in its jacket lay, and ran her finger along the cardboard edge, collecting whatever residue was left.

"How much has she done?"

"I don't know; she's chasing it. Not a good place to be. Can you get me some whiskey?" Barry asked. "I have a few Valium with me. She needs to come down a little."

"Who says I want to?" Claudia called out.

"There's nothing left," Barry replied. Claudia paced back and forth by the window, running her fingers through her hair. "I'm all tapped out, honey."

"Can't you leave her alone?" Robert asked.

"She'd just get it somewhere else," Barry said. "And I won't let anything happen to her."

"How are you so sure?"

Barry's black-brown eyes darted left and right. "I won't let anything happen to her," he said, so softly that Robert could hardly hear him, "because I love her."

"That's rich," Robert mumbled.

"She's the prettiest, classiest girl I ever met," he replied, sounding to Robert suddenly fourteen, the age when women had first puzzled and betrayed him. Claudia paced back and forth in front of the window, holding a Kleenex to her nose.

"She was that way once," Robert whispered.

"You wanted her, didn't you?" Barry asked. "Years ago? And she didn't want you."

"This is all too sick for me. I'm leaving."

"Get us that whiskey I asked for," he said. "Please."

Robert walked down the long hall and out the back door. What was it with Barry and Tracey and all of them, insisting he had feelings for Claudia — the only woman in his life for whom he felt only a brotherly compassion? Was this what happened when you hid your past and kept your secrets from the people around you? They grabbed at pieces of your history and used them to justify whatever conclusion they liked?

The bartender had gone inside and he found a mostly empty bottle, poured a few fingers into a paper cup. Above his head, the last reds and pinks, then blues and greens, exploded in front of him, illuminating the valley in greater and greater bursts, like the last furious lovemaking at the end of an affair. Taking the scotch, he delivered it to the room where Barry and Claudia had been. The door was open and they were gone. He placed the glass on a side table by the bed, then wiped the album cover off with a corner of the bedspread. The Dave Clark Five. The same one Tracey had listened to in their first year of college. He stared for a moment at the smiling, clean-cut young men in their dark ties and narrow lapels, and then quickly left the room.

CHAPTER FORTY-FOUR

Summer, part II

For the rest of the summer, with Crea and Gwen at the beach, Robert was at liberty on weekday evenings. Sometimes he stayed at work, but more often than not he felt restless — even the most ambitious of lawyers didn't tend to stay past 8:00 p.m. after July 4. Prudence Brothers had sent Barry to Hong Kong as a reward for being one of their top brokers, and Tracey was either off with one of his young tennis partners or in Tuxedo with Claudia. Instead of enjoying this solitude, as he'd expected, Robert felt distracted and uneasy.

And so, after work on most Tuesdays, and more than a few Wednesdays as well, he found himself sitting on the cheap cloth couch he'd bought for Sally's use, beer in hand as he sweated in the heat — she had no air-conditioning — and they huddled in front of a rusty portable fan that she'd borrowed from a friend. There was no question of her coming to his place to enjoy the central air; she'd nixed it before he even had a chance to ask. Sometimes they watched television, or played Monopoly, but, though the heat made it hard to eat, he could usually persuade her to get some food in the air-conditioned diner on the ground floor.

She allowed him to pick up the check, that much she would abide, explaining that if he wanted to eat out, he'd have to pay. Her life was not like his, she informed him; she wasn't out spending money every night. Once, he was able to persuade her to go with him someplace better. She put on a dress and heels and they went to the Union Square Café. He thought she'd like it, though he did not say so — she was temperamental, proud; he had to be careful what he did and didn't do for her, and how he introduced it. He said only that he wanted a change of neighborhood. The two-story restaurant, which had opened the year before, was popular, and he'd had to reserve a week in advance even for a Wednesday night, but he didn't fear seeing people he knew. He could look anyone in the eye and say, honestly, that they were just friends.

What he particularly enjoyed was watching her as she looked at the menu and glanced around the room at the well-dressed patrons, the hum of low conversation, the white tablecloths, oak floors, and salmon-colored walls. He remembered his younger self, and what it had felt like the first time he went to a good restaurant and was truly waited on. It was in college, when the parents came to town and he was in a large enough group that he could blend in, awed, observant, anonymous.

He saw her watching him; she mimicked his table manners, put her napkin in her lap, sat up straight. When the food arrived, artfully arranged on large bright yellow plates, she smiled broadly. "They make it so pretty!" she said. But in the middle of the meal, when he asked her how her food was, she replied: "Best fish I've had in my life, but it's dangerous to get used to what you can't afford."

"That sounds dire." Like something his mother would have said. "It's just a meal. And I can afford it." But of course he knew, understood. And it did not stop him from pressing his advantage. No matter what she might say, there was no child anywhere who dreamt of coming to Manhattan to cook a hamburger on an ancient gas range in a Pullman kitchen. All dreamt of the same thing: perfectly orchestrated dinners, Broadway shows, art openings, and glamorous clothes. Success. He could offer her those things. It was something he could do.

They shared a crème brûlée, and he watched her lick the cream slowly off her spoon, willing himself to concentrate on her words. She was talking about Atlantic City. She had gone, too, as a child, was jealous, she said, that he'd known it in the days of the real Steel Pier. She'd only known the Boardwalk with gambling, and its strangely commercial glitz and decrepitude, the ladies in polyester pants playing the slot machines, the high rollers from Japan buying saltwater taffy with their platinum cards. Yet she knew of the old AC, too, from her parents and their photo albums: pictures of family members posing in their best clothes in front of Convention Hall; and a series of images of her mother, on the beach in a plaid two-piece and cat's-eye sunglasses, being lifted into the air by Sally's father, who wore plaid swim trunks and cradled an unlit cigar in his mouth. "I was fascinated by this other life they had," she said, "when they were young. It's so strange to think of parents as ever being young, isn't it?"

Robert, too, had sometimes glanced at those old albums and wondered where those people had gone. His mother had once been a bride. She had spent money on a wedding dress, a nice long one, and carried a bouquet. Back then she could smile with both sides of her mouth. And had long hair. His father was once slim, or almost slim. Healthy. What had happened? Would that slow erosion of spirit — was it even slow? — happen to him? Had it already?

HE TOLD HIMSELF IT wasn't his imagination how she was often home when he stopped by at night — did she stay in on the off chance he'd wander by? Was it because she was saving herself, not going out on what she considered "real" dates, on account of the boyfriend? Or did she simply need to be entertained and treated after a day of lugging that heavy box around? He knew that sometimes she changed into a dress after work, and he wondered if it was for him. Then, if he told her she looked nice, she'd hold up her hands to show him the blackness of her fingers, as if for contrast. But she wanted him to think of her, somehow, as a lady and not a girl who knelt in front of men's crotches all day and serviced their shoes. And once, when he showed up in the lobby on a Thursday, and she hadn't been expecting him, she made him wait in the living room while she showered and styled her hair, and changed her clothes, just to sit with him in the apartment and then go to a diner. He found this moving; it harkened back to his childhood, when people did work in one set of clothes, then came home and changed into a different self, a different set of clothes, for their leisure time—to leave all that behind.

Slowly, he began to tell her other things about himself, and eventually, in early August, he mentioned Gwendolyn. The mention of a woman sparked her interest—again, he wondered, was she interested in a jealous way or a curious one? He could not tell.

What possessed him to tell her—was it the heat, his loneliness, a sense he'd had lately that no one around him knew who he was? She was a good listener, and something about the calm, relentless focus of her blue eyes encouraged him. When, two weeks after he'd first mentioned the subject, he finally got to the end, the suicide, and all that followed, he wondered if he'd done the right thing; he had never told another human being that story. Now, as he'd once been to Tracey, she was the possessor of his secret. Had Tracey once felt this way with him? He had told someone, and the earth had not opened up and swallowed him.

"That's a horrible, terrible story," she said when he was done, and then she got up and moved farther away on the couch. "No wonder you're so confused."

"I'm not confused," he said, wondering why she had suddenly gotten up. Had he repulsed her somehow? "I'm trusting you not to tell anyone. Even Crea doesn't know all that."

"Sure," she said. "I don't see myself running into her at one of those fund-raising luncheons. But why would she care? Gwendolyn's gone."

He did not say a word about his daughter. Did not describe how, holding her in his arms for the first time, he had felt a depth of emotion he didn't think possible ever again. Crea had been in labor for so long and then endured the emergency C-section. In the first hours, when he came to see her, she'd been only half awake. They had talked for months of naming a girl Alexandra, Alexa for short, but it had been easy to get her to sign the birth certificate with a different name; she'd have signed anything, just then, to get rid of him so she could sleep. After she and the baby were stronger, Jack made things easier by hating the name Gwendolyn, Gwen for short, and claimed that Crea had been manipulated. It was, to Crea, another moment of her father sticking his nose in where it didn't belong—when, exactly, she welcomed his interference, and when it was too much for her, remained a mystery to Robert—but soon even Crea had to admit that the name suited the child. Now they could not imagine her as anything but Gwen. But writing Gwendolyn Vishniak on the birth certificate that first night—doing what his people had done for centuries with the names of the dead—he had finally felt able to put his grief to rest.

"Maybe there was a time when I might have told her, but now, too many years have passed," he said to Sally. "She'd know I kept the information back for a reason. She'd know that I wasn't in a state to marry anyone when I proposed—I was still in love with someone else."

"Who'd have guessed that you have such romantic notions about love?"

"I was younger than you are when it all happened," he said, "and not half so tough."

"I'm not tough at all," she said. "If I were, you probably wouldn't have told me all that. But how did someone so romantic turn around and marry for money?"

"Who says I married for money?"

"Hey, I call it like I see it." She got up again and moved from the end of the couch to the other side of the room.

"Sally, why do you keep moving away from me? You're practically in the next room."

"Don't take it the wrong way."

"What the hell's that supposed to mean?"

"Calm down. From my experience, when men tell sad stories from their past, they generally think that they've earned being comforted. And for most of you, that means having sex. 'Look at me, I emoted, now make me feel better.' But I don't have therapy sex with anyone. I was just taking precautions."

He laughed. "I don't know why I even put up with you."

"Am I wrong? Isn't this leading to — 'and that's why my wife doesn't understand me'?"

"I've just entrusted you with something no one else knows about."

"I know," she said, softening for a moment, "and I'm honored by your trust. And I'll uphold it, I swear. But, am I wrong about the other stuff?"

"No," he said, "not really."

"Take that wicked smile off your face," she said. "I want to help you, you know, to do the right thing."

"The right thing," he said, coming toward her, "by whose determination?"

"Don't come any closer with that legal argument. I'm serious."

He felt sweaty and frustrated. "I've never had to work this hard with any woman."

"So I'm a refreshing change," she said, taking his arm and walking him to the door.

THE NEXT DAY, SALLY was at the office to shine shoes. He always brought extra pairs because she had told him that summers were slower, and while she worked they joked and chatted. When she was done she sometimes lingered and, on this day, Wilton Henry walked in and found her sitting in the chair across from his desk, like a client.

"Sally never sits in *my* office like this," he said.

"You never bring in three pairs of shoes for me to shine," she replied.

"And whose office is this, exactly?" he asked, smiling at Robert as he shut the door.

"That was bad," Robert said, and shook his head, but he'd enjoyed the look on Henry's face. He'd been living a very safe life, playing by the rules. Even a small, innocent infraction felt oddly invigorating. "You want to meet me for a drink when you're done?" he asked.

"If you'll pay," she said. "I'm not doing so well today."

"Happily," he said. "I'll even buy you a meal, if you like." Then he held out a twenty. "Take it," he said. "I'm having a good day."

"How do you know when you're having a good day? You don't count out your tips at six o'clock."

"I don't always need to make money to have a good day," he said. "Sometimes I need other things."

She stared uncomfortably at the floor, then left, and Robert plunged into his work, hoping to get absorbed enough to make the rest of the day fly.

AT SEVEN, HE FOUND her in the lobby, chatting with the security guys while throngs of tanned men in cotton trousers and polo shirts, and women in sundresses and sneakers, carrying their shoes in tote bags, rushed toward the doors. When Sally saw him she smiled and waved comically, as if from across a large landmass. Coming closer, he saw that she'd scrubbed her hands, replenished her lipstick, and changed from sneakers to sandals. Instead of the polish-stained blue

T-shirt he'd seen her in earlier, she wore a fresh pink one. The box was gone, too — the shoe shiners kept them in a storage closet at an investment banking firm that had been the company's first client. She looked so bright and optimistic, so fresh and alive. He'd known her for months and had not so much as kissed her on the lips. He slipped his arm possessively around her waist and for a few precious seconds felt her hip against his own. Then, before she could say a word, he shepherded her out the door and down the steps to a waiting cab.

CHAPTER FORTY-FIVE

Robert is up for partner

In the fall his wife and daughter returned, and he went back to working long hours. In September he saw Sally after work a few times for a quick drink, then went back to the office, staying most nights until eleven or twelve. But in October he did not see Sally after work at all—there was no "after work" for him; he worked fifteen-hour days, getting home at midnight and dropping into bed. To make things worse, in October she cut her days at the office and shared the route with another girl, saying that she had rehearsals for a showcase. Her arrival on Wednesdays now became the high point in his week, the one moment that he could shut the door and be fully himself. They knew things about each other now, personal things, and that knowledge created an intimacy that when experienced only once a week, in a small, windowless office, by a man who now granted himself so little leisure, was excruciatingly pleasurable, so much so that he always kept her there longer than he should. This, he knew, was what the self-help books called an emotional affair. In this decade of heightened sexual anxiety—and the inescapable fact that sex could be dangerous, even deadly—the phrase was everywhere. Still, he was a lawyer, and he knew the importance of technicalities. An emotional affair was not, by anyone's definition, the affair that counted, the affair that would end his marriage. Or so he believed. And once she was gone, and he closed the door, he knew how to put his head down and work; he had always known how to do that, and so he worked, blocking out the rest.

At home, everyone was aware that for the immediate future Robert was a kind of indentured servant: within the next nine or ten months, he would make partner or be damned. Crea went off to benefits and charity events alone or with friends, and during the day she and her set met with caterers and party planners, spending their time arranging seating charts and marking their personal touches on hundreds of invitations for worthy causes—it was her busy season, too. He now took Gwen to school in the mornings, sneaking in time with her, watching forlornly as she leapt from his car, already anxious to be on her own. Why not? When they had so often left her with other people and she had been in school since the age of three?

Still, for Gwen's first Halloween, he'd promised to take her around, and he tried to keep his promises to her, if to no one else. The year before she'd been sick on Halloween and they'd spent weeks after, or so it seemed, making up the loss to her, so this year Gwen was doubly expectant. Initially he'd been excited, too, but about ten minutes into the ritual he decided that trick or treat was for the suburbs. Knocking on strangers' doors at night, even in his posh neighborhood, put him on edge. Too many teenagers, too many boys as tall as men running up to yell something in your face, and then the candy—didn't people know by now that it was supposed to be wrapped? He'd have to take half of it away from her.

Dressed as a ballerina, she seemed to have no fear at all, and before he could stop her, she'd walked right up to a homeless man and asked him about his costume, which included one shoe and a shirt with no buttons. The man's response was a mumbled cursing. Robert yanked Gwen into his arms, then dropped a dollar in the crumbled cardboard at the man's feet, and hurried along. Was this what they taught her at that rarefied private school? No street smarts whatsoever? The other parents who passed by were in a state of similar fear. He could see it in their faces, in their restrained greetings and watchful eyes. He hurried her through the collection process, barely getting down two streets and to a few restaurants before rushing her home an hour before bedtime. She pulled at his arm, telling him he was a grouch.

As they got closer to the house, he saw a crowd gathered on his steps, mostly adults and teens with a smattering of children; they held out pillowcases and plastic bags, accepting their candy as they twisted their necks and craned their eyes to see into the first floor.

"Why are you back so soon?" Crea asked from the entrance hall, where she'd been helping May distribute Snickers bars. Robert, carrying Gwen, pushed his way through. Gwen slipped from his arms and ran to her mother, asking for a second try, another few minutes on another few streets, and Crea's face brightened, for once having been requested.

"I don't like it out there," Robert said. "I think she's had enough."

"Gloria Wardell had said to come to her building," Crea said. "Did you try there?"

"I didn't feel like going all the way to Central Park West," Robert replied.

"They go trick-or-treating in the building and then there's an ice cream party in a room downstairs." His daughter jumped up and down now, pleading.

"You want to take her to that, you take her," he said. Gloria Wardell was the daughter-in-law of her father's now-retired partner and Crea's closest female friend, or had become so since she more or less dropped Claudia, disapproving of her new habits. The Wardells had no children of their own and had somehow nominated themselves as Gwen's godparents.

As they left, Robert heard a noise, then noticed a strange woman in the living room, asking about a rocking chair as if she were on a house tour. Quickly escorting the woman out, he told May to stop giving out candy and go home — the nanny, fortunately, was at a party. He closed up the house and locked the doors, then went into his study to do some work and glance, regularly, out the window, waiting for his wife and daughter to return.

He thought of the years driving a cab when he'd been fearless, driving into Harlem and the South Bronx at all hours. He'd had less to lose then, but there was something more to it. Why, with all the money flooding into New York, did the city feel so unsafe? With a disease no one could cure, an explosion of homeless people, and an army of self-appointed vigilantes standing guard on the subway, looking as scary to him as the criminals. He stayed there, staring out the window for what felt like hours, until finally he saw a cab pull up in front, saw Crea's leg half out the door as she paid the driver, then she got out, helping his daughter to do the same. Why now, when his daughter never needed to step inside a subway, and every major possession they owned came with insurance and an alarm, why now did he feel so nervous, as if he had woken up in the wrong life — a life lived from car windows and behind locked doors? He could now see, as he hadn't then, how fragile was the world around him, the world his daughter had entered suddenly and without his permission.

CHAPTER FORTY-SIX

Christmas comes round at last

It was raining men, and the woman's deep, full tenor commanded, "Rip off the roof and staaaay in bed!" as the young lawyers and para-legals stripped off their jackets and shoes and went out on the floor with their hands in the air, echoing back, "Rip off the roof and stay in bed!" Some jumped up high while others wriggled close to the ground, twisting and contorting.

"I thought you said most people at the firm seemed unhappy," Crea whispered.

"Do you think happy people drink and dance like that?" Robert replied.

Crea, her athletic figure shown off to best advantage in a sleeve-less pale blue silk dress, leaned forward, squinting to get a better look. She needed glasses but would not give in. "I suppose you're right," she replied. "They look half mad."

The band had been chosen by the younger partners in the hopes of livening up the annual Christmas party. The Pierre, while con-venient, would always be a staid environment, but the ballroom had been decorated with tinsel and banners reading "Merry Christmas and Happy Holidays, A, L and W!" On each table was a forest of potted foliage, a centerpiece that made things green and festive but also blocked any view of the other side of the table, as if conversation at such events was not already treacherous.

The secretaries and support staff, with spouses and dates, sat at the tables at the edge of the room. Most had been through their share of office Christmases. Some would eventually go out on the dance floor, but that would be at the end, when the older partners had left. You could see a few swaying in their seats, as if warming up, but they stayed put, drinking and talking to each other. Only the occasional lawyer went back there to greet them, and Robert was one such person. He shook hands with Hayward in the mailroom and kissed Lola, his secretary, nodding while her husband, Rafael, showed him wallet photos of a little girl with scant hair and a big pink ribbon around her scalp. Then he signaled Lola over to a corner and handed her the Christmas bonus early so she would be able to meet her holiday expenses — he knew there were complaints each year about how late the money came, and so he generally went into his own pocket early, then got someone in payroll to quietly reimburse him. Lola thanked him, shoving the envelope into her purse while glancing meaningfully at her husband. He knew that look of relief; he'd seen it all his life.

The meal did not pass Crea's standards: the prime rib was dry, she told Robert, and the vegetables were undercooked, but an excellent chocolate soufflé for dessert revived her a bit. He agreed; they almost always agreed in public, were affectionate with each other, appreciative, and would likely go home that night and make love. Some men cheated because they didn't get sex at home, but lack of sex had never been the issue in his marriage — it was more of a bonus amenity, a sweetener that kept the deal from falling apart. He and Crea always bickered more this time of year. She wanted a tree, but he didn't. He wanted to celebrate Hanukkah, and she refused. They'd compromised on an anemic bush, which now stood in the

bay window, its narrow limbs bowed by even the smallest orna-
ments. Robert gave Gwen a dreidel and some chocolate Hanukkah
gelt, but it made no sense out of context, its novelty drowned out
by the twelve-foot tree that sat in Jack's enormous Tuxedo living
room, with countless silver and gold foil boxes, and the promise of
endless toys, stacked underneath.

"Where's Saldana?" Phillip Healey asked. He now stood by
Robert's chair. "I've been looking forward to seeing this year's Miss
Buenos Aires."

Mario's seat was vacant, though he generally got to these things
late. Every year he came with another Latin American fashion
model with a deep smoker's voice and heavy accent, each one thinner and more scantily dressed than the one before her. Rather than
keep track, his colleagues tended to refer to them all as Miss Buenos
Aires. Mario was still a conspicuously dapper dresser with a flair for
bright color, still lived on Prince Street in the loft co-op that he'd
bought in law school, and still drove a silver Porsche Carrera with
little regard for the speed limit. But what had been seen a decade
earlier as fussy, foreign, and strange — his fashionable clothing, lack
of permanent attachment, insistence on living downtown — was
now viewed in another light. Whether Mario had consciously
worked on his PR, which included personal appearances with glamorous females, or had simply been the lucky benefactor of changing
times, Robert was not sure. But these days he was the firm's own
GQ Don Juan, a man who appeared to have grasped the trends of the
decade before they'd even occurred.

Robert's eyes drifted across the room to Jack Alexander, who
moved from table to table, smiling and shaking hands like a seventy-
year-old bar mitzvah boy. Young associates and partners no longer
stopped talking when Robert came into the room — they had figured out years before that Robert did not have Jack's ear — on the
contrary, every step of the way he'd had to fight against Jack's insistent neutrality, and the message that it sent. The less Jack had been

involved in Robert's career, the more Robert was determined to prove himself—which was no doubt what his father-in-law wanted in the first place. No associate at the firm had had a harder time getting supporters, or finding a rabbi. Now, because Robert had thrown in his lot with Mario, or, more accurate, Mario had taken him up, the two of them—youngish, handsome, and with some independent means—attracted attention. As the market revived, the real estate practice group became sexy, much the way that mergers and acquisitions was now sexy in firms with larger corporate practices, and Robert and Mario were its mascots. The two men were envied, and perhaps hated just a little, because their lives *looked* so good to everyone else.

Robert was as aware as anyone that image created its own truth, and so when Healey asked about Mario, he shrugged and smiled sheepishly, as if to imply that God only knows what Mario was up to. Then, with some relief, he spotted the young partner walking around the dance floor, dragging a sylphlike woman in a tiny red sequined dress behind him. As they walked through the crowd, heads turned to watch them.

"You missed the dinner," Healey said, as the couple came closer.

"We ate already," Mario replied, slipping his arm around the girl's waist. "This is Graciella." The young woman offered a limp hand, first to Phillip and then to Robert. Her flesh was ice-cold.

She said something in heavily accented English that Robert didn't make out. She was taller than Mario and leaned down slightly, whispering in his ear.

"She wants to dance to Madonna," he said. "First we have to say a few hellos, *amor*." Despite his cultivated appearance—the slicked-back hair, the black Armani suit, a persimmon-colored shirt, no tie—Mario looked tired, with heavy bags under his eyes. Robert wondered where he had been, but before he could ask, Mario and his date were off again, making the rounds.

Phillip Healey made small talk with Robert, gossiping about

a client who was going through a very public divorce. Healey had implied more than once that he would stand with Mario when he supported Robert for partner, but Robert didn't trust him. He had never really backed anyone unless the person already had the support of the entire room — the only person he stuck his neck out for was Phillip Healey. Robert looked around, wondering, once again, whom he could count on. Was Mario powerful enough, valued enough, to push his case? Jack, who was just then walking toward them, was the real wild card. If Jack would, once and for all, come out for Robert, all would be well; he would be promoted in a shot. If he asked her to, Crea would intervene — she was one of the few people who had power over Jack — but Robert wanted to feel that he'd earned partner, that his hard work had been noted, and he hadn't struggled in vain.

"Phillip, I didn't see you out there," Jack said, gesturing toward the dance floor.

"My sciatica," Healey said. "Men who sit all day long cannot shake their groove thing."

"Merry happy, Father. That singer is the best thing here," Crea said, looking up at him and taking his arm. His face relaxed into a broad smile.

"*Shout, shout, let it all out!*" belted the vocalist and her backup. The crowd on the dance floor stomped their feet aggressively. "*These are the things I can do without —*"

"Tears for Fears," Crea said. "That's the name of the group."

"Sounds like a rallying cry for insurrection," Jack replied.

The dancers looked more like robots than rebels, starting and stopping to the odd beat. Only Mario Saldana's date, dancing within their view, had any evident sense of rhythm. Robert, Crea, and Jack watched her with interest. Her shimmering dress seemed to move with her like a second undulating skin as she shook her behind. Her legs were endless, and though her movements were odd, they appeared to work with the music.

"Is Saldana dating a Martha Graham dancer?" Jack asked, just as a waiter stepped in front of Robert to refill Crea's empty wineglass. By the time the waiter stepped away, the crowd on the floor was mysteriously and suddenly still. Someone shouted: "Call 911!" The lights came up and Jack rushed forward to examine the situation. In the split second when Robert was not looking, Mario Saldana had collapsed and now lay unconscious on the floor.

CHAPTER FORTY-SEVEN

Back at the office

The next morning, as lawyers arrived late and hungover, each found a memo, placed on the desks throughout the office's two floors, explaining that Mario Saldana had contracted viral meningitis and was in the hospital. The firm had already sent a flower arrangement and the memo gave the address of the Upper East Side hospital, and his room number, in case people wanted to send cards or call. The memo was carefully crafted—reminding them that viral meningitis was the less serious kind—that it was contagious, but no more so than any other cold or virus. It told them to wash their hands frequently and see a health-care provider if they developed a sudden fever. Robert arrived just after nine and read the memo over the shoulder of the receptionist before walking down the hallway to his office. On the way, he passed Wilton Henry and two associates whispering in a tight group. They looked at him as he passed, and he nodded and said good morning.

A few minutes after speaking to his secretary, Robert dropped off his accoutrements and walked briskly back down that same hallway toward Jack Alexander's office. It was now nine twenty, and all doors were closed, though through the panels of beveled glass—a decorative element in each doorway that served not only to give the hallways a look of distinction, but also to keep employees on their toes—he could make out that most were on the phone. Unlike his colleagues, Robert had no time for gossip, or a panicked call to the family doctor; he had been summoned. These meetings in Jack's office, few and far between over the years, always made him nervous.

Jack's office had long ago been updated from seventies minimalism to eighties minimalism. On the walls now hung giant abstract canvases splashed with thick circles of brown and black and tan interspersed with angry splotches of mauve. In between two dark brown leather couches was a plain, square steel table. Jack directed Robert to an armless chair facing his now-metal desk but did not sit down himself, instead standing by the windows across the room.

"So I assume you got the memo on Mario," Jack said.

"Yes," Robert said. "Do we know how long he'll be out?"

"At least a week, probably longer," he said, walking back to the desk and sitting down. "I spoke to that woman friend of his, but she's hard to understand."

"Graciella," Robert mumbled.

"Since you and Saldana work so closely, and you can speak Spanish with his Venezuelan clients, you'll have to pitch in with some of Mario's work. I know it's a burden, but it's only for a little while and, well, this is also an opportunity."

Robert nodded, uncertain how to respond.

"Take whomever you want to help you. Elaine is good, isn't she? And of course Phillip Healey will be available for your questions."

Robert frowned. "I'm glad for your confidence in me," he said. "But when you said that this could be an opportunity, I assume you mean because I'll be up for partner this year?"

"I've been meaning to talk to you about that, actually."

"Oh?" Robert sat forward in his seat.

"You're respected around here, Robert, because you've earned respect without my help, which was as I wanted it. I know it's been hard on you. But you're up against several excellent candidates. It will be a tough decision, and frankly, you might watch your step a bit more."

"If I watched my step any more, sir, I'd be standing still."

"Is that what you call inviting a bevy of half-naked girls to come in here and perform?"

"Are you referring to the shoe-shine girls?"

He nodded. "I was not consulted."

Could Jack really be thinking about this now? When the shoe shiners had been around for months? Was he losing his mind? Robert had the sudden, uncanny feeling that it was this, his bringing in the shoe-shine girls, and not Mario's illness, that was the real reason he'd been summoned. Healey was the natural person to assign him work; there was no reason for Jack to be involved. "The girls shine shoes," Robert said. "You like your lawyers to look professional."

"My lawyers can get their shoes shined in Grand Central or out on the street on their own time. They wear suits, but I don't bring tailors into the office."

"The firm does pick up and deliver dry cleaning."

"That's so our people can work late and not have to worry about their clothes."

"The shoe shiners have done so much for morale, surely you've seen that?" he asked. "Everyone is in a much better mood on Mondays and Wednesdays."

"Exotic dancers in the halls might put them in an even better mood. But that's not the kind of atmosphere I want for this firm—word gets out. It's not dignified."

"Then why haven't you gotten rid of them?" Robert asked.

"Because several partners asked me not to."

Robert tried to stifle a smile but could not. "They could help us, really. We are known, for being, well, uptight. I think that reputation hurts recruitment."

"Are you saying we get inferior lawyers?"

"No, I'm not. But the atmosphere, even with the beautiful art, can be, well, depressing. The glass panels foster a kind of paranoia. No one laughs or even smiles much."

"Where are the happy lawyers, Robert?" Jack snapped. "On the beach in Hawaii, maybe you see a few." He sighed and stood up, turning away from Robert and walking back to the windows. When he faced Robert again, his tone was consciously restrained, his voice low. "I don't care if my people are happy or sad—their state of mind is not my business. I only care that they're productive. And staring down some buxom girl's shirt does not make lawyers more productive, it only makes them more distracted!" He motioned to the door, letting Robert know that their discussion was at an end.

WITHIN TEN MINUTES OF his meeting with Jack, Robert was greeted by one of the mailroom guys, who plopped stacks of Mario's files on the floor in his office. Other than the cumbersome computer monitor and its attached keyboard, there was now hardly a spot on his desk or the floor that was not taken up with papers. As the man left, a girl knocked on the door and asked if he wanted a shoe shine.

This one was called Augusta, and she was small and androgynous; her short hair stood out from her head in shiny black spikes, and each ear was pierced up and down the lobe.

"Sally still sick?" he asked, holding out his shoe. Two weeks before, she had altogether stopped coming to A, L and W.

"She was never sick," Augusta said, putting down her box with a thud. "I told you, she's no longer doing this route. You know how many times a day I get asked, 'Where's Sally?' I swear, it's getting on my nerves."

"Sorry," he said, as she placed his foot on her stand and began to spread polish on his shoe, accidentally staining his sock. He pretended not to notice. Sally had not returned his calls to her service — her home number was unlisted — nor would she respond to the notes he'd left with the doorman. One evening he'd sat in the lobby, reading through the work of a junior associate and waiting for her to return; after forty-five minutes, he finally gave up.

"She in another show?" he asked, as the girl moved his foot abruptly to the floor.

"Huh?"

"Sally, in a show?"

"I don't give out personal information," she said, and went back to working.

Her rent checks still arrived each month, a money order in the envelope, a New York postmark, but not so much as a note.

"She's not sick, is she?"

"Look!" Augusta snarled. "I don't *know* a *damn* thing about her!" She looked to be on the verge of tears. "I'm on her route almost three weeks and the tips are still lousy. Even Christmas tips! I gotta eat, too." She placed his foot back on her cloth and began to clean up, not saying another word.

"You're right," he said. "And I'll tell you what. I'll pay you for two. How's ten dollars?"

"Whaddo I gotta do?" she asked.

"It's a gift shine. For the guy with the big office as you come in, on the right. Don't be afraid of the paintings."

"Cool," she said, brightening. "Scary artwork."

"And don't let the secretary keep you out. You're good at asserting yourself." He handed her the ten. "And Augusta, don't forget to tell Mr. Alexander that it's from me."

AFTER WORK, ROBERT WENT to the hospital hoping, among other things, to get more information. He found Mario asleep in bed in a big private room — big by Manhattan standards — while Tracey dozed in a chair by the window. Mario was hooked up to an IV and a machine — oxygen? Robert wasn't sure. Up above them both, on the wall, the television was tuned soundlessly to *Jeopardy*. Visiting hours would be over soon. He walked over to the corner and shook Tracey awake. "Who the hell are you?" Tracey asked, sitting up and smiling.

"It's a nice room," Robert whispered, taking the chair across from him.

"No need to whisper — he sleeps so soundly that I've checked to see if he's breathing."

"I wasn't sure I'd see you here," he said. Mario had not been out to Tuxedo in months, and Robert assumed he'd fallen out of favor, or worse.

"He'd begun to bore me. Maybe because he was always so tired. But I wouldn't abandon a friend in need."

"How's his condition?"

"He's dehydrated, temperature was one hundred and three. They put him on fluids and some kind of pain reliever so he can sleep. The headaches got so bad, his vision was blurry."

Just then, a blond, ponytailed nurse entered, a mask hanging slackly below her chin. She needed to take some blood.

"Why don't we go to the cafeteria?" Tracey suggested. "I haven't eaten all day. We'll get something fast."

"Visiting hours are over soon. I'd like to at least say a few words to him."

"Don't worry about that. I have some influence here," he said. "I got special privileges for Graciella, too."

"What did you say *she* was?" Robert asked, as they walked toward the elevator bank.

"His girlfriend."

"That's one name for it," Robert said softly.

"Graciella's an economist from Paraguay, Vishniak," Tracey said, pushing the button for the elevator. "She's highly intelligent, or so Mario says; I can't understand a thing she says."

The doors opened with a pinging sound. The elevator was empty and the two men stepped on, then the doors closed. Robert turned and looked at Tracey. "Has he been tested?"

"Tested for what?" Tracey asked.

"For AIDS," Robert snapped. It had been a long day. He wasn't in the mood. "You remember that one? New and never boring? No cure? Everyone's talking about it?"

"It's viral meningitis," Tracey said calmly. "The doctors were clear. No test is necessary." The elevator doors opened and they stepped off. Tracey made a right-hand turn down an empty hall and Robert followed. "Start a rumor like that, and you'll ruin his life. You hear me?" His voice was low and tight and a vein stood out on his forehead, like a bolt of lightning. "Do you want to ruin his life? And hurt your chances of making partner, I might add. He's your biggest supporter. And how do you think you got him to support you?"

"Because I speak Spanish?" Robert asked. "And I'm a good lawyer."

"Because I encouraged him to take you up," Tracey said. "I'm sure you're a fine lawyer; Mario has said as much. But from what I hear, it's a lion's den over there, and you need him."

Robert knew Tracey was right, knew also that he'd offended him just by being honest.

"So are you going to stop acting like a worrisome old hen?" Tracey asked.

Robert nodded and put his hands up. "I surrender."

"It's not Appomattox, Vishniak," Tracey said. "And if you don't shut up, you'll miss the pleasure of watching me choke down hospital food. That should amuse you."

Robert followed Tracey past the entrance to the Sanford and Genevieve Trace Cardiology wing, and turned left at the portrait of Judge Harding Trace, as the two moved silently toward the looming, and as of yet unnamed, hospital cafeteria.

CHAPTER FORTY-EIGHT

Crea takes a trip

He'd been surprised when she said yes. But they'd bickered all winter, and she was trying to please him, and as the family set out for Philadelphia, with Robert driving, he felt grateful, even buoyant. Crea and Robert sang folk songs for Gwen, the songs of their generation — Simon and Garfunkel; Joni Mitchell; and Peter, Paul and Mary. Then she wanted songs she'd learned at school, and they all sang "Five Little Ducks" and whatever else she assigned them, like a family in a Disney movie. What a relief to get along, even for a few hours. He and Crea sang out, vaguely off-key, laughing as their daughter made fun of them. Had he known what was coming, he wouldn't have sung, would have saved his voice.

They were old now. When Robert came in the door, they moved toward him slowly but with enthusiasm. He didn't recognize a few of the children, attached to a cousin or two, all with second wives or husbands he'd never met. Crea allowed herself to be kissed, she was not consciously rude, not even capable of it. But she had brought a deck of cards with her, and when the women gathered around the food in the dining room and then in the kitchen, Crea took out the cards and taught Uncle Frank's daughter and Gwen how to play Go Fish. Yes, she was good with children, which they all noted appreciatively. But she sat in that corner much of the night, talking to no one over twelve.

When dessert was on the horizon, Robert left his uncle's side and sat on the arm of her chair. The children had fled and she was playing solitaire. "Have you eaten anything at all? They're all waiting for you over there."

"Your mother doesn't like me," she whispered. "Those women, they're all staring."

He sighed. "They don't *know* you, Crea. But you should make the first move."

"Why? I'm the guest."

"You spend all day cajoling and organizing and small talking," he said. "If you can handle the Black and White Ball, you can handle the Vishniaks."

They were, she asserted, two very different things. "What is it with these paintings, Robert? Are there more, now? I don't remember this many from when I was here last."

"Every few years she likes to change things around. Like you do." He smiled, could not help himself. "You like art, darling. The oldest ones came from green stamps, remember those?" But of course, why would she? "Or people give them to her."

"As gifts?" she asked, her voice high as she flipped over her card, then shook her head. "Bad hand," she mumbled.

He left her to go stand with Gwen, who, away from her mother, shoved a hunk of cherry pie into her mouth, the red filling staining her lips and chin. Gwen wanted to ask Stacia if she would teach her how to bake one for herself but could not make herself heard in the noise. Robert had to stand between them and scream their questions and answers back and forth like some lunatic translator — his mother was going deaf. "Jesus, Ma!" he yelled. "Could you get yourself a hearing aid?!"

His daughter looked at him, not knowing what to do. She was not used to this part of him, the part that came back here to them. He patted her shoulder. Not only were they all loud, the room was so very bright. "Sparkly," Gwen said. Other than Stacia, who liked her practical neutrals, the women of the Northeast liked bright colors and glittering accessories—red velour pants, sequins on shirts, gold lamé purses and other eye-popping details. Next to them Crea, in her dark brown suede skirt and winter-white turtleneck, brown boots, a simple gold necklace, looked like a visitor from another planet.

When the women moved into the kitchen, stuffed themselves into that tiny room to help with the cleaning up, and Crea stayed with her cards, it suddenly dawned on him. "It's the recipes, isn't it?" he asked her. She did not respond, only flipped over another card, pretending not to hear. He knew he was right. Those recipes, the ones that Stacia and Lolly had copied out on those lined three-by-five cards before the engagement party. Crea had put them somewhere before their move into the house and still had no idea where. She did not want to be asked about it. They had yet, in eight years of marriage, to try a single dish. No brisket or *kneidelach*, not even a lousy munn cookie. He didn't care, really, except that whenever a new restaurant opened in Manhattan they were in line, among the first to try Mongolian-fusion, Macrobiotics, and a restaurant that ground up all the food in a blender until it was practically liquid. But mention chicken soup with a matzo ball and her mind went amnesiac.

By nine thirty, Gwen had curled up on the couch, asleep. Unable to stand it, Robert took Crea's hand and pulled her to the food table—she had eaten only a chicken wing, a little kasha. Standing next to her, forcing her to converse with his family, he screamed her replies to their questions, growing increasingly hoarse. Then, in one long yelp, he lost his voice, forcing his wife to speak for herself. She smiled and told them small, dull facts about the house—somehow now, she could make herself heard, and they leaned closer, listening as she described Gwen's school. "The teacher has them reading in kindergarten," she said, and they nodded as if she'd said the children were going to the moon. The room began to relax. "I had a nice time," she declared, then kissed Stacia good-bye, and then the others. They looked at each other, puzzled, and then decided that they were pleased, even, with that much, so anxious to think well of her that it broke his heart all over again.

THE NEXT WEEKEND, Crea was in Aspen, a trip long planned with her girlfriends, who wanted to get in the last decent skiing. There was no question of Gwen going to Aspen. The altitude made her ill, as it did her father. So they were home together for the weekend. Robert had to work on Saturday—Gwen would spend the day with a friend and the nanny—but all Sunday he'd reserved for her, his one day off. When Crea left, she expected tears, but Gwen was used to being left, or leaving—she never cried. And then she was to have her father for a whole day, and this promise trumped everything.

First they went to the Upper West Side to see Barry's new apartment. After he'd returned from Philadelphia, he'd called his brother. He had barely talked to Barry in months, partly because he was so busy and partly because he could hardly stand to hear him talk about Claudia in his disturbing, proprietary way. But Robert also had to admit that he'd missed his brother, plus he was concerned about their mother's hearing. Barry already knew about Stacia's hearing—he went there every month or so, he pointed out, whereas Robert dropped in twice a year. "My trip to Hong Kong was great, by the way," Barry snapped. "Thanks for asking." Still, he was not interested in chastising for long. He had other news: Vishniak the dog had died. He was old but it felt like a blow, even to Robert, who had never even liked the animal. But the name, you couldn't get away from that name.

Barry's condo was at Eighty-seventh and Broadway, a corner unit with two walls of windows in the master bedroom. To Robert, it was like all new buildings put up in that decade — giant boxy rooms, cheap but attractive flooring, and a kitchen with every possible appliance, including a double refrigerator the size of a compact car. In the middle of the tour, Robert heard two children next door screaming bloody murder, then a mother coming in to scold. Even for so much money they couldn't take the time or expense in these new apartments to make the walls thicker. This was what people wanted now — fast to go up, big and anonymous, with terrific views. He did not ask Barry the price, only smiled in a way he hoped looked admiring. After ten minutes, Gwen got impatient and they all left for the park.

They walked to Riverside, and Barry, knowing that Robert was going to ask him questions about the market, as he always did when they were together, began to talk about a trader named Barnett. "His instincts are never wrong," Barry said. "Thanks to him, I just made you a fortune in currency futures. The Swiss franc has been a gold mine."

"Currency trading is risky," Robert said, grasping his daughter's hand as they walked carefully down the long, winding stairs that took them from the street into the gardens at Ninety-first Street.

"You're young. You can tolerate risk. You don't make money any other way. That's what our parents never understood. It takes balls of steel to get rich."

"I worry, that's all."

"Yeah, you always worry. Let me do the worrying."

"What exactly do you give Barnett in exchange for his great instincts?" Robert asked.

"My undying gratitude," Barry replied. "I get you results and you know it. Or you'd never let me handle so much of your money."

Yes, it was addictive, tearing open that statement each month, seeing the numbers climb. His account was up to a quarter of a million dollars, and if he made partner, he'd be well on his way to becoming a rich man.

"Daddy, look!" Gwen said, rushing toward the garden, where they could see the tops of the occasional crocus pushing its way up out of the soil. Nearby, some volunteers were digging up weeds and spreading grass seed. Couples walked hand in hand—it was the first day warm enough to spend outside without a winter coat. They walked south toward a playground on Eighty-third. The water canal in the middle of the playground was empty in March, but there was a merry-go-round, where Gwen met a little Russian boy with his father, who spoke little English, and the grown-ups took turns pushing the contraption round and round while the children, harsh taskmasters, demanded to go faster and faster. When it was his turn, Robert sweated and huffed—it felt good to be moving outside in the fresh air, and then he looked up and saw Sally Johannson coming through the trees at a jog that was closer to a run, her eyes focused straight ahead.

He was so surprised that he let go of the railing. The merry-go-round flew on momentum then squeaked gradually to a halt as he yelled her name. The children whined, and the Russian man took over. Barry and Robert moved toward Sally as she stopped and turned to see who was calling her.

"Isn't *this* a coincidence?" she asked, walking toward them.

"I already got my shoes ready for Monday," Barry said.

"You're going to Prudence Brothers? I thought you've been out of town."

"Who told you that?" She wore baggy gray sweatpants and a pink sweatshirt half zipped over a red and white Phillies T-shirt. Her face was flushed and blotchy, her hair pulled back in a low ponytail, and she had a few small pimples on her forehead. Stripped of so much of her glamour, she looked like any girl from the neighborhood in need of bleaching her roots.

Gwen got off the ride and ran over, took his hand. "Who's she, Dad?" she asked.

"My name's Sally, honey, I'm a friend of your father's."

"Oh," she said. "How come I don't know you?"

"Good question," she said, and bent over slightly, putting out her hand. "Nice to meet you. What's your name?"

"Gwen," she said.

"As in Gwendolyn?" Sally asked, showing no sign of recognition.

Gwen nodded then kicked at the dirt with her foot. "Are you gonna stay here a long time?" she asked Robert. "Talking?"

Barry offered to take her to the sandbox, remembering that there was a mermaid statue in the sand. Robert suggested that they all go, but he hung back a little with Sally.

"I don't understand why you disappeared, and why the hell aren't you listed?"

"I'm listed. But under my real name. Sally Jacobson," she said. "I told you Johannson was a fake name, but you didn't believe me."

"You sure don't look like a Sally Jacobson."

"I was adopted," she replied casually, "by a couple who barely reach my shoulder and wanted a daughter after a son but couldn't have one. So here I am, a genuine dipped-in-the-*mikvah* Jacobson, signed, sealed, the whole thing."

Robert looked for Gwen. She was up to her waist in sand, mugging shamelessly for her uncle, who now held a small camera and was snapping away.

"Anyway, there was another Sally Jacobson in Actors Equity," she continued. "And I like having a secret name. Some jobs, you don't want people to know who you are."

"Aren't there like forty-seven Johannsons in Actors Equity?" he asked.

"I guess not many Swedes go into acting."

"So your number isn't unlisted. It's just in code."

"No, *Johannson* is code. *Jacobson* is who I am."

"But you disappear at will."

"What do you have to complain about?" she said, as they sat down on a bench. "I pay my rent. You want to boot me out for someone who can pay more money?" She paused. "I know I said I'd be out in a few months. But I guess I've gotten used to it. You know, living in a big place? With a doorman? I'll leave if you want me to."

"Don't be ridiculous," he said. "I've missed you is all." He knew now how Tracey had felt. She declared herself his friend and disappeared. And of course he refused to see her as a friend to begin with; that was half the problem. It had been Tracey's, too. "I left messages for you with the doorman. Even came over one night and sat in that lobby. You know how valuable my time is?"

"I did it for your own good," she said. "People were starting to talk."

"No they weren't."

"You don't hear what I hear."

"So I won't invite you to sit down in my office anymore," he said. "I won't bring in so many pairs for you to shine. If you won't see me at the office, then see me outside it."

"You don't have any 'outside' — you're always at the office."

"Just for a few more months," he said. Even unglamorous as she was today, he wanted her. It was unfair to want the life he had with Crea, with its ease and luxury—and intact family for his daughter—and to want Sally, too. He knew that, but he couldn't help himself. Sitting with her now, he wanted everything. "The reason I bought that apartment was to find some peace."

"But then you rented it to me," she said, "and gave up your peace."

"Just the opposite," he said. "And I'm not letting go so easily."

Gwen screamed for him and he went to her, brushing the sand off her clothing. Sally lagged behind him and announced that there were swings nearby, and all three grown-ups walked with Gwen toward them. Gwen chatted to him about the mermaid, and Robert felt relieved that she was not complaining; this was supposed to be their day together, but luckily she liked Barry and didn't get to see him very often.

A swing opened up on the end, and Gwen took Robert's hand, leading him over. She wanted him to push and he obliged. Sally stood with Barry while Robert watched Gwen swing gleefully into the air. He pushed her for a few minutes more before she spotted the Russian boy from the merry-go-round and wanted to get off. The adults let her rush to the boy's side, and then they all walked to some low rocks around the edge of the park. Barry tried to talk to the Russian man.

Robert's brother kept giving him time with Sally; was it that Barry hated Crea? Or was he just in a generous mood from all the money he was making? Robert watched his daughter scamper onto a flat rock and told her to stay close to the ground. Sally stood sentry with him.

"Do you want to look for them?" he asked. "Your birth parents, I mean?"

"Looking at you with Gwen, well, you'd think I would want to, right? I mean, to see who exactly on this earth I look like. But no, I don't. I know where I belong and who I belong to."

"Really?" he asked. "Lucky you."

"I save the drama in my life for the stage. I'm not looking for some movie-of-the-week scenario in my private life."

"Point noted," he said.

"The people who raised me are my parents," she continued. "They played endless rounds of checkers with me when I was sick, went to all my recitals, took out a second mortgage when I got into NYU. You start searching under rocks and mostly what you find is slime."

"I had no idea you were so practical."

"I wouldn't name my kid after my dead fiancé, if that's what you call practical," she whispered. "No wonder you didn't want me to tell your wife. Have you no shame?"

"I told you, no one knows that story."

"So why'd you tell me?"

"I trust you," he said softly, staring for a moment at the ground. He raised his head and called out to his daughter to be careful as she moved to a higher slope. She gave him an argument before moving to lower ground, and he took a few steps back to where Sally stood.

"How's the slip-on?" she asked.

"The what?"

"I have nicknames for all of you. Saldana's 'the sleek Italian slip-on.'"

"He's Venezuelan."

"I know, but he only wears Italian shoes. And he's sleek."

"He's fine," he said. "Back at work, still a billing machine. It was meningitis."

"Really?" she asked. "Because I hear things. Like you and Wilton Henry are in a dead heat for partner along with that woman, Liesel, the one with the thick glasses? And the firm is likely to make all three of you, which would be a record. Business is very good right now."

"Jesus, you haven't been at our place in months."

"The real information, the good stuff," she said, "comes from your competition. People talk in front of us. They think we're illiterate, or idiots, or something."

"Then the joke's on them, isn't it?" He called to his daughter and told her they were going home now. "What about me?" he asked, as Gwen went to say good-bye to her new friend. "You have nicknames for everyone. What do you call me?"

She looked him in the eye. "You? I call you 'dangerous.'"

CHAPTER FORTY-NINE

Mario

The only lie Robert had told Sally that day at the playground was that Mario Saldana was as sleek as ever. He was far from that, but he was clever about his clothes. As a keen observer of people's habits, Robert had watched Saldana's metamorphosis with a combination of concern and admiration. Mario had always dressed with distinction, sparing no expense, but now he had everything made for him. When he'd been blocky and muscular, his suits thinned him down, made him look taller than his five foot eight inches. Now, he wore only double-breasted suits, the clothing staple of the narrow man, with wide lapels and broad shoulders creating the illusion of solidity. People at work seemed hardly to notice that Mario had gotten so much thinner. Or if they did, they did not talk about it in front of Robert. And as summer arrived and the office got cooler, Mario virtually never took off his jacket.

But no amount of careful tailoring could change the fact that Saldana, a meticulous craftsman in two languages, was beginning to screw up at work. Tiny things, issues of concentration, most likely. Robert had to be careful; Mario was his superior, and he could not be seen to double-check him. But Mario could not mess up now, not when Robert needed him.

The spring into summer was occupied, among other things, with work for Pascal, Inc. New York had one of the most complicated regulatory systems of any city in the world. It could take years, sometimes, for a developer to get his architectural plans approved by City Planning and draw down his financing. And at any point along the way, even when things looked optimistic, plans could be stopped, for instance, by the Buildings Department, if they did not have the electrical and highway approvals, or even by the Landmarks Preservation Commission, angry about the way the building might or might not fit into the local style.

But Mark Pascal was optimistic. His father had not been very good at making friends with the right city bureaucrats, greasing palms or patting backs, but somehow Mark had mastered this early, much to the amazement of his family and friends. And so he was aggressive, perhaps even overly confident, in selling off some property to raise capital in anticipation of the TriBeCa purchase, which he planned to go through within the next few months.

The first property he was selling off, at the end of June 1987, was in Queens, an abandoned power station and the surrounding small parcel of land originally bought by Pascal's father in the early 1970s for a future project that never took place. The land had risen in value many times over and would now fetch about $15 million. Proceeds from the sale would be held in a 1031 exchange account so that it could be used toward future property without incurring taxes. The day before the closing, Robert approached Mario's secretary, Inez, and asked to look over the paperwork. The first time this had happened, she'd been protective and refused, but this time, without explanation, she began handing him everything she was to photocopy for the meeting. "Be fast," she said. "He'll be in soon."

Robert looked through the documents, and just as he became convinced that all was in order, he noticed that the direction letter instructed the buyer's lawyers to wire their client's money to the wrong accounts. The payee, Chicano Exchange, did not exist. He'd meant Chicago Exchange. Were these even the correct account numbers?

Mario had been known for his detail orientation, his accuracy; he did not make mistakes or let them slip past him. Inez claimed responsibility, but direction letters were the kind of thing an attorney looked over, or left very careful instructions on. If a mistake happened again, should Robert take it on himself? He looked over Inez's shoulder as the two quickly corrected the errors, then Inez rushed off to the photocopier.

Robert walked back to his desk. If he didn't know better, he'd think Mario was trying to steal. This would be an easy way to do it, diverting money to an account that existed offshore, an account for a company with a name close to the name of the exchange corporation. In law school, Robert had taken an ethics class — they became mandatory after Watergate — and the professor had started the class by saying that they would, as attorneys, likely have access to enormous amounts of money, and that the amazing thing was not how many lawyers embezzled but how few did, considering the temptations.

Mario didn't need the money; he had his own fortune. Robert, who didn't, had thought of theft himself, on those nights when he was at the office until midnight, slaving away for the glory of Phillip Healey and Jack Alexander. Take the money and run. Start over with total freedom. Sitting down at his desk, he imagined Sally coming with him, like a white-collar Bonnie and Clyde; they would go to some tropical paradise, a place with lousy extradition and liberal banking laws. Or there was Paris, the next best thing. He'd gone with Crea, in '83, for the opening of the Pompidou Center, and the architecture of the city had moved him, if the Pompidou — which looked like a bunch of giant pipes in a tangle — had not. Sally would love Paris. They could get an apartment in the student quarter, the area he remembered liking, though maybe he wouldn't like it as much now, being no student. But they could live in quiet, understated luxury among the handsome seventeenth-century buildings, in the city whose neighborhoods are preserved in time, not ripped apart and rezoned, sold off piece by piece every decade or so, as they were in New York. He expanded on the idea, like a game, and felt his mood lift. Sally could transform herself yet again; she seemed good at that, and so was he. Then, suddenly, Sally was standing in front of him, for real, with her shoe-shine box resting on her hip.

"I knocked but you didn't seem to hear me."

"I was daydreaming."

"About what?" she asked. She was back in uniform. The tight T-shirt and jeans, the makeup, the hair, sans roots.

"Oh, the usual," he said, "embezzling money, running away with you to another country."

"I left home for another country, and once is enough. I'll never leave New York. You bother to shine your shoes while I was away? Because they sure don't look it." She put down her shoe-shine box at his feet.

"I avoided cleaning them in protest," he replied. "And you are a disturbingly practical girl, as I've already pointed out. But at least you're back. For good, I hope."

She sat down on the low red seat, took out the flannel rags and other equipment. He hiked up his pants leg and she put his shoe in the metal stirrup. Then she reached in her apron and took out another flyer. "Another show," she said.

"You get cast a lot."

"And paid a little," she replied. "But this is a good part. A good show." She looked away from him suddenly, at the door, as if embarrassed. "So be there, okay?"

"Is that an order?"

"Yup," she said, once again focused on his shoe.

"What about your boyfriend?" he asked, changing feet. "Still on the road?"

"You said you trust me, which meant something to me, so I'm going to trust you: There is no boyfriend. I mean, there've been lots of boyfriends, but no one special now. I say I have one because it's easier that way, you know, with customers."

"That makes sense," he said, smiling. There was no one.

"You mean I look like a girl who has no boyfriend?" She took out her brushes and ran them back and forth over the leather of his shoe, then buffed it with the rag.

"No, you look like a girl whom every man wants but no man will approach seriously." He watched her color vaguely. "So I guess it's not working. The mythical boyfriend?"

"Hard to tell. Don't spread the info around." She had finished his shoes now and was putting her equipment back in the box.

"I'm not giving home court advantage to anyone else," he said, as they stood. Her hiatus had jolted him; so had seeing her that day in the park. He had feared she would go away again. "So are you busy all the time with rehearsals?"

"Most of the time."

He walked closer to her, slipped the money into her apron. "I can't persuade you to have dinner with me?" he asked. "A very good dinner at a very good restaurant?" He missed that smell, the oily polish and watermelon lip gloss.

"You're always tempting me, aren't you?"

"It's just dinner."

She told him she was booked, but her voice was softer. Was he wearing her down? Or had she changed toward him? He would make her change. He would not back down this time. Her face was flushed and he put his palm to her cheek.

"Someone's standing in the doorway," she said softly.

"The door's closed."

"I can see a reflection in the glass."

Robert stepped away from her and yelled, "Come in!" but whoever it was had gone. If they had even been there to begin with.

CHAPTER FIFTY

The summer before the storm

Crea should have been making preparations to go to Tuxedo for June and some of July, but she was late in leaving this year. Gwen's school ended the first week in June, but their daughter had birthday parties and activities and lessons that had to be brought to a satisfactory conclusion. He understood this, but in the past Crea had always been able to get everything organized and together before June 1. He had the feeling she was stalling, that somehow she did not trust him alone. And she was right to feel that way.

He had a reason now not to pick fights with her or get irritated. He had a goal. They did not fight, rarely even made love, and he never asked anymore, never bothered, only accommodated when necessary. Even with all this smooth civility — such a new experience for him, like living with a roommate, really, but an easier one than Barry, a better-smelling one — he still felt himself to be in a strange, unspoken tug-of-war. They walked around each other, did as the other asked, and waited for something to happen.

If they were going to be stuck in the city, she informed him, they might as well keep busy. The social season in Manhattan was over, and yet she somehow dug up a series of small dinner parties and obscure fund-raisers, the kind she'd never had much interest in attending before. It was summer, and he had no desire to spend his evenings in strangers' living rooms, listening to lectures on Italian pottery or antique wrought iron. But contrary to her behavior in the winter, she made it clear each time that she would not forgive him if he didn't at least make an appearance.

She needed him close, demanded it, and he acceded to her demands, hoping she'd finally relax and proceed with her usual plans. On the second Saturday in June, he was working at home in his study when Crea announced that they should have a family outing. Gwen needed a toy for a birthday party the next day, and Crea wanted to go to a gallery that was showing a collection of Max Ernst drawings. They would stop at FAO Schwarz and then go downtown.

"Traffic will be terrible," he said. "The tourists are swarming this time of year."

"You have a habit of sounding like a municipal worker."

"What's a municipal whatever?" Gwen asked. She was six now, full of endless questions.

"Traffic cop? Bus driver?" Crea smiled. "Meter maid."

"We should take the subway," he said calmly, refusing to take the bait.

"You're not driving," she said. "What do you care if there's traffic?"

THEY FOLLOWED HER PLAN, Crea and Robert and Gwen in back and Troy up front, with the radio on and the soundproof barrier up between then. Robert didn't like to use it, but Crea preferred having privacy. It had taken Troy an hour to get twenty blocks, and Gwen was getting impatient. She moved from one parent's lap to the other, too big, really, for either of them to hold her, and so she ended up sitting between them, chomping on a piece of bubble gum.

"Where are we going after Schwarz's?" she asked.

"Max Ernst," Robert replied.

"Who's he?"

"He draws funny pictures," Crea said, "interesting drawings. Sometimes people walk around without heads, sometimes they fly onto roofs. You'll like it."

"Yes, another sunny summer afternoon spent with the refugees from Hitler's Europe," Robert mumbled.

"Why do you always bring up biography and history?" Crea asked. "It's all you care about. There is more to an artist's work than where he came from."

"Why must you focus so utterly on aesthetics? It's a shallow way to look at the world."

"Are you saying I'm shallow?"

"Who's Max Ernst?" Gwen interrupted.

A string of cars honked as they finally turned from Sixtieth onto Fifth Avenue. The city was alive with people, and nowhere were the crowds as dense as here, in the center of the retail Bermuda Triangle that was Bendel, Bergdorf Goodman, and Barneys—the very same block on which Crea and Robert had first wrangled for a cab nine years earlier. At Fifty-ninth, Robert leaned forward and knocked on the glass, signaling Troy to let them out so they could walk. "I don't know where he's supposed to wait for us in all of this," Robert said to Crea.

"I swear, Robert, I think you worry more about Troy's comfort than ours," Crea replied.

"Who's Max Ernst?!" Gwen persisted.

"A talented man who abandoned two ex-wives and a mistress in Germany to run off with Peggy Guggenheim and escape the Nazis," Robert replied.

"How on earth is she supposed to understand that?" Crea asked, as Troy opened the door. People swarmed around the car. A stranger took their picture. Two boys banged on the hood, until Troy, a former high school football player, told them to get the hell off.

"Who are the Nazis?" Gwen asked, as they pushed their way toward their destination.

"Look, sweetheart," Robert said, picking up the child so as not to lose her in the pushing and shoving, "over there, see the giant robot? And the two-thousand-dollar stuffed leopard?"

"Schwarz's!" she said, clapping her hands together.

"Yes, my dear, that's our Xanadu."

Crea slipped her arm through his, less a gesture of affection than a desire not to get pulled away by the crowds as they walked. This was his day off. He sensed it would be a long one.

The next night they had dinner alone because Gwen was at a friend's. But even if their daughter was absent, they still talked about her allergies, her day camp plans, her tennis lessons, and what Crea had heard about next year's first-grade teacher, talked and talked about the child who was not there, as if they could will her back. And then, having exhausted all topics relating to Gwen, they looked at each other across the lemon chicken and found that there was nothing left to say. He had no news of the office; she had no more rooms to redecorate or pictures to replace with other pictures that waited in the wings, and no parties for them to attend. They'd seen what shows they wanted to see on Broadway. All tributaries were dry.

He listened to the quiet tap, tap, tapping of their silverware, the imperceptible sound of his wife swallowing her wine. She looked at him across the table, and he at her, but he did not wonder what she was thinking. He was too tired to wonder, too beaten into submission to care.

"So, I was thinking we would leave next Saturday," she said finally.

"Yes, that's fine," he said, sounding as neutral as he could.

"And you'll come up every weekend?" she asked.

"I'll do my best," he pronounced, feeling that he had won something, though really he had only withstood and persisted. It was a cold victory.

CHAPTER FIFTY-ONE

Sally gives an inch

Three nights later, his wife and daughter gone, he sat in another tiny theater, this one on a floor of what looked from the outside to be a professional building, but on the inside was more a mess of boxes and dirty tables and dark curtains opening onto narrow hallways. At the end of one he found rows of old-fashioned velvet seats that curved slightly around a small stage. The house was half full when he came in, but it began to fill up quickly. If Sally wasn't getting paid much, at least she was playing to larger audiences.

The cast was all women, and the play was set at a women's college in the early 1970s. First the characters appeared in a chaotic dorm bedroom, and then in a facsimile of an elegant but slightly shabby living room. The girls performed rituals—the drinking of tea and the eating of crackers with peanut butter, for instance, and the wearing of flannel nightgowns and pearls. The housemother was a bird-watcher, an old lesbian in the days when no one said the word.

He thought of that first visit to Smith College over twenty years earlier, of those shoes stretched out on the polished floor, and the woman serving punch, the singing groups and Claudia, poor Claudia, at age twenty, as exquisite as a painting, waiting for a man to claim her. Watching a light comedy, he felt a strange foreboding, as if his grave were being walked over.

Perhaps his brother was right and he just took things too seriously. The play, after all, wasn't Chekhov. All the stereotypes of the college dorm were there: the rich WASP with a Protestant work ethic; the working-class Italian who talked too much about sex; the neurotic nouveau-riche Jew whose mother wanted only for her to get married; the insane girl who wouldn't speak; and a comically annoying pair who communicated through a stuffed pig. Sally played the Italian, the tough girl, struggling with her grades and on the verge of flunking out. She cracked gum and wore short shorts and a man's undershirt, used the word *fuck* a lot. She had all the funny lines, got all the laughs, yet injected her character with the only real pathos that the play allowed. And at the end, she stole the show, receiving applause that turned to cheers.

Later, the cast filed out to waiting friends and relations, the makeup still smudged around the edges of their faces. Sally pushed through the crowd, smiling broadly. She had that same glow to her, the sparkle that he'd seen a year before in the lobby of another tiny theater. He reached out to touch her, wanting some of her energy for himself.

"Whaddya think?" she whispered, as her fellow cast members crowded him out, elbowing him to the side, hugging her and squealing. A man claiming to be an agent asked for her number, though he looked more like a horny teenager than a legitimate businessman. Robert recognized a few shoe-shine girls and a pair of young associates from A, L and W, still in their suits, who shook his hand awkwardly and then rushed off as if the building were on fire.

He watched Sally accept her praise, expecting to be forsaken again for a cast party or a bar celebration, but she walked over to him and said coyly: "I'm in the mood for that fancy dinner. You can wine and dine me now." Surprised, he led the way and they went down, down, down in an old, rickety elevator to his car and waiting chauffeur.

"You really want me to get into that?" she asked.

"I don't want you to ride on the hood."

Troy opened the door for them, his face implacable. "Thanks," Sally said to the chauffeur.

"You're welcome," Troy mumbled.

"Let's go to the Village," Robert said, and gave Troy an address just off Perry Street, an area he loved because it felt so Old New York. There was a restaurant he wanted to try.

"Do you tip him?" Sally whispered.

"No," Robert said, "I pay him." He put his arm around her and kissed her, and she kissed him back. It was a long kiss, and he felt the warmth of her body next to his; her mouth tasted of spearmint, like she'd just brushed her teeth. She pushed him away and looked out the window. "You're going to go places," he said. "Someday I'll lose you to the world."

"You don't have me," she said. "You can't lose what you don't have."

Troy pulled over to the curb in front of a tiny restaurant with a large vase of flowers in the window. Not waiting for him, she let herself out, walking to the front door.

"Leave it to me to get the last principled actress in Manhattan," he remarked, half to himself.

The restaurant had only ten tables with romantic lighting. They ordered a bottle of wine and he told her to get whatever she liked; she picked a pasta dish with chunks of lobster. "The second most expensive dish on the menu," she said quietly.

"I don't look at the prices anymore, Sally. I've learned not to notice."

"Wow," she said. "I bet that took years to learn."

"Yes it did," he replied, and sipped his wine.

They talked about the play, about other plays, about her talent, her career. It occurred to him that he had never known anyone with real artistic talent before, the kind you sacrificed for and built a life around — there were the artists he'd helped at the law center, but that was different; he didn't know them or their work. There was a quality of honesty about her acting — she was real onstage, and also, as he'd come to know her, he'd found an honesty about her in daily life. She did not pretend to know what she didn't, or to like what she hated. Her pleasure was genuine and unrepressed, and so was her displeasure. All her emotions were visible on her face, and just then she looked as enthusiastic as a child, complimenting every dish to him as if he had fixed it with his own hands. He focused on her utterly and completely, something he'd always known how to do with women, though he was long out of practice. "Why'd you ask me to take you to dinner? When you were so against it last week?"

"I'll tell you some other time," she said mysteriously. The waiter came and refilled her wineglass and water, and she thanked him extravagantly, as if no one had ever refilled a wineglass before, but the man remained poker-faced, much to Robert's amusement.

"You're allowed to want a night out," he said.

"On your money?"

"Happily, anytime."

"Don't make promises you can't keep." The waiter returned with the dessert menu, and they heard the specials; she ordered a sundae. "In a way I wish I'd never met you. Because then I wouldn't have seen inside places like this, and gotten to ride in fancy cars, and, well, all of it. It's not like my friends live like this, or that I went to places like this as a kid. I never imagined any of it would tempt me. But how can you be tempted by what you've never experienced?"

"Good point," he said. "It's after you experience it that the temptation *really* kicks in."

"Before, I'd never even talked to anyone who lived in a house like yours."

"You've seen my house?"

"I've walked around your neighborhood is all," she said, finishing off her wine. "It's a free city. I saw a picture of your wife in the *Times*, at that museum ball. She's pretty. I know people who could live for a year on what her dress probably cost."

"So do I," he said. "Don't forget that." He would not have her put him on the other side. Even if being there served him in some way. He wanted to take care of her, and part of her wanted it, too; he could feel it. No woman he'd loved before had actually needed him to pick up the check; they had let him do it, to spare his ego. Now, when he grasped the check, she looked at him gratefully and said it was the best meal she'd had, maybe ever. Tracey was the first to show him that there was another world, of elegance and simplicity and quality, a world he could touch and maybe even live in. He wanted to give her that feeling of expansiveness, and he wanted her gratitude as well, enjoyed the power of it.

That night, after he'd walked her inside the building and up the antique marble steps to the second floor, the negotiations began. Before she could open the burgundy door of the apartment, he pushed her against it and kissed her again. She put her arms around his neck, kissed him back, her lips touching his so softly at first, tentatively, and then with more pressure. The kiss was far from indifferent; they moved inside to the hallway, the door slamming heavily behind them, and he undid the two top buttons on her blouse, turning on the hall light, caressing the impressive swell of her breasts, pushed up high in her dark bra. He inhaled the soft scent of talcum; she responded only momentarily, and then wiggled away. "Tea?" she asked, blowing the hair out of her eyes.

"We're adults here, Sally, you can't put me off with milk and cookies." He followed her toward the kitchen. "I've fallen in love with you."

"Uh-huh," she said, picking up the kettle and filling it with water.

"That means nothing to you?"

"It means everything to me," she said, setting the water to boil. Her hair was askew, the tops of her pale breasts exposed, her cheeks flushed. "But I'm still not going to sleep with you." She pulled the top of her blouse closed and buttoned it.

"Are you mortal?" he asked.

She walked over and kissed him again, put her arms around his waist, pressed against him for a few exquisite moments, and then unwound herself from his grasp.

"You're playing with me," he said.

"No!" she replied, her eyes flashing. "*You're* playing with *me*! You think because I have some talent, because I'm unencumbered and put on a cheery, joke-telling face at the office, that my life is so perfect? Nothing I do ever *leads* to anything. Do you know how hard that is? I let you take me out tonight, *asked* you to take me out, because for once in my life I wanted to feel successful. Instead of counting every penny and feeling fucking hopeless!"

"You stole the show tonight."

"I always steal the show," she said, taking out two mugs, slamming the cabinet doors. The dim ceiling lights, ten feet above them, cast a yellow glow. "I always get the most applause, the most attention. Tomorrow, if I'm lucky, a reviewer for some paper or another will review this play and say exactly that. And where will it go? What will it get me? Very likely nothing! You think I want to shine shoes forever? I've tried pilot season, but they keep saying I'm too tall for TV, or too conspicuous, or too God knows what. I finally got an agent and he sends me from one audition to another; sometimes I get the part, but always in the show that's going nowhere. That's my life."

"You're only twenty-four. You have all the time in the world."

"I'm twenty-five next month and no one has all the time in the world!" she said. "Only a man would say something so stupid! Women have a very short shelf life in this career. Every single action and decision we make is about beating the clock. You can go nowhere fast for years, then wake up one day with no health insurance, no money, and no skills that anyone wants. How many jobs call for a British accent or an ability to cry on cue? I can't type, I don't know computers, I'm lousy at math. This is all I'm trained to do. And now you want me to be with you and love you, so that you can feel good about yourself—so that you can touch a kind of passion for life that you know I have and that you probably left behind ten years ago—and I get to be in both a career *and* a relationship that's going absolutely nowhere!"

"Maybe it will," he said, "go somewhere."

"I saw you with that kid. You're not going anywhere." She must have seen something in his face, because her voice softened. "I know you better than you know yourself. You want it all, and then you stand there, offering me nothing and telling me..." Her voice trailed off. She had begun to cry softly. Just a few moments before, in the theater, and then in the restaurant, she'd been ecstatic. Now she was sobbing. He put his arms around her.

"I'm sorry." He stroked her hair. "I don't want you to hate me."

"Well I do!" she said. "I really *hate* you."

He took her face in his hands and kissed her softly. "I mean it when I say I love you, and I'm going to prove it."

"How?" she asked, sniffling.

"I'm going to go home," he replied, as the kettle squealed and they stood watching it, listening to the endless, high-pitched whistling, a sound half passion and half alarm, as the steam pushed up through the hard metal, filling the kitchen with vapor.

CHAPTER FIFTY-TWO

Showdown at the Traces

There were those who said, in the summer of 1987, that had Sanford Trace been able, he would have, metaphorically if not literally, dug a moat and taken up the drawbridge. For months, the Traces had not been seen at any of the usual festivities or any of their regular dinner parties. For their Fourth of July celebration — practically a local institution — the guest list included only ten. Barely a party at all, by the standards of Tuxedo Park.

Robert and Crea had not seen the Traces since February and were as curious as anyone else. Gwen was spending the day with a friend — no other children had been invited, and she would certainly have been bored. The first thing Robert and Crea noticed as they approached the property was that two security guards stood at the entrance, asking for identification. In a gated community, where most of the guests were locals, this felt like overkill.

No waiters moved stealthily around the backyard — with so few guests, Tracey's cook and housekeeper were handling things along with the housekeeper's granddaughter. Robert and Crea walked toward Mark Pascal, who stood with his wife, Biscuit, on the back lawn, which looked strangely empty — there were no children, no sack races or jugglers, just endless green.

"What did you think of the thugs by the door?" Pascal asked Robert.

"Have there ever been crashers at this party?"

"I'm not sure this is about keeping people *out*," Pascal whispered. Biscuit excused herself to go sit down; she felt very tired these days — the Pascals were expecting, though not for some months — and Crea went with Biscuit to keep her company.

"I'm glad we have a minute alone," Mark said. "I've been hearing things about you."

"Can you be a little more specific?"

"Are you screwing that gorgeous shoe-shine girl?"

"That's specific," Robert said. "No, I'm not. Why?"

"Oh, just something I heard."

"Well, if it's a rumor, then do me a favor and quash it because it's not true."

"Lucky you if you were." He paused. "Tell me, after Crea had the baby, how long was it until you, you know?"

"You just asked me if I was screwing the shoe-shine girl, but you can't come out and ask me how long it was before my wife and I could have sex after Gwen was born."

"Well, that's different. It's marital, and Crea is such an old friend."

Robert wasn't going to touch that one. "You'll both be so tired at first, you won't think about much but sleeping," he said, "but that first year is thrilling."

"Well, we wanted this," Mark said wistfully.

"You're just nervous, that's all."

"I better go find my wife," he said, "see if I can get her anything."

Robert stood alone for a moment and then decided to join Mark and the women on the patio. Crea and Biscuit sat just beyond the striped canopy, in the sun. Biscuit was a little heavier than Crea, though she was not showing much, and her hair was blonder. But as he drew closer, he could suddenly see what Claudia Trace had meant that time when she said that the two women resembled each other. Maybe it was the angle he was standing at, or maybe he'd never really looked at them together. The similarity certainly ended with the physical. Had Mark married a sort of Crea stand-in, with a decent-enough pedigree but none of the sophistication of the original? Robert hoped, for Mark's sake, that the choice was unconscious. The couple did not seem unhappy. Just then Mark fetched a club soda from the housekeeper, then returned and handed it to Biscuit, kissing her on the forehead. Perhaps Mark Pascal had finally, after decades of practice, mastered the art of settling. And then Robert, too, joined his wife.

Very soon they were joined by Robert's father-in-law and Trenton Pascal, and soon all the guests were clustered together on the back patio, including the Gordons and the Trumbles, Tracey's elderly neighbors who'd been friends of Tracey's parents. The housekeeper's granddaughter circulated, taking orders for drinks, and Robert was about to flag her down when Jack Alexander moved toward him, took him by the arm, and asked for a moment of his time. Without waiting for a response, he led Robert back in the direction he'd just come from, until the two were standing by themselves in the vast backyard. Considering there were so few guests, everyone seemed crazy for privacy — or, at least, privacy when talking to Robert. This was not a good sign.

"What time did you get in last night?" Jack asked.

"Flat tire," Robert mumbled, "on the Thruway."

"Perhaps start out a little earlier next time."

"Sorry if I woke you."

"You were expected by ten. Have you seen those phones for the car?"

Robert heard his name and turned to see Tracey striding

quickly toward them. The three talked briefly about some new neighbors who were attempting a house renovation that few in the Park approved of. Robert mentioned Gwen's recent request for a Saint Bernard. Jack grew bored—he had come to chastise, not to chat, and having done that, he excused himself to return to his contemporaries.

Robert followed Tracey toward the garden on the side of the house. The tomato plants had capsized, overcome by the weight of their ripening fruit. The cucumbers were so ripe as to be rotting. "I really must get someone to deal with this," Tracey said. "There just hasn't been time." Tracey had aged in the months since Robert had last seen him. His ruddy face was noticeably lined; tiny veins dotted his nose, and his blond hair had grayed into a muddy, indistinguishable shade.

"Where's Claudia?"

"Inside, in bed," Tracey said, "but she'll be down eventually." He paused to pick up a tomato that had tumbled into their path. "I didn't invite your brother, because I can't have Claudia seeing him anymore."

"You don't have to explain anything to me," Robert said. They were at the front of the house now, looking out on the long, empty driveway. The two security guards lounged in their chairs in the distance.

"I don't blame Barry, really. I invited him here, encouraged the relationship. I knew what was going on—was relieved, actually. He made her laugh. He got her out of the house. She seemed happier, more energetic. I figured I had my indulgences and she could have hers, certainly. It made me feel better knowing that she had a few."

"There was no affair, if that's what you're thinking," Robert said. "Not in the technical sense, at least." Barry would have found a way to brag to his brother if there had been.

"Sex? I'd be delighted with something as easy as sex. This is about coke and pills."

"So what are you doing, exactly?"

"Taking matters into my own hands for once. She's going to get clean if I have to sit here and stare at her all summer. Nothing comes in and nothing goes out without my knowing. No guests unless I'm absolutely certain that I can trust them. Hence the security guards."

"I don't know if that's the right approach."

"I'm not going to send her off to one of those places, if that's what you mean. Have her sit in a group with what's-his-name from the Allman Brothers. That's not for Claudia."

Robert didn't think it was Claudia's discomfort that Tracey worried about.

"Took me close to a month to get rid of her stash. She hid it everywhere. And then if we had workers coming into the house — well, I've even replaced some of the staff."

"Is it helping?"

"Some days she's maddening. She whines and begs. It sickens me, to be honest. But I have to bear up. You might do me a favor — go up and see her. She's not talking to anyone in general, but she always liked you." Tracey lit a cigarette; he'd taken up smoking again after a long sabbatical. The two men walked back toward the house.

"If you think it will help, sure," Robert replied. "But I don't see how you can make her a prisoner in her own home."

"What do you know about it?" Tracey asked. "If you'd spent more time with her, she might not have been so drawn to Barry and —"

"Me?" Robert said. "I can barely keep my own marriage together, let alone stand in as proxy for yours. I don't know what's gone on between you and Claudia, or what exactly you expected from this marriage, but leave me the hell out of it!"

Robert walked around the front of the house, wandering the overgrown grounds as he tried to calm down. Tracey's topsy-turvy mess of a life made no sense, but then, did his own? Last night, he'd said good-bye to Sally in front of the building. This was their rule now: he didn't go so much as inside the lobby. They embraced in the dark, away from the prying eyes of the doorman and the glare of the streetlights and foot traffic on Broadway. Holding her in his arms, he'd kissed her for a few exquisite seconds until she pried herself from his grasp and went inside, leaving him frustrated as a fourteen-year-old. Then he'd rushed home to East Seventy-third, changed clothes, and driven himself up to Tuxedo, doing eighty on the freeway, arriving at past midnight. The house was still, and he was long overdue. He'd taken off his shoes and crept down the hall to their bedroom, removed his clothes silently, and slipped into bed. Crea lay beside him, breathing the heavy breath of sleep. He reached for her in the dark and she responded, half conscious. He pushed her nightgown up around her waist and mauled her in the darkness, her muscled legs strong as steel around him, their two deprived bodies taut with hunger. They did not take long. To stifle herself, she put her mouth to his shoulder, smothering her scream with his flesh, her hot breath and anger, her disappointment and desire, mixed together in that silenced sound, which turned into a bite so fierce that he now had a welt the size of a baseball on his upper arm.

He fucked his wife — there could be no other word for what they'd been doing lately, angrily, and in the middle of the night — the two of them barely able to make civil conversation in the light of day; and he made a companion of his mistress, all the while imagining in torturous Technicolor the day she would finally peel off her clothes and give herself to him. How long could all this go on?

Tired of wandering, Robert finally went inside. The drapes were open in the living room, showing off the silk rugs and Renaissance revival chairs and daybed. The room, with its Victorian flourishes, looked just as it might have a hundred years earlier, and it struck him that Tracey and Claudia were oddly old-fashioned people in their tastes, social circles, disinterest in careers (who besides Tracey was still a "gentleman" in the technical sense of the word?), and even their view of the bonds and social proprieties of marriage. But perhaps all people with significant inherited wealth were refugees from another age, and perhaps they had to be — the real work, the dynamic striving, had been done before they ever appeared. Only Jack Alexander refused to be stuck in the past. He didn't start out with their money or have their point of view. In a way, with his tastes in art and his see-through house, he rubbed their faces in it. Robert felt a flicker of admiration for his father-in-law whom he had, over the years, come to loathe.

The upstairs rooms appeared to be closed, but outside one door sat a tray of untouched eggs and toast, left like the aftermath of a bad room service breakfast at a hotel. He went to the door and knocked. Hearing no response, he announced himself loudly and was told to enter.

"I couldn't sleep for days," she mumbled, "and now all I want to do is sleep." She sat up in bed and turned on the light. "Is Barry here?"

"No."

"Sit down," she said, patting the space next to her. He pulled up a chair instead. "He didn't send anything for me?"

Robert shook his head. "I wouldn't give it to you if he did."

She picked up a pack of cigarettes off the nightstand. "Everyone's abandoned me," she said, "including you."

"No, we haven't." Her hands were shaky, and he took the lighter and lit the cigarette for her.

"He's locked me away so he can do as he pleases and not have to look at me." She put her hand out to him. "Couldn't you just call Barry? I've tried him a million times, but if he called back, no one would tell me. Maybe invite him up to your house? Or, you could go into town for me; there's that boy who sells autographed baseballs —"

"You want to kill yourself? Because there are faster ways."

"Yes, it's a regular mausoleum around here. Tracey is our funeral director. And who will bury *him*? You, I suppose."

471

"There's nothing wrong with Tracey."

Claudia smiled, and the skin stretched tightly across her drawn face, in a look that was nothing short of ghoulish. She told him to close the door on his way out.

FIREWORKS WENT OFF THAT YEAR, but Robert would not remember them. Jack left early with Trenton Pascal and Biscuit; Mark stayed behind to see the fireworks. The few remaining guests huddled together in a tight group on the patio. The two elderly couples wore earplugs in preparation for the noise. Crea sat by Robert, eating the last few bites of a slice of ice cream cake. Mark sat on her other side, talking privately to her about a charitable endeavor. Next to Mark, Tracey dozed on a folding chair like an overworked babysitter. In the distance, a band played "The Stars and Stripes Forever." Robert missed his daughter — what was the point of all this ritual without children to make it bearable?

Then Tracey's elderly housekeeper, Famke, appeared and shook Tracey awake. Softly, and then louder, so he'd hear over the music, she told him that Mrs. Trace had disappeared.

She'd gone up to bring Mrs. Trace a tray and found the door ajar, the bed empty. Tracey was upright immediately, and he sprinted into the house. The guests stared at each other, puzzled. When he returned, the sky was filled with color, the fireworks now in full swing. He shook his head and frowned. She was indeed gone. The old people were already making their excuses. Robert told Crea to go home; Gwen would be back soon. He and Mark would help Tracey look, along with the useless, now-chastened, security guards.

"She probably hitched," Robert said. "Plenty of traffic. This will be like looking for a needle in a haystack. You need to call the authorities, get some help."

"No police! Now hurry up and do as I say."

Mark emerged from the house with flashlights. Robert felt

angry, had been angry all day, not at Tracey but at the whole situation. If Tracey for once admitted a problem, exposing it to the light of day, there'd be no need for this. If Robert had never invited Barry; if Tracey had never married. If and if and if. Lie on top of lie, and his own lies the cherry on the iced cake.

They took Tracey's car, but Robert drove because he didn't think Tracey was steady enough. Each of the security guards took separate cars. Mark drove with the housekeeper, who knew the area and insisted on doing her part. They covered Sterling Forest and the area just outside the Park. They all searched the outside roads for hours, first fighting holiday traffic, then putting on the high beams and squinting into the darkness of empty back roads, up and down the hills of Orange County, and then, in what had to be a long shot, they tried the major arteries, the highways, until finally even Tracey had to admit the futility of the exercise. At midnight they drove back to the house, hoping someone had had success.

No one had. The security guards looked exhausted. Mark Pascal paced impatiently. Tracey called the hospitals, but Robert, who should have done so hours earlier, called his brother. Barry had just come home from a night out with some brokers to find Claudia sitting in the lobby of his building in nothing but sneakers and men's pajamas. She didn't want him to drive her back to Tuxedo. She was now sitting on his living room couch, sipping a brandy.

"Don't give her anything else," Robert told his brother. "No, on second thought, give her something to sleep. We'll come for her."

They drove into the city and got Claudia. She lay curled up asleep in the backseat like a child. "It's just going to start all over again if you don't do something about this," Robert said, his voice tired and accusatory as they pulled into the long driveway.

"I know," Tracey said. "No need for that tone, Vishniak. I know."

*   *   *

BY THE TIME THE housekeeper dropped Robert at Jack's, it was past 3:00 a.m. He stripped off his clothes, ready, so ready, for sleep. But as he pulled back the covers and got into bed, Crea turned over and put on the reading light, wanting to know what had happened.

"We had to drive into the city to get her at Barry's. It's been a very long night."

"I've been lying here for a long time, Robert, trying to get past the feeling that if it had been me running away like that, you'd never have been so Johnny-on-the-spot."

"That's silly," Robert said. He was so very tired. "You wouldn't have disappeared like that, Crea; you don't do those things. That's not who you are, thank God."

"Yes, I'm rock solid. Everyone says that. Need to organize your carpool? Find a good price on a Biedermeier secretary? Get your father to the right cardiologist? Call Crea. But no one organizes search parties and drives half the night to rescue the utterly competent, do they? Only the weak and pathetic get grand gestures."

"You're talking craziness."

"You take me for granted."

"Perhaps I do," he said, cringing, and then taking her hand. "Can I get some sleep and we'll talk about this in the morning?"

She pulled her hand away. "You had an affair with her, didn't you?"

"With Claudia?" Robert sighed. "No, I did not."

"You two are always off together at parties in some private tête-à-tête."

"Talking. She's troubled."

"Oh, yes, everyone should have such trouble! A woman with money, looks, and brains, if she has any left, and everyone tripping over themselves to be at her service. Claudia is so depressed. Claudia doesn't eat enough. Claudia never got over Charlie. That was twenty years ago, but you all moon around her and take her temperature. How men love helpless women."

"I swear to you, Crea, that I did not have an affair with Claudia Trace."

"You're having an affair with someone," she spat.

"You're irrational right now," he said quietly. "There's no point in this conversation."

"If I'm irrational, Robert, or if I'm crazy, then you've made me this way. It only took you ten years. Congratulations." And then she turned off the light and they each retreated to their separate sides of the bed, turning their backs.

CHAPTER FIFTY-THREE

The fall of '87

At the end of September, Sally informed him that for once, she'd been wrong. Someone had seen her performance, someone had noticed. And she'd gotten cast as the female lead, Billie Dawn, in a production of Garson Kanin's play *Born Yesterday*, at an Equity theater in Hartford that paid a salary, and provided room and board. She would be gone for six weeks. On her last day shining shoes at A, L and W she was glowing with her triumph, seeming to float down the halls as if on a cloud. She looked as if she'd fallen in love, and it was hard to admit that he was jealous. Was he jealous that her attentions were elsewhere, or jealous of her certainty? A little of both.

"This is good timing, really," she said, finishing up his shoes, then standing up and adjusting the box. "It was getting old, all that push-pull. For you, too, I think. And I'll come back."

He nodded, trying to look agreeable. Maybe this was the beginning of something for her; maybe she'd go from this into something even bigger. Wasn't that the way it happened for actors? Didn't they lead peripatetic lives, going where the work was? But he did not say that because it wouldn't be fair. What did he even have to offer her? Instead he pointed out that he had a lot of work to distract him.

"Maybe when I get back you'll have made partner," she said, "and we'll go out and celebrate." She put her hand on his shoulder and then, looking toward the door, she quickly leaned over and kissed his cheek. "Cheer up."

He handed her fifty dollars and she tried to give it back to him, but he would not take it. Then he watched her go, trying not to feel that the air was being let out of his life, that the next few months would be nothing but bland, unending work, domestic squabbles, worry. In short, what it had been before.

Sally was right about one thing: at Alexander, Lenox and Wardell, a verdict was on the horizon. No one gave a specific day, there was no official meeting, but at some point before December a partner would come into his office and deliver the news. Usually there were hints and rumors beforehand, but Robert had heard nothing. It was the custom in real estate to wait longer to make partner, eight or nine years as opposed to the usual seven. Each passing year was a year wagered in the hopes of a higher-and-higher-stakes happy ending. If you couldn't see that happy ending, if you were a "bad fit," then you were smart to bail out early and go to another firm. Wait too long and you became just a failed aging associate in a boom market, when talent and even simple diligence were claimed and elevated; so what was *your* excuse? Ultimately, politics was the standard answer, or mitigating circumstances, or personality clashes, the endless variations that caused lawyers to be derailed, to not get their names at the top on the stationery. You became a lawyer with a story. And what lawyer wanted to walk around with a story hanging over his head?

Mario Saldana was certainly a lawyer with a story. At the beginning of September, he had left for Caracas to visit his elderly mother, and by the first week in October it had become clear that he wasn't returning. The resignation letter arrived by certified international mail, addressed to the partners, and stated that Mario's mother's health and his desire to be close to family had influenced his decision to take a very early retirement, at age forty-seven. He wrote a strong case in favor of Robert Vishniak's candidacy for partner, but it didn't really matter—now he had no vote.

On the very same day, Robert received a personal note, addressed to his house. To Robert's surprise, Mario told him the truth—he was dying of AIDS. He was apologetic, wishing that he could be there to help secure a partnership that he believed Robert deserved. Robert was deeply touched by Mario's honesty, particularly from such a reserved, proud, and secretive man. But he could not help wondering how all this would affect his own fate.

In the beginning, the other members of the firm honored the truth, or parts of it—Mario was a man with wonderful priorities, so handsome and exemplary, both in his work ethic and his sense of family, his dedication and decorum—but then, after a few weeks, the mythmaking began. The rumor mill worked both ways—it could tear you down or build you up. First, they talked of a potential Caracas office for the firm: maybe Mario could be coaxed back? Then there were rumors of a fiancée in Caracas, a whole other life invented for him—he had given up the crazy hours to live somewhere beautiful and spend time, not only with his sick mother but with the woman he loved. New York lawyers, working an eighty-hour week, could grasp such a dream to their hearts. It kept them going late at night while they stared at their computer screens. Mario's portrait, which Robert did not even know existed, was brought out now from a back room and placed in a spot up front. Usually a man did not get a portrait out front until he'd been at the firm thirty years. Or had done something remarkable.

In October, the firm held a good-bye dinner for Mario Saldana in a large private room at Peter Luger Steakhouse in Brooklyn. That Mario was not there did not really signify—they left an empty chair, as if expecting him, the way Robert's family did at Passover for the prophet Elijah. All the partners and associates showed up, ordering sixteen-ounce prime rib along with dishes of creamed spinach and corn, which they spooned into their mouths like baby food.

Robert had not thought people knew enough about Mario to talk about him — and he was right. The speeches were half praise and half speculation. People talked of favors Mario had done them, presents for children's christenings, jokes he'd made at closings — and Robert was certain that most of what they said never happened. They evoked the phrase *worked hard and played hard* so much that Robert felt as if he were in a commercial for running shoes. They acted like Mario had not been reserved to a fault, avoiding all intimacy, anxious to interact socially only on the soccer field or tennis court, places where men usually did not talk.

If the lawyers in that room knew nothing of Mario's childhood, had never met his family, or even set foot in Venezuela, it did not matter. There were now a series of orphans he had rescued from the streets and was putting through school; a group of soccer players in the South Bronx who had a field to play on and real soccer cleats because of Mario. There was a summa cum laude graduation from Duke, when Robert was certain Mario had said his grades were unimpressive in college. The litigators were the best at these verbal embellishments — few had even worked with Mario, but their speeches brought tears to the eyes of a group of waitresses who'd stopped for a moment to listen.

The older partners did not say much, though they smiled approvingly and clapped at appropriate intervals, like proud parents. But Phillip Healey, the youngest of the old, got up and told a long anecdote, something to do with trying to keep up with Mario on the tennis court — by now, Robert wasn't really listening — and then Phillip sat down, and all eyes turned to Robert. He was the logical one to toast his former mentor, and that was clearly what was now expected — his turn had come.

"Stand up, Robert," Jack whispered.

Grasping his glass of scotch in his hand, as if at any moment he might hoist it for a toast, he found that he had no words. After a long, awkward pause, he said Mario's name aloud. A few lawyers leaned forward in their seats, others smiled—was it with contempt, or the expectation that he was about to do something surprising and witty? But Robert put the glass down, shaking his head. He would not slander the memory of the one lawyer who'd actually been kind to him. Wilton Henry got up from his seat at the next table and approached, put his hand on Robert's shoulder, and whispered: "Having some trouble?" Robert nodded and then sat down. Henry, first saying a few words about how affected Robert had been by Mario's leaving, segued quickly into a monologue so entertaining and yet solemn that he received a standing ovation. Liesel MacDuff took off her very thick glasses in public—for the first time anyone could remember—in order to wipe away the mist on her lenses, then stood up and made her own attempt, admitting that she was in an unenviable spot on the roster.

Robert knew this night might come back to haunt him—he had not done what was expected—but suddenly he did not care. He might have spent more time with Mario than the others, but he could remember only two personal conversations they'd ever had—and only if he counted the first one, when they'd met in the hall in Robert's first month as a summer associate. The one person who knew Mario intimately was not at this dinner, and had he been there, Robert felt sure that he would have fled in horror.

When it was over, Robert got quickly into his waiting car, anxious to avoid his colleagues. "Get me the hell out of here," he told Troy. All the way home, he stared out the window at the aging factories, barren lots, and crumbling row houses of Williamsburg. As the car made its way toward the bridge, it occurred to Robert that Mario's custom suits had fooled no one; neither had his insistence on working long hours to the end, or even the long line of glamorous women he brought to firm Christmas parties. The dinner was not about Mario's accomplishments, or even his character — it was an evening created solely to acknowledge what Mario had done for Alexander, Lenox and Wardell. He had kept them from scandal, kept them or any of their competition from ever having to associate A, L and W with the word *AIDS*.

CHAPTER FIFTY-FOUR

The verdict

When Lola came into Robert's office just after lunch and said that Mr. Alexander wanted to see him, she looked pleased. Robert wished he could feel so sanguine. He had always told her that if he made partner she'd get a raise. "I don't think they're telling us for another month," he cautioned, not wanting her to get her hopes up. Past trips to Jack's office had not always yielded positive results. As he walked down the hall, he wondered: was it his imagination, or were lawyers coming out of their offices and secretaries raising their eyes to stare at him?

Not looking up from her work, Selene told him to go in. He found Jack at his favorite spot at the window, looking out at the view. He turned around and pointed to the chair that faced his desk, then walked over and sat down on the other side. "I don't want to beat around the bush," he said, as Robert quickly took his seat. "You've put me in a very difficult position."

"In what way, exactly?" Robert asked, sitting up straighter.

"With Mario retired, it's a good time for us to take on two real estate partners — a case might even be made for three. We've had an excellent year and our pool of associates has grown significantly. You worked most closely with Mario's clients, but as you know, almost all of them have transferred their business to firms with stronger international practices. Many were family members, as I understand, and he was the draw."

Robert nodded, anxious for him to get to the point.

"You're a solid lawyer, Robert. There's no question you do your job and have brought in business. I've said all along that I'll abstain from voting this year, so as not to give the impression of nepotism. But with Mario retired and Harold Thoms about to step down, we need all the available real estate partners to participate. You can imagine that though I may caution my colleagues to count me as anyone else, my vote holds significant weight."

Spit it out, Robert thought. *Say it already.*

"But I'm not supporting your candidacy."

Robert could feel his chest getting heavier, and so he reached into his jacket for his inhaler and used it quickly. Jack waited politely, his face inscrutable. When Robert could finally speak, his question came out a hoarse croak. "May I ask why, exactly?"

"Because being a partner in this firm is about more than just being a good lawyer. A partner sets an example." He stood up and Robert stood up, too, so that they faced each other across the desk.

"I think I've set a fine example. Are you implying that I haven't brought in enough business, because —"

"You're not hearing what I'm telling you," Jack said, his voice tight. "The whole firm is talking about you and that shoe-shine girl. You've been seen all over the city with her — a group of second-years saw you kissing her under a streetlamp near some downtown bar. You've been seen walking arm in arm with her on the Upper West. And you were seen meeting her, more than once, in the lobby of this building, and described as 'all over each other.' I don't condone gossip, but it's a reality of firm life, and for too long you've been the entertainment around here. The fact that you're not aware of this is shocking in and of itself—and makes me wonder exactly where your head has been these last months, though I suspect I know the answer! But you're also my son-in-law and, unfair as it may seem, I can't separate my personal from my professional feelings here." His voice quivered now. "*You will not* make my daughter the butt of one more damned joke!"

"But I'm faithful to Crea," Robert said.

"Excuse me?"

"I've never slept with the shoe-shine girl," he said. "And I don't see what my personal life has to do with my job. I've given all I could to this firm."

"When you married Crea, your work and personal life ceased to be completely separate."

"But you've treated me no better because I'm your son-in-law, so why should you treat me worse? I tell you that I have not had sex with Sally Johannson. Don't you believe me?"

"Even if I believed you, it wouldn't be relevant. Because everyone *thinks* that you have." He paused. "And given the evidence, I find your claim hard to buy."

"Believe whatever you want, but I'm telling you that we're friends."

"I don't care what they call it nowadays!" he said. "I'm aware that not making partner this year will be very humiliating for you, for the simple reason that everyone expects it."

"And because the entire New York legal community will assume I'm too incompetent to make partner even in my own father-in-law's firm."

Jack seemed calmer now, the most unpleasant part over with, and he sat back down. "Go home and tell Crea what's been going on. The two of you should take a nice vacation. Never see that girl again. In fact you're going to tell her that she can't shine shoes here. When the gossip has settled down, perhaps in a year or two, then we'll reconsider you for partner. But you must tell Crea. If you don't, I will."

"What am I supposed to say?" Robert asked, finally unable to control himself. "That I'm not making partner because the entire firm thinks I'm sleeping with the shoe-shine girl when, in fact, I am not sleeping with the shoe-shine girl?!"

Robert did not believe that all those lawyers had seen him. Manhattan was too big—on the rare occasions that younger associates got out, they went to bars or restaurants close to the office, and he had avoided those. Had his father-in-law had him followed? Or someone else? Wilton Henry or Liesel MacDuff? Anything was possible. "You never liked me, did you?" Robert asked.

"Liking or not liking you has nothing to do with this."

"But you didn't think I was good enough for Crea, did you?"

"That's irrelevant."

"I think it's extremely relevant."

"You have a daughter," Jack said. "Will anyone ever be good enough for her?"

There was a knock at the door, and Jack called out that he was not to be disturbed. But the knocking continued, and he was forced to get up and walk across the room. He walked slowly, his back hunched. He was old, and yet Robert knew that he would never give an inch.

He knew he should leave Jack's office now, but his father-in-law's enormous body now blocked the doorway. Lawyers had affairs every day—only he had somehow found a way to have the public censure without the benefit of the actual pleasure.

Jack whispered to Selene for a long time. What could this be about? A reprieve? Had something changed? His father-in-law thanked his secretary and squeezed her hand. When he turned around to look at Robert, his face had drained of color.

"What is it?" Robert asked. "Has someone died?"

"No," Jack said, walking quickly to the phone. "There's been a crash."

"A plane crash?" Robert asked. "Are there casualties?"

Jack sat down at his desk, staring at the lights on his phone, as if to will a call through. Robert cleared his throat and Jack looked up, surprised to see him still standing there.

"What on earth's going on?" Robert asked.

"The stock market's falling," Jack said, "and there doesn't seem to be any end to it."

CHAPTER FIFTY-FIVE

Where is Barry Vishniak?

A few feet from the entrance, two workmen, their ears plugged and their mouths covered with masks like surgeons, stood on either side of a large jackhammer that burrowed into the earth and filled the street with an endless, pulsing boom and the smell of burning tar. Robert walked past them, rushing through the revolving doors. The lobby looked like the cleanest of ghost towns.

He had not been able to reach Barry on the phone—nobody could reach his broker today—and so he'd come in person. The market had closed now, down 508 points, the biggest one-day decrease in almost seventy-five years. Getting off the elevators and entering the glass doors of the first-floor entrance, Robert walked up to the receptionist, the same Jennifer who had been so friendly a year ago, but now she did not so much as look up. Multiple phone lines beeped, all flashing red, and she pushed one after the other without ceasing, repeating the same sentence in a chanting mono-tone: "He's not available at the moment, may I take a message? He's not available at the moment, may I take a message? He's not—" She did not write anything down on the pad in front of her. She did not look up. Her hair, normally teased so high, now lay flat around her shoulders, as if she had wilted.

In the bull pen, a young man sat in the front row, in his tie and shirtsleeves, mechanically banging his head on the top of his desk in a 1-2-1-2 rhythm. In the last row, the only other occupant had disrobed down to a pair of pants and socks. He paced back and forth, talking animatedly to himself. In between them was row after row of empty desks.

Barry's office was empty except for the cold caller, Justin, who sat at Barry's desk with his feet up, talking on the phone to a girl named Tia-Marie about a movie where blood spurts out of someone's eyeball. Robert cleared his throat and then, still not getting the boy's attention, came up closer and said: "Hang up that phone, Justin, before I strangle you with the cord."

Justin told Tia he'd call back, then took a cigarette out of his jacket and lit it.

"Where is he?" Robert asked.

"Last Thursday two security guards walked him out of the office. Day before that, he was in the conference room with the compliance guys for hours. Your account's been transferred."

"What'd Barry do?"

"You'll have to ask him yourself." The phone rang again, the long rows lighting up over and over.

"So how do I get hold of my money?"

"Contact Joe Harper. But nobody will know how things stand for days. It's a mess."

"And where's Joe Harper?"

"Look out there, you see anyone?" Justin asked. "They're gone. Down at the bar, probably. You know what the problem was today, if you ask me? Technology."

"I didn't actually ask you—"

"The brokers," the boy said, ignoring him, "even when they wanted to, even when everything was going in the crapper, they couldn't sell. Too many trades in the system, no price quotes. Everything froze. You could see the numbers on the Quotron falling and falling and not a thing anyone could do to stop it."

Robert took a hundred-dollar bill from his pocket. "Barry wouldn't hire someone who didn't know how to play the angles. Surely Joe Harper has files?" he asked.

The boy took the money nonchalantly. "I might be able to find out what you had as of last Thursday. That's about the best I can do." He paused. "Today, nobody knows anything."

Robert let him have the money then sat down and waited, listening to the quiet, his pulse racing. When half an hour had passed, and he feared Justin was never coming back, he saw him strolling leisurely across the trading floor. He opened the door and informed Robert that he was in luck; some paperwork had been stacked on Joe Harper's secretary's desk for days, awaiting updating or simply thrown there in disgust.

"What's my total?"

"As of Thursday's closing, seventy thousand dollars."

"*Before* the crash?" Robert asked.

"That's what it says," the boy replied, as Robert snatched the file out of his hand.

"How did he manage to take over two hundred thousand dollars and turn it into seventy thousand?!"

"Hey, I'm not responsible."

"You know what they did in Rome," Robert said. He stepped closer, wanting, suddenly, to fling the kid through the glass wall. "What do I even have left after today?"

"Not much," Justin whispered, and then walked out the door.

Robert used his inhaler again. He heard a rushing in his ears, like the whispering of a crowd. He'd lost. He had no money.

He took the subway from the World Trade Center station up to Barry's place, but his brother was not there — the doorman hadn't seen him in days. He gave the man a twenty-dollar bill — more money Barry was costing him! — got the key, then took the elevator up to the top floor but found the place neat as a hotel. The cleaning woman had done such a good job that had it not been for the picture of himself and Barry with their father, taken on the Boardwalk when they were kids, he might have thought that he had the wrong place. He looked on Barry's Rolodex and called a few names, including Victor Lampshade, but no one had heard from him.

For hours he walked the streets of Manhattan, wandering first along Central Park West, then across the park, and then south, through Midtown, back past his office, and toward Times Square. It was dark by the time he got to those streets where, as a cabbie on the night shift, he'd delivered so many fares. Off Sixth Avenue an explosion of lights blinked GIRLS GIRLS GIRLS. Sheets of newspaper blew about his feet, broken glass littered the sidewalk, and a voice chanted in his head: *Make money, make money, make money.* After all these years and so much hard work, he was back to where he started. Or worse. He thought again of all the cash he handled for other people every day: IOLA accounts, escrow accounts, 1031 exchange accounts such as the one Mario had set up for Mark Pascal. He remembered his fantasy of diverting the money Pascal made from the sale of his next property into an account offshore — Pascal would sell off another investment property of his father's in just a few weeks, this one for $11 million. With Mario gone, Robert was now the senior attorney on the deal. He had set up offshore accounts for clients before — you could do it in an afternoon, over the phone and with a fax these days. He played the idea over and over in his mind, feeling his breathing calm. He could start over and then some, and leave the country a wealthy man. The reason so many people got caught was because they stuck around. Was it such a crime to steal insured money from a wealthy man?

Robert stopped and looked at himself in the display window of a pharmacy. His reflection floated in a sea of face creams, hair dyes, and pain medications. Sweaty and in need of a shave, he tried to imagine changing his name, growing back his beard. When he'd driven a cab, he knew a guy who serviced the cars, but everyone said that he made his real money forging passports. It would not be so hard to disappear. No ties. No money worries. Free.

No Sally.

No Gwen.

The thought stopped him in his tracks. Leave his daughter? How had he not thought of her all afternoon, not for a second? He stared at himself one last time in the window. He could not envision his next move, did not know what his resources were or what he should do. And so he went to the one place he seemed to go when he was up against a wall, desperate and uncertain, and to the one person whose life was just then as complicated and filled with disappointment as his own. He walked east to Park Avenue and up to Fifty-fifth, where he turned into a luxury building and asked the porter, someone new, if Mr. Trace was in and up to seeing company.

He was left to pace back and forth on the mocha-colored marble until, finally, the man waved him through and he took the elevator to the top. Tracey was standing in his doorway, waiting for him. "A day full of surprises," he said. "Only this one is pleasant. Come in."

"So you've been listening to the news?" Robert walked into the apartment, and Tracey, barefoot and casual in jeans and a T-shirt, padded over to the bar to fix them some drinks. "A big drink," Robert said, sitting down, "really big."

"You've lost a lot today?" Tracey asked, his back still to Robert.

"I have no idea exactly how much, or even how much money was in there to begin with. Let's say Barry didn't keep the most accurate of records. He was walked off the floor last week."

"So he wasn't even trading?"

"Nope," Robert said. "The stock market managed to crash without Barry Vishniak."

Tracey walked toward him with the cocktail shaker and two full martini glasses on a tray. He was as calm as Robert had seen him in years.

"You're not concerned by this?" Robert asked, grabbing his drink.

"Win some, lose some. That's the stock market. Barry never had much of my money, and I closed that account before Claudia left. But in any case, I'm sure I lost a small fortune today. I've just never seen much point in worrying."

"I gave Barry most of what I had."

"Your family loyalty is admirable," he said. "Maybe it's not as bad as you think."

"You don't sound very convinced."

"Robert, you're healthy and you have a good job. And a wealthy wife. You'll be fine."

Robert told Tracey what had happened that day in Jack's office, told him about Sally and the state of his marriage, told him, in short, the whole pathetic, confusing condition of his life.

"Will you give this girl up?"

"She gave me up. She's in Hartford in a show."

"She'll be back," Tracey said.

Robert was quickly getting drunk on an empty stomach. He felt light-headed. "Any crackers in this joint?"

Tracey went into the kitchen again and began to grab things off shelves.

"Please don't trouble yourself to cook anything," Robert said.

"It's a day of surprises, Vishniak, not miracles." A few minutes later, Tracey came back with three cheeses on a board, a grouping of crackers, some grapes, and sliced melon, all artfully arranged, along with two small, gold-rimmed china plates. "I'll bet that until this moment you still wondered if I was actually gay."

Robert stared. "I've never heard you say the word before."

"I've closed up the Tuxedo house and put it on the market."

"But it's your family house, isn't it?"

"My brother doesn't want it and my mother isn't ever coming back to the U.S. I can't stand to be there anymore. Too much house for one person."

"You'll live here full-time?" Robert asked, helping himself to more cheese and crackers.

"No, I'm going to sail around the world. Or at least as far as I can stand it. What good is a boat you can live on if you don't use it?"

"By yourself?"

"No, I've hired two strapping young men for my crew. Both very good-looking."

"I envy you," Robert said, "getting away from New York."

"Come with me," Tracey said, sounding suddenly serious.

"I think I have to claw through this mess and figure it out."

"To me, that's about the best time to cut and run," Tracey said, finishing off his drink.

"What about Claudia?" Robert asked, taking some more crackers.

"I believe she'll stay in Paris, once she's out of that place. Her family's there. And the Parisians mind their own business — probably why Rock Hudson went there to die."

Robert had wanted to ask Tracey a question for a long time. The alcohol, and mention of the dead actor, gave him courage. "Are you ever going to, you know, get the test?"

"I don't much see the point."

"Don't you want to know?"

"Aren't I dying to know if I'm dying? Not at all. I'm a coward, and if you haven't figured that out after all these years then you haven't been paying attention."

"What about if you meet someone else?"

"Sex is over. Gone with the bell-bottom and the typewriter."

"Seriously, Tracey."

"I am being serious." He picked up the shaker and stood up. "I'll make more, if that's all right with you."

Robert nodded. Tracey went back to the bar as Robert took more food onto his plate.

"You never did love Crea, did you?" Tracey said. "I didn't want to see it. I wanted to keep you close."

"You could have done that anyway."

"Will she settle anything on you, if you leave?"

"Airtight prenup," he said. "I get nothing if I leave her, not even this watch." He held up his wrist. "I could have renegotiated after Gwen was born, but I was too proud. And I knew I didn't deserve it, frankly. I've been a lousy husband. It feels good to admit that."

"You've always thought too much about money," Tracey said, surprising Robert again, as he set their drinks on the table.

"Easy to say when you've always had it."

"You'll either be wealthy very soon, or you'll be wealthy in twenty years. Either way, you'll have plenty."

"Are you offering me a job?"

"No, but I'm going to die."

Robert put his drink down. "But you haven't even had the test."

"Sooner or later, I'm going to die. We all are. If I have the plague, which is certainly possible, even probable, then you'll get rich soon, within a year or two. If I don't have it, well, the Trace men rarely live past sixty. I could be the exception, but that's not likely."

"I don't want your money."

"You say that now, but I've left you quite a bit. Just a small slice of the pie, but there's an awful lot to go around."

"What about your family?"

"Plenty passes back to them, and to the charities, but that still leaves more than enough. And who have I got to leave it to? You're about the only one."

"You put me in a terrible position."

"Of wishing to speed up my death?" Tracey laughed. "Don't be too cheerful. Right now I'm fit as a fiddle. Not so much as a cold." As if to prove his point, he finished off his fourth martini. "I've always wondered what you'd be like if you actually had enough, or more than enough, to satisfy yourself. Not having to covet and pretend. Not having to work so hard, and be quite so careful or so angry. Just to have more than you need, and to understand that even with so much freedom, a man still has the capacity to be utterly miserable. Hopefully you won't be. But I won't know, will I? I'll be dead."

"Stop it, Tracey. Jesus Christ!" This last piece of news, coming at the end of such a long and horrible day, and then the alcohol — he felt as if he would break in half.

"Oh, calm down. I could live to be a hundred. Wouldn't that be a good joke?"

"I hope you do." Robert wiped the crumbs from his mouth. "When do you leave?"

"Next week."

"That soon?"

"I don't see any point in staying. I could die at sea, you know?"

"If you keep making a joke of this —"

"No, it's not a joke," Tracey said. "Not at all."

Robert stood up, shakily. "I think I'd better get home."

"Yes, it's late. Will you be all right?" Tracey asked. "The door-man can get you a cab."

Tracey walked him to the door. Everything they had to say had been said. Robert told Tracey to take care of himself, and Tracey came toward Robert as if about to kiss him, but instead he put out his hand and smiled. Robert took that hand forcefully and pulled his old friend close, hugging him. Then, as quickly as he'd drawn Tracey to him, he let him go, and walked toward the elevators.

CHAPTER FIFTY-SIX

Telling Gwendolyn

He arrived just before 1:00 a.m. The house was dark. He took off his shoes and socks; the polished wood of the entrance hall felt cool and soothing against his tired feet. Stumbling toward the stairs, he thought only of bed. Then he crept past Gwen's room, and heard her calling out to him. How had she heard? She called him again. He opened the door just enough to peer in; the room was dark except for a few strands of streetlight coming through the blinds and the twinkling of tiny iridescent stars and a moon painted on the ceiling. She yawned. "Daddy, where have you *been?*" she asked, sitting up, her voice still thick with sleep.

"I was at the office, sweetheart," he said, closing the door behind him and walking over to the side of the bed.

"You're always at the office," she said, reaching for the desk lamp. Robert turned it on for her, and the tiny square around her head was flooded with light. "And Mom gets in one of her moods and doesn't talk to anyone and I *miss* you," she added in one breath. He wondered how, at six, she managed to sound like a little girl and an adolescent all at once. Her hair came down in front of her eyes in a curly heap; she parted it with both hands, as if opening a curtain.

"I've been trying to make partner. It means being at the office a lot."

"Did you?" she asked. "Make it?"

"No," he said, sitting down on the edge of the bed. "I don't think I'm going to make it."

She furrowed her brow. The idea of him not getting what he wanted was strange and confusing to her. "What does it mean, Dad, being a partner?"

"Making more money, having more say in decisions. Like when you're a kid and then you get older—and Mom lets you pick your own clothes, or decide sometimes how you want to spend your time. A partner is like becoming more of a grown-up at work."

"If I had more say, then you'd be home all the time. And we'd play on the floor. Like we did last year, remember that day? When we built the Empire State Building out of Legos? And watched *Singin' in the Rain*? When the guy dances up the wall, remember?"

"I remember." If he left, he would have to fight hard for any time he got with her. Would her mother turn her against him? In that moment he imagined staying, making amends at the firm, not seeing Sally again. People made such sacrifices for their children. His father and grandfather had given even more than that for him. They had given their health, their lives.

"Dad, what's wrong?" she asked, and took his hand.

"Gwen-Gwenny-Gwendolyn, did I ever tell you that I named you after someone I loved very much?"

"More than Mom?" his daughter asked, her voice high and uneasy. "Do you and Mom love each other?"

"A person can have more than one love, sweetheart. There's lots of room in the human heart. It's only when you stop thinking you have any room left—that your heart is so broken that you can't love—only then do you make mistakes."

"I don't understand."

"I named you after a girl named Gwendolyn who was very beautiful and smart and the kindest woman I've ever known. We were engaged to be married and we lived in Boston. You know where that is?"

"Where you went to college? With Uncle Tracey?"

"Exactly," he said. "You never forget anything, do you?"

"And what happened to her, Dad? What happened to the girl named Gwendolyn?"

"She died, baby, and some of it was my fault, because I didn't pay enough attention."

"Because you were trying to make partner?"

"No, because for a long time I ignored that she was sick because I didn't want to see."

"Why?" she asked.

"Because it was too painful. I needed her to be well for all the plans I had for us. And after she died, I never thought I could love anyone else, not like that. I thought I was all used up. And then I met your mother, and you were born. And I realized that I was all wrong."

"Why, Dad, why were you all wrong? Because you loved us?"

"Because I knew almost from the day you were born that I loved you more than I've ever loved anyone. More than I thought anyone could love anyone."

"But what about Mom? Don't you love her?"

"I love your mother, but in a different way."

"What kind of way? Different than Gwendolyn?" she asked. Then, ever so quietly, she added, "Dad, are you and Mom gonna get divorced?"

That was one word she certainly understood. She knew who in her class saw a father on weekends, and who spent just holidays and summers. It was too awful to contemplate, and so he assured her of the only thing he could: "No matter what happens, I'll never leave you, Gwen-Gwenny-Gwendolyn." He leaned over, kissed her on the forehead, then reached over and turned out that lamp, but turning it off made no difference. The room was still illuminated by light flooding in from the hallway. And then he saw her, barefoot, in only a nightgown, standing in the doorway.

He got up and went to her. The nightgown was flesh colored, and her hair was pulled off her face, which was extremely pale. Even her lips had lost their color. She appeared to be frozen in that spot in the doorway of their daughter's room, the place he least wanted to have a conversation. He tried to steer her out into the hallway, but she wouldn't move.

"Crea?" he asked. She was shaking. He took off his suit jacket and put it around her shoulders, but she shook it off.

They could hear their daughter stirring in bed. Gwen had lain down and put the pillow over her head, one hand on each side, gripping it around her ears. Crea finally stepped out into the hallway and shut the door. A hand-painted plaque hung there announcing, in green curlicues bordered by a hedge of pink roses: Gwendolyn's Room. Crea stared at it, and her eyes filled with tears. Of all the things he had done to her, this was the worst. The name of the other woman, affixed forever. She would have to say it, over and over, day in and day out. Their daughter's name.

She looked so small and vulnerable in her thin nightgown. The rims of her eyes were red, not from crying, he suspected, but from the force of trying to hold back her tears. He started to ask her if there was anything he could do for her, anything that he could possibly say, but she cut him off, standing up straight, smoothing a strand of hair out of her eyes, and her voice became suddenly businesslike. "I suppose we can tell her tomorrow. Though she knows already, she's known for a long time."

"Known what?" Robert asked.

"That her parents aren't going to live together anymore."

CHAPTER FIFTY-SEVEN

The end of Disston Street

Stacia Vishniak had most of her savings in government-backed securities, a money market fund, and plain old cash. But over the last few decades, and particularly since her son had gone into the business, she'd indulged here and there in the stock market. Barry had put some of her money into an index fund, and she'd had him buy her some shares of General Electric, because everyone always needed lightbulbs, and Sony, because the television she'd bought for the broadcast of the Nixon resignation was still going strong.

Stacia read the *Philadelphia Inquirer,* including the financial page. She watched *Wall Street Week* on PBS. And it did not take a genius to see that something was coming: the decline of the dollar; higher interest rates, creeping inflation, a Republican president who did not believe in regulation. And most of all, the crazed buying of the younger generations, who made expensive purchases when they had little savings and too much debt. Stacia could feel financial doom in her bones, but the appearance of the cat was what pushed her over the edge. A bad omen. The first week in October she called Barry and told him to get her out of the fund and send her the money.

Barry said she was crazy. What did she know about the market anyway? And when had she become superstitious? Who sells stock because of a cat? Was she forgetting things? Did she know what day it was?

She assured him that at seventy, she was still the soundest one in the whole family. And then she told him the story of the black cat, a story that Barry would repeat just weeks later, at the shivah that followed his mother's funeral.

Stacia, notorious hater of air-conditioning, always looked forward to Indian summer. All through September and into October, she slept with the bedroom window open, but this provided no real explanation as to how the animal got into the house in the first place. Barry speculated that the cat had come up from the basement, clever enough to exploit the rotting wood at the base of the garage door, soft, pliable wood—for years he'd been after her to replace it, even if she never used the garage. Likely the cat squeezed underneath, through the basement, up the stairs, and through the house, finding her way to Stacia, who awoke in the middle of the night to such a feeling of heaviness on her chest that she began to panic, sure that she was having a heart attack. Then she heard the soft meow, and felt the animal's paws shift on the light blanket. Sitting up with difficulty, she turned on the light by the bed. The cat dug her paws into the bedsheet and the woman underneath. Cursing, Stacia shoved the animal aside and, seeing that she would not leave, grasped her in the middle, marched downstairs, opened the front door, and threw the angry ball of fur out onto the cement.

She knew exactly where the thing had come from. Her neighbor, Gertrude, a childless widow, had a black cat named Nefertiti, and one of the few things that all Stacia's neighbors could agree on was that Nefertiti was a pretentious name for a cat. Nefertiti ate expensive canned food, and had tiny stuffed-mouse toys with little bells attached to their tails, which Gert sometimes brought out on her patio in an attempt to engage the animal. But Nefertiti preferred to roam. She had been found in many houses on the block, but her attachment to Stacia would be of a more lasting nature. Night after night that fall, the cat found her way into the Vishniak house, only to be tossed out.

Stacia waited, patiently, for something to happen, and when it did, on October 19, she should have felt smug and self-satisfied, safe and secure. Her sister called, asking if she was a psychic, or a genius of finance. Stacia assured her that she had not expected anything this drastic. The fact that she had been so right was not satisfying but terrifying. Who on earth was in charge when an omen was more accurate than a hundred-year-old brokerage house filled with people who had college degrees? What about her savings? Thousands still sat there, unguarded. Lolly tried to calm her down — the banks were not closing — but Stacia, keeping the telephone to her ear, listened to the words spoken over and over again by the anchormen, commentators, and people interviewed on the street. Her sister was listening, also with the sound turned up as loud as possible, so that Stacia and Lolly heard the words in stereo, the same words that had frightened them half out of their wits as girls: *crash, collapse, calamity, careless, catastrophic, costly*. It was only a matter of time, Stacia insisted, before the newscaster moved up the alphabet.

"I have to go check my supplies." She hung up and likely went to examine her basement stash of canned goods. That was the last time Lolly ever talked to her sister.

The next day, Stacia was scheduled to work the cash register for the Oxford Circle Jewish Community Center subsidized lunch for seniors, as she had done every Tuesday, Wednesday, and Thursday, from 11:00 to 2:00, for the past five years. It was a volunteer position, though it came with a free meal. She never showed. At 3:00 p.m., after repeatedly trying Stacia's house, the director of the center called Lolly.

Around the same time, Gert also became concerned — the cat always came home by midday to eat, but not this time. Gert walked the neighborhood, asking if anyone had seen Nefertiti. Finally, though she dreaded the confrontation, she went to Stacia's house and knocked on the door. No one was home. She tried again and was about to give up when she saw Stacia's sister approaching. Lolly used her key, and together they walked through the living and dining rooms and then the kitchen, while Gert called for the cat. Lolly went to the basement, and Gert walked upstairs. As she got to the top of the steps, she heard the familiar meowing, and there she found Nefertiti standing on Stacia's lifeless body as if guarding the tomb of some ancient pharaoh.

NO ONE WAS ABLE to reach Barry, and Robert did not expect him, so he was shocked when, that Thursday morning, he saw his brother walk through the wide glass doors of Goldman's Funeral Parlor on Broad Street. His hair stood out from his head in wild, graying curls, and his pants were baggy, barely held up by a thin belt. His shirt had a stain on it. If not for the added weight he'd put on in his years of plenty, he would have looked exactly the same as before he entered Prudence Brothers. Robert stood in silent disbelief as Barry introduced himself to the balding, freckled undertaker, who pronounced his words slowly, as if speaking to a class of small children. He told them to follow him into his office. Barry put his hand on Robert's arm, pulling him back. "I don't have any money," he whispered, "none available, anyway."

"Neither do I, thanks to you," Robert replied.

"You've got more than I do. It's not like you lost everything."

"Pretty damned close."

"Don't talk about that now."

"I'm leaving my job and Crea has asked me to move out."

"Oh," Barry said. "You got a credit card, don't you? Put it on there. Then when the money comes through—"

"What money?"

"Ma's money," Barry said. "All that saving. We've got to inherit *something.*"

"You heard of something called probate? Let's hear what the man has to say."

"Ma hated these places. She said nothing was a bigger racket than the funeral business."

"We can't exactly put her on an ice float and send her out to sea," Robert snapped, pulling Barry toward the somber man, who stood waiting for them in his paneled office. Robert and Barry took the two chairs across from him. The room smelled of pine air freshener.

"We want the cheapest one you have," Barry said.

The undertaker looked at Robert, who was not dressed like a man who wanted a cheap coffin.

"What do you have on the low end?" Robert asked.

"Low?"

"Five or six hundred dollars?"

"I don't have anything that cheap, not on display."

Barry stood up to leave. Where, Robert wondered, was he going? There were only a few Jewish funeral parlors in Philadelphia, and they were all more or less the same. "We'll have her cremated," Barry said.

"We charge for cremation," the man replied. "I can give you our rates. Many Jews have religious issues with it. Was your mother observant?"

"Not at all," Barry said.

"She had her moments," Robert corrected, as the undertaker flipped through the thick, glossy catalog in front of him. Then he pushed the book at Robert. The coffin was plastic-looking with metal trim and cost $1,200. "This is the Shalom model. It's reasonably priced."

"Sir, I said we have a cash flow problem here."

"There's a plain wooden box. Very popular with the Orthodox," the man replied. He showed Robert what looked to be a refrigerator box made of wood, which cost $875.

"What do you charge for cremation?" Barry asked, as Robert flipped through the book himself.

"We're not having her cremated," Robert replied. "We're burying her next to Pop." The coffin was only part of the deal. They still had to pay for the cost of inscribing the blank half of their parents' double headstone, plus what they were being charged right now, for keeping their mother here, preparing the body for burial and then transporting her to the cemetery. Goldman's also offered prayer books and yarmulkes for the service, an announcement in the paper, and transportation to the funeral, and they could recommend a rabbi, too. The place had a list, which the undertaker called a "menu." He slid it toward Robert, along with the catalog of coffins, and asked if they planned on purchasing custodial services—someone would trim the weeds back from the stone twice a year. The funeral home offered a discount with the cemetery.

It cost a fortune to die, and with Jews burying so fast, you were forced to make decisions at your least rational. But Robert had had so many things to deal with in the past week that his mother's death, oddly enough, had not been such a shock, only one in a series of upheavals, all timed so badly that were he a believer, he might have equated himself with Job. Might have, had he not been aware of just how much of this he'd brought on himself. He shoved the book back at the undertaker. "There," he said. "That one, right there."

"That's not actually a coffin," the man said. "It's a container we use in cremation."

"Is it biodegradable?" Robert asked. "Can we bury her in it, legally?"

"Technically, yes, but this is made from pressed, recycled wood particles. Little more than a packing crate." The undertaker stared down at his lap, looking as if he might cry for the shame of the two sons whose mother had given them so much, and who were repaying her with so little. "I think you could regret this, when the shock wears off. What of your mother's memory?"

"She's dead," Barry said. "She'll never know."

"We've served the Kupferberg and Vishniak families before. What of her sister and brother and their families? We wouldn't want them to think that these are our normal services."

"They already know we're special," Barry mumbled.

"There is a kind of poetry in this." Robert held out his credit card. "You see," he explained, "no one loved a bargain like our mother." And then he and Barry laughed, softly at first and then louder, until the man looked at them helplessly, taking Robert's MasterCard and walking into the next room as the two brothers howled with laughter, tears rolling slowly down their cheeks.

THE FUNERAL WAS QUICK because they had no rabbi — she didn't belong to a synagogue, and they would not pay a rabbi they didn't know, did not think it necessary for a family that read Hebrew badly or not at all. Neither did they post a death notice in the *Philadelphia Jewish Exponent* to alert any distant cousins or old friends who might want to attend or make a donation to charity. Relatives had to find their way by word of mouth.

The temperature that morning was nearly fifty degrees, but many of the people who came to the graveside were elderly and wore their winter coats. Their adult children came with them so that they might help their fragile parents exit cars and walk through the grounds. The two remaining Vishniak brothers were there. One used a walker, another a cane. Aunt Lolly leaned on Uncle Fred, one of the few tall men in the family but bent over now. Only Uncle Frank and his wife were still relatively young, though old enough to have a grown daughter. Frank walked over to the brothers and embraced them, too stricken to speak.

A woman from the Oxford Circle Jewish Community Center

mumbled something about how good Stacia was at making change. Then a man in his thirties said: "She always got the children safely across the street," then added, "and now I'm an osteopath."

Robert thanked people for their platitudes, self-references, clichés. Yet Stacia Vishniak was the least clichéd person he'd ever known. There would never be anyone like her again.

He passed out the books supplied by the funeral parlor. Most of the men reached into their pockets and took out their own flimsy silk yarmulkes, the kind—received free at weddings or previous funerals—that never held its shape and formed a tiny point on top of their heads. To Robert's surprise, Barry still had some rudimentary knowledge of Hebrew; Robert had forgotten. Uncle Frank stood next to Barry and helped him. Barry chanted, "*Yisgadal v'-yiskadash sh'mei raba, b' alma di v'ra khir'usei...*"

Robert read the English: "Magnified and sanctified be the great name of God throughout the world, which He hath created according to His will."

"*... v'yamlikh malkhusei b'-hayeikhon u-v'yomeikhon, uv'-hayei d'khol beis yisrael...*"

"May He establish His kingdom during the days of your life and during the life of all the house of Israel."

The prayer never mentioned the word *death*, only the ideal world, and the kingdom of heaven that God would create after the coming of the Messiah. Only there was no ideal world, no world to come, on heaven or on earth. His mother had known this, and he knew it, too. *There is only the world we make for ourselves, our own private heavens and hells.*

As the service, such as it was, ended, Robert and Barry each took a shovel, scooped up some dirt from the pile next to the new grave, and threw it on the coffin. Then each put his shovel back into the dirt as the other mourners lined up to take their turns. They were supposed to hear the sound of the dirt as it hit, a reminder that death was final. But when the scoops of earth fell on the small cardboard coffin, they made almost no sound at all.

*   *   *

ROBERT AND BARRY HAD hardly spoken in the forty-eight hours between their trip to see the undertaker and the actual funeral. Barry had gone through stuff in the basement, eventually just throwing the junk into piles and calling the Salvation Army. Nothing his mother saved — empty paper towel rolls, chipped glasses, dented cans, broken umbrellas, ancient winter coats, and endless rags made from bedsheets and towels — seemed worth having. On the second floor, Robert went through her bedroom, collecting the financial records that she kept in her chest of drawers — he was executor of the will and would have to deal with the money, as well. Neither intended to stay at the house very long, and there was a lot to clear away. Even at meals, each man ate separately, making sandwiches from the cold brisket left in the refrigerator, eating the cookies and the kasha, knowing it was the last time they would ever taste their mother's cooking.

Only on the food for the shivah did Barry and Robert have no trouble reaching agreement — they had ordered it at the deli, and there was no skimping. Robert paid. It arrived Sunday morning as they were dressing for the cemetery. Corned beef and roast beef and pastrami; piles of rye bread and pumpernickel; coleslaw and pickles and olives; a tray of sliced fruit and another with six different kinds of cookies, nuts, and candy, plus a dark chocolate cake.

The food made everything easier. After the service, people came to the house and gathered around it, grabbing for plates and talking. The crowd grew bigger at lunch. Neighbors came and more cousins, people he barely recognized. All so old now. They asked after his wife and daughter and embraced him, shouting near his ear. Robert piled cold cuts on a plate, then walked to the couch where Uncle Frank, still silent, made room for him. Barry joined them.

"So where are you living?" Barry asked.

"In my apartment," Robert said. "Or I will be when I get back."

Barry lowered his voice. "With the shoe-shine girl?"

"No," Robert replied. "She's away right now. She got a job."

"Oh," Barry said. "I haven't been back to the office."

"I heard," Robert spat. "Tell me, how, exactly, did you happen to lose ninety percent of the money in my account?" When he'd finally gotten the total, the numbers had made him dizzy. From over $200,000 at its height, he now had just over $25,000—exactly enough to pay his debts and be left with about $5,000, most of which would be used to pay the funeral expenses. At least he was not in a hole. "Only *you* could manage to leave me not far from where I started."

"Not here." Barry stood up. "I need some air."

"Fine," Robert said. "I'm going to offer some of her jewelry to the aunts and cousins."

Upstairs, Robert went through the glass and plastic beads that had tangled into a heap, and the tarnished pins and bracelets. He recognized a circular pin dotted with green stones that had once belonged to Cece, and turned out to be fourteen-karat. He saved it for his daughter, along with Stacia's modest diamond engagement ring, then separated the rest of what was not broken into a pile. Slowly the aunts and a few cousins came and sorted through, took what they liked. They wanted keepsakes, though, as Aunt Lolly whispered to him before she made her way carefully back down the stairs, a person would have to be crazy to look at a piece of jewelry and remember Stacia Vishniak. She rarely wore so much as an earring.

Relatives and neighbors drifted in and out; the front and screen doors remained open to accommodate them. The more ambitious used the chairlift to come up and say a few words to him. They needn't have bothered; everyone was so loud down there that he could hear perfectly. About an hour after he'd first entered his mother's room, he became aware of a conspicuous silence on the first floor, and walked halfway down the steps to see what was happening. Two tall black men stood at the bottom. They wore jeans and bright yellow T-shirts with truck logos on them and carried large padded blankets.

"They're the movers!" Robert yelled down. "They're here to move some furniture!"

A loud, relieved "Oh!!" went up from the living room crowd. And then the ceaseless buzzing of the words, "Movers? movers! Almost gave me a heart attack!" Over and over again. And then, "Moving furniture at a shivah?!" This, they would say, was crossing a line, but Robert didn't care. He had other things to worry about that afternoon.

There was the chest of drawers in the bedroom, made of cherrywood, and an oak secretary that sat at the bottom of the steps. His mother had inherited both five years ago, when Cece died. Robert couldn't get a sense of the date on the furniture. It had not been made by anyone famous, but these were the only things in the house worth keeping, and they weren't covered in protective plastic, and he wanted both for himself.

He instructed the movers to take the chest first, and they set to work covering it, then hoisted the thing on their shoulders and walked down the steps. Conversation halted and children scurried. A cousin had made the movers sandwiches — there was so much food — and followed behind them to offer corned beef or chopped liver. As the men returned to pack up the secretary, then took it slowly out of the house, Robert heard Barry return, heard him yelling Robert's name and heard the thud of his footsteps as he ran up the steps. "What the hell are you doing?!"

"Moving the furniture to my apartment," Robert said calmly.

"Today?"

"What are you, religious all of a sudden?"

"You're stealing from me. I deserve half of that!"

"You want to talk to me about stealing?" Robert asked. "Really?" He had restrained himself for two days, working in the same house with Barry, swallowing his anger, but now he could not. He lunged at his brother and the two men fell to the ground. But Barry, who was so much heavier, had the advantage, and he pinned both Robert's hands to the floor.

"She was my mother, too!" Barry yelled. "I am not a stepchild!"

Barry had heft on his side, but Robert was angrier. He raised his knee, jabbing his brother in the groin then grabbing him by the neck as the two went rolling into a nightstand. When the lamp fell to the floor, Robert was on top, hands around Barry's throat. "You ruined my life! You ruined my fucking life!"

"You ruined your own damn life — ," Barry gasped.

"*Where is my money?! Where is my money?!*" Robert repeated, banging his brother's head repeatedly against the floor. Relatives gathered around, calling out to him, but it did no good.

"Stop it, Robert! Stop it now!" Sally Johannson was suddenly by his side, pulling on his arms. "You'll kill him. He's your brother," she said. "You'll kill him."

Robert let go of Barry's neck. Barry coughed and gasped, then sat up, backing into the corner like a wounded animal. Robert's inhaler was in the jacket in his bedroom and slowly he stood up to go get it. Uncle Frank, who had been there with Aunt Lolly and the two old Vishniak uncles, came over and spoke to Robert for the first time all day. "Go downstairs and sit shivah for your mother," he said wearily. "It would kill her all over again to see you like this."

The guests limped and shuffled down the steps. Robert got his inhaler and used it, then went outside. Sally followed.

They might have sat on the patio. There were two metal and plastic chairs folded up against the wall, but like most things in his mother's house, they were old and rusted and torn, and likely wouldn't hold an adult of any significant size. So they sat on the steps. They could hear the announcer on the television in the living room, the volume turned up so loudly that they had to raise their voices just to talk to each other.

"I thought you were in Hartford," Robert said. She was dressed for the occasion, wearing a skirt and a cardigan, and some lipstick. Her hair was brushed off her face. He could hardly take his eyes off her.

"Tech rehearsal tonight. Somebody can walk through it for me." She paused. "My dad told me. He heard from a neighbor. Everyone was talking about that business with the cat."

"Thanks for coming," he said. He needed to say something, but perhaps later was better than sooner. Still, he blurted it out: "Crea and I are separating."

She was quiet for what felt like a long time and he wondered if he had told her too quickly. A divorced man, unemployed, fifteen years her senior, with a child to boot. He could find another job, make more money, but it would take time.

"I got cast in another play after this," she said. "In Denver."

"See," he said, "I told you things were going to happen for you."

"I'm going back to New York tonight to pick up a few things. I hope you don't mind storing some of my stuff in the apartment, until I get back?"

"When will that be?"

"About three months. Before I leave for Colorado, I can come in for a day or two to look for a new place."

He wanted to tell her that she didn't have to do that, she could stay. But he'd always moved quickly with women, taking their love as his due, and he could not do that with Sally. She would have to be courted, won over. "You sure you'll come back?" he asked. He did not know if he could bear it if she didn't. Too many losses.

"You'll have my stuff. Consider it a hostage situation," she said. "How's Gwen?"

"Custody is going to be complicated," he said. "Crea is very angry."

"You think a court can keep that little girl from finding her way to the West Side?"

Robert smiled. For the first time all day, he felt on the verge of tears.

His brother stepped out of the house with an ice pack on his head, a bottle of Chivas Regal, and three paper cups in his hand. "Drinks, anyone?" he asked, and sat down on the lowest step. Sally took the bottle and poured some into each cup. "There's bottles and bottles of the good stuff in there. Unopened. Years of Christmas gifts from the PO." He turned to Sally. "None of them drank much."

"Mine neither," she said, swallowing what was in her cup in one gulp.

"There'll be a little from the sale of the house," Robert said, "and there's about two hundred thousand in savings and treasuries."

"All that skimping, all those coupons and sleepless nights." Barry took a long swallow of whiskey. "My half won't even pay my legal bills. Looks like I'll be away for a while."

"I heard."

"Sometimes I wasn't exactly accurate in my depiction of the risks. Or the companies."

Robert didn't say a word.

"Maybe I exaggerated how much money I was making you," Barry added, "jacked up the numbers a little. I liked how it felt, being the big man. Going to the parties."

"Me too," Robert said, finishing his drink. "And after you get out?"

"I don't know," Barry said. "Maybe I'll go back to my old business. At least there, the technology was reliable and the rules were clear."

Dusk was nearing, the sky fading to pale gray and indigo, and the tiny yellow patio lights came on up and down the block, creating jaundiced little halos next to each doorway. A group of girls started a game of double Dutch between two parked cars, the ropes slapping hard at the asphalt. Across the street, somebody honked a car horn over and over. Two houses down, a man in an undershirt, blue shorts, and heavy black shoes limped up the sidewalk, his footsteps squeaking as he walked. He was greeted by two little boys, one dark-haired and the other blond, and each took one of his hands. In the distance, Robert could smell meat roasting. His brother belched loudly; Sally smiled at him. And for a moment, a strange and wonderful moment, Robert Vishniak knew where he belonged.

Acknowledgments

Words are inadequate to express my gratitude to my agent, Bill Clegg, who, over endless drafts, and many years, never gave up on this novel or its author. *Rich Boy* could not have been in better hands than those of the very wonderful Jonathan Karp and his team at Twelve, who grasped so quickly what I was trying to do and helped me make it better.

Jonathan Freedman has read every draft and fragment related to this novel since 2001; thank you especially to him and to Sara Blair for publishing an early story about these characters in the *Michigan Quarterly Review*. I am grateful for the support of all my teachers and colleagues at the University of Michigan, especially Nicholas Delbanco, Peter Ho Davies, and Eileen Pollack. Many thanks to the generous, talented writer friends who served as readers for drafts of this novel: Natalie Bakopoulus, Sara Houghteling, Aric Knuth, Valerie Laken, Patrick O'Keeffe, and Raymond McDaniel. Also, Peggy Adler, Margaret Lazarus Dean and Chris Hebert, and Karen Outen. Before there was Ann Arbor, there was New York. Thank you to Wendy Lamb, Min Jin Lee, and Andrea Louie. Meir Ribalow, who does his father and family proud in his constant and unselfish support of his fellow writers and artists, not only read drafts and offered comments, but also encouraged me to preview a very early chapter of *Rich Boy* at New River in Healing Springs, North Carolina — a big thank you to him and to everyone I met there. Some funding for this novel was generously provided by the Ludwig Vogelstein Foundation; over the years, the Virginia Center for the Creative Arts has provided me with important space and time.

Lawyers who helped me with the legal and real estate information in this novel: Elliott Meisel, Michael Mervis, and most especially, the very patient Ronald Burton. They are all brilliant, and any mistakes are fully my own. Robert Barandes read this as a lawyer, a dear friend, and a huge supporter — thank God I didn't miss that Hampton's jitney back in 1998. Thank you to Lori and Arie Abecassis for their Northeast Philadelphia knowledge, and Diane Saltzman, who came to my aid on last-minute art questions — it's a lucky woman whose friends are also resources.

I was helped in my research of New York in the 1970s by the archives of the *New York Times*, especially articles written by the inspiring architectural critic Ada Louise Huxtable; also by the books *Living Poor: A Peace Corps Chronicle* by Moritz Thomsen; *The Peace Corps Experience: Challenge and Change, 1969–1976* by P. David Searles; and *740 Park* by Michael Gross. Thank you also to Nanci A. Young at the Smith College archives, and to the folks at Merchant's House Museum in lower Manhattan.

Many people helped keep me going over years of writing this novel; I can't thank them all, but I must thank a few more: Rachel Aranoff and Neil Zuckerman; Mark Eisman; Ricki and Josh Lowitz (and the entire extended Chicago clan); my partners in crime since college, Julia Harrison and Monique Skruzny; Mindy Mervis; Naomi Morgenstern; Harris Rosenweig; and Marcie Wald, who has witnessed my life, ministered to my problems, and made me laugh for over thirty years. Thank you also to cousins Robin Berman,

Steven Pomerantz, Jill Bucinell, and Steve Swerdlow for service beyond the call of duty.

Last, but most of all, thank you to my mother, Estelle S. Pomerantz, who read to me, sacrificed for me, and always told me stories. And to Bill Richert, who enriches my life in more ways than he knows.

About the Author

SHARON POMERANTZ's short fiction has appeared in a variety of literary journals, most recently the *Missouri Review, Ploughshares,* and *Prairie Schooner.* Her story "Ghost Knife" was selected for inclusion in *Best American Short Stories 2003*; another story, "Shoes," was read as part of the Selected Shorts series at Symphony Space in 1996 and broadcast on National Public Radio in 1998. Sharon has also contributed nonfiction to the *Chicago Tribune,* the *Village Voice, Hadassah Magazine,* and many other publications. She is a graduate of Smith College and the University of Michigan and currently teaches at the University of Michigan in Ann Arbor. *Rich Boy* is her first novel. She can be contacted at sharon@sharonpomerantz.com.

ABOUT TWELVE
Mission Statement

TWELVE was established in August 2005 with the objective of publishing no more than one book per month. We strive to publish the singular book, by authors who have a unique perspective and compelling authority. Works that explain our culture; that illuminate, inspire, provoke, and entertain. We seek to establish communities of conversation surrounding our books. Talented authors deserve attention not only from publishers, but from readers as well. To sell the book is only the beginning of our mission. To build avid audiences of readers who are enriched by these works—that is our ultimate purpose.

For more information about forthcoming TWELVE books, please go to www.TwelveBooks.com..